THE
SECOND RULE
OF TEN

ALSO BY GAY HENDRICKS AND TINKER LINDSAY

The First Rule of Ten

The Third Rule of Ten

The Broken Rules of Ten (e-book only)

Available from Hay House

Please visit:
Hay House UK: **www.hayhouse.co.uk**
Hay House USA: **www.hayhouse.com**®
Hay House Australia: **www.hayhouse.com.au**
Hay House South Africa: **www.hayhouse.co.za**
Hay House India: **www.hayhouse.co.in**

THE SECOND RULE OF TEN

A TENZING NORBU MYSTERY

GAY HENDRICKS
& TINKER LINDSAY

HAY HOUSE

Carlsbad, California • New York City • London • Sydney
Johannesburg • Vancouver • Hong Kong • New Delhi

First published and distributed in the United Kingdom by:
Hay House UK Ltd, Astley House, 33 Notting Hill, London W11 3JQ.
Tel.: (44) 20 3675 2450; Fax: (44) 203675 2451. www.hayhouse.co.uk

Published and distributed in the United States of America by:
Hay House, Inc., PO Box 5100, Carlsbad, CA 92018-5100.
Tel.: (1) 760 431 7695 or (800) 654 5126; Fax: (1) 760 431 6948 or
(800) 650 5115. www.hayhouse.com

Published and distributed in Australia by:
Hay House Australia Ltd, 18/36 Ralph St, Alexandria NSW 2015.
Tel.: (61) 2 9669 4299; Fax: (61) 2 9669 4144. www.hayhouse.com.au

Published and distributed in the Republic of South Africa by:
Hay House SA (Pty), Ltd, PO Box 990, Witkoppen 2068.
Tel./Fax: (27) 11 467 8904. www.hayhouse.co.za

Published and distributed in India by:
Hay House Publishers India, Muskaan Complex, Plot No.3, B-2,
Vasant Kunj, New Delhi – 110 070. Tel.: (91) 11 4176 1620;
Fax: (91) 11 4176 1630. www.hayhouse.co.in

Distributed in Canada by:
Raincoast, 9050 Shaughnessy St, Vancouver, BC V6P 6E5.
Tel.: (1) 604 323 7100; Fax: (1) 604 323 2600

Photo of Gay Hendricks: Mikki Willis
Photo of Tinker Lindsay: Cameron Keys

A catalogue record for this book is available from the British Library.

ISBN 978-1-78180-270-0

Printed and bound by TJ International Ltd, Padstow, Cornwall

Lama Yeshe and Lama Lobsang
Dorje Yidam Monastery
Dharamshala, India

Venerable Brothers,

I find myself reaching out to you because my
heart lies heavy in my chest this evening.
A few weeks ago a pair of cops in a city
just south of here answered a call about
a vagrant breaking into parked cars. They
arrived on the scene and found the culprit
at a bus depot nearby. He resisted arrest.
They threw him to the ground, shocking
him multiple times with their stun guns.
Backup cops arrived, mob instinct took over,
and soon six cops had Tasered and clubbed
him into a coma as he cried out for his
father . . .
    . . . who was at home, mere miles away,
oblivious to the unfolding catastrophe.
    . . . who was, it turns out, a retired
member of the police force.
    Three days later, this heartbroken
retired cop took his son off life support,
finishing what his brethren had started. And
today's paper tells me the perpetrators are
themselves under investigation by the FBI.
    Multiple tragedies built on false

assumptions. A homeless young man with a mental disorder, beaten to death by my other brothers, the ones in blue who carry badges. And all because they couldn't see what was actually in front of them—a suffering human being gripped by paranoia, in need of medical attention. They saw the ground-in grime and ragged filth of the chronic vagrant, and assumed "homeless" meant abandoned and disposable, like trash. Maybe even dangerous. Their preconceived prejudices stripped the victim of all humanity.

His confused brain must have told him these officers were monsters. They obliged by responding monstrously.

Here's the thing. As I sit here on my deck, watching the sky darken, I understand. I understand how those officers got caught up in the moment. How the flood of adrenaline swept aside reason and fellow feeling. How the twitch of an outstretched limb could seem as threatening as a cocked trigger. I want to believe that I am incapable of that kind of delusion, but I know better. As do you, my dear Yeshe and Lobsang, who know the deceptive capabilities, the hidden mines of the mind, better than most.

Lately I've been seeing more clearly how I use my false beliefs to deceive myself. I'll notice self-critical thoughts running through my mind, labeling me as incapable of discipline, when suddenly I'll realize that it was my father who'd always labeled me lazy. Or I'll look at a beautiful woman and assume she is needy, then suddenly recognize it's my mother's neediness I'm seeing. It happens in my work, too. I found a missing 16-year-old I was searching for—found her pushed against a wall by a man twice her age, and assumed she was being raped. Nothing could have been further from the truth, but my unconscious assumptions kept me from seeing reality as it was.

So, I'm making a new rule for myself—a reminder, really, of a truth I tend to forget: From now on, I'm going to be on the lookout for unconscious beliefs, the kind I hold so closely, I mistake them for reality. As familiar as they are, as safe as they make me feel, too often these convictions serve as blinders. They prevent me from understanding what is actually happening in my life. I'm taking a new vow to challenge my old, limited models of thinking. To be willing to release them. Their job may be to protect, but more often than not they mislead and in some cases, even endanger. In the split second it takes you to figure out the difference between your perception of reality and reality itself, a lot of bad things can happen. In my chosen line of work, that split second can mean the difference between living and dying.

The lost-and-found teenager Harper Rudolph was my latest such lesson in humility. I'm not complaining. The job paid well enough to see me through several lunar months. I can now report that I am more than holding my own as a private investigator. I'm grateful for that. And I guess you could say I closed the case successfully, though Harper didn't see it that way. She may have been missing in her father Marv's eyes, but the last thing she wanted was to be found.

After maybe three minutes of face time with Marv Rudolph, I felt like heading for the hills myself.

But that's another story for another day. The air grows cool and moist against my skin. An eyelash of moon has just materialized, low on the horizon. Can you see it as well? I like to think so.

I miss you, my friends, even as I hold you close in my heart. Not a limiting assumption. Reality.

90

Ten

CHAPTER 1

I flipped the envelope over, rechecking the address in Dharamshala, making sure I had it right. But of course I did. How many letters, over how many weeks and months and years, had I mailed to my friends in just this way?

The original postmark was still there, stamped and dated almost three months earlier. Yeshe's and Lobsang's names were x-ed out. *Return to sender!* blared across the envelope in black ink, with a slash of arrow pointing to my Topanga Canyon address.

I recognized the handwriting. I had grown up with it, the jagged letters gouged into small index cards summoning me to the monastery headquarters once or twice a week, so that my father, or should I say my father the senior abbot, could chastise me for yet another infraction. His stiff, angry scrawl was permanently etched in my brain. I would know it anywhere. Raw pain flared, deep within my solar plexus. From across the ocean, my father had hurled yet another judgmental spear. And once again, he had hit his mark.

I refolded the letter and slipped it back inside its paper pocket. A low sigh escaped, originating deep in my chest. Now that I knew Yeshe and Lobsang hadn't received my latest letter, I felt a little lonelier than before. Nothing had changed, yet everything felt different. The sweet feeling of clarity I had been savoring, the one that often lingers after a deep afternoon meditation, was clouded now by a sense of loss.

I allowed it in.

In the distance, the ocean was quiet and majestic, the lights of distant boats just beginning to twinkle in the fading dusk. I took a sip of green tea. It had cooled in its cup as I sifted through my mail, turning tepid as I mulled over this unexpectedly returned letter.

Marvin Rudolph and his daughter, Harper. What a pair.

I felt my lips purse with taut disapproval, and I forced myself to relax into a half smile. Whenever my mouth tightens in judgment like that, I look a lot like my father. That tells me I'm thinking like him, too.

I tried to recall the case. After half a year, it had turned somewhat tepid in my mind as well. I closed my eyes and opened my other senses. Sometimes I have to let them do the remembering for me.

An acrid scent filled my nostrils.

Bad breath and potholes, that's how it started. . . .

"Find her. She's just a kid." Marvin Rudolph leaned close, wheezing from the effort of walking the ten yards from his car to my living room. I wanted to recoil from the fetid combination of sushi and cigar smoke. My 18-pound Persian housemate, Tank, darted under the couch, probably for the same reason.

"Don't you mean, find her again?"

"Whatever."

Marv had already filled me in on his elusive daughter, Harper—at 16, a newly converted connoisseur of the seedy and the derelict. Six months earlier she'd made her first escape, bolting the family mansion to savor the dark side, in this case Adams Boulevard, near Skid Row. He'd discovered his daughter hunkered in a downtown loft with a drug dealer by the name of Bronco.

Marv handed over a photograph of Harper. I studied it. She must have gotten her looks from her mother. Dark wavy hair framed a heart-shaped face dominated by huge gray eyes.

"How did you know where to find her?"

Marv settled back in his chair. His long-sleeved black linen shirt, one size too small, encased a belly that billowed over his jeans. He was close to 70, but he dressed much younger.

"Good story. We were open casting for a dope dealer when in saunters Bronco. Bronco Portreras. Think early Banderas meets Robert Pattinson, plus tats, minus the fangs."

I must have looked as baffled as I felt.

"Hot," he clarified. "I'm just sayin'. He nailed the reading, too. Anyway, the insurance company balked, because it turns out it wasn't an act. He really was dealing dope. Everybody wants to be a star, know what I mean? A week later, when Harper didn't come home from school, I logged onto her Facebook page. Bingo. She'd put a link to Bronco's audition on her wall, posted it on YouTube, too. He'd already gotten like twenty thousand hits." Marv's voice grew wistful, probably envisioning yet another gilded statuette that got away.

"So you tracked her down?" I prompted. It was almost ten o'clock at night. Way past Tank's bedtime.

"Yeah. He'd given his contact information to the casting agent. A crack dealer, leaving his digits on file. Dumber than a stick, right? I found Harper and him in his loft downtown, high as kites on weed, coke, maybe a little E. I threw a coupla grand at Bronco to shut him up, dragged her sorry ass home, and cut off her allowance until further notice."

It seemed to me that Marv was better equipped to deal with his daughter than I was, and I told him so.

"Not anymore," he said. "She's blocked me. Fuckin' privacy settings. My wife and I can't get on her page. And she won't answer her phone."

Marv's mouth twisted, and for a flash I saw the ruthless producer whose reputation for intimidation, especially when crossed, was legendary, even in an industry known for bullies. Then it was gone. His face sagged. With his grizzled day-old beard and loose jowls, he looked like a disappointed mastiff.

"Please," he said. "She needs to come home."

"Why not go to the cops?"

"Are you on crack? This whole thing would go viral before the cops even left the building."

I had one last question.

"How did you get my name?"

"I talked to one of your buddies down at police headquarters."

I immediately thought of my ex-partner, Bill. He was always worrying about my finances.

"Bill Bohannon?"

"Who? Nah," Marv said. "The Captain. Told him I needed a private detective, someone discreet. He told me you're more than discreet. You're some kind of Buddhist monk. Tight with the Dalai Lama and all. That right?"

"Something like that," I said.

"So, you into poverty, then?" Marv's expression grew shrewd.

"Five grand a day, three day minimum," I said. "Plus expenses."

He wrote me a check then and there. Three days, prepaid.

With that kind of discretionary income, you'd think he could afford mouthwash.

Whump! Tank thudded onto my lap, startling me out of my reverie on the deck. He draped his chunky body across my knees. I scratched under his chin, and he made a deep, gentle *prrrttt* sound. He tilted his head and eyed me, lids half closed, as if to say, "Don't let me stop you."

"Where was I?" I asked Tank. He flicked his tail like a whip.

"Right. Potholes." Like the Randy Newman song says, "God bless the potholes down on memory lane."

Devouring contraband mysteries every night as I hid under the covers of my monastic pallet in Dharamshala, I tended to romanticize the life of a detective. I'd open Raymond Chandler, read "Down these mean streets a man must go," and picture dark, smoky alleys with music drifting out of open windows, and beautiful women leaning in doorways, their long legs toned, their eyes glinting at me. I say "me," but in my mind back then I wasn't a skinny Tibetan teenager living in a Buddhist monastery, with a shaved head, maroon robe, and sandals. I wasn't Lama Tenzing Norbu. In this fantasy version of me, I lived in a big city. I solved crimes. I was armed, and I was dangerously good at what I did. Fedoras were involved, as well as a sexy car and sexier gun. My street handle was "Ten."

A lot like my current life, come to think of it, though I discovered I look ridiculous in a fedora.

Anyway, the mean streets in my imagination didn't have potholes the size of garbage cans threatening to break my Toyota's axle and hijack one of my kidneys, like the ones en route to finding Harper Rudolph that night.

After Marv left, my first and only call had been to Mike Koenigs. It was late, close to midnight, so he'd be having breakfast right about then. Mike is my personal "information security contractor"—according to Mike the word "hacker" is now considered passé, if not slightly insulting. I helped him out some years back, keeping him out of federal prison for dabbling with someone else's data. In return, he was my go-to man for digital matters, big and small.

"Can you get past Facebook blockades?" I asked.

"Boss, where's the love? Where's the respect?" he replied. "Name?"

I gave him Harper's name.

Pause.

"Okay, I'm on."

I waited.

"Hunh. She's posting as we speak. Whoa. Some serious partying pictures." Mike let out a long, low whistle. "Is that Keith Connor?"

"Keith who?"

"Ten, even you must have heard of the guy. He was the

lead singer for Blue Heron. Ex-rocker-turned-actor? Bad-boy heartthrob? Daily fodder for TMZ?"

Oh.

"She says here, and I quote, 'Keith's place is off the hook.'"

I heard light tapping.

"Yeah, and guess what? He's about to start work on a film produced by Harper's daddy, Marvin. Seven-digit salary. No wonder Keith's gigging it up."

Half the time I have no idea what Mike is actually saying.

"Can you give me his address?"

"Give me a mo'. Celebrity cribs are tricky."

In Mike-time, a mo' usually equals two deep breaths, in and out. Sure enough . . .

"Okay, here it is." He gave an address on Hartley Crest in Beverly Hills. "I'm also sending you a link to Keith's IMDB page."

In another moment, my iPhone screen was filled with a Caucasian male, late 20s, light brown hair, hazel eyes, and a reddish sexy demibeard that looked like he'd "forgotten" to shave for exactly the right number of days. He was gazing to his left, scowling slightly. He may have been going for a bad-boy heartthrob effect, but to me he just looked silly.

I sent Marv a text: LOCATED HARPER AT PARTY IN BEVERLY HILLS. ON MY WAY THERE. STAY PUT.

I grabbed my Wilson Supergrade from the gun safe in my closet and headed out.

First decision: which set of wheels to use? I quickly settled on my faithful workhorse, the Toyota-that-would-not-die, but not without regret. I hated leaving my real car, the thoroughbred, stabled at home, but a bright yellow '65 Shelby Mustang lends itself to surveillance about as well as a maroon monk's robe would.

There wasn't much traffic at that hour. Soon I was lurching along Wilshire Boulevard, traversing my way into

Beverly Hills. I would be at Keith's soon, if the drive didn't put me in traction first.

I know. Beverly Hills and cracked pavements don't seem to mix. And in fact, if you take Sunset Boulevard, the minute you approach Beverly Hills proper, the pavement magically loses its pockmarks as a thick profusion of multicolored flowers suddenly burst into bloom along the medians. Like an A-list actress, that area of Beverly Hills wouldn't be caught dead in public without makeup and blond streaks. But drop south of there and it's one big bad hair and acne day.

According to the latest city infrastructure assessment, there are over half a million unfilled potholes in Los Angeles at any given time, and maybe a dozen patch trucks to deal with them. Once a year the mayor announces Operation Pothole, and maintenance crews fan out across the city to patch and plug. They usually manage to repair 30,000 holes over a single weekend. That's 30,000 down, 470,000 to go. It's like doing battle with a wrathful Tibetan deity, the kind with never-ending multiple arms waving thunderbolts and skulls. When I was still a rookie on traffic detail, one jaded city official put it this way: "Potholes, like diamonds, are forever, son. So you tell me, how do you stop forever?"

Welcome to my brain when I'm driving around, dodging troughs, working a case.

I checked the map on my phone, zigzagging my way north and west, and eventually turning onto the bumpy byway known as Hartley Crest, set in the wooded hills off Benedict Canyon, where the houses are in the four-million-dollar range. As my beater car and I labored up the steep, winding street, a dim drizzle of wet fog slimed my windshield. The Toyota had a bum wiper on the driver's side, which I kept forgetting to replace.

I started passing high-end luxury coupes and SUVs parked nose-to-tail along the narrow road. Considering the company, maybe I should have taken the Shelby after all. I squeezed into a space between a dark blue Mercedes and a silver Infiniti. I considered grabbing the .38 Super out of the locked glove compartment, just in case, but thought better of it. First of all, technically, I wasn't allowed to carry it yet. Secondly, guns and teenagers don't mix. I climbed out of my car and took a moment to collect myself.

A bottom-heavy hip-hop beat shook the night. *Boom Boom thud, Boom Boom thud, Boom Boom thud.* Raucous laughter. A girl's high-pitched bray. I had found the party.

I passed between a pair of tall wrought-iron security gates, wide open and inviting any and all to enter, and picked my way up a driveway paved with antique cobblestones. Sherlock would have felt right at home. The house was a large two-story Mediterranean, stucco and red tile, with a second story turret. It looked like it had been built in the '20s and renovated this morning.

First things first. I tested the door to the attached garage. Unlocked. I looked inside. I was curious to see what an ex-rocker-turned-actor drove. I saw a gleaming black sedan I couldn't immediately identify. I slipped inside. I had to take a look. Well, well, well. A Maybach 57 S. Maybe the most expensive car in the world. You don't see that every day. I gave its flawless German features a respectful bow and continued on to the heavy, ornately carved front door.

The sound inside was deafening. I changed course—no one in the middle of that was about to hear the ring of a doorbell. I moved around to the manicured pool area in the back. Light spilled out of a large kitchen window. I took a closer look.

A young couple was engaged in a prolonged mouth-to-mouth exchange of oxygen and saliva. He had her pinned against a marble kitchen island, and she had her legs gripped around his waist like a monkey. Neither one paid me any attention as I slid open a glass door and slipped inside. I passed a row of gleaming, top-of-the-line appliances and moved into a large, arched entryway. To my right, a gigantic flat-screen television loomed over an oak-paneled den that was bigger than my house. Several young people, glassy eyed and still, were fixated by the flickering images on the screen. To my left was a step-down living room, where more kids sprawled on leather chairs and sofas, passing around an elaborate bong. If good looks were illegal, they'd all be locked up. I caught the eye of one young temptress, and she gave me a glazed once-over, followed by a dismissive smirk. I was barely 30, but already a fossilized life form to her, a curious leftover from the late Paleolithic. Ouch.

I scanned all the faces. No Harper. No Keith, for that matter. I mentally stepped into his shoes. If I were a rising hot actor about to hook up with my producer's daughter, I'd want to do my hooking up in private. In the master bedroom, for example.

I bounded up the curved and carpeted marble staircase and was faced with three doors. Two of them were ajar. I headed for the closed double doors at the end of the hallway. I pressed my ear to the wood. Animated voices, one low, one high. Arguing? I cracked the doors open and spotted a muscular, naked man groping at a slight young woman, tearing her clothes off as she gasped and cried out. My mind screamed, "Two-six-one! Two-six-one in progress! Sexual assault!"

Adrenaline coursing, I threw open the doors and flung myself across the room. I peeled off the brute—Keith—and tossed him to the floor.

I turned to the victim—Harper—expecting to see relief and gratitude.

With a high-pitched scream, Harper launched herself at me, arms flailing. I had to hold her wrists aloft to prevent her from gouging out my eyes.

"Who are you? What do you think you are doing?" Harper shrieked. "I was about to fuck Keith Connor! *Keith Connor!* Are you *completely insane?!*"

I moved to a window seat, well out of reach of Harper's talons. Keith watched me from the floor with a kind of stoned curiosity. He was stark naked and seemingly too high, or uninhibited, to care. My eye was drawn to a blue heron, tattooed just above his groin. *Ooph*. I turned my attention to Harper.

"My name is Tenzing Norbu. I'm a private investigator," I told her. "Your father hired me to find you and bring you home."

"I hate you," she said.

"Dude," Keith's voice piped up. "For real?"

I met Keith's reddened eyes. "For real. Dude. And you should be ashamed of yourself," I added. "She's sixteen."

His eyelids drooped. His facial expressions flickered as several fuzzy concepts formed their way into an unpleasant pattern:

Marv.

Movie.

Underage daughter.

Detective.

He sat up.

"Shit, man," he said. "You really know how to mess with a guy's buzz."

Irritation made the back of my neck itch. *Entitled jerk.* I glared at him, daring him to make a move.

Keith remained unfazed. He looked at me with interest.

"So, what, you're like Jackie Chan? Chinese or something?"

"Tibetan," I snapped.

"Awesome. Save the yaks, right? Some guy asked me to sponsor one last year. So, tell me, what's it like in the Land of Snows?"

"I wouldn't know," I replied icily. "I was raised in a monastery in India." *Moron.*

He blinked in confusion.

I opened my mouth to continue. Then I closed it again. There was no point giving him a history lesson about China's brutal takeover of Tibet. One: the systematic destruction of Tibetan Buddhist culture and the exile of thousands of monks and nuns happened more than 30 years before I was born. And two: China's war with Tibet was not to blame for my current state of mind.

Harper jumped in. "Hey, I've got an idea. How about if we just pay you some money and you go away?"

"Babe, he's not going to do that. He works for your dad, okay?" Keith's voice was patient.

He stood up and closed the doors. Scooping a rumpled pair of gray cashmere sweatpants from the floor, he stepped into them, cinching them with one hand. Harper's minuscule panties and featherweight tank top left little—no, make that nothing—to the imagination. With her slim hips and small, firm breasts, she was beautiful, in a waifish orphan kind of way. My taste in women tends toward the voluptuous, not to mention legally aged, but there was no denying it: the girl was hot.

I was a monk, not a saint.

I quickly turned my attention back to Keith. He gave me a half wink, as if to say, "See what I have to deal with?"

"So, detective," he drawled. "What's Marv paying you, anyway?"

I found myself wanting to impress him. "I get five grand a day for jobs like this, three-day minimum."

His eyes widened. I guess he momentarily forgot his own day rate. He gave me a friendly nod. He'd decided to have a little chat, man to man.

"Okay, so now, let me see if I've got this straight. You're pretty much obligated to go back to Marv and tell him you found Harper here, and me about to bone her, right?"

"Pretty much," I said.

In actual fact, I wasn't sure about getting into the details. Fathers like Marv with sexually precocious daughters like Harper have enough to worry about. The fact that Keith was on Marv's payroll further complicated things. I wasn't exactly sure what my next move needed to be.

"Dude," Keith said. "I've got twenty-thousand in cash in the top drawer of my dresser. I'll hire you for four more days to forget all about this, and you can refund Marv's money. Or you can keep his money, and take my twenty as a little bonus. I don't care. I just don't want to fuck up the movie. I don't want any bad vibes between me and Marv."

A $20,000 "little" bonus? He must have remembered his day rate after all.

Before I could respond, loud noises erupted down in the foyer. Heavy footsteps pounded up the stairs.

The double doors burst open for the second time, and there stood all 300 quivering pounds of Marv Rudolph, face clotted with rage.

As he swayed in the doorway, I was fascinated to see how wrath had transformed him. His left eyelid twitched, and a vein on his forehead swelled into a caterpillar of pulsing anger. Hot fury rippled from him like poisonous waves. Behind me, Harper whimpered.

An old monk's teaching flickered through my mind: *When in doubt, breathe. When not in doubt, breathe.* I focused on my breathing. One. Two.

Before I got to three, Marv exploded. Screeching like a wounded pig, he broke for Keith, who desperately tried to scoot backward. Harper threw herself between her father and Keith. In the resulting collision, she and Marv tumbled to the floor. Keith leaped nimbly over them and trotted out of the bedroom, still holding his sweatpants up with one hand.

I stepped outside after him. He was at the stairs when Marv hurtled past me and made a diving tackle. No contest. Now Harper was screaming, *"Daddy Daddy Daddy"* at the top of her lungs, as Daddy and Keith bumped and slid down the stairs locked in a mutual choke hold. Finally they rolled to a halt on the landing. Both collapsed onto their backs.

"Fuck," said Keith.

Marv was too winded to do much more than groan.

I was feeling pretty calm, calmer than they were,

anyway. I took a seat on the bottom step and waited for Marvin's panting to subside. Time for a little family mediation.

"You shouldn't be here," I told Marv. "But now that you are, you need to cool it. You're going to hurt somebody, and the somebody I'm worried about is you."

Marvin twisted his stubbled face toward me, then glanced away. "I can take care of myself," he muttered. He pushed upright.

Keith, too, sat up, wincing.

"Does this mean I'm fired?" he asked Marv. I found the question absurd. Of course he was fired. Marv considered Keith's answer longer than I would have.

"You do her?" Marv finally said.

"No!" Keith answered. "Swear to God, no. Ask the monk."

Keith had assigned me a role in his personal movie: I was The Monk.

Marv grunted, mulling it over. Keith's eyes entreated. Some wordless understanding passed between the film producer and his lead actor. Then: "Thanks, man," Keith said. "I won't let you down."

Marv grunted again.

When it comes to how the movie business works, I know nothing.

I surveyed the scene: Marvin hunched on the floor, Keith clutching his ribs. A sullen, sniffling Harper, her cheeks striped with mascara, leaned against the banister, seemingly unconcerned with her father's well-being or with the fact that she was the half-naked cause of all this.

Weariness fell over me like a heavy blanket. I wanted to go home. The sooner I took charge, the sooner I could leave. I stood up.

"Harper, go get dressed, please, then come right back."

She glared at my authoritative tone but headed up the stairs.

"Marv, take Harper home and put her to bed. Then get some sleep yourself." Marv stood, groaning under his breath.

"Keith, go into the kitchen and make yourself a cup of tea, if you know how. Sip it, and count your blessings."

He shuffled into the kitchen, the too-long legs of his sweats dragging behind like reversed flippers.

"How did you figure out Harper was here?" I asked Marv.

"Two plus two equaled Keith," Marv said. "She's a star-fucker, just like everyone else in this town."

I was sorry I'd asked. I marshaled the remaining revelers into the foyer. They were scattered throughout the down-stairs like so many discarded empties.

"Party's over," I said. "And if I see one word of this on the Internet, I will not only track you down and have you arrested, I will serve your name to Marv Rudolph on a plat-ter. And you don't want Marv Rudolph as an enemy."

They hustled out the door.

That was worth at least $5,000 in P.R. repair and main-tenance right there. Operation Pothole, at your service.

It took me a few more minutes to shepherd the Rudolphs into Marv's smoky gray Lexus, parked askew in the drive-way. Touching. He drove an LS Hybrid. For over $100,000 he could be comfortable, as well as politically correct.

Father and daughter drove off together in stony silence. I went back inside for one last sweep. Everyone but Keith was gone. The house felt very empty.

"Hey," Keith called from the kitchen. "Want a cup of Darjeeling?"

"I'm good," I said. He rejoined me with his steaming mug.

With a sheepish smile, Keith offered, "I still want to pay you."

"What for?"

"I owe you, man. Three more minutes and my big break would have gone right out the window."

I thought it over for one, maybe two seconds. "Send it

to the Tibet Foundation," I said. "Twenty grand sponsors a lot of yaks."

Brrtttt! My cell phone vibrated in my pocket, buzzing me back to the present. Me. Deck. Returned letter from my friends. The air was chilly, the sky as dark as ink. Tank leapt off my lap and stalked into the house. I rotated my neck and shoulders. I was a little stunned at the almost total recall I had just experienced, especially after months had passed since I had closed the case.

I grabbed my phone and glanced at the screen.

"Hello, Detective," I said.

"Hey, Ten. How goes it?"

"It goes, Bill. It goes. I was just out here on the deck, taking in the view, winding down."

"Rub it in."

So I did. "Let me ask you something, Bill. Can you feel deep down in your bones that this is the only moment there is?"

Without missing a beat, Bill came right back with, "Yeah, I was sitting here looking at crime scene photographs, when suddenly this little voice inside me says, 'Hey Bohannon—this is the only moment there is.'"

"And what did you say to that little voice?"

He adopted the thundering voice of a Pentecostal preacher. "I just said, *'Thank ya, Buddha!'*"

Bill Bohannon, newly appointed LAPD Detective III, Robbery/Homicide, is my former partner and one of my oldest friends in Los Angeles. He and I weathered a lot of weirdness together as Detective II's, including the ultimate male-bonding experience, shooting back at thugs who were trying to kill us. He'd recently moved to a desk job. Me? I'd just moved on. Bill didn't waste any more time getting to the point—one of his many virtues.

"We're working a homicide, Ten. Messy one. Came in late last night. Some big Hollywood producer."

My skin began to tingle.

"The Captain thought I should give you a call."

Of course he did.

"The victim is a guy by the name of Rudolph. Marvin Rudolph."

Of course he is.

CHAPTER 2

I pictured Marv the last time I saw him, face grim as granite as he drove his daughter home. All that angry bluster, and now he was dead.

"Any guesses on the COD?" I asked. Often the cause of death was pretty easy to determine at the crime scene.

"See, that's what's weird, Ten. Nothing is quite adding up." Bill's voice sounded strained, as if his chest muscles had constricted. I heard a high-pitched wail in the background, immediately joined by a second one, a lusty duet of protest from his twin toddlers, Maude and Lola.

"Damn it, Martha, I can't think!" Bill yelled. Cop shoes clunked across the floor, and a door slammed shut.

My own chest tightened. This behavior from my normally unflappable friend was completely uncharacteristic. "Everything okay over there?" I said.

Either Bill didn't hear me, or he wasn't in the mood to respond.

"Bill?"

"Yeah, well, like I said, the crime scene makes no sense. Autopsy's first thing tomorrow. They've put a rush on it—family's super traditional Jewish, and the wife's hoping to get the body buried before Saturday, though that will take a fucking miracle. Meanwhile, Marv is such a big shot in Hollywood, the media are swarming like a poked nest of hornets. I'd like to know how the hell I'm supposed to do my job when I can't even walk into Headquarters without twenty microphones getting shoved in my face." Bill's voice was climbing the scales. I waited. Heard the unmistakable sound of chugging and the clink of a bottle being set down. Bill was drinking something. I was betting on beer. I thought yearningly of my own six-pack cooling in the fridge.

"Anyway, the Captain seems to think you might have known Rudolph."

"I do," I said. "I mean I did." I gave Bill a recap of my interactions with Marv and his runaway daughter, Harper. If he was impressed with my total recall abilities, he kept it to himself.

"Okay. That helps," he said, and hung up.

I stared at my phone in disbelief. Not even a thank you? Tank spilled off my lap onto the deck and executed one of his nose-down tail-up, full-body stretches. In yoga they call it the "downward dog," but that's just wrong. It's a cat move, all the way. Tank padded over to the door and gave me his "where's dinner?" look.

"Sorry, guy," I said. "Not until I figure out what's up with Bill." Tank determined that the only proper response was to sit in front of the door and glare at me. It was like getting pinned by a pair of green headlamps.

I rotated my shoulders to dispel some of the muscle irritation as I called him back.

"Yes?" Bill sounded exhausted, and annoyance morphed into concern.

"Listen, I'd like to help," I said. "I'm happy to take a look at the crime scene photos. How about I come to you first thing in the morning? I'll even bring breakfast."

Bill hesitated. My concern grew. The Bill I knew never turned down a free meal.

"I know I'm rusty, but maybe I'll see something. Two sets of eyes and all that," I added.

Bill sighed. "Okay. But for God's sake don't come here." Bill's laugh was more of a small, grim bark. "The girls are eating real food now, and half the time the kitchen looks like a grocery grenade went off. How about Langer's?"

Langer's, home of all manner of deliciously greasy meat products. The bane of vegetarians. "Sounds good," I said. "I'll bring the official investigation report I wrote up for Rudolph."

"Unofficial, you mean. You get your license yet, Sherlock?"

"I passed the second retest, Bill. I told you."

I fought off the urge to defend myself further. The truth is nine out of ten L.A. cops fail the P.I. exam. It turns out we know plenty about criminal proceedings but almost nothing about civil matters, which is all the state cares about. I'd like to see Bill correctly identifying all 58 counties in California, or what agency department manages marriage licenses. (Public health—go figure.)

"Now I'm just waiting for my liability insurance to come through," I grumbled.

"Never mind," Bill said. "I don't want to know."

"Wise response." A second tart ripple of irritation spread through my body, this time aimed at idiotic bureaucracy. It seemed like every time I turned around, something else was standing between me and making my lifelong dream a permanent reality. My first two paying (well-paying, thank goodness) cases—the result, it now seemed, of beginner's luck more than anything else—had turned into a good long stretch of nothing. Nothing, that is, but flunking the private investigator exam not once, but twice, at over $100 a try. Nothing but finding that the Captain's final good-bye present, my LAPD "permit-to-carry," didn't preclude my owing another hefty gun permit fee to the California Bureau of Security and Investigative Services. Nothing but having to take out a $1 million liability policy, merely because I had permission to own and conceal that same firearm, my Wilson Supergrade, which was costing me more than my mortgage. And finally, nothing but crawling to Simi Valley, steeped in humiliation, for private tutoring from another private eye, so I could actually pass the test, hang a shingle on my door, and join the 30,000-plus other private investigators now populating Los Angeles County who could actually charge for their services. Not for the first time, I thought longingly of Keith Connor's $20,000 offer, long gone to a happy herd of Tibetan yaks.

Bill didn't know how good he had it.

No, Ten, you're the one who doesn't know. You never did, and you never will. And there it was, right on schedule: my inner, incriminating father-voice.

A fresh chorus of girl wails broke out over the phone, interrupting the slide into self-judgment. I could hear Martha's voice climb over her daughters', sharp with desperation, no doubt calling for backup.

"I'm too old for this," Bill said.

He was gone again, just like that, sucked back into the chaotic undertow of young children. After a moment of appreciation for the relative peace and silence of my twinless Topanga Canyon world, I gathered Tank up in my arms and gave him a lift back inside the house. The deck is off-limits to him at night unless I'm also there, due to the increasing boldness of the coyote population. In the hills of Topanga Canyon, coyotes have been known to squeeze through the little pet-doors people have for their cats and dogs. Just last month, one of my neighbors heard a shriek and woke up to find a coyote chasing his cat around the living room.

Safely inside, Tank leapt from my arms and sped across the hardwood floor, pulling up short a yard before his empty food dish. He walked the final three feet in stiff dignity and allowed himself one low cat-growl.

My stomach gave an answering growl: sympathetic hunger—right up there with the sublime Buddhist state of sympathetic joy. I opened a can of mixed grill and a fresh can of tuna. He's not crazy about tuna itself, but tuna-water is his favorite, so I started with that, squeezing it into his bowl. Tank gave me a quick beam and began lapping. I cracked open a frosty bottle of pale ale for my own treat. I tilted the bottle back and chugged. My exhaled *"Aaahhhh"* wafted across the room.

Tank glanced up.

"One of life's sacred experiences, Tank."

Tank lowered his face back into his dish: such thoughts were irrelevant to his feline needs. At times like this, I found myself acutely missing my ex-partner, Bill, and our daily ritual of late afternoon beer-and-casework reviews.

I reheated some leftover Thai food, washed it down with the rest of my beer, and moved to my home office, basically an interconnected snarl of digital equipment personally selected and installed by my tech guru, Mike. At first I'd resisted buying any of it. Now I couldn't imagine functioning without all of it. Nothing new, there. I'd been experiencing that emotional seesaw regarding technology ever since I first arrived from Dharamshala, 11 years ago. The Buddha urged his followers not to crave material possessions, to seek knowledge instead. But in his wildest imaginings, he couldn't have anticipated the eventual necessity of digital technology in the pursuit of that same knowledge.

Because Mike believed in following feng shui, my computer lived and slept oddly angled on my long, flat desk. I sat down and woke up the beast with one light tap of the finger: magic. I located the case file marked Marvin Rudolph, and opened and printed out my report for Bill. An eye-watering yawn escaped. I'd changed my bed this morning in a burst of virtuous housecleaning, and the crisp sheets were calling to me.

Don't do it. Don't do it, Tenzing. You haven't been asked, and you're not getting paid.

My hand snaked over and grasped my mouse. I called up my new best friend and assistant, Dr. Google. I entered Marv Rudolph's name and pressed SEARCH. My eyes widened. Marv had been a very busy boy over the last several years, not to mention the six months since I'd met him.

News of his death was just hitting the Internet, but I skipped past those items to earlier articles—I prefer to get my facts on a celebrity's sudden demise from those who actually know what they're talking about. Scanning other relevant subjects, though, I managed to deduce that Marv Rudolph, who had been considered "finished" five years ago, was now "back." His photograph was everywhere, often in a tuxedo, arms around various luminaries from the worlds of entertainment, civics, and politics, most of whom I didn't recognize. I did note that Keith Connor and Marv seemed to be together a lot this past month, promoting *Stung,* their just-finished film. From what I could decipher, the "buzz" on *Stung* was good, no pun intended. I also found several earlier articles trumpeting a small "indie" film Marv was casting right around the time he hired me to find Harper—a reinvention of the Romeo and Juliet story called *Loving Hagar.* But then all mention of it seemed to have just disappeared.

Things that disappear interest me. I put in a quick call to Mike. It was just late enough for him to be awake, working on his second cup of coffee.

"Yo," Mike answered.

"Mike, I have a request."

"Cool," he said. Mike was a man of few words before midnight.

"Can you look into the past five years of Marv Rudolph–produced film projects, including any that got dropped? I need to know details, if possible: who backed him, who backed out, who he was in bed with, who he might have pissed off. That kind of thing."

"What's ol' Marv done now?" Mike drawled over the tapping of keys. There was a pause. "Oh, oops. Bummer. So I'm guessing you need this ASAP?"

"Yes, please. And Mike, I may have to defer payment on this one. Sorry. Just keep track of your hours."

"No worries, boss." Mike yawned. "Later."

I hate asking people to work on spec, but Mike was earning six figures as a high-tech data-retriever these days, and he'd probably be in prison doing push-ups if it weren't for my early intervention. I wasn't too concerned.

I returned to my screen. When I'd Googled images of Marv, one particular press photograph from two years ago appeared again and again. A portly, tuxedoed Marv, arm and arm with a thin woman who resembled Harper, only older and more muted, smiled into the camera. They stood next to a distinguished older man and his gaunt but elegant companion. This second woman had the hollow eyes and turbaned head that suggested a long battle with an illness, probably involving chemotherapy treatments. I opened the article. The Rudolphs were at a charitable event, apparently raising funds to renovate a Bel Air synagogue, Temple Beth Adel. I squinted at the caption under the photograph. "Marv and Arlene Rudolph greet fellow Temple Beth Adel supporters Julius and Dorothy Rosen." Julius Rosen: even I had heard of him. His name was plastered on museums and theaters, up there with arts benefactors like Dorothy Chandler and Eli Broad. I printed out the photograph and accompanying article.

Next, I zeroed in on a news item from last year, an incident involving Marv's notorious temper and a paparazzo called Clancy Williams. It seemed to include a black eye, a smashed expensive camera, accusations of racism and paparazzi brutality, and an out-of-court settlement to Marv from a high-profile celebrity gossip agency, x17. I jotted down Clancy's name.

Finally, there was a very long feature in *Vanity Fair* entitled, "You Can't Keep a Good Marv Down," too long to read.

For every piece extolling Marv's creativity and talent, there seemed to be three describing angry directors, actors, or fellow producers claiming he had cheated, stolen from, or ruined them in some way. My list of industry people with gripes grew, though I got the feeling that while they might hate Marv, they also feared him and couldn't afford to shun him. Interesting. If, in fact, Marv had been murdered by a business associate, there were plenty of potential suspects, but how many were rich enough not to need him, powerful enough not to fear him, and vengeful enough to want to kill him? That was the list I'd start with.

I sighed. Who was I kidding? First of all, no one had hired me to look into Marv's death. Secondly, Marv Rudolph inhabited Hollywood, an entertainment arena of glitter, fantasy, wealth, and power incomprehensible to a lowly Tibetan ex-monk. I had spent most of my youth locked away in a monastery, and the gaps in my early education regarding popular culture were huge. Even now, I knew next to nothing of this world. I might finally have a good computer, but I still didn't even own a television. Even getting myself to a movie theater was a rare ocurrence. Movies were for dating, and dating for me, currently, was nonexistent. My big concession to new media was to purchase a Kindle last month from my dwindling reserve of funds, and load it up with my usual weird mix of reading material, from ancient Greek philosophies to modern noir mysteries. I figured it was a good investment for an avid reader and would serve me well for stakeouts.

All those long, lucrative stakeouts I was not getting hired for.

The glum direction of my thoughts told me I was too tired to keep working. I staggered to bed, my grateful Persian hugging my ankles, a thick file of printouts stacked neatly by my once-again slumbering computer.

CHAPTER 3

Bill opened the manila envelope and slid a photograph across the table to me. My favorite waitress at Langer's, Jean, had ferried us to a corner booth for privacy. Graphic images of corpses don't do much for people awaiting their breakfast pile of pancakes and bacon.

I pulled the photograph of the crime scene closer and leaned in to take a look. A belly-tightening chill of nausea swept through me. Even after all these years, I've never gotten completely comfortable with images of homicide victims, and I had met this corpse while it still housed a personality—in this case, one larger than life. I breathed in and out, long, deep breaths to disperse the queasiness; in a moment my mind cleared enough for me to look at Marv's body through Ten-the-detective's eyes rather than Ten-the-human's.

The victim was slumped in a semisupine position, knees bent, arms spread wide, reclining on some sort of heavy wicker lounge chair. An empty wine glass was set on the ground to his left. His long-sleeved black shirt had hiked up over his belly, and the great mound of flesh was dimpled and pasty white. His eyes were half closed, his mouth wide-open, tongue protruding slightly. An 8-inch black-handled chef's knife lay to his left.

Bill pushed another photo over. In this one, the knife and Marv's shirt had been removed, no doubt bagged and tagged as evidence.

"See anything interesting?" he asked.

I mentally divided the photograph into quadrants and

scanned each one carefully. I pointed to Marv's left fore-arm. "That?"

A ragged strip of skin was missing from his inner fore-arm, maybe the length of a business card. In its place was a red, raw patch of exposed flesh. I could only hope Marv's skin had been removed after he was already dead.

I looked up at Bill. "Before or after?" He shrugged.

I pointed to the knife. "That's the weapon used?"

"That's where things get even weirder, Ten. According to forensics, no."

Marv had wound up dead in a crime scene mysterious enough to warrant a visit from Sherlock himself. I returned to the photo. The lounge chair was on a black, tar paper surface, lightly graveled. Three faint sets of parallel drag marks, crisscrossed in places, led from the exit door to the area where the chair was placed.

"Where is this, anyway?"

"Rooftop terrace of Robinsgrove Apartments, that old art deco building in Hancock Park. Not far from my house, in fact. Built in the '30s. Pretty pricey rentals. They say Mae West used to live there. Rudolph's car was parked around the corner, on a side street."

I knew the place. I passed its ornate façade every time I cut north up Rossmore from Wilshire to get into Hollywood proper. At night, the letters of its name glowed red, a neon invitation looming over the city.

"A couple from a first-floor apartment found him. They were up on the roof having a romantic, late night canoodle and heard this buzzing sound every time they came up for air. It was Marv's phone. Popular guy, your Marv. He'd got-ten maybe fifty, sixty calls in a matter of hours."

"That'll keep you busy," I said.

"Not me. I'm a D-Three now, remember? I'm in charge. I passed the phone numbers along to Sully and Mack."

"You're kidding me. They're your lead investigators?"

"I know. I know. What can I say, they got the call."

Homicide detectives Richard "Sully" O'Sullivan and B. J. Mack, known as S & M to their friends, were good guys, but not endowed with an abundance of native intelligence. Bill was going to have his hands full solving this one.

I returned to my study of the crime scene photo. I pointed to the second set of drag marks. "What happened to the other chair?"

"Good question. Not to mention . . ." he cocked his head, waiting.

" . . . the person sitting in it," I finished. "And what do you know about the knife?"

"It's a Wüsthof. Only one of the most popular kitchen knives around. We have a whole set of them at home."

"Me, too, come to think of it. But you can rule me out. I was home in bed all Wednesday night. You can ask Tank. Fingerprints?"

"Lots. Mostly smudged. One partial we maybe can use."

I moved back to the wound on Marv's arm. "And this. I'm thinking maybe a telltale tattoo, removed to throw us off?"

"Twisted minds think alike," Bill said.

A swell of happiness flooded me. It had been a while since Bill and I had talked through a case. I'd given up one of my true pleasures in life when I left the force, and therefore, Bill.

"Oh, no, no, no. Not more dead people," Jean's southwestern twang broke in, her voice stern. She stood over us, mock-scowling, as Bill put the photographs away, then set a plate of crisp, fragrant potato pancakes in front of me and a massive pile of bacon and eggs before Bill.

"You're looking good, Jean," I said. She was. Her gray-blonde hair was freshly cropped at her chin-line, and her hazel eyes twinkled. She may have been in her 60s, but her energy was decades younger.

"Don't change the subject," she said. "Ten-zing, I thought you were through with that bad guy stuff."

"Just helping out an old friend." I smiled across at Bill.

"And how's your other old friend doing, not the cat, the other one. The one who wants to be a chef?"

My smile died. I tried to stave her off by stabbing a bite of potato, but Jean wasn't finished with me.

"Oh, don't tell me. You scared that girl off, too? What happened?"

Bill was getting way too much pleasure out of the direction this conversation was taking.

"Yes, Ten, do tell us what happened," he said.

I dipped the hot potato pancake in sour cream, added a little applesauce, and popped the whole thing in my mouth. The combination of earthy, sour, and sweet was superb. Maybe they'd both just go away.

"What? Nothing to add?" Bill turned to Jean. "As it so happens, Julie-the-chef is my wife, Martha's, half sister. I have it on good authority that she is back in Chicago, happily living with her previous ex-boyfriend, the sommelier."

"I thought she hated him," I burst out. "I thought he was a crazy lush."

"He got sober, apparently."

"A sober sommelier? How's that supposed to work?" My temples were throbbing.

Jean jumped in. "No, I've heard of that before, Ten-zing. They just smell everything." Jean had once confessed to me that she hadn't touched alcohol or drugs in years. What Scientology couldn't fix, a recovery program apparently could.

I gathered what little dignity remained. "Give Julie my best," I said to Bill. My voice sounded stiff, even to me. "She wasn't a good fit for me, anyway."

Jean patted my arm. "You know what they say about failed relationships, Ten-zing. 'Put down the flashlight, pick up the mirror.'" With that, she sailed off to her other unsuspecting diners, no doubt to offer more brilliant, unsolicited advice.

We ate in silence for a few moments. As Bill swallowed a big forkful of bacon and eggs, he grunted with pleasure. Then he frowned.

"If Martha saw me eating this she'd kill me," he muttered. "All she does these days is nag. She's turning forty, and somehow it's my fault. As if I didn't have enough stress with this new fucking job."

I'm always surprised how little actual joy we humans allow ourselves before we feel compelled to do something that brings us down again. Bill gave himself at most ten seconds of bacon ecstasy before starting the guilt-game, before some little part of his mind said, "Okay, that's enough happiness for now—time to bring up a subject sure to bum me out."

I met his eyes. Waited.

"Ah, never mind. It's all good," Bill said. "Don't forget—Miceli's tomorrow, for Martha's fortieth. Her parents are flying in from Germany tonight. We're defying the gods and bringing Lola and Maude, too. They've only been out to a restaurant once before, and it wasn't pretty." He signaled to Jean as he pulled some bills out of his pocket, waving my own money away as he tossed two 20s on the table. "Unh-unh. This one's on me. I'm heading over to the autopsy next. You?"

I shrugged. I didn't want to tell Bill I would probably be spending the rest of the day polishing my already gleaming Shelby Mustang and cleaning my already immaculate Wilson Combat .38 Supergrade. I certainly wasn't going to beg to be invited.

"Okay. Well, I'm off, then." Bill tightened his tie and tucked his manila envelope of crime scene photos and my Marv report into his briefcase. He started for the door, then turned and came right back. "Ah, hell. I'll just tell them you're consulting, helping me out a little with the investigation."

I pictured the big pile of Marv material on my desk back at home. In a way, I was.

CHAPTER 4

The L.A. County Coroner's Office was surrounded. At least six news trucks were parked in the lot, with maybe 15 reporters and cameramen milling around the front of the building, like ants waiting for the picnic to begin. When I pulled up, Bill was in their midst, trying to wade past, or through, or something. I couldn't tell. His cheeks were looking pretty ruddy, though.

I skirted the crowd and slipped into the building on the left, 1102, where the forensic labs were located. The main coroner's building was all brick and flounces. Decorative, and more for show, good for notifications and the release of personal property. But 1102 was where the real work happened. Here, medical examiners conducted autopsies on a continuous stream of suspicious deaths, sometimes as many as a dozen a day.

I sat down in a chair in the tiny waiting area, located to the right of the entrance. Across from me, a young man in a dark suit and yarmulke was camped out in another chair, rocking slightly back and forth. His eyes were closed and he was chanting continuously under his breath. I don't know much about the Jewish faith, but I'd once questioned another such young man on another case, this one a hit-and-run involving a Rabbi and a van. He'd told me keeping the body company, guarding it from harm, and soothing it with prayers until it could be put into the ground, was central to the Jewish burial process. He'd said the human soul can feel somewhat lost and confused between the time of death and burial, and so they offer companionship and comfort. I'd told him this practice was not unlike my own Tibetan tradition of chanting to help guide the dead through the confusion of the *bardo* and beyond.

I respected the fervency with which this young man was praying. This was a building filled to the brim with discarded lives, and most of the deceased had only homicide detectives and the County Coroner's Office to advocate for them. I closed my eyes as well: *May all beings, as many as exist in ten directions, be always well and happy. May all beings live in harmony with the dharma, and may their every dharma wish be fulfilled.*

"Vultures. I thought I'd never get away," Bill said, touching my arm. He'd survived the onslaught of media. I stood and followed him to the security window. He showed his ID to a woman behind the glass, and then leaned toward the slotted opening, gesturing to me. "You remember Detective Tenzing Norbu—he's with me," and that was that, we were buzzed right in.

We walked toward the autopsy room, pulling on our standard-issue latex gloves, paper aprons, and face-shields. "Just to let you know, there's gonna be a crowd in here—a case this high profile." He stopped at a door. "Okay, here goes nothing."

We stepped inside the refrigerated room. Bill was right again—this was a standing room only event. I looked around at the gloved, masked, and aproned attendants. The chief medical examiner, Dr. Padman Bhatnager, was there, as were Sully and Mack, plus a second autopsy technician, a stenographer, and a staff photographer whose job was to carefully chronicle every cut and swab for the Prosecutor's office, should this case ever go to court. They were all familiar to me from past autopsies, though I'd never seen them in one examination room at the same time like this. A tall, willowy blonde hovered by Bhatnager's elbow. Her I'd never seen before, with or without a mask. She must have felt my glance. Clear blue eyes behind delicate wire-rimmed glasses locked in on mine and then looked away. I checked out her hands. Her long, latex-gloved fingers were gripped tightly together. No rings. Hmmm.

We exchanged brief hellos all around. I barely caught her name—Heather something. She and Bill nodded like they already knew each other. I shot Bill a look: he'd been holding out. He ignored me.

"Let's keep going," Bhatnager said. He glanced at Bill. "We've already reviewed the medical records from his physician," he read from a clipboard, "a Dr. Davitz. He confirms Mr. Rudolph was on a number of medications typical for a male in his late sixties. He had slight heart issues, high cholesterol, moderate plaque, the usual. Nothing to indicate an acute myocardial infarction might be imminent."

I'd thought Marv looked like a heart attack waiting to happen, but nobody was asking me.

Bill and I moved to one corner as the ME began a meticulous visual scan of the body, reciting his findings into a tape recorder. The assistant marked a body diagram on his own clipboard, and the stenographer took notes. They were being triply careful with this. The external autopsy started to give up its first round of data. It was just as puzzling as the crime scene photos. The absence of major bleeding around the skin wound indicated it was inflicted post-mortem. Marv got skinned shortly after he died.

But how did he die?

There was no other visible trauma, no needle sites, no gun shot wounds, no lacerations, no blunt force trauma, no hematomas, no evidence of strangulation. Nothing.

"No visible external cause of death," Bhatnager concluded. "I'm going to have to open him up, at least do a partial on his sternum. We still can't rule out a cardiac event."

He opened Marv's chest with a V-shaped incision, from shoulder joints to mid-chest. Using surgical shears, he cut along both sides of the chest cavity and lifted up the entire ribcage and breastbone as if it were a single chest-plate of armor.

I looked over at Heather. Her eyes connected with mine for one brief moment before returning to Marv's remains. I did the same. I was pretty sure this was my first flirtation initiated over an opened cadaver.

After the usual visual recitation of organs, and some careful cutting away of muscle and cartilage, Bhatnager placed both hands in the chest cavity and lifted out a heart. Contrary to the opinion of some in the entertainment world, Marv Rudolph actually had one.

Bhatnager gently deposited the organ on a metal tray to be weighed and measured, sliced and scrutinized. I was both fascinated and slightly repelled by the fleshy pump before me. How could this lump of muscle and tissue be the seat of so much joy, and so much trouble? I glanced at Heather again as terms like "subscapular fat thickness" and "mild myocardial hypertrophy" swirled around us. She was studying the removed heart. Her eyes blinked several times.

"Can't be sure yet, but it doesn't look like a heart attack, either," Bhatnager muttered. "This is going to take a while. We're going to have to open the cranium as well. Somebody let the family know, please. I mean, we're looking at numerous tissue samples, stomach contents, toxicology screenings, maybe even bringing in my histo- and neuro-pathologists. Oh, and get me the ultra-violet light, as well." Bhatnager rotated his shoulders. "He's not getting out of here any time soon. Cause of death deferred, pending further results. Let's take a little break."

Bill and I shed our autopsy-wear and walked back through the lobby, where Marv's young guardian was still deep in prayer, chanting words of consolation. I was glad he wasn't privy to the events taking place inside that chilly room. As Bill and I stepped outside, Heather was right behind us. She peeled off her mask and lifted her face to the sun, breathing deeply.

She was very beautiful.

"Thank God for small favors," Bill said. I followed his

gaze. The Assistant Chief from the Operations Bureau, Ted Summer, was making a statement to the clustered media. Their cameras were fixated on his trim goatee, not us.

"What a mess," Bill added. "If this goes the toxicology route, it could take weeks. How you holding up, Heather?"

"So-so," she admitted. "Still trying to get used to everything . . ." She shook her head.

I nudged Bill. Nudged him again, harder.

"Oh, Heather, this is my former partner, Tenzing Norbu. Ten, Dr. Heather Magnuson."

She pushed her glasses to the top of her head, held out a hand, blushed, snatched it back to peel off a latex examination glove, and tried again. "Hello."

"Pleased to meet you, Dr. Magnuson." We shook hands. Hers was cool to the touch. Her fingers were long and delicate, musician's fingers. The bones felt fragile to me.

"Not used to 'doctor' either. Better just make it Heather." Right away I liked the sound of her voice. It was deep and calm, a perfect "bedside manner" voice. On the other hand, I wasn't crazy about the fact that she was an inch or two taller than me. On the other, other hand, maybe I wasn't finished growing yet.

"Detective Bohannon!" Chief Summer had spotted Bill and was waving him over to the media mob.

"Great," Bill said, and crossed the parking lot to toss a few bland and noncommittal fact morsels to the insatiable reporters.

Heather and I stood. The lengthening silence felt awkward. My monastic training left me very unskilled at the art of prolonging a conversation with a woman of interest, especially without being obvious.

"So you, um, you're into forensics?" I felt my own fleshy pump of a heart speed up its tempo.

"I'd better be," she said. "I got my medical degree this September and just started a year-long residency at the county coroner's office." So she was just about the same age as me. Interesting. She looked younger. "Yesterday was my second day at work, and my first ride-along, and today's my first assist, in case you didn't notice my hands shaking in there. Talk about jumping into the deep end."

I was preparing to launch into a fascinating discourse on the number of high profile autopsies I, myself, Tenzing Norbu, had attended, when Heather looked at her watch and let out a little yelp.

"I can't be late," she said, and scurried back into the building. I stared at the door as it closed behind her. It had been seven months, seven long months since Julie drove off, her car stuffed from floor to roof with her belongings, and a good part of my heart. For the first time since then, I felt the possibility of romantic regeneration.

Bill rejoined me.

"A beautiful blonde ME named Heather Magnuson. Who'd a thunk?" he asked.

"Thunk what? That she's a beautiful woman, or she's interested in pathology? That's borderline politically incorrect, my friend."

"That she's a *Heather*. People who choose to spend all day cutting up dead bodies are not supposed to be tall and blonde and have names like Heather or Tiffany or Amber. If you're a tall, blonde Heather, Tiffany, or Amber you're supposed to shop all day."

"Dumb blonde jokes? Really, Bill?" My tone was sharper than I'd intended.

"Hey, give me a break, Mr. Single Male Cat-owner. I'm the one who's home life is overrun by females, and don't think eighteen-month-old twins don't count." Bill's look was shrewd. "Anyway, since when did you become the staunch defender of blondes?"

Bill had a point. I'd only known Heather for a few minutes and already I was feeling protective. Warning sensations pricked. Duly noted.

"Where to next?" I said.

"I'm going over to interview the widow. I don't know what kind of shape she's in. Why don't you come? I could use an extra shoulder for her to lean on. Yours seems to work particularly well in these situations."

"What, you mean next-of-kin situations?"

"Nope. Needy women situations."

He jumped out of reach before I could swat him.

Chapter 5

I followed Bill to the Rudolph house, enjoying the throaty snarl of my Mustang as I let her stretch her muscles a little on the surprisingly fluid freeways, since Friday traffic hadn't started clogging all the drains yet. We took the Sunset exit off the 405, wound our way past the Bel Air byways, turned north on Beverly Glen, and after a few quick turns, onto Madrono Lane. The Rudolph house was a two-story, butter-yellow Mediterranean, surprisingly modest for a man of Marv's means. It had a neat lawn and was set back from the sidewalk at the end of a quiet cul-de-sac.

Bill climbed out of the unmarked Ford Taurus, gave his back a satisfying crack, and started up a narrow paved path to the front door. I had parked a half block away and was a few steps behind Bill. As I headed for the house, I noticed a black, four-door sedan, some sort of Chevy, an Impala maybe, parked across the street, engine idling. It sped off.

Bill pressed the doorbell, and we heard a chime of bells inside.

"You met Mrs. Rudolph before, right?" he said

"No," I said. "Just Marv and the daughter, Harper."

"Well, hell, what good are you, Norbu?"

I ignored him as I studied a narrow antique brass object, rectangular in shape, tilted inward on the right side of the doorframe. The door opened a crack and then swung wide as a dark-suited man in a black yarmulke stepped outside. He peered into our faces, his own expression grave.

"Is there news?" he said. "I'm their Rabbi, Rabbi Aaron Fishbein. The body, is it available for burial yet?"

"Not yet, sir," Bill answered.

Fishbein nodded. "Please, be gentle with her. She is in shock." He kissed his fingertips, transferred the kiss to the brass object, and hurried across the street. I watched as he continued down the sidewalk to the intersection and turned toward Beverly Glen, still on foot. The door started to close again.

"Mrs. Rudolph?" Bill said.

"Go away. Please." The voice quavered with quiet emotion.

Bill flipped open his badge-case and held it up to the crack in the door. "I'm Detective Bohannon. We spoke briefly this morning." He nodded in my direction. "My colleague Tenzing Norbu is here with me. Can we come in?" After a moment, the door opened. On an impulse, I glanced behind me, across the street. The Impala was driving past again. I followed Bill inside.

The house was much larger than it appeared from the outside. A grand foyer opened into an even grander living-room area to the right. The formal dining room on the left boasted an antique table that could easily seat 20, and a huge hinged mahogany door that led into what I assumed must be the kitchen. A curved staircase led up to an equally spacious second floor. All the doorways had similar small, rectangular boxes, tilted at an angle.

The rooms were spotless but decorated with a somewhat jarring mix of modern and traditional. As I trained my eyes on Mrs. Rudolph, my first impression was that she and her husband were an odd study in contrasts. From my own experience, coupled with everything I'd read, Marv was an explosive person, prone to arm-waving bursts of rage. He had stormed through life like a blustering monsoon, destroying anyone in his path. The woman before me was meek, thin, and unassuming; she seemed almost to disappear into herself. Her brown wavy hair was threaded with silver, and it stopped just short of her hunched shoulders. A deep worry line was etched vertically between her eyebrows, and her mouth was pinched with pain. But her oval face and dark eyes hinted at an earlier beauty, and I flashed on her daughter's fragile appeal. I was looking at the 55-year-old, worn-out version. Mrs. Rudolph wore black slacks, a gray cardigan, and a pair of dark flats embroidered with a muted Moroccan design. Her face bore the stark, flattened expression I had seen again and again on relatives of homicide victims. She led us into the living room. A few silver-framed photographs, some of a younger, happier Harper, some of Marv and her, dotted the tables. A large, ornate mirror hung over a fireplace mantel. The rest of the walls were covered with framed posters of past Marv Rudolph films.

As Bill and I sank into a pair of modern, overstuffed leather armchairs, I found myself wondering, as I often did with married couples, *What did they see in each other?* For some reason, this time a possible answer popped into my head: *Something they couldn't find in themselves.* Marv probably needed her quality of hardly-there-ness to balance out his quality of here-the-fuck-I-am-and-you-better-get-used-to-it-ness. As for what she saw in him, I guessed it had something to do with survival—she who mates with the biggest gorilla in the jungle gets the most bananas, or something like that.

Not that I'm an expert on this subject. I was taught to view females, and, it follows, sex with females, as harmful, if not disastrous, distractions on the road to enlightenment. One of the creation myths drummed into us in the monastery even claimed that Tibetans were descended from a wise monkey and a wily, rock-dwelling demoness.

Now that I'd read Darwin, I had to admire the fact that my Tibetan ancestors at least got the monkey part right.

Bill's calm voice tugged me back. "We just have a few questions we need to ask, Mrs. Rudolph."

"Yes, yes." She waved vaguely at the dining room. "I should offer you something to drink."

"We're fine," Bill said. I thought longingly about coffee,

but I knew he was right. She pulled over the most uncomfortable chair in the living room, a straight-backed antique number, and perched on its edge, facing us. She sat very still, looking at the floor, neither patient nor impatient. Everything she did seemed to be a beat or two behind normal, and it was hard to get a read on her. Grief does strange things to people.

Then again, so do pills. I remembered the last time I'd seen her daughter, stoned to the gills. Maybe Mom was her role model.

"Is Harper home?" I asked, gently. She looked blank for a moment, and then said, "Harper? No, no, she's at school. I thought it was best that she go. She's doing so much better at her new school." Her expression brightened at the thought of her daughter then sagged again, as if weighted down by the recollection that her husband was dead. She met my eyes. Hers were huge, but the pupils didn't seem dilated.

Bill said, "I'm very sorry for your loss. Please accept our condolences."

"I asked my Rabbi, why? Is this a punishment from God? For him? For me?" Her eyes filled. "Marv wasn't always like this, you know," she said. "He wasn't always so . . . " She blinked, and tears spilled over.

"I'm very sorry for your loss," Bill repeated. I was silent.

Homicide detectives are trained to say, "I'm sorry for your loss," to the next of kin, but I seldom connect to these words. Maybe it's a Buddhist thing. I know it's important to acknowledge another's pain, but if I tune in, deep down inside, I usually don't feel comfortable using the word *sorry*. Why apologize for someone else's loss, especially when all involved are strangers? It borders on egotistical. In this case, it would also be a lie. I did not feel sad. Not for the demise of Marv Rudolph and not for his surviving wife. Most of us are in for a rough ride as we get older, even more so if we're overweight, chronic cigar-smokers. Maybe Marv got lucky;

his limited time on earth came to a fairly painless and swift end rather than a long, slow, painful one. And as for Arlene, I had a hunch she was well rid of him.

Marv's wife wrung her hands. "This is all such a shock. I don't know what to do." Her voice rose. "I need to bury him. I need to put him into the ground, so he . . . so he can have some peace, and we can sit shivah. It's almost Shabbat. Why are they keeping him so long? What are they doing to his poor body?" She doubled over, moaning.

And now, I did feel a surge of compassion. I walked over to her and put my hand on her thin shoulder, but she pulled away. After a moment, she straightened up, folding her hands in her lap like a schoolgirl. I returned to my chair.

"This won't take long," Bill said. "I apologize. There's no easy way to ask these questions, ma'am."

"Ma'am," she said with a thin smile. "Ma'am makes me feel so old. Please. Arlene."

"First, and again, ma . . . Arlene, I apologize, but we have to ask. Can you tell me where you were late Wednesday night and early Thursday morning?"

She blinked. "I was, I was at a lecture at my temple on Wednesday night. Temple Beth Adel. It was a talk about redemption—Jewish Women and Redemption. I took Harper. Then, I went to bed early. A few hours later, Harper woke me up. She wanted to know when her father was getting home. I said I didn't know. Late." Arlene's voice faltered. She licked her lips. "She said she needed his signature for something, umm, some school trip coming up." She smiled a little smile. "She's doing so much better at her new school," she repeated.

I was glad. She needed to be doing better.

Bill was jotting down Arlene's information for later corroboration.

"Anyway," she said, "I went right back to sleep. The next thing I knew, it was light out, and those two detectives were ringing the doorbell. That's when I realized Marv never came home." A small "oh" escaped her mouth, and she curled tighter, around the pain.

"And where did your husband say he was?" Bill said.

"Some sort of business meeting, he said. I really don't know."

"Did your husband seem preoccupied in any way? Worried about something, maybe?"

"No. No, in fact he's seemed much happier lately. Excited about his new movie, of course. And he loves awards season, all the parties and premieres. Especially now that he feels successful again. He's been out almost every night. It's that time of year."

Bill scribbled a few more things. He looked up from his notebook.

"Right. Now, Arlene. You were given some details by Officers O' Sullivan and Mack, concerning an . . . injury to your husband's body, yes?"

A rush of blood turned her throat pink. "They said someone took his skin," she whispered. "Is that how he died?"

"We're still not certain how he died, I'm afraid."

She waited, anxiety coming off her in waves.

"The piece of skin was removed from your husband's inner forearm. Someone seems to have cut something off of there. Do you know what it might be?"

Her flush deepened, staining her pale skin. How odd. She looked ashamed.

She made a small choking sound and started to gasp for breath. Bill shot me a "do something, we're losing her" look.

I squatted in front of her, a little awkwardly, as if she were a small child. "Breathe, Mrs. Rudolph. Breathe." I took a deep inhale and exhale, hoping it would prove contagious, like a yawn.

It seemed to work. Arlene, too, took a deep shaky breath, and let it go. We breathed together for a few moments. I should have quit while I was ahead, but I decided to go one step further.

"That's right," I said. "Just feel what you're feeling."

She stiffened, aiming her words at the floor like darts. "How am I supposed to know what I'm feeling? One day I'm sitting here doing what I've done every day forever, and then my doorbell rings and I've got some strangers telling me my husband's dead, maybe murdered, and now I've got another one saying somebody defiled him, tore off his skin!" She met my eyes, a wild-eyed look. "Can you imagine that?" Her voice rose. "Can you?"

"No," I said. "There's no way I could ever know how that felt."

She ignored me and turned to Bill.

"Somebody cut his tattoo off his arm? Is that what you're saying?"

Bill and I met eyes. Bingo.

"I'm afraid that's it," Bill said. "Please, Arlene, can you tell us about the tattoo?"

"Numbers," she said. "Numbers."

"Numbers? Do you happen to know what they were?"

"No," she whispered. "No. I, I can't . . ." She started to twist the heavy gold wedding band on her finger. "It was wrong of Marv to violate his body like that. Terribly wrong. I told him so, but he wouldn't listen."

"Was this recent?"

"Two years ago."

"And you're sure you don't remember the numbers?"

Her face cleared. "I wrote them down." She excused herself and hurried upstairs.

"Violate his body? That seems a little harsh," I said.

"I think tattoos are taboo for Jewish people," Bill answered. "Same reason they don't want autopsies . . ."

Arlene came back downstairs, a piece of lined note paper in her hand. She gave it to Bill. He copied some numbers off of it and handed the paper to me. I wrote them down as well: 481632.

She took back the paper and stared at the numbers.

"Now I remember," she said. In a singsong voice she recited, "Double four, makes eight. Double eight, makes sixteen. Double sixteen, makes thirty-two. I used to be a whiz at numbers when I was Marv's bookkeeper, back in New York. When we were happy."

She's losing it, I thought.

"What do the numbers refer to?" Bill asked.

"I don't know," she said. "He wouldn't tell me. He got angry that I didn't already know. Know what? Know what?"

Bill studied her with the flat unsentimental gaze only acquired by being lied to a few thousand times. He turned to me and flared his eyes. I knew the look: I think she's telling the truth. What do you think?

I nodded slightly to him. I agreed.

Mrs. Rudolph stared off into space. "Marv wasn't the same after the tattoo. Something in him got . . . hard. I mean, he was always ambitious, but after that, there was no getting in. Pretty soon, all he thought about, cared about, was Hagar."

Bill stiffened, on high alert. "I'm sorry? Hagar?"

I knew that name. Why did I know that name?

Arlene's eyes flashed. "*Loving Hagar! Loving Hagar!* He was obsessed."

"Who is Hagar?" Bill's voice was gentle, but there was steel underneath.

Arlene said nothing.

"Ma'am, are you saying Marv was having an affair?"

She stared at Bill.

"You don't know anything, do you?" she said, and that's when the penny dropped for me.

I put my mouth close to Bill's ear. "I'm pretty sure that's the name of a film Marv was trying to produce," I murmured. "*Loving Hagar.*"

"Oh. Great," Bill muttered. "That's just great."

"Anyway, none of this matters now." Arlene's voice was dull.

"It matters if we're to find out how your husband died. Who or what might be responsible . . . " Bill answered.

"No. No, detective. That's not important."

I could almost hear Bill's mental teeth grinding in frustration. Ever the diplomat, though, he said, "What is important, then, Arlene?"

Arlene picked at a loose thread on her cardigan. "How Marv lost his way," she said. "How he got to a point in his life where somebody needed to kill him. How the sweet devout goofball salesman I married came to die a lonely, angry crook with too many enemies to count." Her words hung in the air like storm clouds, fat with rain.

"I'm tired," she said, the tears spilling over. "I have people coming, friends, from my temple, and my daughter will be home any minute. Can you leave me alone now?"

Bill hesitated. "Sorry, one last question."

Her voice shook with exhaustion. "What is it?"

"You said *crook* a moment ago. Was your husband involved with criminals in some way?"

Now it was Bill's turn to receive a long look, this time from the weary wife's eyes. Arlene's smile was bitter. "You must be joking, detective," she said. "He was a *movie producer.*"

CHAPTER 6

As we stepped outside the house, a chorus of strident voices accosted Bill. "Detective Bohannon? Detective! Bill! Over here, Detective!" A fresh gaggle of photographers and news reporters had landed on the sidewalk in front of the Rudolphs' lawn, no doubt hoping for a saleable glimpse of wifely grief.

They are vultures, I thought. *Carrion-eaters. Useless, hateful creatures.* My hands tightened into fists. *I'd like to . . .*

I caught myself mid-surge: righteous indignation is the straightest route I know toward blind ignorance and away from any possibility of insight.

Vultures, too, have their place in this world. They recycle rot, rot the rest of us help create.

Bill said, "How the hell did they find me here?" His phone beeped notice of an incoming text message. He checked his screen.

"Shit. I'm due at the airport right now. Martha's parents land in half an hour." He pushed through the media mass, tossing off "No comments," jumped in his Taurus, and took off. A couple cars sped after him, and I smiled, imagining them tailing Bill all the way to the airport, praying for a scoop. Well, if any journalists actually made it there, Bill's German mother-in-law would soon make schnitzel out of them.

The remaining reporters looked at me hopefully, but I didn't register as anyone important, and they resumed their vigil on the house. As I walked to my car, I noticed the black Impala, parked a block and a half further ahead. I continued on foot, until I was next to it. A light-skinned African

American slumped in the driver's seat. Something pinged in my brain. I looked more closely. It was the photographer, the one from x17 who'd gotten into the dust-up with Marv. Clancy Williams, fast asleep. His front seat was crammed full of disturbingly familiar items: a laptop computer, empty fast food containers, crushed coffee cups, a pair of binoculars, and a digital camera with a huge telephoto lens. If I didn't know differently, I'd have assumed he was a fellow PI, staking out Marv's house.

In the back seat, I noted a banged-up boogie board, a well-thumbed catalog for high-end digital equipment, and a glossy trade magazine, *American Cinematographer.*

I tapped on the glass. He startled awake. We met eyes—his were bleary and suspicious. He lowered the window.

"Clancy Williams?" I said. He nodded, even warier. "My name is Tenzing Norbu. I'm a PI. Can we talk?"

He was momentarily distracted by another news van pulling up in front of the Rudolph house. He shrugged. "Why not," he said. "I've obviously fucked up any chance at a grieving widow shot."

Strike one, Clancy, I thought. One count of felon-ious insensitivity.

He cleared off the front seat, transferring the trash and equipment to the back, and released the door locks. I climbed inside. The car smelled faintly of fried potatoes and sweat.

I handed Clancy my business card. Mike had printed up a box of them for me after my Marv job, and I had taken to carrying some around, in anticipation of my actually getting licensed sometime this decade. Clancy studied my card, and I studied him. He was a good-looking fellow, despite the dark smudges of fatigue under his eyes. Early to mid-thirties, muscular, light brown skin, fine-featured, with a halo of curly black hair. When he looked up, I saw his eyes were hazel flecked with green.

He was a hybrid, just like me.

"Tenzing Norbu. What is that? Korean or something?"
Strike two.

"Tibetan," I said.

Light flooded his features, evaporating the tiredness. He looked like a totally different person. "Tibet! Fuck, man, I'd sell my left nut to shoot there. I pretty much nailed a gig assistant-DP-ing a documentary about Tibet straight out of Alabama State. I mean for real, it was a lock." His face fell. "But there was no green in it. None. Had to turn it down." He shook his head. "Nope, this is me now. Chasing people down, exposing their shit, so other people can feed on it."

I had never been this close to a vulture before. I wasn't passing up the chance learn more. "Why do it, if that's how you feel?"

He pulled out a pack of cigarettes and offered me one. I shook my head. "This is one of the few recession-proof jobs left, you know? People will give up their car payments before they give up the gossip. Why do I do it? Two words: *Student. Loans.* Lady Gaga and Madonna in a lip lock? Miley Cyrus sucking on a bong? Fifty grand. Boom. Freedom! I am one big money shot away from getting out from under." He lit his cigarette and cracked his window, dangling his hand outside, where the smoke spiraled into the blue sky. "Or I was, until I walked into that piece-of-shit firestorm called Marvin Rudolph. My agency dropped me, none of the others will touch me, and all my contacts have completely dried up. Even the other paps treat me like I've got herpes." He stubbed out his cigarette. He'd hardly taken a puff.

"Trying to quit," he said, at my look. "I got a little girl now. Meanwhile, the competition keeps getting worse. Ever since Rupert Murdoch's people got nailed, we've been swamped by European scumbags willing to do whatever it takes to claw their way in. Used to be, you could make six, even eight K a month. Now?" He shook his head. "Jesus, listen to me. Whining like a baby. So. What's your story?"

"I'm a private investigator," I said, leaving out the

"licensed" part. "I did a job for Marv Rudolph a while back. Right now I'm helping a friend investigate his death." Enough truth to satisfy, I hoped.

"That's cool," he said. "Listen, man, I didn't mean to sound so harsh about Marv. I feel for his wife, a-right? She seemed like a nice lady, the few times I saw them together. But that dude? He was nothing but bad news. So, yeah, I mean, I came straight here soon as I read he'd bought it. I already knew where he lived, a-right? I wasn't going to harass Mrs. Rudolph or anything. I was just hoping for a 'human interest' shot, before the others showed up. Make a few bucks, ahead of the herd."

I nodded. I now had my own herd of 30,000 private dicks to compete with.

"Truth, dawg? My heart isn't in this anymore. I just want to pay off my loans, so I can maybe start doing some good in the world with my camera. Make my wife and kid proud of me."

I couldn't believe it. I was starting to relate to this guy. A hairline fracture weakened my rock-hard prejudice against paparazzi, and a crazy idea snuck inside. My scalp tingled, a sure sign I should pay attention.

"Listen, Clancy," I said. "I'm just getting started in my business, you know? And the thing is, I could use another set of eyes."

"Doing what?"

"Doing what you already do. Watching. Noticing. Taking pictures, even. I can't pay you, not right now, but in my experience, these things have a way of working themselves out in the long run."

He shook his head. "Naw, man. I already got a long line of people pissed off at me for what I do."

"It's not what you're doing that's the problem, Clancy. It's what you're doing it for."

Clancy thought this over. He shrugged. Pocketed my card.

"Whatever. I'm sick of my life. Maybe this'll change things up."

I smiled as I got out of his car. "Where I come from, it's called karma. And as for things changing? Guaranteed, my friend. Guaranteed."

I took Sunset all the way to the ocean, turned right on Pacific Coast Highway, and pulled into one of the Santa Monica parking lots bordering the public beach. I had an old set of cut-offs and running shoes in the back for just such moments. I was starving—somehow I had completely missed lunch—but a run sounded even better than food. My muscles were twitching from a day of enforced inactivity.

I changed in the car. A smattering of bike riders, roller bladers, and power-walking parents with strollers navigated the pedestrian pathway in both directions. I decided to run on the sand. I started off with a slow jog down to the water's edge and turned north, toward the pier. The setting sun glinted on the slow-breaking waves, and pelicans circled, occasionally making a vertical dive to snag a wriggling snack.

I thought about the day as I ran: Arlene, nursing her grief; Clancy, postponing his dreams. And me, dancing around my own job-related fears. *What if the insurance company turns me down? What if it doesn't, and I can't afford the premiums? What if I never get hired again?*

I picked up the pace. As I glanced ahead, I saw a tall blonde woman in the distance, walking toward me. Her hand was tucked in the arm of an even taller blond man. She tipped her head back and laughed, her teeth so white they flashed in the afternoon light. The couple stopped, kissed, and started to walk again.

Heather.

What did you think, Tenzing? Did you actually think you could be with a woman like her?

My feet pounded the sand.

Too smart. Too beautiful. Too smart. Too beautiful. My mind chanted to the rhythm of my feet hitting the ground. *Loser. Loser. Loser.* Sweat dripped between my shoulder blades. I was closing the gap between us quickly, but I couldn't bear the idea of turning around. She'd know I was just trying to avoid her. So I kept running, closer and closer, focusing my eyes on the damp sand in front of me. At the last minute, I looked as I passed her, passed the perfectly pleasant-looking blonde woman who was not Heather, not even close to being Heather, unless you were me, once again distorting reality so it would fit a negative mindset.

I don't need any outside enemies. I have a perfectly good one residing right between my ears.

I ran another mile or so. Stripping off my T-shirt and shoes, I ploughed into the icy ocean and windmilled through the waves like a maniac. For the next ten minutes I churned back and forth, parallel to the beach. One good thing about swimming in ice water is you don't spend much time thinking about anything else. I charged back out, gasping from the frigid bite of saltwater on my skin. A lone surfer in a full wetsuit, bobbing on his board, hooted at my lunacy. The shock of cold was bracing. As I pulled on my shirt and shoes, a wind kicked up and I broke into a sprint, feeling its welcome force helping from behind. I poured it on, exhilarating in the feeling of lungs and heart working together at high speed. I came to rest, panting, on the sand near the parking lot, and stretched out my thrumming muscles.

I strolled back to my car a new man.

I exchanged wet clothes for dry ones, using the Mustang's passenger door for cover. I felt so much better as I drove up Topanga Canyon that I decided to practice changing my mental channel as well, to one that played more positive tunes. I envisioned myself with a ridiculously high-paying PI job, working for someone I respected. I pictured myself doing such good work that my phone started ringing off the hook with clients. Then I pictured myself enjoying a really good meal at a romantic restaurant with the lovely Heather, wine and dessert included, and nary a blink at the tab.

I pulled my Mustang into the carport, gave its marigold coat a quick once-over with a chamois to remove any sea salt, and strolled up the path to my house.

Tank was on his favorite cushion, busily licking his fur, the perfect self-cleaning oven.

"Hello, my friend. Miss me?" I said. "I missed you." Tank's green eyes narrowed with pleasure, as he got to work on his paws.

I grabbed an apple and moved onto the deck. A warm furry body, soft and alive, rubbed up against my ankles, and I felt a wave of happiness as I stood and munched. Soon I would step back inside, fill Tank's bowl, treat myself to a nice long meditation, cook up some brown rice and stir-fry, and settle into bed with my Kindle and my cat. I allowed myself one more thought. Maybe, just maybe, everything was pretty fine, just the way it was.

Tank lived that way. Why not me?

CHAPTER 7

Mike's text had come in around 6 A.M. I try not to look at my phone until I've stretched and meditated, and it was almost two hours later when I checked my messages and called him back.

"Dude. You're insane." Mike's voice was more of a croak. "I said I was going to bed, to call me late this afternoon."

"If you slept at night like a normal person I wouldn't have to wake you up," I said. "So what did you find?"

I heard groans, and a lighter, female voice murmuring in the background. Mike and his girlfriend were still cohabiting happily together, after almost a year. Tricia was a graduate student, and quite the night owl as well. I'd recently asked him what their secret was. "She's the only person I've ever met who's smarter than me," he'd admitted. "No offense, boss. Plus, she's hot, and she laughs at my jokes." I'd filed the conversation away for future consideration.

Mike finally started talking. "Right, so I looked into Marv Rudolph, like you asked. Interesting story. He came out of nowhere in the early seventies and was making a fortune within ten years. His business model was pure genius. Find little gems at foreign film festivals, get them for a song, turn around and remake them for almost nothing, with stars who want respect in the form of little gold statues called Oscar, rack up nominations, sell lots of tickets, and use the profits to buy more little gems at foreign film festivals. The guy had a nose for the winners, too. Where other people smelled crap, he smelled gold. It was his zone of genius, you know? He should have stuck with it."

"Go on."

"Well, he must have gotten bored, or greedy, or something. He sold his library to Warner Brothers for a nice piece of change and spent the next decade putting the profits into all sorts of things he knew nothing about: five-star restaurants, high-end nightclubs, luxury apartments, stuff like that. Then the recession hit. Bottom line? He lost his shirt and virtually disappeared from the Hollywood scene. Hang on, I need to take a leak."

My coffee maker beeped. I leaned over the coffee pot and inhaled the rich, earthy scent of freshly brewed Sumatra. I poured the coffee and took my first sip. Delicious. *May I live with ease, and may I always be able to afford good coffee.*

"Okay. Where was I?" Mike asked.

"Marv went bust."

"Right. Big time. So fast-forward five years. He still had a little cash in the coffer. His name started popping up here and there. Perez Hilton. Nikki Finke, just a mention or two. He was hawking a new little indie movie he wanted to make, *Loving Hagar.* Word was the script was edgy. A hard sell, but brilliant. Romeo and Juliet, only instead of Montagues and Capulets, it was Jews and Palestinians, you know, granddaughter of holocaust survivor falls for West Bank refugee. This was surefire Oscar material if it ever got that far—and classic Marv Rudolph. The heat from the script alone led to Marv beating out everybody in town for the option on a bestselling thriller called *Stung.* Marv took another chance, and let the author adapt his own novel. Then he landed the biggest fish of all. With Keith Connor signed on as the lead, suddenly Marv was back, you know?"

I thought about our interview with Arlene yesterday. "So what happened to the other one, to *Loving Hagar?*" I asked.

"I'm still trying to find out," Mike said. "According to Nikki Finke, two years ago Marv was all gung-ho and full speed ahead, with guaranteed backing from that billionaire Rosen. Julius Rosen."

"Hang on." I moved to my desk and shuffled through

the printouts until I found myself looking at Rosen's benign smile. "Okay. Go on."

"Marv'd already cast an unknown for the Hagar role, Tovah Field, make that Fields with an 's,' and was in the process of looking for another unknown to play the dude. The plan was to surround two up-and-coming stars with a bunch of big names for the supporting roles. Then, suddenly, there was talk of rewrites happening. Never a good sign. Then more rewrites. Then, nothing. Marv was all *Stung*, all the time."

"How the hell did you learn all this in twenty-four hours, Mike?"

"Oh, you know, start with IMDB Pro, cross reference some data, check the trades, this and that." Whenever he got cagey, I got less curious. With Mike, some things are better left unknown.

"Thanks. This is really helpful," I said. "Listen, I hate to ask, but can you look into . . ."

". . . Julius Rosen. Already did, boss. I'm busy with gigs the next two nights, so lucky for you I'm trying to clear my plate. Rosen's somewhat of a recluse these days, hard to find, but I dug up an old feature *Architectural Digest* did on his compound and put two and two together. Once I had an actual location, I was able to track down his digits. I'm texting his phone number and address to you now. Oh, and I'm e-mailing you photos of some of the other major players in Marv's life for the past five years or so." His voice took on the accent of a gangster. "See? I'm schmart! I can do things!" I heard Tricia giggling.

"What?" I said. "What's so funny?"

"I'm doing Fredo. Godfather Two. Jeez. Word to the wise. If you're going to tango with the big boys in Hollywood, you'd better start streaming Netflix. Later, Terminator." He hung up.

I looked over at Tank. "Mike thinks we're culturally deprived," I said. "What do you think, Tank?" He rolled to one side and closed his eyes, as if the notion of "streaming" anything exhausted him. "My feelings, exactly."

I called the number Mike had texted me. To my surprise, it was Julius Rosen's personal phone—his voice mail picked up after five or so rings. I listened with attention. Rosen's voice was clearly that of an older man, but the tone was strong and warm. I identified myself, somewhat vaguely, as a detective, and said that I needed to come by, hopefully this morning, to ask him some questions regarding the late Marv Rudolph. I left my number.

I took a glass of orange juice, a bowl of Greek yogurt topped with almond-date granola and sliced banana, and my pile of Marv Rudolph reading material to the deck. My phone stayed silent, as I steeped myself in the further adventures of Marv. Much of what I had downloaded yesterday confirmed what I had just learned from Mike. Good. I was finally getting better at using the Internet. I'm schmart, too.

It was 10 A.M., and still no reply—not from Rosen, not from Bill. Time was a-wasting. I decided to drive over there. From what Mike told me, Mr. Rosen was likely to be home. I checked the address on my phone. Big surprise. I was going back to Beverly Hills.

I also called Bill, but his voice mail picked up as well. He was sure to be neck deep in in-laws and Martha's birthday plans. I filled him in, and gave him Rosen's address, just in case.

"Oh, and tell Martha happy four-oh, and I'll see her tonight," I finished.

I exchanged my sweats for my best pair of jeans and added a nice long-sleeved cotton shirt. I checked the mirror for any obvious faux pas.

I'm almost five-ten, and weigh about one-eighty. I guess you could say I caught a few genetic breaks from my sturdy Tibetan father and my willowy Midwestern mother. Some days I look Asian, others, American, with more than a dash of European brio thrown in. I got his muscles and her height, his dark brown eyes and her high cheekbones, his tawny skin, her full lips. My hair seems to have come from a place all its own. It's thick and black and ridiculous if it's more than a few inches long. One time I tried growing it out, but the guys in Robbery/Homicide started calling me Magic Marker. I went back to my near buzz right away.

I looked okay. Nothing stuck in my teeth.

I printed the photographs from Mike, made sure Tank had food and fresh water, looked longingly at the locked gun safe in my closet—I hate going anyplace new, where I don't know what's waiting, unarmed—and climbed into my Mustang, with only my scintillating personality for protection.

As I headed down Topanga, I thought more about Mike's comment. He was right. I did have a lot of gaps in my Western cultural education. Neither my mother nor my father had believed in television. To my hippie mother, commercial entertainment was a corrupting influence and sure to lead to rampant consumerism. To my austere father, it was distracting and sure to lead to delusion. Neither of them gave a thought to where such an extreme upbringing might leave a little boy, swinging back and forth between Paris and Dharamshala.

Then my mother died, ironically you might say, of over-consumption—too many drugs and too much alcohol in one sitting. I was sent to live with my father and entered the cocooned life of a Tibetan lama-in-training full time. Not a lot of Hollywood breached those walls. By the time I arrived in Los Angeles, at the age of 18, I was a full-on cultural misfit. Once there, I'd played catch-up with books, basically reading everything I could get my hands on. But as far as television and movies went, well, it seemed hopeless. I'd never catch up, so why even try?

Truthfully, I'd maintained a certain amount of pride in my media naiveté. I'd even been known to hold forth myself on the subject, labeling commercial entertainment as both corrupting and distracting.

Hmm. Something to think about.

I opened up the throttle, keeping my eye out for patrol officers as I sped along the coast highway.

No, my childhood entertainment took a different form. Every night, right after evening chants, and right before the monks sent us off to bed, we'd get a "dharma talk," some tale revealing some helpful or not-so-helpful hints as to why we shouldn't stray off the path to self-realization. The Buddha's way was our life purpose, and these talks helped guide us. How else would we learn how to apply the Eightfold Path to daily life? While kids on the other side of the world were streaming Netflix, or whatever the equivalent was back then, I was streaming dharma.

I stopped at the Sunset traffic signal. The ocean was spectacular this morning, dark green, with little snowy caplets dancing across the swells. The light changed, and I turned left, snaking north.

One night, a special visitor, Serje Rinpoche, came into the hall to give us boys a talk. The whispers had swirled when we'd caught a glimpse of him at dinnertime. He was special to His Holiness, one boy said. Visiting from America, another added. I kept the fact that he and my father were close friends to myself. It was hard enough fitting in when your father was one of the three head abbots running the monastery.

Serje Rinpoche had walked up to the front of the hall and taken a seat, facing us. He sat very still, and soon the room settled.

"*Namo Buddhaya. Namo Dharmaya. Namo Sanghaya,*" he chanted. "I take refuge in the Buddha. I take refuge in the Dharma. I take refuge in the Sangha." He smiled, looking out over our little sangha, a sea of small bald-headed boys, seated in rows on round meditation cushions. I was close to the front, but I could feel the electricity all around and behind me: We never got Serje Rinpoche all to ourselves like this.

"Imagine water everywhere," he said, "water as far as you can see in every direction. Huge. Without limit." He waited. The room itself seemed to grow and swell with the image he was painting. "This is the ocean. Can you feel how vast it is?"

I had seen the ocean. I nodded.

"Now picture an ancient turtle that lives deep, deep in this ocean."

I pictured the turtle, his snout scaly, his neck a tight mass of wrinkled folds.

"There is something strange about this turtle. This turtle only rises to the surface for air once every one hundred years."

A hushed "ooooh" rippled among us. Serje Rinpoche knew how to tell a good story.

"So once every century, up, up, up he swims, until his head pops to the surface. He takes a deep sniff of air and down he dives again, back into the depths, not to return for another hundred years."

I found myself taking a deep lungful of air.

"Now, on the surface of this same huge ocean floats one small, round life preserver. Do you know what that is? Children in America wear them around their waists, so they can float in the water." He curved his arms, to show the size and shape. "Year after year after year, one lone life preserver. Floating in the vastness of the ocean. Can you imagine that?"

I pictured the tiny, bobbing thing. I nodded shyly.

"Oh, I almost forgot!" he smiled. "The turtle is also blind." His smile widened. "Yes, the poor old turtle cannot see a thing. It simply must feel its way up to the surface as best it can."

Another long pause, as he let us absorb this new fact. Then he leaned toward us, his voice gathering power.

"Now, I wonder. How many times do you think this blind turtle must come to the surface, how many hundreds and thousands of times, and years, must pass, before it happens to push its nose up through that life preserver?"

I remember shaking my head. I didn't know how many years. Definitely a whole lot.

"The odds are great, so great as to be almost impossible. But they are no greater than the odds against a soul landing in a human incarnation. And *you*," Rinpoche was staring right at me, "*you* have beaten those odds. And so I ask you, what are you going to do with this opportunity?"

No pressure, right?

I checked my iPhone and turned north on Benedict Canyon, past the perfectly tended lawns and gardens of the Beverly Hills Hotel, climbing the hills, merging with San Ysidro, then Summitridge Drive, climbing and climbing to a crest with a spectacular view.

It's about persistence, I thought. Just showing up and doing the work. Keeping your eye on the task at hand and letting go of whether or not it leads exactly where you want to go. If you do that, the Buddha says—if you just keep working with passion and attention—auspicious coincidences are bound to occur.

In other words, even a blind turtle comes up in the right place once in a millennium.

A high stucco wall, its fortlike presence slightly softened by some sort of creeping vine, appeared on the road to my left, delineating a massive property that took up the better part of the street. I was here. I stopped at a small stucco guard house attached to a pair of ornate black, wrought-iron gates.

Sun glinted off the mirrored sunglasses of the gate guard as he stepped forward. His eyes raked my car, and he motioned for me to lower my window. I was glad I hadn't come in my Toyota beater.

"May I help you?"

"I'm here to meet with Julius Rosen," I said. "My name is Tenzing Norbu. I believe he's expecting me."

He stepped back inside and made a call. He talked, and then listened, nodding a couple times. I figured I had at least a 50-50 chance of pulling this off. Better than a blind turtle, anyway. He hung up and leaned out the little doorway.

"Just take the driveway to the top of the hill. Someone will be waiting for you."

The gates swung open, and I made my way up a long, steep, curving lane lined on either side by twisted California sycamores, a drive long enough to make me wonder if I'd missed a turn. Sprawling private estates are common in Beverly Hills, but even so.

Then I saw Rosen's house.

Whoa.

It loomed over the manicured landscape, a modern pile with stucco walls and a steel pitched roof. I parked the Mustang at the far end of the semicircular driveway next to what I guessed was a Bentley or Rolls; it was hidden under a custom weatherproof cover. As I crossed the outer courtyard, I linked eyes with a gardener, trimming an olive tree at one end of the drive. He was built like a fireplug, a swarthy Latino man in his late 50s with ebony eyes and a moustache shaped like a scimitar. He wore a narrow-brimmed woven straw hat. I nodded and smiled. He looked away.

The front of the mansion was dominated by a rough stone sculpture set within a circular pool of water. The sculpture was modern, free-form, a potent mass of gathered curves and angles, with suggestions of jutting wings. It strained upward, as if trying to take flight from the water: an eagle, maybe, or the mythical creature Garuda, frozen in mid take-off.

A beefy man in a dark suit stood at the front door watching me. Not fat beefy, strong beefy. I instantly dubbed him Señor Beefy.

I gave Señor Beefy a little wave. Why not?

Before I reached him, the front door opened. A slight,

elderly gentleman in a red checked shirt and baggy tan pants, belted high and tight, waved Señor Beefy off and tapped his way to me, wielding a pair of canes like they were his own personal chopsticks. He was dapper and slim, about five foot nine, and he crackled with energy. A necklace of bright woven beads draped his neck and disappeared down the front of his shirt.

"Hello, sir," he said, pumping my hand. "I'm Julius. Julius Rosen." He peered through black-rimmed glasses. He had almost no wrinkles, and his thinning brown hair, swept straight back, was barely streaked with gray. The age spots on his hands, and the papery skin at his neck, indicated a man in his early 80s, but he looked 20 years younger.

I handed him my card. "Tenzing Norbu," I said.

He barely glanced at it before slipping it into his pocket. Good, I wouldn't be forced to explain the lack of an actual number next to the word "licensed."

"What do you think?" he asked, holding one cane to my face. "I just got 'em."

His canes matched. They were painted black, and decorated with neon constellations.

"Galactic," I said.

"I thought so."

"I appreciate you seeing me."

"Not at all. Not at all. At my age, I don't get many visitors. I've stopped giving away my money, so that narrowed the field of suitors, and all my real friends have moved. Or croaked."

I couldn't help laughing. His eyes gleamed at me from behind the dark owl-like rings of plastic.

"Want to come in, or would you like to take a little tour outside, Mr. Norbu?" I glanced down. He was wearing leather walking shoes with Velcro straps.

"I'd love to look around." I said.

"Great. Great."

He gathered himself, as if for launching, and took off

for the sculpture, waving his canes like the antennae of a giant insect. I had to trot to keep up.

"I had this piece created for my wife, Dorothy," he said, stopping at the pool. "She was a great friend of this sculptor." I nodded. My research this morning had revealed that his late wife had been a much beloved benefactor of the art world. The Museum of Contemporary Art downtown now owned several works donated from her private collection.

I studied the sculpture more closely. "It's beautiful," I said. "Fierce, like a winged goddess."

"Interesting," he said. "I asked the artist to capture my wife's intensity. 'Fierce.' Yes. I'm impressed you picked up on that. Are you an art lover?"

I shook my head. "I enjoy art, but I've never taken the time to learn much about it. Something about this piece, though, reminds me of the slightly ferocious images painted on Tibetan thangkas."

"You're from Tibet?" Julius asked.

"By proxy," I said. "I grew up in a monastery in Dharamshala, India. His Holiness the Dalai Lama set up there, after he escaped from Tibet, just ahead of the Chinese, in 1959."

"Yeah, I remember all that. 1959. I was . . . " His eyes drifted off. "I was 31 years old. You believe that?"

"I don't," my 31-year-old self said. "You look too young for that to be true."

Julius reached both arms to the rim of the fountain. At first I thought he was just touching it, but then I realized he was leaning against the stone, his body oddly stiff.

"Mr. Rosen?" I said. His face was immobile, and his eyes stared fixedly at his hands, pressing against the edge. "Mr. Rosen, are you okay?"

His mouth tightened with some supreme effort, and then, just as I was about to call for help, he took a small, jerking step back, as if released from a spell.

"Sorry about that," he said. "Parkinson's. Makes you

freeze at the worst damn moments. And please, call me Julius." A series of harsh squawks sounded from his chest area. He fished up a pink metallic phone dangling from the beaded necklace. He opened it and held it in front of his mouth.

"Shut up!" he barked, and snapped it shut. He smiled at me. "Don't worry, it's a recorded reminder. Almost time for my mid-morning pills. Shall we?" And he scuttled back toward the house.

I had to walk quickly to keep up. Suddenly, he veered onto an impeccably raked pathway of rose-colored gravel. He waved one cane at a circular structure set in the far corner of the side lawn. "That's what I call my workshop. Come see." We crossed the lawn at a brisk clip. The gardener, now on his knees trimming vines, looked up at our crunching footsteps. He touched his hat to Julius.

"Good morning, Señor Manuel. *Como estas?*" Julius said.

"*Muy bien*, Señor Julius."

"Everything's looking beautiful, as always, Manuel."

"*Gracias.*" As Julius caned his way past, Manuel's eyes followed him.

When we reached the cottage, Julius leaned over and un-Velcro'd his straps. He stepped out of his shoes and opened the door. Following his lead, I slipped off my slip-ons and walked in behind him.

My breath caught. The room was round, and completely white—ceiling, walls, and carpeted floor—except for a black, curved easy chair on a chrome-painted stand, located, like the pupil of an eye, right in the center. Next to the chair was a low, white table with a silver framed photograph on it. My eyes adjusted to the muted light. The interior design was masterful. Somehow the all-white décor was fully textured and diverse. The white of the carpet interplayed magically with the soft light off the walls, creating a sense of airy openness. I felt I was standing in a cloud.

Julius beamed. "So what do you think?"

I shook my head. "I'm not thinking, just feeling."

"Feeling what?"

"Wonder," I said.

"Wow, kid, you're on fire this morning!" Julius said. "I assigned three different designers the task of creating a room where I could think. This was the winning design. Know what she called her concept? 'A Room for Wondering.'"

"Wondering," I said. "Where I come from, we call it meditating."

"I call it using the noodle, though wondering works, too, because the things I like to think about don't usually have answers."

He swayed in place a little. A small droplet of saliva slid down one corner of his mouth and landed on his collar. "Excuse me," he said. He fished out his phone, pushed a button, and had a low conversation with someone on the other end. He tucked the phone back inside his shirt. "Sorry. Pill call." A confused look crossed his face. "Where were we?"

"Using your noodle?"

Julius shook his head. He crossed the room and opened a large closet, gesturing for me to come over. I grabbed a second easy chair—this one, all white. Following his instructions, I parked it, facing his, and sat. He lowered himself into his own chair, settling into the curved contours. He picked up the photograph, touching the glass gently.

"My wife, Dorothy, was a force of nature," he said. "And a joy to behold—as full of life as anybody you'd ever want to meet."

I sensed the air in the room grow heavy. I just listened and breathed.

"I was twenty-four when we married, and she was barely nineteen. We had fifty-six years. She was all I ever needed."

He handed me the black and white photograph. A vibrant young woman with dark hair, flashing eyes, and a wide smile gazed up at the camera, her lashes long and thick.

"Beautiful," I said, handing it back.

"It was just a day, like any other. Until she asked me if I'd seen her cup of cocoa. 'Cocoa?' I asked. 'I've never seen you drink a cup of cocoa in your life.' Her voice was so patient. 'You know mama brings me a cup of cocoa this time every day.' Then she put her hands to her temples and let out a cry. I'll never forget that cry."

I said nothing. He'd tell me more if he wanted to.

"The tumor was right in the middle of her brain. It took her from full of life to no life at all in three months." He tucked his chin in slightly, to hide the trembling.

There were no words, so I bowed, honoring his grief with my body. He seemed to appreciate it. He fixed his attention on me. His eyes flashed with what I could swear was anger. "I'm old, but I'm not useless. I'd like to give you some pointers, maybe save you some trouble over the next thirty or forty years. Interested in some advice from an *alta kaka*?"

"An *alta* . . . ?"

"Sorry. Yiddish for 'old fart,'" he said.

"Yes. I am definitely interested," I said. Julius reminded me of the older lamas in my monastery, not the rigid ones, but the sage few who seemed to grow in wisdom, vigor, and flexibility as they aged. After a lifetime spent in meditation, they radiated the kind of power that came from confronting life head-on, with no illusions. They were living proof that wrestling inner reality is as challenging as confronting the outer one.

My phone vibrated in my pocket. Bill, probably. I ignored it. I didn't want to break the mood. It felt like we were moving onto sacred ground of some kind. I wanted to see where all of this was going.

Julius frowned. "Where are they?" He peered at me. "I am getting to the point. I promise, Mr. Norbu."

"Ten," I said.

"Ten." He swayed again.

"No hurry," I added.

Tiny beads of sweat started to form on his forehead. He let out a little moan.

"No hurry? Maybe when you're thirty."

Shoes crunched on the gravel path. Whatever Julius's advice was, it had come and gone. There was a tap on the door, and a tiny woman, Hispanic, early 60s, in a light blue housekeeper's uniform, padded inside on stockinged feet, holding a tray of little paper cups and a glass of water. Sharp eyes glared at me from underneath a fringe of metallic gray hair. Right on her heels, a younger Hispanic woman in a crisp, tailored pantsuit carried a bulging red nylon sports bag. She'd kept her ankle boots on. When she saw me, her eyes widened for an instant.

She set her bag on the table, unzipped the top, and lifted the lid like a trunk. Clear plastic pouches and adjustable compartments overflowed with medical supplies of every kind—syringes, patches, bandages, blood-pressure cuffs—I even spotted a small oxygen tank. The woman was a walking emergency room. Triage to go.

Julius had a small army of Latin Americans caring for him.

"Ladies, this is my new friend, Ten. Ten, these are the ladies who keep my PD at bay. Otilia and Dr. Alvarado."

Otilia held the tray out in front of Julius. He dutifully tipped a series of pills into his mouth, washing them down with sips of water.

"Thank you, Otilia," he said. "I don't know what I'd do without you." She gave Julius a smile of pure affection, then shot a look at Dr. Alvarado, as if to make sure she understood who was at the top of the pecking order.

"Mr. Rosen, would you prefer some privacy?" Dr. Alvarado said. Otilia crossed her arms. She wasn't budging.

"Yes, maybe that would be better," Julius said. His voice sounded weaker, even a little shaky. "Otilia, take Mr. Norbu into the house, please. Dr. Alvarado and I will join you there in a few minutes."

We reclaimed our shoes out front. The silent Otilia led

me back toward the house, her back stiff with disapproval, though whether at me or the doctor, I didn't know.

My phone buzzed again. This time I answered.

"Hey, Bill."

"Are you already there? Don't tell me you started interviewing Rosen," he barked.

"Steady, Bill. Deep breath, my friend. Not really. I mean I'm here, but we've just been chatting."

"Good. Don't. Not until I get there, okay? I'm on my way." He hung up.

I shoved my phone in my pocket, a little harder than necessary.

Otilia waited at the front door of the main house like a tiny martinet.

"I'll be there in a few minutes," I called. She wheeled around and disappeared inside.

I needed to take a stroll, let the heat behind my eyes dissipate. I walked all the way to one walled perimeter—a quarter-mile, at least—to an arbor of several dozen carob, pear, and oak trees. The wall was covered with thick hydrangea vines. Nearby was a two-story guesthouse, clearly built at the same time and by the same architect as the main house, with its own little garage. It was bigger than my actual home. I lingered at the edge of a fishpond, fat with koi, the red-orange color of sunset. My shoulder muscles loosened as I executed a sequence of long, deep breaths. Bill was under a lot of stress: first big case as a D-III; in-laws in town; press breathing down his neck. The light October breeze brushed against my cheeks, crisp and a little cool. I decided to give Bill the benefit of the doubt. He'd done so for me plenty of times in the past.

As I ambled back toward the house, the base of my neck prickled. I stopped. I scanned the lawns and terraced gardens. Lots of succulents. No people.

But the certainty that I was being watched trailed me like a shadow all the way to the front door.

CHAPTER 8

Otilia whisked me into a cavernous living room, its oversized proportions warmed up by the reclaimed-wood floor and ceiling beams.

"You want coffee?" she asked.

"Thanks," I answered, and she huffed away. I looked around. A Roman bust stared at me with blind eyes from one corner, and a modern painting, raw and bold—a skeletal figure with upraised arms and a barbed-wire crown—shook its fists at me from the other. Photographs of Dorothy, some with Julius, some alone, adorned every shelf and table, and a large oil portrait of his wife, still beautiful late in life, hung over the fireplace. On the mantel below was a small, framed black-and-white photograph of what I assumed to be Julius as a skinny, knock-kneed kid, a toddler in his lap. They shared the same big eyes.

As I settled into a deep embrace of an overstuffed sofa, on cue my phone signaled an incoming text.

I'M HERE, I read. HOLY SHIT.

In a moment, Bill joined me, escorted by a still-grumpy Otilia.

"You want coffee?" she repeated, and left without waiting for an answer. Bill raised his eyebrows at me, but we didn't have a chance to talk before the whirr of a small motor signaled more company. A glowering Señor Beefy helped guide a fancy, state-of-the-art wheelchair into the room, Julius enthroned in it like a king.

I tried to control the shock on my face. This Julius looked his age, and more so. His head lolled slightly to one side, and his body swayed back and forth, like a cobra

77

following a flute. What had happened to him? As he waved his keeper out of the room, Otilia marched in with another tray, this one bearing mugs of coffee for Bill and me, and a small sandwich, cut into quarters, for Julius. She held a section up to his mouth. He took a bite.

"Next time, you no wait so long for your medicine, Señor Julius," she scolded. "You see what happens."

"I promise, Otilia." Julius's voice was meek and hard to understand. "Thank you. I can eat the rest on my own." Before Otilia left, she grabbed a small throw pillow from an armchair and tucked it behind Julius's back. Her stern mask dropped, leaving a face blazing with protective love. Interesting.

I introduced Bill. Julius was gracious, though his energy level was noticeably dimmed.

"Yes, yes," he said. "You're here about Marv Rudolph, Tenzing told me. What do you want to know?" The words ran together, as if he were speaking through mesh.

"Anything would be helpful," Bill said. "For starters, what was your relationship with Mr. Rudolph?"

"My relationship?" Julius snapped. "Marv Rudolph was a thieving, lying sonofabitch, and I'm glad he's gone. I'm not exactly proud of that, but, hell, if Los Angeles had a law against *Schadenfreude* the jails would be overflowing."

Bill and I smiled as Julius swiped at the corners of his mouth with a napkin, his hand shaking. "And in case you're wondering, I have an alibi."

Bill shot him a look. "Sir, we haven't told you Rudolph's time of death yet."

"Doesn't matter. I haven't left this property in three years."

Bill's cop-eyes narrowed at that. He decided to move on. "Do you know how he died?"

Julius shook his head. "The paper said 'under suspicious circumstances.' That's all I know, or care to. Why?"

Bill said, "Well, it's just that there are still quite a few missing pieces." He sat back and opened his notebook. I decided to jump in.

"According to Mrs. Rudolph, her husband was quite passionate about a film project, *Loving Hagar*."

Julius stiffened.

"I understand you might have been one of its backers . . ." Bill shot me a look: *News to me,* it said.

Julius's neck flushed red. "That fucking liar! I never put one penny into that movie. After that scumbag did what he did, I wouldn't touch the movie, or him, with a ten-foot pole." Julius's right hand rubbed at an area just under the left forearm. Almost exactly where . . .

"Julius," I said. "Did Marv ever show you his tattoo?"

Julius stared at me, his head swinging left to right to left to right. "After doing business in this town for fifty-plus years, I thought I'd seen everything, but Marv and his tattoo, that took the goddamn cake." His fingers fumbled with the button at his left cuff.

"Do you mind?" he asked me. "The dyskinesia messes with my coordination."

I unbuttoned the cuff, and he pushed up his shirtsleeve, exposing a faded blue tattoo on the pale underside of his forearm. Numbers.

His right thumb brushed across them, as if trying to rub them out.

"What were you doing when you were ten years old?" he asked Bill.

Bill's smile was wry.

"Encino. Mrs. Landreth's fifth grade class, God help me," Bill said. Julius turned to me.

"Ummm. In a monastery in Dharamshala, memorizing Buddhist texts," I said.

Julius pulled down his sleeve. "I was teaching my little sister, Sadie, that two times two equals four, in a hayloft near the Polish border. A fine place to hide, if you didn't mind frostbite and rats. We lasted maybe six months before the Nazis caught us."

"Where were your parents?" I asked.

His eyes flickered. "Smoke and ash," he said. "The last memory I have of them was my father stuffing my pockets with oatmeal, raisins, and some gold coins, and my mother screaming at me to take Sadie and run." His voice faltered. He glanced back and forth at Bill and me. "How did we get to talking about all this?"

"The tattoo on Marv's arm." Bill's voice was gentle.

"Right, the tattoo," He looked at the floor. "I'm sorry," he mumbled. "This sort of thing has been happening to me a lot lately. What was I saying?"

Most of our experience with interviews entailed getting people to tell us things they didn't want to. Our training didn't cover what to do when somebody wants to tell you something but can't figure out how to do so.

"Something about Marv Rudolph," Bill offered.

Heat flooded Julius's face. "That fucking liar! Three, four years ago, Marv called about pitching me a movie, a real passion project. Nothing new there—I probably listen to twenty or thirty pitches a year. This one did sound special: a love story between a Palestinian refugee and a third-generation Auschwitz survivor. Right up my alley, and I told Marv so. But Dorothy had just been diagnosed, so I wished him luck and passed. He and his wife, Arlene, had met Dorothy. In a moment of weakness I opened up, told him a little of our story, and that bastard used the information to connect with me. Right after Dorothy died, here comes Marv. He plants himself right where you're sitting, puts his head in his hands, and starts sobbing."

Bill and I exchanged looks. Didn't sound like the Marv we knew.

"I'm sitting there wondering what the hell is going on, and all of a sudden Marv's rolling up his sleeve and showing me his tattoo."

Julius paused to take a small bite of sandwich. My breath caught. *Please, we're so close. Don't lose track again.*

"So then he says we're like brothers because we were both in the camps, and now he's lost everything again, and this movie's probably career suicide, but he has to make it to honor everyone we lost and to show the power of love over evil."

Julius spat the next words out. "And you know what? He hooked me. Dorothy had just died, and the son-of-a-bitch reeled me in like a fish. If I'd thought about it for ten seconds I'd have realized he was too young to be a survivor, but I wasn't thinking straight, was I? And the truth is, I've done business with the best brass-ball bullshit artists in the world. Wasserman, Kerkorian, Shainberg, Weintraub—you name them, I've danced with them. But not one of them would have had the goddamned chutzpah to tattoo numbers on his arm and pretend to be a survivor, just to close a fucking movie deal!"

He made a sound of disgust. "I committed five million then and there, including a million up front to get things started. *Shmendrik!*" His mouth was ringed in white.

"How did you discover the tattoo was fake?" I asked.

"You mean when did I come to my senses? The next morning. Something wasn't sitting right. I called my lawyers," Julius said. "Within hours one of them calls me back. 'You're right. Marv Rudolph was nowhere near the camps. He was born and raised in the Bronx. Plus, he's been lying about his age.' 'So what else is new?' I said. 'Everyone in this town shaves a few years off.' 'No,' my lawyer said, 'Marv's started listing his age as ten years *older.'*

"I had to hand it to that asshole. Unlike your normal craven person working in Hollywood, where thirty is the new fifty, and anything older might as well be a death knell, he tacks ten years *onto* his age." Julius leaned close. "Want to know the worst-kept secret in Hollywood? Surviving the Holocaust brings you great . . . " Julius used his fingers as quotation marks, "'. . .street cred' out here. Even better than rehab." His mouth twitched with humor, and the anger drained out of him. "Marv confessed he'd gotten the tattoo somewhere in the San Fernando Valley."

"The San Fernando Valley?" I jotted that down.

"Yeah. A long way from Auschwitz. I pulled out of the deal, then and there." His voice slurred. I concentrated. I didn't want to miss a word. "Marv and I never spoke again."

Julius ducked his chin into his chest. His eyes drifted shut. "Anything else I can help you with? I'm sorry; I'm feeling a bit tired."

Bill stood up and I followed his lead. "Just to recap, Mr. Rosen," Bill said, "You didn't kill Marv Rudolph, and you have no idea who did."

"I like you two," Julius answered, his voice dreamy. "You don't beat around the bush like most people."

"Thank you, Mr. Rosen." Bill said. "So, that would be a 'No,' would it?"

"Yes. That would be a 'No.'"

On our way out, I paused. "If you don't mind me asking, sir," I said, "why haven't you left the property for the last few years?"

Julius roused himself. One trembling hand offered a vague wave in the direction of the oil painting of Dorothy hanging over the fireplace. "That woman was my lifeline," he said. "She was the one facing out, running interference for me. After she died, I just . . . I couldn't . . . " His mouth twisted. "The truth is, I don't like people all that much. Never have." His body shrugged. "Ironic, isn't it? Me being such a big philanthropist and all. Anyway, there it is. What can you do?"

My jaw tightened. I dislike that phrase *What can you do?*, or, as my highly eloquent contemporaries put it: *Whatever*. The shrug, the attitude, dismisses any possibility of things changing. It's self-perpetuating paralysis.

And one of your own worst character flaws, Tenzing. So have a little compassion.

I relaxed my jaw muscles. My heart reached toward the frail man in his wheelchair, a gentle and tentative reminder that lifelines can come from more than one source. But Julius was fast asleep, awareness doused, like a lamp. He snored gently.

Bill had parked his car next to mine. We traversed the curved driveway together. His cell phone rang. He glanced at the screen, and his expression flattened.

"Yes?" he said into the phone. "Yes, chief. No, no we haven't, chief. We're still waiting on the ME's report. We're hoping to release the body later today." He glanced at me. "Yes, sir, he is." He listened, his neck turning a dull red. "No, sir, that won't be necessary. Sully and Mack are already on it." We reached our cars. Bill's phone was still pressed to his ear, and he shifted from foot to foot. Finally he said, "I understand, Chief, but we're moving as fast as we can." Bill ended the call. He kicked at the gravel. "I fucking hate fucking celebrity homicides," he muttered.

"So listen," I said. "I spent a little time on the Internet getting more information on Marv, and . . ."

"On whose authority?" Bill interrupted.

"What?"

"On whose authority? Did the Chief call you?"

"No," I said. "I just thought you might like a little help."

"I'll let you know when I need help, Ten. I've got too many cooks as it is."

Too many . . . cooks? What was he talking about? "I don't understand."

"Fuuuck," Bill groaned.

I waited.

"Ahh! Never mind." He shook frustration off like a wet dog. "I'll see you tonight, okay? You'll be happy to know Martha made me invite what's-her-name. Blondie."

If he was trying to distract me, it worked.

"Heather? Heather's coming?"

"Yeah. Heather. So happy birthday to you. Oh, wait. That would be my wife who turned forty today." He clapped me on the shoulder, climbed into his car, and sped off.

I leaned against the Mustang, absorbing this new piece of information. On balance, I was glad, though it meant I wouldn't be nearly as relaxed tonight. I made a vow to leave enough time this afternoon to meditate, as well as shower.

I checked my messages before I started driving. I had three. The first was from Verizon, letting me know I could save more money by spending more money. I deleted it. The second was from my new best friend, Clancy Williams.

"Hey, Ten, yeah, so, I've been thinking things over. And I guess I want to help. Just to let you know, Arlene Rudolph hasn't left the house all day, but the kid, Harper? She took off in one of the family cars this afternoon. Yeah. So, I decided to follow her. Maybe get some grief-shots, or why-isn't-she-grieving shots. Like that. But anyway, she's led me somewhere interesting. Call me."

My heart rate accelerated from stroll to jog. I called Clancy, but it went straight to voice mail. *"Yo, Clancy here. Wassup?"*

"Clancy? Where are you? Call me back."

The third message was from Heather.

"Hi," she said, her voice shy. "So Bill invited me his wife's fortieth tonight, and, umm, I was wondering if you knew what Martha might like for a present? I've never met her, so . . . Anyway, if you could help with that, I'd appreciate it. Thanks, oh wait, here's my number, oh wait, I'm calling your cell, so, well, just call this number, okay? God. Okay, then. Bye."

I smiled at her awkwardness. I knew that clumsy-message feeling well. You might even say I invented it. My smile faded. I'd completely forgotten about getting Martha a present.

Before I devolved into full-scale panic, I closed my eyes, sensing my way into the essence of Martha.

Her warmth—that was key. Also her humor and innate creativity—Martha's flower arrangements, culled from her own garden, were little works of art. She was a fabulous cook, too, famous back in the day for her gourmet gatherings for close friends and hungry detectives. And her stamina was legendary. Martha had worked full time as a court reporter right up until she had the twins. I used to tease her, call her Durga, after the Hindu many-armed goddess. And she was stylish, though maybe a little less so since the twins came along. Come to think of it, I couldn't remember the last time I saw her dressed in anything but sweats.

Right. Something to wear. Something elegant and fiery. One-of-a-kind. A reminder that her Durga-like flame wasn't out, just banked by motherhood for a little while. I knew just where to go look.

Julius's front door opened. I looked over. Señor Beefy moved into the doorway and leaned against the frame. He crossed his arms, and his bicep muscles bulged against his suit coat.

I hopped in my Mustang and left Julius's estate, intent on my gift-finding mission. I drove just over the speed limit, parked in an alley off West Third Street, and walked into freeHand Gallery, a store committed to selling handmade crafts, a scant hour later. I described what I wanted. The saleslady led me to a wooden rack against one wall, and within minutes I found almost exactly what I'd envisioned: a vibrant hand-dyed silk and wool shawl of swirling yellows, oranges, and reds. Most unmomlike. I threw in two little sparkling, beaded headbands for the twins. I had hoped to pay with cash, but the total was twice what I had in my wallet. I hesitated—maybe I should just go with a funny card.

No, this was Martha. I had to trust I'd be an earner again soon.

I handed over my little plastic debt-maker. The joy on

Martha's face would be worth forgoing months of Belgian Trappist beer.

I called Heather from the store parking lot, and got her voicemail.

"It's Ten. Martha loves Gewürztraminer, or any good Pinot Noir. You can't miss with either of those. Okay. See you tonight." I hung up feeling smug. Nary a stutter out of me.

And nary a word from Clancy. I tried him again.

"Yo, Clancy here. Wassup?"

Yo, yourself. Answer your damn phone! my mind snapped. I shook the irritation off. Clancy wasn't my employee. Not yet, anyway.

"It's Ten, again. Call me."

I stopped by the Urth Café, wolfed down a portobello panini, and raced home. Halfway up Topanga, my iPhone buzzed. I veered into a private driveway to take the call.

"Hey. It's Clancy."

"Clancy? Where the hell have you been?"

There was a long pause on the other end of the line. Great. I'd managed to piss off my first possible lead on Marv's death before I even got the information.

"Really sorry," I said. "Long day. Let's start over. Hey, Clancy, thanks for your message. I really appreciate your keeping my proposal in mind. I could use a resourceful man like you in my life right now." I paused. "And if you don't tell me what the hell is going on I may jump right out of my fucking skin!"

Clancy laughed, and the tension between us drained.

"I told my wife about you," he said. "How you're, like, a monk, but then, not at all like a monk."

"And what did she say?"

"She said, 'Don't look a gift monk in the mouth.' Did I mention she hates what I do for a living?"

"I believe you did."

"Right. Well, moving on. Like I said, no sign of Arlene all day. Just a lot of older women coming in and out with food and shit. But this afternoon the garage doors opened and Harper—she was wearing a baseball cap and shades, but it was definitely her—pulls out in a little red Mini Cooper. And guess where she winds up?"

"No idea."

"Robinsgrove Apartments. And get this. Either she knew the code or she knew someone else in there, because she punched in a code and was buzzed inside. She came back out a few minutes later. I wasn't sure what else to do, besides snap a few photos."

"Are you still there?"

"Close. I went into Larchmont for a late lunch break. If I don't eat every few hours, I smoke."

"Meet me back at the Robinsgrove."

So much for lowering my blood pressure before I saw the good Dr. Magnuson again.

CHAPTER 9

I was back on the road by 4:30 P.M., leaving just enough wiggle room for traffic and a quick stop at Robinsgrove Apartments. Much as I loved my canyon retreat, on days like this it felt like I lived in Siberia. As I slalomed down Topanga, I did a body-check. I was still wound up pretty tight. I had scheduled a full half hour to sit on the meditation cushion, but by the time I'd typed up the barest essentials of the meeting with Julius, fed Tank, gathered material for Clancy, and thrown on my blue-striped cotton shirt, there was no meditation window left. I would have spent the entire sit looking at my watch anyway.

I checked the gauge on the Mustang. Her tank read empty. Well, guess what, so was mine.

I worried this knot of a thought as I pulled into a 76 station. I had quit the LAPD in part because the bureaucratic demands had left me with a constant sense that I would never catch up, that there were never enough hours in a day.

What was my excuse now?

I needed to take a good long look at how I was spending, or wasting, time. Usually when I feel like there's no time, it really means I haven't made time *for myself*. I decided to explore this topic further, soon. As soon as I had time.

Clancy's black Impala was parked a block south of the Robinsgrove's front entrance. I circled around and tucked my Mustang in a private church lot just north of the apartments. The last thing I needed was one of Bill's little cop-helpers eyeballing my car in the vicinity—might as well wave a flag announcing my continued interest in this case. I strolled back to the Impala and tapped on the passenger window. Clancy leaned across and opened the door. I slipped inside. A fresh supply of empty Styrofoam coffee cups and a few crumpled receipts littered the seat. I set the pile of trash on the floor.

A vague idea plucked at my brain but refused to materialize.

Clancy reached behind and pulled up a smallish square camera, weighted down with a howitzer of a telephoto lens.

At my questioning look, he volunteered, "Canon Mark IV. This baby burst shoots at up to ten frames per second. It's a beautiful thing."

"What about the tuba on top?"

"I like keeping a low profile. With this 500mm Sigma and a 2x extender I can shoot from a quarter mile away if I want to." He patted his lens. "eBay," he said, "back when I still had scratch."

"Can I see the shots?"

"Sure. No other paps around, that I can see. They must have moved on to greener pastures. So far I've caught maybe twenty-five in-and-outs. Here."

Clancy pulled the compact flash card from his camera, plugged it into an adapter and slotted it into a laptop he'd retrieved from the back seat. Soon, a series of images marched in little squares across his screen. Sure enough, here comes Harper up the sidewalk, checking over her shoulder. Punching a code into the apartment entrance pad. Maybe talking to someone, couldn't tell from the back. Entering. A few men and women of various ages and ethnicities followed, entering or exiting the Robinsgrove. They alternated between the elderly and the young-and-hip, what Mike calls doo-dah metrosexuals. And then Harper, leaving, head down, hat pulled low.

Clancy started to close the laptop.

"Wait," I said. I scrolled ahead to a familiar pair.

Sully and Mack: bent close to the security speaker by the entrance, and then pushing through the front entrance, buzzed in by the manager, no doubt. How did they do it? They were famous for always showing up right after last call at the bar, or just missing the moment when the bad guy confessed. And these were the lead detectives on Marv's case. Poor Bill. A few photographs later, out they came again, scowling. I wasn't interested in the S & M show, though. It was the other residents who piqued my curiosity.

"Really good work," I said. "Now, I have a big favor to ask you. It may be a dead end, but . . ."

I passed over the printouts of significant people from Marv's past, downloaded from Mike's research.

"These are the major players in Marv's world. Producers. Actors. That kind of thing."

He shuffled through the images. "Okay?"

"Any chance you can stick around here for a while longer? See if these jibe with anyone?"

"You mean figure out who let Harper in?"

"Smart man."

"Why not?" Clancy stretched and smiled. "Beats circling Keith Connor's hideaway or Brad Pitt's gated estate 24/7, dodging fucking security guards," he said. "It's all good. I have a hunch about this whole deal."

"A hunch?"

Clancy glanced at me, then away.

"I . . . I get these, premonitions sometimes," he said. "Or I used to, when I was still kicking ass, nailing exclusives. Before Marv fucked things up for me. It's like . . . I wake up early, barely have time to scratch my balls, much less kiss the wife, when I get yanked out of bed by a righteous thought. Like, one morning it was: Angie's going to be at the Farmer's Market in less than an hour. So off I go, and sure enough, there's Angie, hiding behind sunglasses the size of Frisbees, kids hanging off every limb. Another time? I'm eating dinner with my wife and little girl when an image pops in my head: Tom, treating little Suri to Sunday brunch at the Scientology Celebrity Center. Sunday morning, swear to

God, I positioned myself on Franklin Avenue—it's all about the set up, man, staying three steps ahead—and *boom*. There they were, slipping into the back gates. Once in a while I doubt myself. Two days later I'll open *InTouch*, and I'd see it. Same exact shot as I'd imagined, courtesy of some other lucky fucker's camera."

As he talked, Clancy kept one eye on the late afternoon traffic moving up and down Rossmore. "I mean, I was raised Baptist, but this is more, like, spiritual, you feel me?"

"Yes," I said. "I feel you. I feel you a lot." I considered telling him about my number one rule, to trust intuitive flashes, but it sounded like he was already living his own version of it.

Clancy's eyes narrowed as a luxury SUV with darkened windows sped past us.

"Bieber's people," he said. "He's in town all week. *Access Hollywood, Leno*. Full court press. Christmas album coming out."

"No kidding." I wasn't sure who "Bieber" was, much less what "his people" drove, but I was still impressed. The more time I spent with Clancy, the more I realized how complimentary our jobs were and what an asset he could be.

"I got at least four hundred license plates in my head," he added. "Lot of good it does me now." He sighed. "Anyway, like I said, Ten, I'm betting tonight's the night."

"But we don't even know who we're looking for," I said.

"Tonight," he repeated. "Believe it."

Before I climbed out of his car, I tried to recall my earlier thought-twinge, but nothing clear materialized. I'd figure it out later.

Meantime, party time.

I had planned my arrival at the restaurant carefully: early enough not to miss the main event, but late enough to avoid the awkward, prefood small talk. My hope was to slip in unnoticed.

The elderly host at the front had a wide smile and a

stooped back. As he led me through the raucous crowd of diners, I glanced up at the hanging clusters of straw-covered Chianti bottles. They looked like they hadn't been dusted since the restaurant opened—1949, or so the neon sign proclaimed.

The walls were lined with old-school Hollywood glamour shots, and the tables sported red-checkered tablecloths and flickering votive candles. A man was banging away at a grand piano parked on a raised dais in the center of the room. As I wove between crowded tables and booths, I caught a glimpse of Heather, wearing a party hat, sitting at the end of a long table in the far corner. She looked up, and her eyes met mine. Then hers widened. Before I could wonder why, a perky waitress sashayed to my side, microphone in hand. I caught the words *teaser* and *burning*. She was joined by two other waitresses. They surrounded me, wagging their fingers at my frozen face as they warbled about a dancing queen in three-part harmony. Martha's entire birthday group burst into cheers and applause. So much for slipping in unnoticed.

Maude and Lola, up way past their bedtimes, sat in wooden high chairs on either side of Martha. Maude's face was covered with red sauce. Lola gnawed on a piece of gummy bread. Martha, cheeks flushed with Chianti, appeared shell-shocked. She looked at the tables, filled with people who loved her, as if she didn't know quite what to do. I added my present to the pile.

"Happy birthday, my friend," I said, and kissed her cheek.

"Thanks," she answered. "This one's a little hard to process. But we're having fun now," she flung her arms around the twins, "aren't we, girls? Look! It's Uncle Ten!"

"Unh Tey! Unh Tey!" Maude chortled.

"Can you believe these monkeys are almost two years old?" she said. Both girls threw back their heads. "Chee, chee, chee!" they chattered. Martha hugged them close.

"I love you, you know," she said, and planted one kiss each on their rosy, reachable cheeks.

I gave the girls their sparkling headbands. Maude grabbed hers, yanked off her party hat and stuck the band on her head. It nestled in her cloud of red hair like a tiara. Eighteen months old, and she already knew her headgear. Lola, ever the thoughtful one, studied her headband, turning it this way and that. She felt her head, confirming that it was already occupied. Then, as if coming to a major decision, she hung my present around her neck like a collar.

"That works, too," I said.

"Say thank you to Uncle Ten," Martha said.

"Ta, Unh Tey."

"You're most welcome," I said. I wish all communication with girls could be this simple and satisfying. Bill walked up, two steins of beer in hand. "Dancing queen," he crooned in my ear.

"Very funny."

"It was." Bill handed over one of the beers. "This'll take the edge off." He ushered me to an empty chair at the other end of the booth, right next to Heather.

I sat.

"Hi," Heather said.

"Hi."

Bill squatted between us. "So Heather, what do you think of my friend Ten?" he said.

"Don't answer that," I said to Heather. Luckily, she was laughing. "Exactly how much have you had to drink, Bill?" But Bill had already spotted another latecomer and was off.

"I hope it's okay. I ordered you the veggie lasagna," she said.

"Perfect. How'd you know?"

"I'm psychic, didn't I tell you?" she said. "Well, and a little birdie may have also told me you don't eat meat."

We surveyed the group. I pointed out a group of detectives I knew from Robbery/Homicide, as well as Martha's mother and stepfather. I knew Bill and Martha were part of some sort of parents-of-twins support group, and I guessed another table consisted of couples from there. I deduced this for two reasons. One, a second set of twins, little boys, also in high chairs, were the center of attention. Two, the adults surrounding them wore the same stunned we-don't-get-out-much-anymore looks on their faces as Martha. As I watched, one of the little boys accidentally dropped a slice of salami on the floor. His lip trembled. The probable mother comforted him as the probable father snagged him another slice from the antipasti platter. No shaming involved. Remarkable.

Heather let out a big sigh. "I am so happy to be here. This week has been rough."

"Marv?"

"Marv, plus rotations, plus another autopsy. A thirty-five-year-old mother of two. No mystery there. She died from a thorn-prick on her arm. She was gardening, deadheading roses. The site got infected, and sepsis set in before she realized how bad it was and started on antibiotics. Sometimes you just have to wonder."

"I'm sorry."

"Yeah, well . . ." Heather seemed to shake the heaviness off. "I knew the job was tough when I signed on for it! Like I said, glad I'm here. Thanks for the Martha tip, by the way." She lightly touched my arm. "I went with a Pinot Noir."

I liked how her hand felt, resting on my wrist. I impulsively covered it with my own. My heart beat harder against my chest. Now what?

"Now what" was a waiter sliding two plates of steaming hot lasagna, bubbling with cheese, in front of us. Rescued by pasta. We concentrated on the lasagna, which was piping hot, stuffed with spinach, ricotta, and mozzarella cheese, drenched in a fresh marinara sauce, and very delicious.

Heather used a hunk of garlic bread to sop up the extra sauce. I did the same. Heather was a hearty eater. I smiled.

I like a girl with a good appetite. Another waiter, a tenor, belted out a song about sending in clowns. For a song about clowns, it was pretty sad.

Bill staggered back with an empty bottle of Bell'agio Chianti, its woven straw covering now scribbled with messages. He set it down, and handed me a Magic Marker. "Write a birthday wish for Martha," he said. "Keep it clean."

I thought and wrote, "May you live with ease." Not so original for an ex-monk, but heartfelt. I handed the pen to Heather. She rotated the bottle until she found a blank spot. She studied it, tilting her head, catching her lovely lower lip between her teeth. Finally, she drew a small, drippy pizza, decorated it with tiny candles, in the shape of a heart, and wrote *love* inside it. She caught my eye.

"When in doubt, make it cheesy," she explained. I laughed.

Bill reappeared, fresh beer in hand. He squatted between us again. Uh oh.

"So, Dr. Magnuson," Bill said. "I know you're a very hard worker. What do you do for fun? And don't say go to Dodger games, because the team is fuckin' bankrupt." Bill winked at me, and I realized this was his slightly clumsy way of giving me an opening.

"You mean outside of carving up corpses? Let's see. Once in a while I like to go dancing," Heather said. "But mostly I'm pretty happy curling up in bed with a good book."

I liked the sound of that, too.

"I knew it! You and Ten here are kindred spirits. Aren't you, Ten?" Bill was eyeballing me. *Leap!* his eyes said. Hard to leap, when you're legs are made of lead. A familiar jumble of thoughts piled on: *too smart, too beautiful, you're not ready, you'll never be ready.*

A waiter pulled Bill away. Heather picked up her fork and pushed it around her plate.

"Heather," I said. Her eyes met mine, and I glimpsed a little girl peeking out. *She's just as scared as I am.*

I jumped, lead legs and all.

"I'd really like to see you sometime. Maybe have dinner, or something."

I waited. *Breathe. Breathe.*

"Okay," she said. "Yes, I'd like that, Ten."

We smiled at each other, suddenly shy.

Heather leaned close. Was she going to kiss me?

"Be right back," she said. "Pit stop."

She disappeared into the back of the restaurant.

Someone clinked on a glass as a dozen waiters and waitresses formed a semicircle around Martha. Maude started yipping and bouncing in her high chair, and Lola popped her right middle fingers into her mouth and sucked furiously, as Bill set a big blue-and-white cake shaped like a Dodger cap in front of Martha, ablaze with forty candles, plus one. I guess he hadn't completely given up on his team. Martha found me with her eyes. She lifted one corner of my birthday shawl, wrapped around her neck, glowing orange in the candlelight. She waved it at me. She looked spectacular.

"Thank you," she mouthed. The piano player banged out a crescendo of cascading notes, and it was on. The birthday song rocked the rafters, and the entire restaurant joined in.

Heather slipped back in her seat. My nose picked up the minty scent of toothpaste.

Uh oh, was she was one of those obsessive brush-after-every-meal types? She leaned against my shoulder, singing lustily. I decided I couldn't care less.

Raucous cheers and claps greeted Martha's blowing out of the candles. Lola shrank in her seat from the din and started to wail. I watched as Bill plucked her out of her high chair and held her tight to his chest, covering her ears, kissing the top of her head. *What a good father.* Martha leaned over to blow out the candles, and Maude, headband askew, poofed up her cheeks, a perfect little mimic. I laughed again, and my eyes filled.

Remember this. This is family.

Heather reached for my hand and gave it a squeeze. My phone buzzed in my pocket. I had to let her hand, and the moment, go. "Sorry," I said, and I was.

I checked my phone. It was a text from Clancy.

GOT SOMETHING.

I caught Bill's eye. Pointed to my phone and the door. He pointed to Martha and the girls. Priorities. We both understood. I explained things to Heather and said I'd call about getting together soon. If she was disappointed, she didn't show it. I didn't know if that was a good thing or a bad thing, but I was in a hurry to go, so I dismissed it from my mind.

Within half an hour, I was sitting next to Clancy as he clicked through another series of close-ups, this time of a slight figure leaving the Robinsgrove. *Click, click, click.* Tiny incremental shifts, stepping outside, looking up and down the street. *Click. Click.*

Clancy angled his computer screen closer to me.

"Here," he said. "Here's the best one."

"Can you make it bigger?"

He expanded the image. I squinted at the slight young woman, dark hair hanging straight down her back like a curtain, face creased with anxiety.

My pulse quickened.

"Yes," I said. "That's her. Really good work, Clancy."

Two years ago, Marv Rudolph, in a bold move, had cast an unknown to play the lead in *Loving Hagar.* I was looking at his Hagar. Tovah Fields, with an "s."

"What happened after this?"

He showed the next sequence of images. She turned right, walked along the sidewalk maybe ten yards, and turned right again into a canted entryway. She was wheeling a large suitcase.

"That's the Robinsgrove's outside lot," Clancy said. Moments later, a series of photographs showed a white

Toyota Scion pulling out and driving north on Rossmore, toward who knew where.

I had found the link between Marv, Harper, and the Robinsgrove. And maybe, just maybe, I had found the key to his death. *Click.*

Driving home, I was surprised to note a dull ache behind my heart. I inhaled, feeling my way past it to what hid behind. Sadness. Loss.

What do you have to be sad about? You were laughing, eating cake with a beautiful woman a short while ago. What's wrong with you? Get a grip!

I was doing it again. How many times had my father chided me with that exact tone? *Don't feel that. Don't think that. Don't be that.*

I was attacking myself with the same behavior I despised in my father. Limiting myself, now that he was no longer there to do it for me. *Second rule, Ten.*

I took a second, deeper breath. *Let. It. Go.*

I focused instead on the sadness, allowing it to just be, with no mind-story attached. The experience was quite painful, and my breath caught. But then, the ache softened.

I imagined cradling my sore heart, like Bill. . . .

Yes. Like Bill, holding Lola close, kissing her. The image plucked a dull, untuned string deep inside me, the source of the hurt. To have a father like that: one who guided you, protected you. Whose face lit up whenever he saw you.

To have a father like that.

I couldn't remember my father ever smiling at me, except maybe the day I told him I was moving to Los Angeles. That smile didn't count for much: It was twisted, full of disapproval and contempt. It was confirmation that I'd never amount to anything.

I drove up the hill to my house. I turned into the tree-lined driveway. A crescent moon hung low in the sky. I turned off my car lights, leaving the graceful Japanese lines and curves of my home bathed in night shadows. A sigh escaped me, this one braided with joy. Sometimes my solo existence felt lonely, but right now, after the din of celebration, the dose of romantic possibility, the thrill of discovery, and the stab of sadness, a little solitude seemed very welcome.

I parked in the carport and walked into the kitchen. Tank was at the door, ready. With one slow, luxuriant roll-over, he exposed the soft white fur of his belly. I sat next to him and rubbed the downy pelt, feeling, as much as hearing, his deep purr of contentment.

"Good cat. Good cat," I said.

I gave him a small scoop of treats. As I walked into my bedroom, I could hear him crunching in the darkness.

Chapter 10

A sharp *crack!* penetrated my sleep, and for a moment I thought I'd been shot. I pushed upright and switched on the light, fumbling for something, anything, to use as a weapon. My pulse raced. I had to take several deep breaths to bring my body back to a state of stasis. I listened. Inside, my house was quiet; outside, the night air cool and still. Tank lay nose to paws at the foot of my bed, his belly rising and falling.

My hand rose to my cheek. My jaw was killing me. I wriggled it back and forth.

"Owww!" My left jawbone let out a second, audible crack. Tank raised his head, suddenly alert.

"Really?" I said. "My jaw? That's what woke me up?"

Tank lowered his head and closed his eyes.

"Your housemate is a bit of a mess, Tank," I said. I checked my phone for the time. 3:20 A.M. The hour my demons love to come out and play. Well, I could either order them to stay outside, where they would keep me up all night tapping at the windows, or I could invite them in and try to befriend them. I pulled on some sweats and a long-sleeved T-shirt, and took my aching jaw and hammering heart into my meditation room for some healing time.

I closed my eyes.

Heather. Did I actually ask her out? Did she actually say yes?

I opened my eyes. Not helping.

I closed my eyes, this time letting awareness roam through my body, looking for any particular areas of tension, of holding on.

Great. Basically, that would be everywhere.

For the next hour, I moved a light feather of attention

from jaws to neck. Shoulders to chest. Down the spine, up through the belly, just resting on each clenched muscle and rigid bone, allowing, coaxing, breathing acceptance, leaving just enough space for things to shift slightly.

When I felt into the opening spaces, what I found was loneliness.

I reached out to Yeshe and Lobsang, using my quieted mind to seek connection with my friends on the other side of the world. It had been far, far too long. Whatever time it was there, they were probably also meditating, or about to be. I probed for their welcoming presence, but came up empty; the emptiness quickly filled with a small wave of anxiety. Why had my father returned the letter I had sent to my friends? Why were they no longer in contact with me?

I opened my eyes. Maybe I was the problem. Maybe I was too wired. Too much static in my system. I tried to remember the last time I had successfully met them in meditation, but I couldn't. My small stone Buddha gazed back at me from my meditation table. I wanted to read compassion in his face, but in truth, he looked a little stern.

I stood and stretched, trying to mimic Tank's fluid movements, to calm my body so I could try to mentally reach my friends again, when my iPhone chimed in the bedroom. Now what? Who was calling this early on a Sunday morning?

Bill, that's who.

"Hey there, partner," I said. "Great party last night. I'm surprised you're not still sleeping it off."

"You and me both," Bill's voice was hoarse. He sounded in pain. "Listen, they're releasing Marv's body."

"Now?"

"Yeah. Only way to avoid the media. I'm almost there. Any chance you can bring me a Venti Americano with a double shot?"

I thought about his several steins of beer.

"How about a bottle of Advil?"

Bill grunted. Then, "I don't need a wife, Ten. I already have one."

I was one customer away from the cashier when Bill sent a text: ALSO A NONFAT VANILLA SOY LATTE. THX.

What was he up to now?

The coroner's parking lot was empty and still in the pre-dawn darkness. Three white vans, their blue lettering and county coroner seals easily identifiable, sat vacant in their allotted spaces. A fourth white van idled in the middle of the lot, this one unmarked. It was identical to the vehicle used to spirit Michael Jackson's body away. I noted a silver Honda Civic Hybrid, new plates; an older model Acura RL; and Bill and Martha's Dodge minivan, a pair of empty car-seats belted in the back. I parked in the visitor's slot and climbed out, balancing my little cardboard carton of coffees. As I hurried around the corner, three funeral home atten-dants wheeled a body, carefully wrapped in white cloth, out the back entrance and over to the unmarked van. A young man in a yarmulke, maybe the same one from the waiting room, I couldn't really tell, trotted beside the gur-ney. Arlene's rabbi, what was his name? Fishbein, Rabbi Fishbein, followed, hands clasped, head down. Both were dressed in black suits. The chief medical examiner, Assistant Chief Summer, and Bill watched from the door. I glimpsed a blonde cap of hair behind Bill. Registered the lady-drink in my carton. Clever man, that Bill.

He caught my eye. "*Wait*," his expression seemed to say.

I waited.

The attendants opened the back double doors of the van. Grunting and straining from the weight, they lifted the gurney and loaded the shrouded figure inside.

The van sped off. Rabbi Fishbein and the other young man climbed in the Acura and followed. I scanned the shadows. No telephoto lenses. No inquisitive journalists. No vultures. They'd pulled it off.

I joined Bill and Heather by the building entrance. The ME and Summer were back inside, conferring.

"Here's your caffeine," I said to Bill. "Hope I'm not too late with it."

He grabbed it like a man starved.

"You look like roadkill," I said.

"Thanks, honey."

I handed the other cup to Heather. "I believe this one's for you."

"You're a saint." She cupped her hands around the coffee and sipped.

"They've issued the certificate of death, pending," Bill said. "At least the family can bury Marv later today. That's something."

He drained his coffee.

"I'm not looking forward to the press conference, I can tell you that. Talk about a big goose egg. They still don't have a fucking clue how he died. And neither do I."

"So what's next?"

"It pretty much rests with the toxicologists, and that could take months. Needle in a haystack, you know? If they don't know what to look for, they don't know what to test for. There were no drugs on the scene. Nothing out of the ordinary in Marv's medicine cabinet. His medical records checked out with what the early blood tests show. I mean, he'd been drinking a lot, and there was some very high-grade pot in his system, but contrary to what our mamas told us, those drugs don't kill." Bill scrubbed his face with his hands. "Whoever did this to Marv was one slick fucker, that's all I have to say. We'll keep poking around, but it's more or less up to these guys for the time being."

"What about the knife?" I said. "What about the tat?"

"What about them? They didn't cause his death, Ten. And until we know what did . . ."

"What about the daughter, Harper? This guy I met, one of the paparazzi? He said . . ."

"Jesus Christ, Ten! Now you're talking to the paparazzi? What the hell is going on in your brain?" Bill's face was the color of a beet.

"Bill, slow down."

"Right. I know. Take a deep breath. You know what? I'm beat. I'm going back to bed. I recommend you guys do the same." He stomped off.

Heather was staring at Bill's receding back. "He doesn't do well when he's tired," I explained, though my insides were stinging.

Heather nodded. She lifted her coffee and drank. I noticed the knuckles of her right hand were a little red and chapped. She shuddered.

"Are you okay?" I said.

"I'm fine," she said. "I just hate that this case is so . . . unfinished." She crumpled the coffee cup. "It's freezing. I thought L.A. never got cold."

"Do you want my coat?" I started to take it off, but she shook her head.

"I'm exhausted, Ten. Sorry, but I guess I need sleep more than anything." She threw me an apologetic smile and followed Bill to the lot.

"So glad I came," I said, to no one in particular.

I stewed about things all the way home. Thankfully, the freeways were empty, and I was back under the covers by 8 A.M. An hour later, my phone woke me up all over again. It was just going to be one of those days.

"Lox and bagels, Mr. Norbu," I heard.

"Excuse me?"

"Lox and bagels from Nate 'n' Al's."

"Is this Mr. Rosen?"

"Yes. Yes it is. So. I've been sitting in my favorite room, thinking," he said.

"Ruminating."

"Yes. And I ruminated up an image of lox and bagels

from my favorite deli. Now, I could call and get them to deliver, but I thought instead you might visit me and bring with. I have something I want to discuss." His voice sounded slurry. If I didn't know about the Parkinson's, I'd assume the guy was high on something. "How's that sound?"

First soy lattés, then bagels. Maybe the universe was training me for my next career, as a delivery boy.

"It sounds fine," I said. I pulled on a fresh pair of jeans and left Tank scrutinizing his bowl of crunchy treats for hidden messages.

"Back in a few hours," I said. Tank flicked his tail, unconvinced.

I fired up the Mustang. Extended unemployment meant I could drive her whenever I pleased, and I pleased. I pleased a lot. Nate 'n' Al's was wall-to-wall with Sunday morning enthusiasts. I took a number and watched the passing parade of humanity for 20 minutes, trying to guess their stories. I walked out with half a dozen bagels, lox and cream cheese, and a container of egg salad.

Ten minutes later, the same guard waved me through, and I was rolling up the drive to the Rosen mansion. This time Julius was out the front door before I'd finished parking. No sign of Señor Beefy. Julius slowly caned his way over—he was noticeably less spry today—and surveyed my car, swaying slightly.

"Nice-looking Mustang," he said. "Not a mark on it. You buy it like this?"

"More a matter of spending a couple hundred hours restoring her," I said. "Me, and some expensive geniuses in Santa Monica who specialize in Shelbys."

"Carroll Shelby?"

"Yes."

"I used to know Carroll Shelby," Julius mused. "Good man." His eyes drifted. Then he focused on mine again. "What was I saying?"

"Carroll Shelby," I prompted.

His nod was vague. "I used to know him. Good man," he repeated. Then, "You want to see my baby?"

He led me to the large, covered behemoth parked nearby. He patted the hood. "Here. Take a look."

I set down the bag of bagels and lifted up the front flap of the nylon cover. The gleaming creamy brown nose of a classic Bentley emerged, chrome grille topped by the famous flying B, feathered wings and all. Julius Rosen did like his wings.

"T-two. Three-speed automatic," he said. "I bought her in nineteen eighty."

"Beautiful," I said. "How does she drive?"

His face clouded. "She *drove* like a dream. It's been a few years since I got behind the wheel of anything."

I touched the front panel. "I love the color. Rich. Like chocolate."

"Ha!" Julius said. His eyes narrowed. "I don't say this often, but maybe you'd like to take her for a test drive one day."

"I'd be honored." I rolled the cover back over his Bentley with care.

Julius pointed to the deli bag.

"I see you got the goods," he said. "Let's eat."

He led me through a large kitchen, and then a pair of sliding glass doors, to a sunny, enclosed breakfast nook. The air was filled with the dense, smoky fragrance of fresh-brewed coffee. If there's a better scent on five hours of sleep I haven't found it.

Otilia was at a round wooden table, setting two mugs next to a coffee carafe, a pitcher of cream, and various sweeteners.

Julius said, "Have you met my dear Otilia?"

"I have," I said, and bowed in her direction. Otilia cracked a half smile, which was about 50 percent more than I'd gotten last time. Maybe she was warming up to me. She took the bag and disappeared into the kitchen. "Otilia's been with Dorothy and me for twenty-five years," Julius said. His eyes filled. I busied myself with the first sip of coffee.

Otilia reappeared, bagels and fixings beautifully arranged on a large platter. She placed a slender vase with a perfect pink rose at the center of the table. I bowed again. Her eyes narrowed, saying, *Don't push it.*

"I bring your pills in one hour, Señor Julius."

Julius spread a generous smear of cream cheese on half a pumpernickel bagel, added a translucent slice of onion, and topped it off with two thick, slightly oily slices of lox. I admired the colors, the contrast of salmon pink and creamy white, the loving attention he put into assembling his bagel. I spooned a big dollop of egg salad on my own slice of chewy rye dotted with caraway seeds.

"Bon appétit," I said.

I glanced over at Julius. His jaws were already at work. For a slight man, he ate heartily. He waggled his eyebrows at me and kept chewing. We ate in contented silence.

I poured us each a second mug of coffee. "In the monastery, breakfast consisted of a small hunk of bread and a cup of yak butter tea." I shuddered slightly. "This is better."

"Takes me right back to Brooklyn," Julius said. "When I still lived over Aunt Esther and Uncle Abe's candy shop. I helped them out after classes. Then Uncle Abe dropped dead of a heart attack, and I quit school to run the shop. Times were lean, but we still managed to have lox and bagels every Sunday."

"A candy shop?"

"I know. Death camp to candy store—talk about bizarre." He shook his head. "Less than a year after my uncle left us, my aunt started wasting away—cancer, just like Dorothy, only in her stomach. Before she died, she told me to look under her bed, she had a surprise for me. I pulled out a pickle jar, stuffed with bills. She'd put away close to forty thousand dollars, can you believe it?"

He shot a look at me. The amount seemed high, for a candy shop, but what do I know? I nodded.

"I ended up buying the building, plus the one next door. I converted them into low-rent apartments." He shook his head. "A pickle jar. Good old Aunt Esther."

I felt a wave of affection for this odd, endearing person. He might have one of the highest net-worths in Los Angeles, but it was his personality that struck me as rich. Which reminded me . . .

"Julius, yesterday you started to give me some advice, insights you thought might save me a bit of trouble in the future."

"I did?" he said. "What were they?"

For a moment I thought he was joking, but his eyes were blank. He truly didn't know what I was talking about. Too bad. I'd been lucky. Except for one glaring exception, the elders in my life had been great sources of wisdom. These days, I could use some.

It was not to be. Not today, anyway.

"I want to show you something," Julius grabbed his canes. The man did not like to stay put for long. I followed him down a hallway off the kitchen. He propped open a swinging saloon-type door with one cane, and motioned for me to go through. I stepped into a little kid's fantasy: shelves of candy, glass counters of candy, and bins, hundreds of bins, all filled with colorful varieties of candy.

I walked around, marveling. "Is this a replica of the store in Brooklyn?"

"Nope," he said. "This *is* the store in Brooklyn. Had it taken apart and packed up when I remodeled the old building." His words ran together in a stream. I had to concentrate to understand him. "A team of carpenters put it back together here. Most of the candy's from the original store, you know, for show." He picked up a small brown square, wrapped in waxed paper. "Not these. Caramel marshmallows," he said. "Delivered fresh. My favorites. Sadie's, too."

"Sadie's?"

"What? What? Sorry, no. Dorothy's. Dorothy loved her caramels right until the end."

He looked at the candy as if wondering how it got in his hand.

"You want one?"

I shook my head. I could see the autopsy report: Cause of Death—caramel-salmonella. Julius unwrapped his and popped it into his mouth.

"Julius, what happened to Sadie?"

Panic illuminated his face, disappearing as quickly as it came. He swallowed. "They tracked us down. Came for us. The soldiers threw me on a truck." A slight sheen of sweat coated his forehead. "Her face. Her little face. Women and children staring from a cage like animals." He looked at me, his eyes pleading. "What could I do?"

As a young monk-in-training, I'd spent hours with the older, ailing lamas; some sick, others dying. My father thought it would be good for me. I read to them, chanted with them, but mostly I listened. I listened to them talk, of course, but I also learned to listen to their breathing, to the flickering energy of their being; to read the subtle messages their aging bodies were trying to tell me. At times I resented the work—what child wouldn't?—but I acquired my keenest tools of attention from the practice. I brought that attention into play with Julius. I focused on his breath. It was thready—the breath of a frightened man. Maybe also a guilty one.

"I can't imagine what that time must have felt like," I said.

He lifted his head. "I quit feeling a lot of things the day I lost Sadie."

"I have times like that. Times when I shut down because I can't tolerate the pain."

He made a gruff sound in his throat. "Yeah, well, plastered a whole damn wall over mine. It took Dorothy to bring me back. And now . . ." He pushed himself up. "Enough. Give me your elbow?"

Now what? I glanced at my watch. I'd been here for almost two hours already. Clinging to my arm, Julius led me down another hall and into yet another room, this one lined with wooden shelves crammed with books—thousands of them, floor to ceiling. A massive mahogany desk dominated the center. I helped Julius into a leather office chair behind his desk. He waved me into the chair opposite.

"I've got a business proposition for you, Ten." He pushed a file across the desk to me.

I leafed through the contents. *What is this?* Snapshots of Dorje Yidam Monastery, as well as my mother's apartment building in Paris. My official LAPD ID. Case reports on burglaries and homicides through the years. The missing persons report regarding Harper Rudolph. Even my two recent failing scores on the P.I. exams. Photographs, articles, pages of print, all concerning a single subject. Me. I tasted anger, with a backwash of shame. I was too exposed.

"Thorough," I said. "You know more about me than I do."

"Due diligence." If Julius noticed the edge in my voice, he chose to ignore it.

"Somebody worked overtime," I said.

"Double overtime," he said. "Plus weekend rates."

"Why?"

His eyes shifted away. He licked his lips, and I sensed a quickening of his pulse. *He's nervous.*

"I've got an eye for people, Ten. Always have. But maybe more important, I've got an ear. I listen to people. Not the talking, but when they're quiet. People give off a hum. That hum tells me everything I need to know."

I had just been practicing my own version of exactly that technique on Julius. Weird. But he still hadn't answered the question. "Why the extensive due diligence on me?"

He shrugged. "You don't give off a hum. Could be you've

done so much meditating it canceled yours out. Or maybe you give off a hum, and I just can't perceive it. Either way, I had to make sure you were legit. I want to offer you a job, a consulting arrangement. Something right up your alley, I should think."

A job. An actual job. Maybe Julius couldn't hear my hum of interest, but it was there, and getting louder.

He pulled a second, thicker file from a side drawer. He slid out a detailed drawing of a broad-faced, stocky woman in a dark cloth coat, a scarf covering her hair. Her expression was part fear, part defiance. She pulled at the hand of a little girl who was turned away, straining to get loose. Dark hair cascaded down the child's back.

I pointed to the child. "Sadie?"

Julius nodded. He slid a second drawing across the desk. Sadie, from the front. Round face, clear eyes, and a radiant smile. Same cascading hair.

"Tell me," I said.

"That was the moment—the last time I saw Sadie. It seared itself into my brain, invaded every waking moment, haunted every dream, even followed me here from Brooklyn." Julius shuddered. "I was going mad, and Dorothy was getting desperate. Finally, she sat me down with a sketch artist. It took forever, me describing, the artist drawing, but she finally got it right. And I finally had something to work with." Julius sighed. "I spent hundreds of thousands of dollars on detectives, historical search firms, anything else I could think of, to see if I could find out what happened to Sadie and that woman." Again, his eyes shifted away.

"Ten years ago, I called off the search."

Again, I felt a little twinge of off-ness. *He's lying. Why?*

"So, why now?" I asked.

"Some days I'm the real Julius," he said. "Some days I don't know who the fuck I am." His head dipped forward. "All my life I've been the smartest guy in the room. Never any doubt. Now, I'm not even in the room half the time."

"I can't imagine," I said.

"You know that old poker saying—if you've been in the game for half an hour and you haven't figured out who the pigeon is, the pigeon is you?" His eyes flashed. "Well, I don't plan to go out as anybody's goddamned pigeon. Understand me?" His eyes lost connection. Had he slipped off the rails again?

A chilly ball formed in my belly. *I need this job.* I breathed warmth into the anxiety. The sensation eased.

"Anyway. This just arrived." Julius passed me a photocopy of the first drawing, a message hand-scrawled in blue ink across the middle. "I know what happened." A business card was paper-clipped to the photocopy, a single name, in bold black type: **HELMUT ZIGO.**

Another notation was hand-scribbled on the card, same writing, same blue ink: Contact me. After eleven pm best at Skype ID HelmutZigo.

"Have you contacted him?" I asked.

He shook his head. "You're the first person I've showed this to. It arrived exactly one day before you walked into my life. Do you believe in coincidences, Tenzing?"

"Not really," I said.

"I find it fascinating the very day I needed some detecting done, a detective arrived at my doorstep." He pointed at the card. "Any idea what 'Skype ID' means?"

"No," I said. "But I know someone who does."

"Then you're one step ahead of me."

"So you'd like me to contact Helmut Zigo and see what I can learn?"

"I suspect it's a scam, but you never know. In any case, I'm not able to run this down right now. Want the job?"

I briefly wondered why he wasn't using his own people. They'd done a pretty fucking good job of running me down. Down, and back up the other side. But I needed the job. I wasn't going to push it. As for hiring me . . .

He hasn't asked. Don't tell him.

"I've got to tell you something," I said. "I'm still waiting for my liability insurance. Technically I'm not licensed yet."

"Yes, yes, I know all about that," Julius brushed my words aside. "I didn't get where I am by being a stickler."

"I've also never worked a missing persons case where the person has been missing for such a long time." Might as well get it all out now.

The sheen had reappeared. He swiped at his forehead. "Please, Tenzing. My mind is Swiss cheese half the time. I need you to be my full-time brain on this one." He opened his desk drawer and pulled out a business check. "I took the liberty of improving slightly on Marv Rudolph's rates," he said. "He's a notorious skinflint." He handed the check over. I had to lean close to make out the tiny handwritten letters and numbers. I blinked, sure my eyes were deceiving me. Nothing changed. The check was made out to Tenzing Norbu, in the amount of $25,000. Twenty. Five. Thousand.

"This is too much," I said.

"I'm a childless billionaire, Ten. Indulge me. Give it everything you've got. If you don't find anything in, say, ten days, we'll call it quits."

I couldn't stop staring at the check.

"Good, then." The phone dangling around Julius's neck let out an alarming squawk. He started to stand and fell back into his chair with a little grunt. He fumbled for the phone, but his fingers weren't working either. He looked at me, his eyes scared. "Otilia," he said.

I found her in the kitchen. One look at my face and she grabbed the wheelchair. It took our combined strength to get Julius into the chair—his body had hardened, like concrete. I pushed and Otilia fussed as we rattled our way down a series of corridors. I took the final corner too fast, caught a footrest against the wall, and almost dumped Julius. Otilia flung open a pair of doors leading into a large bedroom, furnished almost exclusively with a small hospital bed. Otilia took firm hold of the wheelchair handles.

"Goodbye, Señor," she said to me.

I turned to leave. Julius grabbed my arm and pulled at me. I bent to hear.

"I changed my mind, Norbu," he said, his voice soft. My heart sank. I reached for the check in my pocket, but he pulled me even closer. "You're not getting near my Bentley. You drive like crap." Then he winked.

Chapter 11

I climbed into the Mustang, inhaling its musky scent of worn leather and time. Before I placed the key in the ignition, I allowed myself a few moments to simply sit and absorb the change. I had a ridiculously well-paying job with a man I admired. When solutions like this arrive, seemingly out of the blue, but more often than not after I've at least made space for their possibility, they carry with them buoyancy, a lightness of heart. Such moments affirm that hope is not a dead end, and joy is often just a small perceptual shift from despair. The hard edges of my body softened and expanded. I smiled. Gratitude, that's what I was feeling.

Before I left the estate, I sent Mike a text. NEED YOUR HELP TONIGHT. I'LL COME TO YOU. 10PM OK? ALSO, WORK YOUR WONDERS ON HELMUT ZIGO. EUROPEAN. Ten at night was midday for Mike. I'd bring my laptop. He'd get me Skyped up in no time.

Until I met up with Mike and communicated with this Zigo fellow directly, there wasn't much else I could do for Julius.

Which left me with the murder mystery known as Marv. I still didn't have any official connection to the case. If anything, Bill was actively discouraging my involvement. I should move on, right? But. But. But. Once my mind gets a hold of something, I have a hard time letting it go. My spiritual life may embrace nonattachment, but when it comes to unnatural deaths, I'm doggedly persistent.

What did we have so far? A dead producer, whose death was caused by someone smart enough to conceal its source but stupid enough to leave not one, but two calling cards, therefore completely wasting the original secrecy. One event, Marv's mysterious death, felt calculated. Another, the skinned tattoo, seemed vindictive. And the third, the dropped knife, was impulsive. The only thing these three had in common, so far, was Marv Rudolph's obese body.

I knew that S & M were tracking down all Marv's incoming calls—checking alibis, interviewing his entertainment associates. But I had a hunch these would be dead ends. Studio honchos didn't kill you outright. From what I had just read about Marv's world, they were more likely to cut off your balls, metaphorically speaking, and leave you only wishing you were dead.

But the knife meant something. So did the skinning. They may not have been the cause of death, but they were an indication of *something*. I grabbed the little notebook I kept in my glove compartment and jotted down some thoughts:

Who would want Marv Rudolph dead?

1. Pissed off family member. (Harper. Arlene. Others?)

2. Jealous girlfriend. (Tovah?)

3. Angry underling/associate/employee. (Julius? Tovah? Keith Connor?)

Like Bill, I felt we could probably rule out Arlene. She had an alibi and seemed genuinely distressed by Marv's death, and frankly, she was too wispy to pull such a thing off. It looked like Harper was out as well, if her mother was to be believed, though their alibis were conveniently interdependent. Though Harper's little return jaunt to the Robinsgrove vaulted her to the top of my suspect list. I underlined her name. I wondered if Sully and Mack had even questioned her?

4. (Talk to Harper?) I added.

Julius, Parkinson's or not, had some fire in him, and I felt he was lying about something, but his dismissal of Marv felt genuine. I also believed him when he said he never left his compound. And Keith Connor needed Marv alive, it seemed to me. Tovah, however, was also a real possibility, for obvious reasons. Availability, motive, you name it. I had no idea what her current relationship was to Marv, though I could guess. But Tovah was gone for now, and I couldn't track her down through her license or credit card use without letting Bill know I was still deeply involved in his case.

An idea nudged its way in.

Maybe, with a little help, I could bring Tovah to me. Then I could deliver her to Bill on a platter, no questions asked. I put in a call to Sully and got his voicemail.

"Hey, Sully, it's Ten. How's it going? Listen, I have a question about your door-to-door at Robinsgrove, for the Rudolph case. Also wondering if you questioned the daughter, Harper, yet. Call me, okay?"

I made a note: "10/29 - Called Sully re: Robinsgrove/Tovah. Harper."

I paused. I should call Bill and tell him about Harper's visit to the Robinsgrove. But his sharp words had left residual sting-marks on my heart. I wasn't ready to let them go.

And then there was Arlene's reference to "crooks"— her implication that anyone in the movie business, Marv included, was automatically in bed with gangsters and criminals.

5. Criminal element? Mafia? Gangs?

Which led me to the tattoo. Where had Marv gotten it? What did it mean?

6. Tattoo.

I turned the key and the engine growled to life. As I put my car in reverse, something caught my eye: two figures, a man and a woman, hurrying across the lawn from the direction of the guesthouse, beyond Julius's cloud-room. They appeared to be arguing. The man was stabbing the air. He stopped abruptly, as if he'd just caught sight of me. He was broad-shouldered, his face shielded by a hat. Manuel, the gardener. Even from a distance I sensed hostility radiating off him in waves. He wheeled around and hurried back toward the guesthouse. As the woman got closer, I saw the red nylon medical bag. Dr. Alvarado, making a house call.

I was relieved—Julius had looked in need of medical attention. I rolled down my window to acknowledge her, but she passed by without a glance.

I rested my hands lightly on the mahogany frame of the steering wheel, and it responded to my touch like an old friend, as I wound my way down the long, curved drive. About three-quarters of the way out, I passed a familiar stocky figure, built like a fireplug, kneeling by a sprinkler valve. Manuel looked up and tipped his hat, his curved moustache framing an unsmiling mouth.

Impossible. Unless the man could teleport his body, there was no way he could be back there and also here.

So who was the other Manuel, the one back at the house?

I tucked the question next to all the other unanswered ones currently crowding my mind and drove home.

I changed into my running clothes. Now that I was back on somebody's payroll, I was somehow more inspired to keep my muscles toned. Before I ran into Topanga Canyon Park, I hauled a protesting Tank outside for a quick tree-climbing lesson. He pretends to hate this, but once I deposited him on the peeling bark of a eucalyptus branch, Tank acted quite happy to scratch his way upward for a few yards. I felt encouraged. Silly me. He stared from his perch, flicking his shaggy tail, as if to say: Up is one thing, buddy; down is another.

"C'mon, Tank. You can do this. Use your claws."

He turned away, peering into the distance to contemplate the absurdity of this idea.

I had to climb up after Tank and drag 18 pounds of furry, boneless deadweight off the branch. The minute we were back on firm ground, he erupted out of my arms and darted to the deck, where he proceeded to groom himself, as if none of this had happened. The lesson, for me, was 2 percent progress, 98 percent humility.

After a long run and a short shower, I was ready to browse the Internet. Julius had said Marv got his tattoo somewhere in the San Fernando Valley. I got to work.

There were well over 100 parlors. Where to start?

As Julius would say, time to use my noodle. If I were Marv, getting this particular tattoo, what would be my priorities? Quality: It had to look authentically old. Hygiene: I couldn't afford an infected arm, and all the accompanying embarrassments. Most of all, I'd require confidentiality. If this tattoo was to be my Holocaust calling card, no one could know when or where I had actually gotten it.

I assumed cost was no object.

I got to work, and soon had narrowed the list to a dozen high-end parlors located in and around there. All catered to a celebrity clientele, promised a superior artistic product, and, most important, guaranteed complete privacy. I browsed their websites. Several had online galleries displaying anonymous limbs, festooned with ornate tattoos. I scrolled through jeweled images scaling torsos, wrapping around biceps, decorating muscled backs. I clicked past a snarling dragon, a pipe-smoking cat in a pinstriped suit, a skull nibbling on a rose. My attention got roped into an endless loop, surveying multiple renditions of the Buddha: rotund buddhas, emaciated buddhas, laughing buddhas, praying buddhas.

I had to close the computer and pick up the phone, before I lost an entire day staring at bodhisattvas inked on skin.

I called all twelve parlors and bombed out on twelve fronts. No one had tattooed Marv. No one had heard of anyone else tattooing Marv. I was told to fuck off several times, and those were the polite responses.

I was back to square one. I had to get smarter here. Okay, if I were *me* getting a tattoo, what would be my priority? Easy. A personal connection. I'd want to go to a tattoo artist who came highly recommended by someone who had used him or her.

Marv rubbed shoulders with a lot of stars. What star in Marv's life had a tattoo?

A long-legged bird stiff-walked through my consciousness, settling on the groin of someone famous whose groin I had seen, someone Marv also knew. Keith Connor.

I tapped in a few key words and up popped a short article in *L.A. Weekly* from six years back, featuring Keith Connor, the rock star's pelvis, and a tiny tattoo parlor in Sherman Oaks. My eyes lasered in on the name: T-Bird Tattoos. The proprietor's name was Thurman Bird, aka "Thunder." Thunder Bird. I took the muscle car connection to be a good sign.

I dialed the number.

"T-Bird Tattoos."

"Mr. Thurman Bird?"

"Who's asking?"

"My name is Tenzing Norbu. I'm an acquaintance of Keith Connor."

The voice warmed up several degrees. "How is the SOB? I keep waiting for him to come in for that butt-tat he wanted. I still have the sketch. Mayan Sun God. Left cheek."

I wrenched my mind away from the image. "I'd like to come see you about something. Today, if possible. Is there a good time, Thurman?"

"'Thunder.' Jesus. No one calls me Thurman but the fucking IRS. Yeah, sure, you can come by. Be my guest. I got no one scheduled until later tonight."

"I'll be there within the hour," I said.

Adrenaline carbonated my blood. *Slow down, Ten. You have an actual paying job to attend to, remember?*

I hadn't heard back so I texted Mike again. NEED. HELP. YOUR PLACE. TONIGHT. That counted as work.

I toasted a thick slice of seven-grain bread, spread an even thicker layer of olive tapenade, piled on chunks of ripe avocado and chopped Persian cucumbers, and ate as mindfully as I could, given that I was done in six minutes. I zipped my laptop in a hard travel case and slid it next to the Sadie file in my official Private-Investigator-Man backpack. I forked a can of mixed grill into Tank's bowl and topped it with a splash of tuna water. Guilt water, more like it.

"Lunch is ready," I told Tank. He was curled in the kitchen windowsill, catching the afternoon sun, one of his favorite pastimes. I sent him a mental message that I'd be gone for a while.

If he got it, he wasn't saying.

On a whim, I changed into a pair of not-too-rumpled khaki pants, a proper cotton shirt with a collar and buttons, and my die-hard navy sport coat. I even stuck a tie in my pocket. You never know. I grabbed a fleece-lined windbreaker from the closet, in case I was out late, and left the house whistling. It felt good to be employed—to have tasks to complete and a nice fat check in my pocket.

I took the Toyota—it was time to ride the everyday workhorse, rather than my conspicuous thoroughbred. I decided to avoid possible beach traffic and navigated Topanga Canyon Drive away from the ocean, picking up the 101 at Woodland Hills. Thankfully, I'd guessed right. The Sunday freeway traffic was light, and I was parking at a meter on Ventura Boulevard, just off Woodman, within 40 minutes. I felt in my pants pocket for quarters and came up with three. Enough for a 12-minute visit these days—inflation hadn't skipped over Sherman Oaks either. I fed the meter. Then I remembered it was Sunday. Parking was free. Now I was doubly irritated.

I put on the tie. Might as well. Easier to pass as a homicide detective, should the need arise.

T-Bird Tattoos was a small shop tucked between a Psychic and a Cigar, Pipe, and Hookah Boutique. A psychic tip, a tat, or a toke: take your pick. I picked the tat. I stepped under a scalloped white canvas awning boasting a drawing of a large pink lotus with a tiny skull in its center and T-Bird's website address. I also counted at least five variations of the word "Tattoo" on the shop entrance: painted, stenciled, etched in glass, hung from a wooden shingle, and glowing in orange neon. In case I was confused.

I entered a dim, jumbled array of hanging plants, painted masks, gumball machines, and numerous black and white posters in gilded wooden frames—detailed drawings of buxom women with tassels dangling from their nipples, buxom women with iconic political figures on their laps, and rock 'n' roll deities, among them, buxom women. Statues of other deities, the Hindu kind, perched on homemade shelves, waving multiple arms and uplifted elephant trunks. The walls were painted bright blue, and a small fridge and microwave oven completed the decor. Two black leather chairs, the kind you'd find in a barber's shop, awaited customers at the back of the shop. In front of them, a brocade curtain was bunched to one side, held in place by what looked like a wizened monkey's paw. It was rigged to pull across and attach to a claw on the other side of the store, thus blocking the vision of whatever took place in back. That solved the privacy issue.

I tried, and failed, to imagine Marv sitting in one of those chairs, Thunder hunched over him with a buzzing machine. Marv must have really, really wanted Julius to invest.

"I'm eating a late lunch," a voice said. "Hungry? There's plenty."

"Thunder?"

"That would be me." He was sitting behind a desk to my left, eating out of a cardboard container. I recognized the carton, and the smell: frozen cheese enchiladas, zapped in a microwave. Bachelor cuisine. I'd eaten more than my share. He lifted the carton in my direction.

"No, thanks," I said. Thunder looked to be nearing 40. His head was shaved, and a neat moustache and goatee framed an easy smile. Of medium build, but muscular, he was wearing a black T-shirt, and my eyes were drawn to the tiger creeping down his right bicep, like Tank descending a branch, only much more surefooted.

"I called earlier. Tenzing Norbu," I said. "Ten, for short."

"Cool," he said. A phone on his desk rang. He glanced at the screen on the handset. "Never mind," he said. "Probably my mortgage calling. Fuckers. Have a seat. Here. Leaf through this while I clean up." He crossed the room and stuffed the container into a black trash bin, overflowing with similar containers. Again, a thought flicked past my brain. Again, I couldn't catch it in time.

I pulled up a wooden three-legged stool and paged through an album of laminated photographs of tattooed body parts, most of them anonymous. I paused at one—a striking green Gila monster curling around a man's neck. Two pages after, sure enough, there was a groin I knew well, sporting a long-legged bird.

I turned the album toward Thunder.

"Keith Connor?" I said.

"I'll never tell," he winked, and sat across from me again. "So, what gives? I'm guessing you're not here for ink."

"No. Not today. I'm actually here with a question concerning another tattoo, one I believe you gave a mutual acquaintance," I said. "A Marvin Rudolph?"

Thunder's face darkened, and for the first time I put his name to his form. "Yeah, well, I'll tell you the same thing I told the other a-hole who came in asking about Rudolph. No fucking comment."

"I'm sorry, who came in?" I found it hard, no, make that impossible, to believe Sully and Mack were onto this guy. Not unless they'd had an intelligence transplant.

"Some asswipe on a bike. He said he was a cop, and I laughed. Sorry, he just didn't seem the type. Plus, the guy had the worst skull tat on his wrist I've ever seen; we're talkin' fuckin' Casper the friendly ghost. He wasn't too happy with me when I offered to ink it over, either."

"And he questioned you about Marv?"

"He tried." Thunder shook his head. "I've spent more time talking about that tattoo then I did inking it. First some suit was all over me about it three years ago, about a month after I inked it. Next day, Marv called me up, all pissed off, read me the riot act for two fucking hours. How was I supposed to know it was a secret? Yesterday morning, I read that Marv's dead, and it starts up all over again, guys in ties with questions. Twice in two days? Dude, give it fucking rest."

"I would," I said, "but a man's dead. And the tattoo might help lead us to whoever's responsible."

Thunder eyed me. I met his gaze. Finally, he nodded. "Right. Fair enough. What do you want to know?"

"Whatever you can tell me."

"Okay, so three years ago, Marv calls me on my private line, tells me he's a friend of Keith Connor. And he asks me what it would cost to close my shop for an evening, just for him. He needs a tattoo, on the DL, like I did for Keith. 'Name your price,' he says. So I do: one thousand, plus the time it takes to do the tat. Two nights later, I close early, pull the curtains, and set him up in the back. He'd brought in a picture of one of those number tattoos, from the Holocaust. Kind of creepy, actually. Anyway, he wanted to make sure I could duplicate the exact color of faded blue. It was a holy bitch to match, but I finally got it by diluting blue-gray dye with rosewater and a little witch hazel. The tat itself didn't take long—maybe an hour. I think I charged him about thirteen hundred, total. I warned him it would take two or three weeks before it really looked authentic—that there'd still be a little bit of glisten while it healed. He went off happy, though."

"What about the actual numbers? It would help me to know what they meant."

"No idea," Thunder said. "Only that they were important to him." He shook his head. "You cops even talk to each other? The guy yesterday wanted to know the exact same thing."

So Thunder assumed I was a cop. I decided to let that go for the time being. I was much more interested in the other possible imposter. "Was the other detective a tall, lanky guy, white hair, blue eyes, name of Sully?"

"Wrong," Thunder said.

"How about Mack, or Bill Bohannon?"

Thunder made a sound like a buzzer. "*Annhhh.* Wrong again. Dude was kind of short, with a goatee and ridiculous wraparound shades. Hispanic." He started to fish through a pile of business cards in a brass bowl on his desk. A very familiar brass bowl. A Tibetan singing bowl, in fact. Rub the rim with a wooden dowel and it creates a liquid sound, pure as prayer. I resisted the urge to rescue the poor thing, held hostage in a tattoo parlor.

"He had serious guns though, I'll give him that," Thunder went on, oblivious to my moral struggle.

"Guns? He was armed?"

"No, dude. *Guns.*" Thunder flexed his biceps, illustrating. He went back to rummaging through the bowl and pounced on a card. "Yes! I rock!" He handed it over. I glanced down at an official-looking LAPD calling card, one that I was 99 percent sure was fake, since (a) I didn't recognize the name, Raul Martinez, and I hadn't been gone from the force that long; (b) the card was printed on cheap stock, and the colors of the city seal looked suspiciously garish; and (c) who else from the division would be working the tattoo angle but Sully, Mack, or Bill? Or me, but that was another story.

"Can I have this?" I slipped it in my pocket before he could object. Another question worked its way to the surface.

"Did I hear you correctly? Did you say he arrived on a motorcycle?"

"Yeah. A chopper. HD."

"HD?"

"Hardly Drivable. Low hanging bars and a shitload of shiny extras. Not your normal cop bike, am I right?"

Now I was 100 percent sure the man wasn't a cop, not

unless he was dead. That's the only way you'd catch an LAPD officer on a souped-up chopper.

"One thing was weird, though. We were shooting the shit about Harleys, and I mentioned a buddy who had a bad spin-out on the 134 a few years back. Left him with a permanent limp. Some rich douche bag in a BMW didn't see him, but my friend wound up booked on suspicion of reckless endangerment. Nobody likes Mexican Harley riders covered in tats. So anyway, this Martinez dude remembered the court case perfectly, only it sounded like he was on the side of the biker. I mean he backtracked pretty fast, but it sure seemed as if he was defending the guy at first—like maybe he was his lawyer or something."

Finally, something I could work with.

I handed Thunder my own card. "Thank you for your help. If you happen to think of anything else, give me a call, all right?"

"No problem," he said. "Hey, tats are half off on Sundays. You want a Chinese dragon or something?"

"Not today," I said. As I left the store, I saw him toss my card into the singing bowl. I listened, but I didn't hear a sound.

There was a ticket on my Toyota's windshield. *What?* I looked around for an official in a uniform, but he or she was long gone, and anyway, I wasn't playing for the home team anymore. I scoured the ticket and finally discovered what I'd done, or in this case, not done: "Non-Display of Current License Tabs." The actual tab was in my glove compartment, waiting to be displayed. I could feel a small bubble of annoyance rise inside, swelling with justifications as to why I was special and why this was undeserved. I rotated my shoulders to reset: I had a lot of work hours ahead of me, and clinging to righteous indignation might bring brief satisfaction, but it would only increase fatigue in the long run. I affixed the new tab and tucked the ticket in my wallet.

After jotting down my conversation with Thunder, I checked the time. It was 4 P.M., and still not a peep from Mike. I again weighed putting in a call to Bill. I wasn't sure he would welcome hearing from me. I called him anyway. Force of habit.

"Hey," Bill's voice was low, almost a whisper. "I'm just leaving Marv Rudolph's burial service. He's in the ground, and they're all heading back to the house. "

"Are you going there next?"

"Can't," he said. "Bhatnager and Summer are releasing their preliminary autopsy findings at a press conference in a couple hours. They want me there, just so everyone can know that the LAPD has no fucking cause of death and no fucking suspects. Did I tell you I hate my job? Because I do. It's Sunday, for Christ's sake. I was supposed to meet everyone at the zoo. I love the zoo. And I hate my job." He sighed. "So, what's up?"

I wanted to tell him about Marv's starlet Tovah, about Thunder Bird, about the mysterious cop wannabe Raul Martinez, I really did, but my mouth wouldn't form the words. *It's not the right moment. He already has too much on his plate.* The tight ball forming in my belly told another story. I was anxious. If Bill railed at me again for exceeding my authority, I wasn't sure I could handle it. I didn't even dare ask for a copy of the coroner's report.

For the first time since Bill and I had become partners, and then friends, I withheld information that could be important to a case. Instead, I played it safe.

"I just wanted to pass along some good news. Julius Rosen's hired me to find his sister, Sadie. Really nice money, too. I have an actual job." I wondered if he could hear the bright, false note in my voice.

"That's good, Ten," Bill said, distracted. "Listen, I'll catch you later, okay?" He hung up, leaving me to absorb the sour aftertaste of guilt.

I jabbed Mike's number on my iPhone. His voicemail picked up.

"Where the hell are you, Mike? I need to see you! Check your text messages."

That's useful, Ten, taking your guilt out on your one other friend in Los Angeles. This was becoming a bad habit. Before I could ring Mike back and apologize, he called me, his voice sleepy.

"I miss something, boss? Somebody start a fucking fire in your pants?"

"Sorry," I said. "I've been up since three this morning. I'm running on fumes. Listen, the good news is I have a job, so we both can get paid. The bad news is, I need your help with some technical stuff. Right away. So can I come to your place?"

"Oh, man. No can do, not today. I have a deejay gig later, and I have to pick up an extra turntable in Calabasas first."

My only task for Julius was going down the proverbial drain. There was only one solution—I would have to do what I had vowed never to do. "Then I'll meet you there, okay? At your gig. Where is it?"

Mike lowered his voice to growl. "If I toldja that, I'd have to kill ya."

"What are you talking about, Mike?"

"Little joke, Ten, okay? It's just, the concert's, umm, let's just say it's way underground, you know? I mean, it's not exactly—what's the word—legal? Even I don't know where I'm going yet, you know?"

"The only thing I know, Mike, is that I'm in a bind here."

Mike sighed. "Look. I'll e-mail you the link, and the promo code for this thing. Just register online, and someone else will e-mail you the actual address later. But boss, you can't tell anyone about this, like Bill for instance, or post it on Facebook, okay?"

"What is this, some kind of deejay terrorist cell?"

"I mean it, Ten. These are my friends, and they're finally letting me in on their deal. I don't want to blow it. I go on at ten. Ironically."

"That's when you *start*?" This day was sliding from bad to worse. I could probably find someone else to help with the technical aspects of contacting Zigo, but I knew no one as skillful or discreet.

"Fine," I said. "I'll meet you there." I couldn't resist a small dig. "Gosh! My first rave."

Silence. Then, "No glow sticks, boss. I'd never live it down."

The e-mail from Mike arrived moments later. I opened the link to www.iluvchaotica.com and entered the promo code, my thumbs clumsy: iBluvingTechno.

i B feeling ridiculous was more like it.

One $20 credit card "donation" later, I was promised a text message at 8 P.M., complete with location and further instructions. Would Sherlock have gone to these lengths? Probably, probably.

I recorded the website address and code in my little notebook, just in case. As I leafed back through the pages, I zeroed in on my suspect list: item number 1, in particular. *Pissed off family member. Arlene. Harper. Others?*

I knew where to go next. Maybe Bill couldn't make it to the Rudolph family reception, but I could. Heck, I even had a tie.

Chapter 12

Cars lined the front of the Rudolph home. I recognized Rabbi Fishbein's Acura; soon I'd have as many vehicles in my mental files as Clancy Williams. Speaking of which, there was no sign of Clancy's Impala, or any other photographers or media members. They must all be at the press conference.

I parked in the street and trailed behind an elderly woman walking up the Rudolph's drive, holding a covered casserole dish. The front door was slightly ajar, and I could hear the murmur of voices within. Like the rabbi, this woman kissed the fingertips of her right hand and pressed them to the piece of wood on the doorsill before slipping inside. I paused, hesitant to enact a ritual I knew nothing about, but wanting to honor a house in grief. I settled on a small bow and followed her.

I slipped off my shoes and added them to the pile just inside the front door. The older woman carried her casserole into the kitchen. I headed right, toward the living room, carefully stepping around a small basin of water and a stack of linen hand towels set by the entrance. The living room curtains were drawn. My eyes adjusted to the flickering light of several large candles. About 20 people, men and women, were sitting on or near the floor, I couldn't quite tell which. All the photographs and framed posters on the tables and walls were shrouded with pieces of cloth, as was the large mirror hanging over the fireplace. The effect was of a room itself wrapped in sorrow. I could feel my body softening, settling into a quieter, purer space. Any thought of interrogation evaporated. *Not the time.*

I spotted Arlene, arms wrapped around her knees, near

the middle of the room. Her skin and lips were pale, her eyelashes almost invisible. She was scrubbed clean of make-up, and she seemed younger and more vulnerable without it. The left sleeve of her silk blouse was torn, and I realized other people had tears in their clothing—here, a jacket, there, a shirtsleeve. I was touched by this visible symbol of the emotional fissure a sudden death can cause. Arlene glanced over at me, confused by my presence, I thought. I bowed slightly. She looked away.

Low wooden stools were scattered throughout. *Ahh, these must be their special mourning seats.* I walked over to the little stool closest to Arlene and sat.

I heard a hiss, a collective intake of breath indicating I had done something wrong, and I scrambled to my feet. I'd committed some sort of *faux pas*, not at all my intention. I stood awkwardly, until Rabbi Fishbein took pity on me. He got up and led me to the empty sofa. I perched on the edge, self-consciously looming over the others in the room.

"Why are you here, detective?" Rabbi Fishbein's voice was quiet, and not unkind. "We are sitting *shivah*. This is a sacred time."

"I understand," I said. I included Arlene in my next words. "I've come to pay my respects. I won't stay long."

She offered me a wan smile. "My husband's soul is at peace now," she said.

I nodded, and relaxed my posture, settling into the sofa. I closed my eyes: *Om mani padme hum. May you have serenity and happiness in the afterlife and in all your future lives.*

I rested in the silence. My breath slowed, and spaciousness flowered in my heart, as the men in the room started to chant, a beautiful, haunting melody in a language that sounded both ancient and wise. I dropped deeper into a state of stillness. The universal practice of honoring the dead was expressed in a tongue absolutely foreign to me, but it was perfectly understood.

As the prayer faded, I opened my eyes. My throat

tightened, not with sadness, but alarm. A young woman, startlingly beautiful, toned and strong, was sitting on a low stool across the room, staring at me. Her eyes blazed with hate. Harper, seven months later, and all grown up. My face registered shocked recognition; she quickly covered her own with her hands and began to wail. Comforting adults surrounded her.

I turned to Rabbi Fishbein, who was again pushing to his feet, this time to tend to Harper.

"I'll get her a glass of water," I murmured.

I hurried through the foyer and dining room, skirting the long wooden dining table, where a handful of women were busy unwrapping platters of fruit and cheese and setting them next to noodle casseroles, mounds of chopped liver, and bowls of egg salad. I pushed through a swinging wooden door into a pristine kitchen, which was smaller than I'd imagined, but a jewel. From the antique tile to the honeyed wood, everything looked exquisitely original—vintage and yet brand new.

I couldn't help myself. I scanned the stone counters for any signs of knives, and soon located a slotted wooden block of them, by the gleaming Viking stove. I crossed over to investigate. Wüsthofs. *Yes.* But every slot was occupied by its designated knife, including the 8-inch chef's knife. All cutlery present and accounted for.

A woman backed her way through a second swinging door, on the far side of the kitchen, balancing a pungent platter of carved meat.

"Smells delicious," I lied.

"Brisket," she said, and continued to the dining room.

I plucked a small plastic party glass from a stacked tower on the counter, filled it with water, and retraced my steps to the room of mourners. I offered the water to Harper. She gulped it down.

"Thank you," she said, her voice low. But when she raised her eyes to meet mine, a wild, panicked look distorted her lovely features, gone almost before it arrived. I took the glass.

Rabbi Fishbein appeared at my shoulder.

"Will you be joining us for *seudat havra'ah*? It is our meal of healing."

"Thank you, but no," I said. "I must be going."

He touched my arm. "I wish you well," he said. "Shalom."

"Shalom," I repeated. Again, the language was universal. Peace, my brother.

I sat in my Toyota, loosening my tie. Thinking. Maybe Harper just didn't want me to expose her sordid past, now that she was "doing so well in her new school." She certainly looked better—her skin and body glowed with health, and she had added needed pounds, mostly of muscle. She was stronger now. And she was capable of hate—I had just been on the receiving end of it. I circled her name in my notebook. She remained an unanswered question for now. Then I plucked one of the spare evidence bags from my glove compartment, leftovers from my homicide cop days. Inside it, I carefully placed the plastic party glass I had conveniently forgotten to throw away.

I still had two hours to fill before I received my underground instructions to Mike's techno-rave, in this, my longest of days. What to do in the meantime? When in doubt, I ask my body. I ran my attention over my insides like a wand. The impromptu meditation had soothed the jangled tiredness and settled my heart, which was great. But a hollow space remained. Hunger. I was hungry. Hungry for food, no doubt, but also something else. *Companionship.*

Should I call Heather? I'd experienced two serious romantic debacles in as many years, with a string of short missteps before that. Much as I wanted to lay the blame elsewhere, both Charlotte and Julie were now in committed relationships with other men. The overlapping factor in their failure, maybe in all the failures? Me. Let's face it: I was afraid to engage again, to risk my heart in yet another entanglement, leading to yet another round of blame and betrayal. It was always the same. It never ended well.

Always. Never. There they were, like gongs, warning me that I was stuck again in limited thinking. Breaking my second rule. Jean's words echoed: *Put down the flashlight, pick up the mirror.* I replayed the thousands of squabbles and upsets, the arguments, the miscommunications I had both invited and inflicted over the past decade. Watched as "she never" and "I always" moments piled up, forming a barricade around me, a prison of my own making. Better to be safe than hurt. Better to be right than happy. Ten's working mottos.

But what if they were based on misinformation? The Buddha says to question everything. "Everything" includes mottos.

I was struck with a realization so powerful that it stopped my breath. *What if I haven't had thousands of fights? What if I've been having the same fight, thousands of times?*

What if my mother's betrayal and my father's scorn made up the foundational underpinning for every romantic relationship I've ever entered? What if I was breaking my second rule over and over and over again? *Don't do it, Ten. Don't allow yourself to be imprisoned by past betrayals, disguised as your protectors.*

I let my breath out slowly, as something shifted, deep inside. I had work to do—that much was certain. But maybe, just maybe, Heather could be a starting place to do that work. How would I ever know, if I didn't have the courage to try?

I fished out her business card and typed her name and number into my contact list.

I touched her number on the screen.

She picked up on the third ring.

"Hello?"

"Heather," I said. "This is Ten."

"Hey."

I heard traffic humming in the background. "Sounds like you're on the road."

"Yup. Heading home after a very long press conference and debriefing."

"Where's home?'

"Santa Monica."

I liked the sound of that. In Los Angeles, where the looming specter of gridlock hovers over just about every conversation, geography can play a big role in a budding romance. Santa Monica was just down the road from Topanga, an easy commute. I was glad she didn't live in some buzz-killing location like Simi Valley.

"So you're on the ten?"

"That's me. Talking to Ten on the ten," she said.

I smiled. "How about talking to Ten in person? Would you like to get together for dinner? I'm in Beverly Hills, and I've got hours before my next appointment."

Heather took her time answering. "You know what? I'm a little beat, and I'm not crazy about most restaurants out here to begin with. All that hipster strutting exhausts me. Would it be okay if we met down at the beach? It's a gorgeous evening."

I made some quick calculations. Even if Mike's gig was as far away as Thousand Oaks, I'd be able to have a picnic at the beach and make it to him by 11 P.M. I guess insanely late gigs did have their value.

"Let's meet at the parking lot across from Patrick's Roadhouse, by Entrada Drive. I'll pick up some food. Anything you don't eat?"

"I don't eat anything that has eyes," she said. "Except potatoes."

I laughed. "Shouldn't be a problem."

I bought two large Greek salads and a side of hummus from the Urth Café, my go-to restaurant for eyeless foods. I parked next to Heather's little Honda. She was sitting inside, headphones on, bopping her head to something on her iPad. I tapped on her window. She climbed out, and we gave each other a friendly SoCal half hug. She grabbed a blanket from her trunk, and we carried our matching eco-friendly bags down to the beach.

I unpacked our little picnic. Heather handed over a chilled bottle of wine and a corkscrew. Puligny-Montrachet. Nice. I worked the cork out of the bottle while she spread her blanket and set down the food.

"Oops," she said. "No glasses."

"No problem," I said. I handed her the bottle, and she took a sip. She handed it back to me, and I did the same. The wine was crisp and dry; its flinty edge woke up my taste buds.

"To health and happiness," I said.

"And everything else good," she answered. Heather popped a kalamata olive into her mouth with long, slender fingers. Up close, they looked stronger than I'd remembered.

"Do you play an instrument?"

Her eyes widened. "Classical guitar. Ever since I started med school," she said. "How did you know?"

"Your fingers. They're the fingers of a musician."

She studied them. "I started taking lessons to relax, you know, as a kind of stress-release. But one day I hit a chord—it was a big, open G chord—and it sounded so amazing, I must have strummed it a hundred times. Now I'm hooked. If I could, I'd play every day."

"Do you have a favorite guitarist?"

"Andrés Segovia," Heather sighed. "He's the gold standard. I dream of sounding like him some day." For once, instead of blurting out something trite like, "I'm sure you will," I just smiled. I also refrained from discussing work, hers or mine. I just wasn't in the mood. Neither, it seemed, was she. We ate in companionable silence, Heather matching me bite for bite, opting out of the usual flurry of first-date chitchat. What a relief. After we finished eating, I stood up and stretched.

"Walk?" I held out my hand.

"Sounds good." I pulled her upright. We kicked off our shoes, stowed them in our bags, and strolled barefoot in the cool sand, serenaded by the crash and pull of the waves.

We stopped to watch the dark green water, the curls of foam almost phosphorescent. "Can I ask you something?" Heather asked. "Something personal?"

Here we go, I thought. "Sure," I said, and braced for romantic commitment questions. But Heather had a different kind of commitment on her mind.

"Bill tells me you're Tibetan. That you trained to be a monk."

"Half Tibetan. And almost-monk."

"But you're a practicing Buddhist, right?"

"Yes. Well, kind of. Yes."

"How does that work? I mean, how do you do what you do and stay true to what you believe?"

Chitchat suddenly wasn't looking so bad. I dug my toes in the sand, a tiny postponement.

"I don't, at least not all the time. I just do the best I can."

"And how does that feel, inside I mean? To be committed to nonviolence, and working in a profession that concentrates on the opposite?"

I let the question settle, and soon, the answer floated up.

"Lonely," I said. "It feels lonely."

She nodded. "I sensed that."

My iPhone pinged. Good timing. "Sorry, I have to check this," I said. I opened the e-mail from ilovechaotica.com and quickly found the location details. I was heading downtown next, way downtown.

"You have to get going," Heather said. I nodded. "To be continued?" she said.

"To be continued."

As we strolled back, Heather slipped her hand into mine. "Two Ten-sightings in one day," she said. "This is nice."

A jogger ran past us in the dark, and I flashed on the

morning before, when I was the jogger and my crazy brain had concocted a very different Heather scenario.

"Yes," I said. "Yes, it is."

We reached our cars. We faced each other. The awkward time was at hand.

"Thank you," she said. "I like being with you." She delivered a soft kiss to my cheek.

"Me, too," I said. My pulse raced. "And, and if I were a cool California dude, I'd know what the next step should be."

She cocked her head. "But?" she said.

"But I'm not. I'm a Tibetan transplant who hasn't quite mastered the whole 'cool' thing."

"Well thank God for small favors."

We shared a smile. I touched her cheek.

"Heather . . ." My voice trailed off.

"We'll get there," she said, still smiling. "These things take time," and climbed in her car.

The e-mail instructions to the event on 11th and Main had been terse. Doors open at 10 P.M.; park on the street; no cameras allowed; *Don't Loiter!*, followed by a list of set times and performers. My eyes widened. The last set *started* at five A.M. What was wrong with these people?

I hit traffic on the Harbor Freeway and got off on Sixth. I took Main south, one way all the way, past a doggy day care that I wouldn't put my worst enemy's mutt in, past the Topshape Training Center, which looked anything but. As I neared the location, I skirted around a patrol car askew in the street, red and blue lights flashing. Two cops had a young banger cuffed, pressed against a warehouse wall. His baggy shorts reached almost to his ankles, and his body radiated defiance. Don't loiter, indeed.

Finally I reached a squat concrete bunker of a building, ominously deserted. But then I noticed the small row of windows across the top: They flickered and flashed red and blue lights. Unless a cop car was inside, I'd found my event.

I was very glad I had come in the Toyota. My Mustang would have been stripped down to its bare chassis in minutes around here. I parked on a side street around the corner, grabbed my laptop, and walked into a small courtyard, where a cluster of smokers were talking and laughing.

"I pop-locked and broke it down!" one of them brayed. "Ridic!" another yelled, and they all bumped fists. I was entering Mike Koenigs–land, one more situation where I didn't know the customs, and I didn't speak the language.

A young woman with a slender ring through her right nostril and a red *bindi* marking her forehead guarded the door. I'll bet she had no idea she and her *bindi* were telling the world she was married. I showed her the e-ticket on my phone, and she waved me inside.

The sound-assault was instant, and shocking: the loud, deep drone of a bass line, overlaid with multiple streams of electronic sound, reverberating between the exposed brick walls. About 20 couples writhed and swayed to the music, most of them reading their smart phone screens at the same time.

Another young woman—multiple piercings, a thatch of neon pink hair—was tending a well-stocked bar illuminated by a little pink lamp. I wasn't expecting liquor—a vat full of powdered horse tranquilizer seemed more likely. A swarthy young man in a baseball cap crouched on the floor to the left, working a sound board. A single blinking spotlight roamed the room, bathing the swaying bodies in blue, green, red, and back to blue again, as a mechanical, sirenlike wail looped around the rhythmic pounding.

I located the nexus of sound. And found Mike, or "dj mk," as the e-mail referred to him, headphones askew, traversing a long table of blinking orange lights and electronic equipment: laptops, turntables, iPods, iPhones, mouses, soundboards. Hunched over, his fingers flew over various keys and buttons, a tall skinny maestro. I caught his eye. He smiled, held up five fingers, tapped his watch, and returned to his rocket-ship dashboard. Five minutes was good. I can tolerate anything for five minutes. I leaned against one wall and closed my eyes. The blanket of sound began to separate into different tonal threads, some human, some not. Layers within layers, streams within streams, repetitive, meditative. A deep underlying chord of male voices began to vibrate, overtaking the other sounds. *Oooowahhhh*, the glottal texture amplified, vibrating with my insides like a tuning fork, and just like that, I was transported to Dorje Yidam. Twelve years old and experiencing for the first time the reverberating chants of a trio of Tibetan throat singers. Now, as then, the base notes throbbed, resonated, and probed directly into my chest. For a moment, suspended between two realities of time and place, I slipped into boundlessness, where neither one existed.

A dancer jostled my arm, and I startled back into the brick-lined warehouse. Mike transferred his headphones to another DJ, a shorter, stockier version of Mike, the transition seamless. The pulsing sound continued uninterrupted.

Mike grabbed a bottle of water and joined me.

"Wow," I yelled. "I get why you like this music! It's tantric! I may have just experienced techno-induced *samadhi*!"

Mike grinned and leaned close to my ear. "You sure you're not riding some k-love down the rabbit hole, boss?"

"I have no idea what you're talking about," I said, "and for that, I am grateful."

He grabbed my arm and pulled me to the outside courtyard. A sweet-faced, pretty girl with a shiny cap of chestnut hair and bright, blue-green eyes stepped to Mike's side. A pair of red sparkly devil's horns nested in her hair. She wore a miniscule black dress over red tights and red and black plaid high tops. The tip of her head barely reached the middle of Mike's chest, not counting the horns. Bending slightly, he encircled her with one arm. "This is my girl, Tricia. Tricia, this is Ten." I stuck out my hand. She darted under it to give me a hug.

"Happy almost-Halloween," she said.

I liked her. She was unexpectedly normal. A communal whoop emerged from the doorway of the venue. She kissed Mike on the lips and danced back inside.

"Nice girl," I said.

"I'm so lucky," he replied, without a shred of irony. "So, what do you need, boss?"

I explained about Zigo and showed him the business card. He shook his head.

"This is about setting you up on Skype?" he said. "That's the emergency?"

"Yes. Why?"

Mike grabbed me by the shoulders and leaned close to my face.

"Ten, you have got to get over this computer phobia. Dude, getting on Skype is like, like . . . I don't even know what to say. Like learning how to count to one."

He set up my laptop on a low wall surrounding the courtyard and opened the screen.

"I'm going to make you do this all by yourself," he said.

Five minutes later, I had a Skype account. Note to self: next time, at least try learning something new before you take a drive in the dead of night to a sleazy no-loiter zone for help.

Following Mike's directions, I then clicked on "Add a Contact" and typed "Helmut Zigo" into the box. I clicked on "Search" and his account name popped up right away.

"Now what?"

"Now, you send him a message," Mike said.

I clicked open the chat-box and typed in "Are you available to talk?" I took a deep breath and sent the message. Ten seconds later I got a reply:

HELMUTZIGO: DON'T RECGNZE U. WHO R U?

TENZINGNORBU: I REPRESENT JULIUS R.

HELMUTZIGO: OK. R U A LWYER?

TENZINGNORBU: NO, THANK GOD.

HELMUTZIGO: HAHA. WHT THEN?

TENZINGNORBU: PRIVATE DETECTIVE. YOU?

HELMUTZIGO: BSNESS. I ND TO CHCK U OUT. LV SKYPE ON AND WLL SND U MSG ABT NXT MTG.

His icon disappeared from the screen. So that was Helmut Zigo. All I knew about him so far was he didn't like to use vowels. I needed to check him out as well.

"See? Easy as pie," Mike said.

"Could he see me?"

"Nah, but that's easy to do, too." Mike showed me how to click on the video icon. "It only works as a video-phone if you and the other person have webcams. I'm surprised you haven't used this to contact your buddies in India, it being free and all."

I smiled at the thought of Yeshe and Lobsang trying to find their way around a computer. I was Bill Gates compared to them, unless things had changed drastically.

"Okay," Mike said. "You sticking around? The three A.M. set's going to be huge." He registered the look of horror on my face. "Right. Catch you later." He ducked inside and was instantly enveloped by a wall of sound.

I staggered through my front door an hour later. Tank skated between my legs, rubbing against my shins and meowing. Tank never meowed. I scooped him into my arms.

"I'm so sorry," I said. "I had no idea I'd be gone this long." Cradling him with one arm, I scrounged around the pantry for a tin of chicken liver pâté I'd stored for just such an emergency. I set him down next to his dish. His tail broomed the floor as I emptied the tin. I sat cross-legged beside him, holding his feathery tail as he ate, telling him about my long, crazy day.

I checked my computer one last time, but Zigo remained silent. I was glad. I didn't think I could take another interaction with another human being tonight.

I fell into bed. The last thing I experienced was the dense thud of cat landing beside me.

CHAPTER 13

I slept so long and deep that Tank had to nudge me awake with his paws. I got out of bed a new man. Today was going to be Julius Rosen day. All day. I checked my Skype account first thing, but there was no word yet from Zigo. I tried Googling him, but the scant information there was came up in German. I bookmarked what was there. I fed Tank, made myself a yogurt and banana smoothie, and suited up for a good long run. My body was barking for exercise like a cooped-up rescue dog.

I jogged into Topanga State Park by way of Trippet Ranch and ran the Musch trail hard, working up a good sweat despite the cool, misty air. I stepped off the trail for some reps, mostly curls and push-ups, and then started jogging at a nice easy pace.

I thought about Heather first. After Julie left, I wondered if I'd ever have another chance. Now, appearances seemed to suggest I might. It was exciting and alarming at the same time. What if this didn't work out? What if it did? After ruminating on both thoughts for an unpleasant several yards, I filed them in the giant mental file folder labeled "Things I Cannot Control," which sits right next to "Things I Can Control." The former file is a lot fatter. I felt the usual wave of relief after letting go of the idea I was in charge of the world. As for Heather, I was determined to take things slower this time, and so far, so good. As she so aptly put it, we'd get there, if we were meant to.

No, the person I was worried about right now was Bill. He didn't look like himself, and he wasn't acting like himself. I couldn't put my finger on what was wrong, though.

147

His complaints about his job weren't anything new—griping about the LAPD came with the territory, for all of us. So did frustration. I remembered one of my first conversations with Bill. We were halfway into a pitcher of ale, in that brief window of consumption when you're feeling brave enough to broach personal questions, and happy enough with the *Ah-So*-ness of everything not to care what the answer is. Bill had already been a homicide detective for almost ten years, long enough to know the job in his bones.

"What's it like?" I'd asked. "Really like, I mean."

"You want to know what being in Homicide is like?" He'd studied the head on the beer, as if the foam contained the secret to life. Maybe it did. "Here's the job, Ten. Ninety percent boredom, just putting one foot in front of the other, and one percent pure panic."

"Ninety percent boredom, one percent panic." I reflected on the proportions.

"Maybe panic isn't the right word, but it's pretty close. Things break out all at once, and you're taking hairpin turns on the fly, inventing shit as you go, just hoping you stay inside the guard rail."

I liked the sound of that. "So what's the other nine percent?

"Fuck if I know." Bill took a long swig. At that moment I realized we wouldn't just be partners, we'd be friends.

And so we have been, watching each other's backs, making each other laugh. As partners, our differences were unimportant, our similarities essential. Neither of those things had changed. So why was I feeling so cut off from him?

I had planned on capping off my run with a good long sit-down in my meditation room, but I made the mistake of checking my computer first. This time, the Skype icon was blinking and bouncing to get my attention. If it had arms, it would have been waving them frantically.

"All right, all right, I see you."

I clicked on the icon and sure enough, I had a message from the mysterious Mr. Zigo.

HELMUTZIGO: OK TO CLL NW. USE PHNE.

I glanced at the time stamp. He'd sent the message fifteen minutes earlier. I followed Mike's highly complicated instructions: I clicked on the phone icon. I heard a distinctive ring. For fun, I also clicked the video icon so Zigo could presumably see my Tibetan mug. *It can't be this simple.*

Apparently, it could. He answered right away. "Hello, Mr. Norbu." A voice, but no visual. I regretted my impulse to try both features at once. I now felt at a disadvantage.

"Greetings. Can you see me?"

"Yes," he said. "I see you just fine." His English retained a trace of an accent. German? Swiss?

"Where are you located, Mr. Zigo?" A pause.

Finally, "Belgium."

"Would you mind turning on your webcam so I can see you?"

"Yes," he said. "I mind."

My gut twanged at that.

"You're acting like a man with something to hide," I said. "Are you contemplating something illegal, Mr. Zigo?"

He chuckled. "What's that expression? 'You don't beat at the bush.'"

"That's right," I said. "I'm not beating around the bush. You are dealing with the painful past and tender emotions of an elderly gentleman. A very fine man who's done a lot of good in the world. So I hope you aren't thinking of wasting anybody's time, Mr. Zigo."

"Your zeal is admirable," he said. "And the answer is no, absolutely not."

"Then let's get right to it. What do you have and what do you want?"

"I've got proof that Julius Rosen's sister, Sadie Rosen, is alive."

"That could be interesting. What is the proof?"

"Slow down, Mr. Norbu. I'm getting there."

I breathed through a contraction of irritation. He was right. I needed to shift gears.

"All right," I said. "Let's try this. How is Sadie? Is she well?"

"Reasonably well for a person of her age."

"And what age is that?" I asked.

"You know very well how old she is," he said.

"Humor me."

He sighed. "Seventy-three," he said.

I actually had no idea how old Sadie was, but 73 sounded right. I'd do the math later. "Okay," I said. "What's next?"

"What's next is I outline my terms and you respond to them. There are other people involved in this transaction."

"Transaction," I said. "The magic word has been uttered."

"You have an irritating tone of moral superiority, Mr. Norbu."

I pictured Julius, his face lined with pain over his lost sibling.

"Maybe I do," I said, "but you're the one trying to sell something that an ethical person would give freely, for the pure joy of it. Maybe in this situation you actually, genuinely, are morally inferior."

"Fuck you." His icon disappeared from the screen.

Another stellar moment in my detecting career. Somewhere out there, in the sphere inhabited by kindred spirits, Sherlock sighed. "Next time, meditate first," he seemed to say.

Should I try to call Zigo back? I vacillated, but in the end decided to wait.

It hadn't helped that I was starving. I pulled my loaf of whole-grain bread out of the fridge and hacked off a couple thick slices. While they toasted, I was faced with another tough decision. Peanut butter was a once-a-year luxury in the monastery where I did most of my growing up, and I still found it amazing that I could walk into my local health food store and find six different brands of organic peanut butter.

I lined all six on the counter. I went with light-roasted crunchy.

After my snack, I moved to the deck, Tank padding after me. A little repair work was in order. I closed my eyes and settled into my body's rhythmic ebbs and flows. The morning fog had burned off, and my skin warmed in the sun's warm touch. After 20 minutes of quiet breathing, I opened my eyes, automatically searching for Tank. He was at the far end of the deck. I had to laugh. Tank likes to stretch on his back and catch rays with all four feet in the air, a position I have yet to master. He was snoring lightly, limbs aloft, en route to his first big nap of the morning.

I had brought my Julius Rosen file outside with me. I opened it and went through its meager contents again, wondering whether I should call him about this first contact, or lack of contact, with Helmut Zigo. I wasn't sure what my policy with clients should be yet—I'd only had a few. My inclination was to give as much detail as possible, down to the nitty-gritty, boring details of the failed phone calls and dead-end leads that are part of every investigation. In other words, to include the 90 percent. I might drive them crazy, but at least they'd know I was earning my keep.

I called Julius. Predictably, given my train of thought all morning, his phone rang for a long time, without going to voice mail. I made a note in the file. I'd try later.

I paced the deck, fretting about my aborted communication with Zigo. This quickly led to worrying about my ongoing half status as a private investigator, which led to wondering what other productive careers existed where I could put my energy.

My deck isn't that big; after a few laps I began to feel ridiculous.

"I need a sign, Tank," I said.

I went back inside to check my computer. And sure

enough, Helmut Zigo was back, this time offering a conversation in the flesh, or screen-flesh, I guess you'd have to say. A moment later I was face to face, digitally speaking, with a tanned, good-looking fellow of about fifty, a few days worth of fashionable stubble on his face. A pair of reading glasses perched on his head. He was sitting at what appeared to be a kitchen table. In the background I could make out a flowery curtain, dim light shining through the folds.

I asked him, "Still in Belgium?" Neutral enough.

He indicated the curtain. "Yes. And a very gloomy Belgium it is. Rain and thick fog for three straight days. I imagine it's considerably different in Southern California."

"I won't torture you with the details," I said, "but yes. Are you ready to talk business?"

"I am," he said. "But, first, let me say that I took offense at your tone the last time we spoke. As a result, I allowed my emotions to get in the way."

"Me, too," I said. "And I appreciate . . ."

"Let me explain, please," he interrupted. "I'm a businessman, Mr. Norbu—not some kind of criminal. Other than an unfortunate night of celebration back in '99, leading to me and my car sitting in a ditch, I have never once been detained by the police. I sell information for money, and if you or Mr. Rosen don't want my information, you don't have to buy it."

"I'll try to keep that distinction in mind, Mr. Zigo. And please, feel free to raise a warning finger if I get on my moral high horse. Now, what's your information, and how much does it cost?"

He lowered his reading glasses and lifted a few sheets of paper. "I am holding the records of a tiny orphanage in Germany. It folded a few years after the end of the war. Sadie Rosen is mentioned in their records, as well as an indication as to how she might be traced. That is what I am selling, Mr. Norbu."

"How did you know to look into the records of an

orphanage, Mr. Zigo? How did you know to look for Sadie Rosen?"

"Excellent questions," he said. "Some years ago I came across Julius Rosen's inquiry regarding Sadie Rosen. It seemed like a useful business prospect. After all, if there was one Julius Rosen, there might be others. Wealthy survivors, I mean, looking for relatives. I filed the flier away, for possible future use. A few weeks ago, an associate of mine in Germany turned up these records. He gave me a call." He spread his hands and shrugged. "No big mysteries."

"Have you followed up, to find out if there's anything to this new information?"

He shook his head. "I don't want to get that far into it," he said. "You're a clever man, Mr. Norbu, so you probably have a sense of the kind of communication I deal in. Most of it inhabits the borderline area between business and extortion. Distinctions can be blurry, do you agree?"

I try not to blur too many distinctions, but I resisted the temptation to tell him. I wasn't in the mood to be invited to fuck myself twice in one day. "You could get a lot more for this information if you had some verification that it was valid."

"True," he said, "but then I'd be in a different business, wouldn't I? One a bit more like yours, perhaps. I'm happy with the niche I occupy and the commissions I can earn from it, Mr. Norbu. Let's get on with it, shall we?"

"Just to be clear, what we're buying is the written record of Sadie's time spent in an orphanage, as well as what happened to her after she left."

"I'll be even more specific. You get the name of the family who adopted her."

"And this is recorded on original documents I can see with my own eyes?"

He nodded. "That is correct. In broad terms, do you want to make this deal?"

"How much?" I asked.

"One hundred thousand dollars."

Whoa.

"I'll need to get authorization from Mr. Rosen," I said.

"I'll stay here while you contact him." Zigo smiled, and sat back, as if he had all day.

I walked into my bedroom, far from the webcam's reach, closed the door, and called Julius from the landline.

This time he picked right up.

"Mr. Rosen, it's Ten."

"Tenzing! Just who I was hoping it would be. Any luck?"

I explained the situation. Call me silly, but with $100,000 at stake, I'd want to sleep on Zigo's offer. But I guess Julius didn't get where he was by spending long hours mulling over financial decisions. He didn't hesitate. "Offer him ten grand up front, no strings, and the remainder in two equal installments, two weeks apart, if, and only if, the information pans out. Tell him this isn't a negotiation. He can take it or leave it."

Right. I went back to my desk and sat down in front of the computer. Zigo's face still filled the screen. He arched an eyebrow. "Well?"

"Mr. Rosen wants to make it clear that this is not a negotiation and that this is a one-time-only offer."

He nodded. "I understand."

I told him the terms. He pursed his lips. "What does that mean 'if the information pans out'? Does that mean if you find Sadie Rosen?"

I felt like a minnow in a tankful of sharks. It was rapidly becoming clear I wasn't cut out for a career in business, especially at this level. I ran back to my bedroom, had another quick chat with Julius, and returned.

"No," I said. "It means if we find the family that took Sadie Rosen in. If that link turns out to be good, you get your money."

He thought it over. "Okay. Deal." He cocked his head at me. "Mr. Norbu, I need you to confirm."

"Deal," I said.

He dictated wire transfer instructions. I gave him my contact information, and said I'd get in touch when everything was finalized. I called Julius, who passed me on to an assistant to handle banking details. Then Julius came back on the line.

"What's your gut telling you? You think there's anything to this?"

I was tempted to hedge, to blur the line, as Zigo put it, between spinning the truth and speaking it. The temptation passed.

"I don't have a good, clear read yet," I said. "Maybe it's too early for my gut to weigh in. Or maybe it's never going to. I don't know."

"Fair enough. My lawyers will get everything in writing. I want to move fast on this. If all goes well, the money transfer should be complete sometime late tomorrow. You should have what you need in two days, max. Good work, Ten. Keep me posted."

Everything was moving along smoothly. Too smoothly for comfort. I'd better deposit my check today, in case, as Mike liked to say, it all went pear-shaped.

Meanwhile, I needed Mike to help me with a deeper background check on Zigo. But Mike was out of commission. I could call it a day.

Or . . .

I could find out more about Thunder's mysterious biker-cop, the one asking the same questions about Marv as I was. I pulled out the card of the supposed cop and called the number. It went directly to voice mail, not even a voice message. I hung up. Then I Googled Raul Martinez. There was an artist, a boxer, and a former mayor, none of whom fit my needs.

Think, Tenzing. Think.

I called Thunder.

"T-Bird Tattoos."

"Thunder, it's Tenzing."

"Yo, change your mind on the dragon?"

"Not yet. Listen, I have a question for you. When did your friend get in his motorcycle accident? The one you and that biker cop both knew? The one that went to court?"

"Shit. Let me think. I'd just opened up my own shop, so it must have been . . . seven? No. Eight years ago. June, because I'd invited him to my open house, and he had to be in court instead. So yeah, the first week in June."

"What's your friend's name?"

"Daniel Morales, but we've lost touch. I have no idea how to reach him."

"Don't need to. You are amazing."

"That's what they say," Thunder answered, and hung up.

I got back on the Google-express, cast my net, and after a few false starts, pulled up a June 2004 *L.A. Times* squib on an accident between a BMW and a Harley, ridden by a Daniel Morales. I followed the trail up to and including a wrongful injury lawsuit, and finally landed on Morales's defense lawyer, one Charles Montoya, Esquire. One more click, and I was on his web site. Charles Montoya, founder and owner of the Law Offices of Charles Raul Montoya & Associates, specializing in, wait for it, personal injury lawsuits involving motorcycle accidents. His nickname? The Low-riding Lawyer. He used the word *aggressive* to describe himself, as in: "I am an aggressive lawyer who likes getting results."

Charlie Montoya was the proud father of four girls, and the proud rider of an S&S custom Harley. I clicked on the link to contact his office. Interestingly, it connected me to the Internet equivalent of "no such number." Next, I called the telephone number listed on the site. This time, I received the actual message, "The number you have reached is not in service and there is no new number." I noticed he also had a Law Biker blog. I clicked on that link. His last entry had been about four years ago. Since then, silence.

He'd disappeared. Or maybe just changed identities. His picture was prominently displayed on the top of his blog. He was a middle-aged Latino, trim beard and moustache, in a suit, tie, and wraparound sunglasses. One bulging arm rested on his S&S custom twin. *Nice guns.*

I called Thunder again.

"You in love with me or something? Because I'm already taken."

"I'm e-mailing you a picture. Can you look at it please?"

I sent him the Montoya link.

"Folks, we have a winner!" Thunder announced. "That's him. That's the dude who came by here."

Finally, I was getting somewhere, though when I thought about it further, I had no idea where that somewhere might actually be. I could call Bill and run things by him, or I could take the riskier but perhaps more direct route to some answers.

I called the "Raul Martinez" number a second time.

Beep.

"My name is Tenzing Norbu. I'm a private investigator, and I'm calling regarding the recent death of Marv Rudolph. I have reason to believe you are involved." I left my cell number. That should stir things up.

I like getting results as well.

I checked my e-mail and immediately zoomed in on one from Heather. She had sent me something under the somewhat ominous subject: Retreat. *Who's retreating?* The knot in my stomach was instantaneous. I almost opened the e-mail, then stopped. This called for emotional reinforcement.

"Tank? Where are you, buddy?"

I checked all his usual napping locations. Finally, in the bedroom, I saw a blue-black nose and a fine set of silver whiskers poking out from under the bed. I reached with both arms and hauled close an armload of fur.

"Sorry, guy, but I need you. I'm probably overreacting, but I might be getting dumped."

He protested slightly, but I placated him with a cat treat, before settling in front of the computer, his comforting weight sprawled across my lap. I opened Heather's e-mail, braced for a gentle brush-off.

It was anything but.

"Hi, Ten. Happy Halloween. Really enjoyed our picnic last night. A fellow intern just sent me the following re: a one-day retreat this Friday. He said there are still spaces available, and asked if I would like to go. I thought of you, natch. Want to join me? H."

I opened the attachment. It was an invitation to any and all individuals connected to any and all aspects of law enforcement to attend a one-day silent meditation retreat on "Fierce Compassion," where like-minded people would somehow mutely explore the balance between upholding the law and achieving inner peace.

It sounded like a total nightmare.

I looked up the organization sponsoring the retreat. It was a little meditation center tucked in the Elysian Valley, between Griffith Park, Dodger Stadium, and the 5 Freeway. The head monk, Niem Kelsang Dechong, was a Westerner who grew up in Northern California and spent a number of years studying Buddhism in France with his teacher, Chocktrul Pema Dorje Rinpoche. I knew nothing about either man, but my resistance was immediate—and immense.

To make matters worse, if I understood things correctly, the visiting retreat leader was a woman, a Buddhist nun-in-training and an ex-cop.

I reread Heather's e-mail and zeroed in on a couple suspicious items, namely, *fellow intern* and the pronoun *he*, as in "*He* said there are still spaces available." I'll bet. Whoever this intern was, *he* had designs on Heather.

But a daylong silent retreat at some random monastery in Echo Park, listening to Buddhist newcomers telling me how to meditate? How to relax while doing my job?

"What do you think, Tank? Is she worth it?" Tank was the wrong cat to ask. He believes a Persian Blue should be more than enough company for any sentient being.

I e-mailed Heather back. "Thanks. Looks interesting. I'll call you later. T." Neutral, and it bought me time to think up a valid excuse, if necessary.

I poured myself an iced green tea and downed a small container of macaroni and cheese, zapped in the micro-wave. Not my finest gourmet meal, but I was distracted by thoughts of Heather and her mystery suitor.

I walked to the end of the driveway to pick up my mail and clear my mind. The afternoon sun shone through the waving trees, dappling the road with shimmering coins of gold. I pulled out a thick packet from the insurance com-pany. I opened it, and fist-pumped the air. For a small fortune, they were willing to cover me. Finally, my glacial path to respectability could move forward. I was officially a private investigator. More important, I could legally carry again. Next indicated action? Deposit Julius Rosen's check, so I could pay the outrageous premium. If I hurried, I'd make it to the bank before 6 P.M. And as long as I was out, maybe I'd check on the meditation center and see if that helped with the decision.

I filled Tank's bowl and hustled into the bedroom to grab a fleece from the closet. I paused. Technically, I was almost insured. Technically, I had my permit to conceal. I unlocked the gun safe and took out the blue nylon Wilson Combat carrying case. I unzipped it. My custom .38 Supergrade gleamed, its burnished cocobolo wood grip and stainless steel barrel nestled in a form-fitted bed of foam. My palm itched to hold the handgun again, shaped perfectly to the contours of my hand. I so wanted to take it with me.

"Soon," I murmured. I locked the case back in the safe, alongside my Halo automatic knife. If I was going to do a recon of a Buddhist monastery, I shouldn't be carrying. Why invite bad karma?

CHAPTER 14

I felt good. My checking account was now $25,000 healthier, less a couple grand in cash. I took the Stadium Way exit off the 5, turned right onto Riverside Drive, left onto Altman Street, another quick right onto Altman Place, and parked. I half remembered the general area. Bill's ongoing mission had been to find new and ingenious ways to get us to Dodger Stadium for games. He'd recently boycotted the team, a combination of disgust at the vicious beating of a Giants fan by some thugs on opening day, and rage at the owner who let it happen on his watch because he was too busy divorcing his wife and living off the team's revenue to take care of little things like parking lot security. For the rest of the year they'd upped security, but it was too little and way too late. Happily, that season of baseball disappointments was over. But I'd noticed a suspicious build-up of traffic around the stadium freeway exits, so some kind of event was going on. Maybe a Dodger fans protest march.

I locked the Toyota, double-checked the address, and strolled up the block about 300 yards to Kelton Way, a small side street on the right. The neighborhood was peaceful, a little suburban oasis not too far from the L.A. River. I slowed as I neared a two-story clapboard structure with a peaked roof at the end of the street. A small bell hung over the front door, below it a sign declaring this to be the Sweet Spirit Buddhist Meditation Center. A garbage truck ground its gears somewhere nearby, followed by the beeping and whining of mechanical arms grasping and dumping trash. The truck moved on, its noisy engine fading.

Garbage. The little lost thought that had been bugging

me for days finally surfaced. I grabbed my iPhone, logged onto the Bureau of Sanitation website, and entered the address for the Robinsgrove. Hunh. Nothing came up. I made a call, and after a few frustrating runarounds, discovered a private firm did their pick-ups there on Wednesdays. I still had time. I called Clancy.

"*Yo, Clancy here . . .*" Yeah yeah yeah, wassup. I'd call him again later.

The area settled into silence once again. The setting sun bathed the little center in pink and gold. The whole thing felt like a set-up, a tease from the universe: *Bliss lives here.* Their spacious fenced-in garden boasted a large stone Buddha set between winding footpaths, all leading to a second structure further back, this one long and flat. A few pairs of shoes lined the entrance: a meditation hall, I was guessing.

I paused. Was it my imagination, or did the quiet here have a denser quality than elsewhere, like an atmospheric version of "heavy water"? A sapphire hummingbird dipped its beak in a little feeder hanging from the branch of a small olive tree next to the fence. The air was fresh and still. Now the harsh cough of a two-cylinder motorcycle cut through the silence. I smiled. Like it or not, this was an urban environment, and I suspected its members had to develop a strong ongoing practice of accepting noise. But there was something deeply familiar about the stillness. I resonated with it. I had been raised in it, and I felt its pull.

I heard voices. I turned. A young Caucasian monk with a shaved head and orange robe strolled out of the center, laughing and chatting with a middle-aged woman in jeans. They hugged briefly. He went back inside, and she started to walk in my direction. Time to go. I scurried past her, head lowered, avoiding eye contact. *What are you resisting?*

I turned the corner. As I approached my car, my detective-antennae quivered. At first, I thought maybe I'd gotten another ticket, but the piece of paper under my wiper was the wrong size and shape. I pulled it out.

It was a grainy, black-and-white photocopy of my image, taken from a distance. I couldn't tell where or when. My face was circled, with an X scored right through the middle of my forehead.

I was fairly confident this was not the work of the monk.

I looked around. Altman Place was empty of pedestrians. I jumped in the Toyota, cursing my reverse pride—at the last minute I'd decided to take the modest Toyota instead of my brash Mustang. If any practicing Buddhists saw me get out of my car, I'd wanted to appear suitably humble.

I started the car, my mind clicking through options, which were meager. I was unarmed, and my ride was a broken down pony. I pulled onto Riverside, debating my next move, when I saw something in my rear-view mirror that caused my belly muscles to cramp. A big black and orange Harley was closing fast on me from behind. I pressed hard on my gas pedal to put some distance between us, but he accelerated right along with me, closing to about a hundred yards. The rider was wearing a minimalist helmet with a little pointed top, faux Nazi headgear from the 1940s. Ridiculous. I couldn't make out his face behind the goggles and bandanna. He was close enough now for the snarl of his big twin engine to dominate.

There was no way I was taking this chase back onto the freeway. As soon as we got into high-speed pursuit territory, we were playing with lives, and not just our own. I had to win with my brains, if possible.

I pulled a hard left onto North Broadway and another quick turn onto Bishops Road. For a brief second, the Harley shot up beside my Toyota. I glanced over. The rider jutted his chin toward the shoulder, as in "pull over." My calculation went something like this: Do I really want to pull over for a guy in a Nazi helmet riding my tail in an unfriendly fashion? My inner Security Council took about a tenth of a second to come up with a unanimous "Heck no." I took a hard right onto Stadium Way, which seemed a better bet than doing close range battle with a mystery hog.

I sped around the outer rim of Elysian Park. Where was the traffic? Where was all this new security I'd heard so much about? A couple potholes sent shockwaves up my spine. I looked back. The Harley was wallowing around a curve, right behind me. Up ahead I spotted the juncture where Stadium Way crossed Elysian Park Boulevard. Finally. Three fat lines of vehicles were slowly working their way toward the entrance booths. I broke every rule in my good-driver book, cutting in front of SUVs and pick-up trucks, swerving across three solid lines to the farthest lane. Drivers laid on their horns, and I didn't blame them one bit, but the Harley was now at least seven cars back, stuck in the thick of the traffic, very visible, and therefore very vulnerable. I tossed 20 bucks to the parking attendant, with mental apologies to Bill, who thought the parking fees were high-way robbery. My brain scarcely had time to register the fact that the guy in the booth was wearing a clown nose and a multicolored wig, when he said, "Enjoy the monster rally. Happy Halloween."

What had I gotten myself into?

Attendants in neon vests merrily waved me to Lot 3, at the far end of the stadium. I was directed to tuck my Toyota between two huge pick-ups. The lot was packed with super-sized SUVs and trucks built for giants, with jumbo tires and massive grilles. I guess I didn't get the memo. The stadium was alight, the crowd roaring, big engines answering with roars of their own. A deep, hearty, manly-man voice barked announcements over the P.A. system. I could think of no better way to stay good and lost, until my new friend got tired of looking for me, so I melted into the crowd flowing toward the stadium. They were the usual sports event blend of flotsam, jetsam, and gentry; only in this case many were dressed in their Halloween best. I grabbed a Dracula. He reeked of pot and his eyes were as red as his bloodstained lips.

"What's going on here tonight?" I asked.

"Monster Jam Rally! I'm stoked. Big machines, man, dueling each other." He peered at me. "What are you?"

"Undercover monk," I said.

For me, Halloween was a personal nonevent, and always caught me by surprise. In my seven years living in Topanga, I'd never had a single trick-or-treater, and anyway, the whole point of the holiday was bizarre. I mean, dressing up like a ghoul and demanding candy hardly seems like a meaningful way to honor the dead.

There was no sign of the chopper or his rider, but just to be safe, I bought a ticket from a scalper just outside an escalator that led to the main entrance. Another $20, gone. I rode the escalator up, sandwiched between Captain America and Green Lantern, or so they informed me.

I slowly inched my way up one last line to the main entrance. My breath had returned to normal. Maybe I'd get a veggie Dodger Dog and watch a few cars spar with each other, or whatever they did at these things. The stadium attendant scanned my ticket. As I started to push through the turnstile, one tiny part of my brain registered the four designated motorcycle spots just to the left of me, in the preferred parking area, the black and orange custom Harley, dead still and dead empty in one slot. *Danger!*

My Harley-riding nemesis was waiting for me, leaning against the chain link barricade just inside the entrance. He saw me and reached to his ankle, where I glimpsed a Microtech stiletto. I recognized it, because I had one just like it. Back at home, locked in my gun safe. He began to move, and my feet started going before my brain had a chance to catalog much else.

I was running pretty well, considering the crowd. I debated finding a security guard, but slowing down would expose my ribs. One jab, and I was done, at least for this lifetime. I veered right, weaving between vendors hawking monster jam gear and families with young kids waving flags emblazoned with Grave Digger and Maximum Destruction—I tried not to read too much into the names.

Someone cried out. I threw a look back. My pursuer had knocked over a little kid. Now I was pissed. I wheeled around and ran right at him, not what he expected. I grabbed his wrist and gave it a vicious twist. The knife clattered to the ground, and I pinned his arms to his side, hooking my own arms hand-to-wrist behind his back. He thrashed against my tight embrace. It took all my strength to keep him immobilized.

He had swapped his helmet for the bandana, which he'd tied across his forehead like a pirate. His neck was inked. He was young, maybe early 20s, with chestnut-colored skin, aquiline nose, and full lips: startlingly good-looking, if you like pretty boys. But his eyes? Gang eyes. Any veteran cop will tell you the same thing. Eyes that become flat from killing people or helping other people kill people.

"We don't want a scene, do we?" I tightened the squeeze.

He struggled against my rigid hold.

"What do you want?" I said.

"You," he said, and in one strong full-body twist, he wrested from my grasp and bent to the ground. I leapt back, as a blade flashed through the air, just missing my neck. I heard a woman scream. I had to get out of there, before someone innocent got hurt. To my right was a set of stairs leading to the lower decks and eventually to the field-level seats. Where were all the fucking cops? Where were the security guards, normally posted at every stairway to keep riffraff from going to the lower levels? I hit the stairs running, Pretty Boy right on my heels. I took the steps three at a time, down, down, until I burst through the field level entrance to what Bill called the high-baller sections. Which were empty, and blanketed with thick red and yellow nylon tarps.

I swan-dived onto a tarp and crabbed my way across, using the seat backs underneath for support. I was vaguely aware of the sound of souped-up engines revving and roaring somewhere in front of me. I reached the front row and took a flying leap, landing on all fours on a dirt surface covering the playing field. I scrambled to my feet, dodged between slanted runaway vehicle ramps, and pounded up a steep incline to a wide platform right in the middle of the track. An electronic board directly across from me blinked red, its digital clock counting down seconds. I was at the starting gate, and the next race was moments away.

"Get off of the course," I heard over the P.A. "*Get off of the course!*" I had three seconds to take in the semicircle of monster trucks, suspended on humongous tires, pawing and snorting like angry bulls that couldn't wait to gouge and toss me. Then I was tackled and cuffed by five cops, or maybe five random dudes in cop costumes. What did I care? I was safe at last.

Two hours later Security released me from the Dodger Stadium slammer, or "holding area," as they prefer to call it, a bleak space between two upper decks, behind where home plate should have been. The two moonlighting detectives working the rally were from the Burglary division. They knew my name, and knew Bill's even better. I got off easy for my stunt: they didn't even slap me with a fine. As I left the concrete holding cell, two security guards muscled a soused and belligerent fan past me—my first and hopefully only experience seeing a bumblebee with an overhanging gut in handcuffs.

By the time I'd finished explaining myself, Pretty Boy and his chopper were nowhere to be found. Anyway, how would anyone know if he was a gang-banger, or just dressing like one?

It was past ten when I got home. I was exhausted and wired at the same time. I listened to a brief, sleepy message from Heather. She'd called my home phone at 9 P.M. to say she was turning in. Good. I wouldn't have to make excuses about the retreat until tomorrow. I gave Tank a late-night snack, shoveled down a banana smeared with no salt Valencia chunky, and fell into bed.

Tired as I was, I lay awake, my blood buzzing from the chase. I traced tensed body parts with light attention, beginning with my toes, to unwind the knots. I had barely reached my kneecaps when my heart constricted like a fist. *Someone's outside.* I slipped out of bed and was at my closet; in seconds, I had my Wilson in my hand.

There it was again—a bumping sound by the front of the house. It was pitch black inside, but I wasn't about to turn on a light.

I slid along the bedroom wall to the door. Tank raised his head from my bed.

Stay here, Tank.

I dropped out of window-level sight and crouch-walked across the living room. I pressed my ear against the front door. I heard sibilant whispers. There were at least two of them. If they really wanted in, they could smash right through that hollow core door . . .

The knob turned, left, right, just a test. My adrenal gland dumped a metric pint of endocrine into my bloodstream. In about three seconds, my hands would start shaking: *fight or flee, Ten?*

I stood up, stepped back, planted my feet, and took careful aim at the closed door. I imagined my target on the other side, heart level. I released the safety, lightly hooking my index finger around the trigger. *One . . . Two . . .*

A pair of giggling voices called out "Trick or treat!"

Fear rippled through my body like iced water. I engaged the safety, laid my .38 on the floor, and stepped away, as if the gun was timed to explode.

I turned on the light and opened the door. A couple of teenagers, camouflaged as His and Her corpses, stood grinning at me, their painted features slightly askew. The yeasty scent of beer—too many beers by the looks of them—wafted from the swaying pair in a sour cloud.

"Get the hell out of here," I said.

The young man glanced at my shaking hands. I stuffed them in my pockets. He looked past me into the house, where my gun lay in full view. He took a quick step back.

"Sorry," he said. "Shit!"

He grabbed the girl's arm, and they hustled down my driveway. She stumbled once, and he steadied her without breaking stride.

"I'm sorry, too," I whispered, but I don't think they heard me.

My heart was pumping so hard and high I couldn't swallow. I backed inside, my step unsteady. *What was I thinking?* I wasn't. I was assuming, running on leftover fear. I had broken my second rule once again and almost shot an innocent child because of it. I turned off the light and sat very still, breathing in the dark room until my hands stopped trembling. Then I went over to my computer, opened the on-line application form, and signed up for the retreat.

CHAPTER 15

I still felt shaken in the morning, even after a run, a weight-lifting session, and half an hour of yoga stretches. The terror at what might have been reignited whenever I stopped moving.

I called Bill. He would understand.

"Hey, Bill."

"Ten." His voice was tight. Angry-tight, not anxious-tight.

"What's going on?"

"Why don't you tell me?" he said.

I tried to laugh it off. "Ummm, I'm not sure what you mean. Did the Dodger-cops call you this morning?"

"No," Bill said. His voice hardened. "Sully did. He told me you're still sniffing around my case."

"Bill . . ."

"I asked you nicely to back off, Ten. Now I'm *telling* you to back off. Is that clear? Stay the fuck away." I had heard this level of anger in his voice once or twice over the years. But never aimed at me. "Jesus, I'm sorry I ever brought you into this!"

Heat boiled through my body.

"Yeah, well, thanks for nothing," I snapped. "What gives you the right? You're not my partner anymore, and you sure as hell aren't my father!"

"Thank God, because I sure as hell wouldn't want you for a kid!"

"Go to hell," I said, and hung up on his answering, "Fuck you."

I stood by the phone, eyes scalding with fury. I ran out

to the deck. "Arrghhhh!" I yelled into the valley. I peppered the air with quick punches until sweat dripped. I leaned against the deck railing, breathing heavily. Now righteous indignation flooded my system. I let it.

I'll show you. I'll show all of you.

Tank meowed from the kitchen.

"Not yet!" I yelled.

I called Clancy and told him to meet me at Robinsgrove in half an hour. We'd get inside, somehow. *Screw them.* Inside, I dumped a full can of tuna into Tank's bowl. It was ridiculous and a total waste of money, since he only liked the water.

I rode the Mustang hard. Every time I tried to breathe through the fist of feeling, I heard Bill's *I sure as hell wouldn't want you for a kid,* and my chest clenched tight. A tiny part of my brain waved an even tinier flag signaling that I was having a tantrum. That puffing myself up, vowing to show everyone how competent and superior I was, might be yet another reaction to a dearly held limiting idea. I brushed the warning aside. I needed to feel superiority to function right now.

I pulled in behind Clancy's Impala, parked in its usual spot. I looked up the block to the Robinsgrove. We were in luck. A large moving van sat in front, hazard lights blinking. A cardboard mover's box propped open the glass doors.

I grabbed the two pairs of disposable latex gloves and eight 35-gallon garbage bags I'd thrown into the back of my Mustang.

Clancy climbed out of his car, tossing a crumpled coffee cup onto the new mound of takeout containers on his front seat.

"You ready to do a trash cover?" I asked.

"I don't know. Am I?'

"Absolutely," I said. "You'll feel right at home."

We walked to the Robinsgrove entrance. Two clean cut, muscular young men, one fair, one dark, both with crew cuts, and both wearing Meathead Movers shirts, juggled a heavy bed frame into the back of their van.

"How much longer will you be here?" I made a move to help them with the frame, but they waved me off.

Blond Crew Cut answered. "We'll be here maybe an hour more."

An hour was good. First task? Locate the trash bins. We crossed the shabby-elegant lobby, a small sitting room on either side, and faced a maze of stairs, elevators, exits, and entrances. You could easily get lost in a building like this. I told Clancy to wait. I trotted up a short flight of stairs to the first floor and checked the hallway. Most older buildings like this had incinerator chutes, and this one was no exception. The chute was no longer functional, but told me what I needed to know. Buildings, like people, don't like change. The bins were probably located directly below.

I rejoined Clancy and found the elevators, a pair of heavy wooden doors, painted white and stenciled with little star-shaped holes. I pushed the down button and stood waiting. And waiting. The blond mover called to me from the lobby.

"You have to look through the holes. "

"What?"

"The elevator doesn't ping. You have to look through the holes to see if it's there."

I looked, and it was. I heaved open the righthand door, and we stepped inside. I pushed the B button. We creaked downward. The door pushed open to a dark basement corridor, running east to west. I could hear the swish and hum of washing machines to our right. I looked left, and spotted another very short flight of stairs, leading upward this time, to a metal door and an exit sign. I pulled it open. We were standing in the underground parking lot, home to a row of six black dumpsters and six blue recycling bins.

"I hope you're not squeamish," I said to Clancy, pulling on my gloves. I scanned the lot. Lots of cars. No people.

One by one, I flung open the dumpsters and did a quick rummage. I ignored moving-type cast-offs like a broken umbrella and three torn sofa cushions. I grabbed assorted small garbage bags, moist, fetid, and loaded with potential clues, stuffing them into the extra-large ones I had brought for this purpose. Clancy stared with something approaching disgust. I handed him the second set of gloves and two more big bags.

"You do the recycling," I said.

He hurried to the bright blue bins, and loaded his bags with comparatively clean paper and plastic.

We lugged eight bulging sacks back to the lobby. If anyone had stopped us, I would have just said "Moving sucks, eh?" and carried on. But no one did. We hauled our loot to my Mustang and piled the bags on the fiberglass shelf in the back, where a second seat should have been.

The entrance to the Robinsgrove was still propped open.

"Let's take a quick look at the roof, okay?"

Clancy shook his head.

"You go," he said. "I'm starting to feel pretty skeeved out about this. You sure it's cool?"

I'd forgotten Clancy was intuitive. Well, I wasn't about to tell him the truth, that my actions weren't cool. That they were fueled by hurt feelings and bruised pride. I might lose impetus.

"Thanks for helping," I said. I opened my wallet to pay him.

"No, man," he said. "We're good."

"I owe you then, Clancy."

He waggled his hand over his shoulder as he hurried away. I added the pang of remorse to a growing pile inside.

As I started back to the apartment building, my phone chimed. I didn't recognize the number.

"Tenzing Norbu."

"You've been nosing around some things that interest

me." The Latino edge was worn soft from years of speaking English.

"Who is this? Is this Raul Mendoza?"

"We need to meet."

"I might want to hear what you have to say, but why in person?"

"I want to discuss something. Privately. Having to do with Marv Rudolph."

I'll show them. "Okay. Where?"

"Getty View Park, just off the four-oh-five. I'll be there in one hour."

I reached the entrance in half that time, but it was blocked off, the lot crawling with workers in hard hats undergoing yet another futile attempt to widen the freeway. I called Raul back and got his voicemail.

"The park's closed. I'll be waiting for you at the sculpture garden by the lower tram station at the Getty."

I parked in the underground lot. I slipped my Halo Microtech in my pocket—I wasn't making that mistake twice. I took the stairs to the tram station, where a large group of tourists stood in line, waiting to be transported to the sprawling collection of buildings. Like so much else about Los Angeles, the theme-park tram ride to the museum perfectly combined culture and kitsch. I stepped around a retaining wall to the Fran and Ray Stark sculpture garden, a small, private gem mixing natural and manmade works of art. I skirted thick rows of dark purple succulents, shooting lime green blooms, and passed a gigantic hanging bronze nightshirt, near a small bench at the far side of the garden. I sat facing a large marble sculpture, stone curves hinting at a reclining mother, baby in her arms.

I half closed my eyes. Other than the distant white-noise roar of the freeway, it was quiet. Birds twittered. A dog barked out a message and was answered by another's woof.

The crunch of footsteps warned me of company. He was here. I slipped my hand in my pocket.

Raul was older than his website photograph. His muscles had softened into paunch. A graying braid trailed down his back. Black leather motorcycle jacket and black jeans tucked into black cowboy boots. Raul wheezed from the short hike, a smoker's rasp. I sniffed the air. No nicotine reek. Maybe he'd quit.

My cell phone buzzed. I glanced at the screen. Bill. No way was I taking that call, especially considering my current activities.

Raul glanced at the dangling bronze nightshirt.

"What the fuck is that?"

"Art. I know. Probably cost more than a house," I said. "Two houses. Yours and mine, both." I was trying to put him at ease

"I'm a pacer," Raul said. "You okay with walking?"

I stood up. "Fine with me." A concrete pedestrian walkway led to the Getty, paralleling the tracks. As we started up on foot, a tram sped past. Faces pressed against the glass.

Raul shot me a sideways glance. "I'm going to stick my hand in my pants pocket and pull out a piece of paper. Don't do anything stupid."

"I won't, if you won't," I said. "You carrying?"

"No. You?"

"No. Except for the Wilson Combat Supergrade."

He stiffened.

"Relax. It's in my car. In the lot."

"Mine's in my S&S saddlebag. Forty-four Mag autoloader." Just as I suspected, he couldn't resist.

I thought about his gun. The .44 Magnum kicks like a horse but it can blow a through-and-through in one side of a car and out the other, like it was nothing. "So, you like to shoot elephants, do you?"

That got a smile. "You're one to talk. Wilsons sight like a mother."

I faced Raul. "Okay," I said. "Enough male bonding. Why are we here?"

He glanced around, suddenly nervous—not that there was anywhere on this concrete walkway for a bad guy to hide.

"You know what? I've changed my mind," he said. "Something doesn't smell right."

I smiled. "Is that Raul Mendoza the fake cop, or Charles Raul Montoya, the Low-riding Lawyer, talking?"

He looked startled.

"Relax," I said again. "I'm not here to harm you. I think maybe we can help each other."

"Charlie Montoya," he said, shaking his head. "Yeah, that used to be me, but old Charlie's gone. You're looking at the new me."

I doubted that, but I wasn't going to push it.

He hesitated, clutching his piece of paper. He seemed to make a decision. "Listen. I know who Marv was poking," he said, "besides his wife, I mean. I'll give her up to you if you tell me why you're so interested in a dead movie producer. Who hired you?"

I was faced with a small integrity dilemma. Such moments are inconvenient for a private investigator, but that's how I was raised. Should I tell him I was pretty sure I already knew who Marv's mistress was? Or should I play along, see if I could extract more information?

I thought about my fight with Bill, and the bags of garbage piled up in my back seat, like so many betrayals.

There's no such thing as a small integrity dilemma, Ten. They're all the same size.

"I already know Tovah's name. And nobody's hired me to look into Rudolph. Let's just say I have personal reasons for doing so. As for why I'm interested, why are you?"

We had started walking again; we were almost at the museum.

"Look," he said. "You seem like an okay guy. It's like this. I work for some of the nastiest sons-a-bitches you'll ever run across. They do business, very big business, out here," his voice rose. "And they are very fucking committed to staying in that business for a long time." He swallowed. "So when some slanty-eyed *vaquero* rides into their territory, they take note. Paranoia? You haven't seen paranoia until you've met these *pendejos*. I'm on the fringe, but they still pay me a butt-load of money just to sit on my ass, unless and until they need me for something."

"So what are you saying?"

"Disappear. Lose your curiosity. Go be a detective somewhere else. You got no business with these guys."

"And if I don't want to?"

We had reached the museum. The beige, rough-hewn buildings of stone gleamed in the sunlight. Raul gazed at the sparkling surfaces, but he didn't seem to see them.

"I'm telling you, you don't want to be on their radar." He tried to keep his voice casual, but his forehead broke out in sweat. "You're close to your ex-partner. Bill, right? His wife, Martha? His two little girls?"

My jaw clenched. Hot anger, so recently tamed, spilled through my body again. My hand reached to my pocket for my knife, almost involuntarily. Not here. I took a deep breath. Exhaled, slowly, before responding.

My voice was steel. "Are you threatening me? Are you threatening my friend, his family?"

He met my eyes, and for the first time, I caught sight of the fear hunkering behind the bravado. "I have twins, too, amigo," he said quietly. "Girls. They're in high school now. I'm trying to do you a favor, okay? Think of this as a polite invitation to back off."

"Does it come with a stiletto? Like my visit from Pretty Boy yesterday?"

He went white. "I don't know what the fuck you're talking about," he said. "We're done here."

He scurried back down the walkway, his braid swinging from side to side as he inspected the grassy borders, as if looking for rattlesnakes.

The sweep and curl of a building to my right caught my eye, like stacked grand pianos formed from limestone bricks. Everywhere I turned, the central plaza offered a glimpse of one of Los Angeles' myriad faces. Here, the pink and brown San Gabriel Mountains, there, the slate glow of the Pacific Ocean, and everywhere, a vast quilt of city- and landscapes. The hilltop site, with its magnificent complex of fossilized architectural structures, satisfied some longing in me for beauty. The exhibits themselves would have to wait—this was all the uplift I had time or tolerance for today.

Gridlock, all the way home. I was in a foul mood by the time I pulled up my driveway. I stashed the garbage bags in the back of the carport, retrieved my gun from the glove box, and stomped into the kitchen. Tank's bowl full of tuna chunks lay lukewarm and untouched, a silent reproach.

"Tank?" I checked the windowsill and under the table. He wasn't in the kitchen.

"Tank? Where are you?"

I heard a piteous meow from the living room, a call bordering on "I'm dying."

I hurried in, and found him crouched on the hardwood floor, frozen between the sofa and armchair.

"What is it? Show me."

His green eyes widened, and he lowered his head. His tail swept back and forth.

What was going on? I tuned in to him and shrank inside. Tank's world, normally centered and inviting, had turned foreign and unsafe, like a hostile planet.

I softened my voice, made it more inviting. "Show me?"

Tank hopped onto the armchair, and stared at me, willing me to understand.

Make me safe. Build me a safe space.

He jumped off and waited. I got a spare blanket from the bedroom. I draped it carefully over the arms of the chair. The front edge trailed to the floor.

No. I need to be able to escape.

I repositioned the blanket, so only a small flap hung over the front of the chair. Tank gave a soft *prrrttt* and slipped under the flap. He curled up, eyes closed, nose to paws, protected by his makeshift fort and finally at ease.

I retrieved my Wilson from the gun bag and checked the perimeter of the house. Everything seemed fine, but Raul's threats hung in the air like a rancid smell, disturbing my normal sense of peace. Maybe Tank had picked up on that.

Or maybe he was just mad at me for yelling at him.

I came back inside.

Over on my desk, my message light was blinking. It was Heather. I called her back, postponing the other, harder call awaiting me.

"Hi! I was just thinking about you." Her warmth actually pained me.

"Hello," I said.

"What's wrong?" How could she tell anything was wrong? We barely knew each other.

"Nothing. I'm just tired," I said. "I've had a couple of long days."

"Tell me?" Her voice was soft, inviting. *Show me?*

But I gave her the shorthand, and it was very short indeed, as I edited out the Dodger Stadium stiletto encounter, the near-shooting of a trick-or-treater, the dumpster dive, and the fight with Bill, especially the fight with Bill. In other words, anything that mattered. The more I censored, the more separate I felt. One secret piled on top of another, until I was trapped inside my own kind of fort, only this one didn't make me feel safe at all.

Heather was silent.

"Hey, so anyway, guess what? I signed up for the retreat," I said. "I even drove by there, to check it out."

"That's great," she said, but her voice was subdued. "Listen, I have to go. Thanks for calling back."

After we hung up, I felt terrible. I realized I hadn't asked her one thing about her day.

I checked on Tank again. He was sound asleep.

I grabbed his food bowl and dumped the uneaten contents into the trash. Then I washed and dried the dish with care, and refilled it with fresh-squeezed tuna water, and nothing else. I loved Tank. Why had I felt the need to disregard him, to impose my will?

Because I, too, felt disregarded, by someone who I'd thought had loved me.

I stepped onto the deck. A thick fog had obliterated any sunset, and the overcast sky bled into the dark gray water. The irony of my situation stung: I might lose Bill if I told him how hurt I was; I *would* lose him if I didn't. I was afraid to call Bill back; I was more afraid of becoming the kind of man who never called anyone back, because he was so afraid.

I pulled out my cell phone. "Call Bill Bohannon," I commanded. "Mobile." As my phone dialed automatically, I heard a beep indicating an incoming call. "Bill's cell" appeared on my screen. We were calling each other at the same time.

I answered first.

"Bill, I'm sorry," I said. "I've been, I'm . . ."—for some reason the French phrase flashed through my mind first: *je suis bete.* "I'm an idiot."

"And I'm a horse's ass," he answered. "Can I come by first thing in the morning? I'm on bath-and-bed duty with the girls tonight. And I need to see your ugly mug to do this properly."

Relief wet my eyes.

"Wherever and whenever you want."

"Good, because I'm pretty far up shit creek right now, and you may be my only paddle."

I called Heather back immediately.

"Hello?"

"Hi. I would like to acknowledge, fully, and without reservation, that I'm not great with phone conversations, especially when I'm starving and exhausted. I would like to invite you to dinner. I happen to know the perfect restaurant for people who don't like restaurants."

She didn't answer right away.

"It doesn't have to be an actual date. It can just be a friendly meal, okay? I'd really love to see you."

I sensed her smile. "Okay, but I'll meet you there, big guy. I need my own wheels, in case you go AWOL, emotionally speaking, and I need to make a quick escape."

"I know a cat you'd love," I said.

I told her the address, and to dress warmly. I called ahead for a reservation, took a long, hot shower, and changed into a long-sleeved flannel shirt, my favorite deep blue cashmere sweater and my best black jeans. I checked my reflection in the mirror for any obvious fashion faux pas.

"Big guy." I liked the sound of that, especially coming from Heather. I ran a damp hairbrush through my cranial hedge, gave Tank a handful of dry treats, and I was good to go.

Ten minutes later, I was parking in a space right off the street, above the larger lot. The "creekside dining" arrow on the rustic carved wooden restaurant sign pointed me toward a wrought iron archway, announcing the name of the restaurant, Inn of the Seventh Ray, the metal scroll embroidered with small violet lights. A hearty chorus of creek frogs supplied a natural rhythm section to the gentle flute and violin duet piping away over the sound system.

Heather must have broken a few speed limits getting here—she was already waiting at a little table next to the hostess, opposite a large stone Buddha cupping a flickering votive candle in one palm. The heady scent of jasmine permeated the air, though whether it emanated from Heather's glowing skin or a squat purple candle by the hostess, I couldn't tell. Heather, too, was in jeans; hers were dark blue and did something to her hips that was surely illegal. Thigh-high brown suede boots and a brown leather jacket completed the impression of casual elegance and sexy confidence. She met my eyes and smiled, her face cupped by shining curtains of blonde hair. My heart did a little flip in my chest.

"Hello," I said.

"Wow," Heather answered, her arm including the whole setting.

I had asked to be seated by the creek. Our hostess led us down rustic steps and past two more Buddhas. We crossed the central dining area where scattered tables of murmuring guests surrounded a large, bubbling stone fountain, thick with flowers. Branches danced with points of white light, and gauzy white canopies created cloistered pavilions. White tablecloths, violet napkins, white wrought iron chairs, wispy wildflowers, here a Ganesh, there a Mother Mary, and everywhere, invitations to be touched by natural beauty and open to timeless mysteries.

I thought I'd chosen the inn with my stomach, but once here, I realized I had also chosen with my heart.

The hostess sat us at an intimate table for two, overlooking the chuckling creek. Heat lamps blanketed us from the chilly air.

"Enjoy your meal," our hostess said.

Heather fingered her violet napkin. "What's the color supposed to represent?"

"Celestial fire," the hostess answered, her eyes shining. "Some say, new beginnings." She filled our glasses with water.

"Double-reverse-osmosis," she said. "Filtered with alkali. Enjoy."

She left the table. "Whoa," Heather said. "Should I drink it or worship it?"

We dug into a basket of bread that was still warm from the oven

"There's a teeny tiny part of me that is tempted to leap on the table right now and juggle pom-poms," Heather whispered to me, after a waiter had taken our wine and appetizer orders. "Spiritual settings do that to me sometimes."

"Pom-poms?"

"Ah, yes. I'm a girl with secrets," she replied. She touched my hand lightly. "Seriously, though, this is amazing, and you're right, I love it."

"It started out as some sort of mountain retreat in the thirties," I said. "Died and came back as a gospel church, then a garage, then a junkyard, until these guys took over. Now it's a gourmet restaurant, dressed as a happy hippie bride. I live ten minutes away, so I do take-out when I want to treat myself. How'd you get here so fast, by the way? I thought you lived in Santa Monica?"

"I do. But I'm staying at a motel in Malibu for two days, right off Topanga Canyon. I just had my condo painted, and I'm giving it a couple of days for the new paint smell to get cleared out."

That sounded promising.

The waiter returned with our appetizers and a bottle of Adelaide cabernet. I sipped, nodded, and he filled our glasses.

"I love the cabernets from Paso Robles," I said to Heather. "Something about the soil there seems to give the reds a combination of lively zip and deep earthiness."

Heather gave me a curious look.

"What?"

"You're an odd monk, that's all."

"Ex-monk."

The waiter delivered our shared appetizers: raw flax seed crostini with some sort of olive, pesto, and macadamia nut spread, and a salad of organic baby lettuces, spiced walnuts, and figs.

I spread a crostini thick and handed it to Heather. I made another, and crunched. My mouth exploded with crisp and creamy, soul and spice.

"Oh. My. God," I heard from across the table.

For a few minutes, we communicated with low, appreciative moans. Heather was still an enthusiastic eater, I was again pleased to note.

I took a sip of wine and studied the lovely woman sitting opposite me. She wasn't wearing glasses tonight, and it made her face somehow more vulnerable. Her azure eyes sparkled in the flickering candlelight. She grinned at me, and then returned to her food with focused pleasure. I wanted to know more about her.

"How did you find your way into pathology?" I asked. She looked up from her last bite of salad. Her expression made me want to say it differently. "Let me rephrase," I said. "Why pick a career that deals with death? You seem like one of the most alive people I've ever met." She smiled at that. Her smile faded as she considered her answer.

"I loved my grandfather very much," she said. "He was a widower, and he lived with us in Minnesota. He died when I was twelve, very suddenly, in his bed. No one would, or could, tell us why. 'Natural causes' is what our family doctor finally concluded, but it didn't make any sense. Gramps was healthy as a horse; Doc Gordon said he had the heart and lungs of a much younger man. Anyway, he was only in his late sixties when he died, and it sucked my father into a tailspin, one he's still riding." Heather's hands gripped each other. She put them in her lap. "Dad's about the same age my grandfather was when he died. Every time we talk on the phone he acts as if it may be the last time. It breaks my heart." She took a small sip of wine. I listened with every pore. "That experience shaped me. Some might say warped me, but I feel like this is my calling. Someone has to speak for the dead and maybe bring peace to the living, you know?"

"I do," I said. "I really do."

"Plus, I find it weirdly fascinating," Heather added. "Especially the mysteries, like Marv."

I didn't want to get into shoptalk. Not tonight.

"So your father's still alive?" I asked.

"Oh, yeah," she said. "He and my mom retired. They live out here now, in Manhattan Beach. I'm their middle child, the only girl. I see them once or twice a month. They're really sweet. I think you'd like them." She laughed. "My mother is obsessed with celebrities. She can't believe I don't run into Keith Connor or Angelina Jolie every day. Sadly, the only celebrity I've laid eyes on is Lindsay Lohan when I was emptying trash at the morgue, and Mom doesn't think that counts."

Our main courses arrived. Heather had ordered a sweet pea risotto, with a medley of mushrooms mixed in. I had settled on an angel hair arrabiatta; I was craving the fierce bite of chili flakes. Again, we ate with shared concentration.

"Whatever seventh ray-gun vibe they're laying on this food, it's working," Heather said, after a bit. "I'm getting totally stoned, and it's not just the wine." She dipped another hunk of bread in olive oil and waved it at me. "Okay, your turn. From what Bill says, your childhood was pretty out there."

I was reeling a little, trying to keep up. I asked her what Bill had told her.

"That you grew up in a Tibetan monastery, and your father works for the Dalai Lama."

"Close," I said. "My father's one of three head abbots at the Dorje Yidam Monastery. That makes him part of a council of lamas who advise the Dalai Lama on theological matters."

"A spiritual version of the Joint Chiefs of Staff?"

"Exactly."

"But aren't monks supposed to be celibate?" she asked.

"Yes," I said, "but there are exceptions. My father was married to a Tibetan woman when he was very young, long before he became a lama. She died in childbirth, along with the baby, and that's when, and probably why, he became a monk."

"Poor man."

"Yeah, well, he's also a brilliant man. He rose through the hierarchy fast. Then along came my mother . . . " My tongue turned to felt. I sipped water.

Heather touched my wrist lightly.

My voice tightened. "My father was forty, living his dry, monkish life, when temptation arrived at his doorstep in the form of a dewy-eyed American less than half his age. Valerie was a free spirit, and she walked right into a huge irony. She came to India on fire with a desire for spiritual liberation, and ended up pregnant and yoked for the rest of her short life to the chilliest of men." I pushed my plate away. All I could taste now was bitterness. "My father's first wife was a cousin of the Dalai Lama's birth family, so he got an official blessing to re-marry. Not that the marriage lasted. She fled to Paris to have and raise me, and he went on with his life as if nothing had happened."

"That's quite a story."

"It gets better. I'm pretty sure my father regretted my existence from the moment he got wind of it. As for my mother, she did her best, but she was young, single, and totally overwhelmed. She sent me to Dharamshala for six months out of every year as soon as I could walk and talk, but she never found her own feet. Instead, she replaced her dream of spiritual transformation with chemical substances." I rearranged my silverware on my plate. "Valerie was a daily drinker and pill-taker. She overdosed when I was thirteen. I moved to Dorje Yidam full time."

"Oh, oh, you poor thing."

I couldn't meet Heather's eyes. "Yeah, well, I took my vows, and made a formal commitment; it was the only way my father would have me—as a novice monk. I worked and studied for five more years. If it hadn't been for my two best friends, Yeshe and Lobsang, and a nightly escape into my contraband copy of *The Complete Works of Sherlock Holmes*, I would have lost my mind." A small twinge in my chest reminded me—I still hadn't solved the communication issue with my friends. They didn't even know about Heather . . .

"So what happened?"

"Oh, well, I finally escaped to Los Angeles when I turned eighteen. Another irony. I was sent to America to teach teenagers how to meditate. Instead, I guess you could say I learned how to retaliate, by going to the police academy. I'm not cut out to be a monk—I never was."

Heather touched the scar on my left temple. "Apparently not. Is that a bullet graze?"

I smiled. "Another long story."

"We'll get there," we both said at the same time. "Anyway," I said. "All I ever wanted to be was a detective. And here I am."

"And here you are. I'm glad your dream came true." Her gaze deepened, and the invitation was clear and strong.

"So, um, would you maybe like to come stay with me tonight?"

She smiled. "You read my mind, detective." She stood up. "Be right back."

I added a pint of lavender ice cream to our tab and included a hefty tip, paying without a twinge; another recent aspiration come true.

Heather traversed the dining area back to our table, leaving in her wake a pattern of admiring—or assessing, depending on the gender—glances. I stood, proud to be the target of her smile. We walked out hand in hand.

The drive was short, one quick turn off Old Topanga to Topanga Boulevard proper, and a couple of winding curves up the canyon to my driveway. Heather's lights remained close behind me.

As I drove, I wanted to reach across time and space, grab my father by the shoulders and shake him. *See?* I wanted to say. *See how great my life has turned out?*

"You know nothing," my father had roared at me, the night before I left for Los Angeles. "You cannot possibly understand the implications of your actions!"

"You mean the way you did, with my mother?" I had shot back.

"Quiet! Have some respect. You are too young and ignorant to know the truth of things!"

"Maybe you're too old to remember what truth even feels like!"

I could still taste the rush of glee I'd experienced proclaiming my rightness. But this time I felt a second rush, the hot, dark tang of shame. My father and I had been equally caught up in the great drama of needing to be right. He was acting out of that need, but so was I. Underneath each of us lay whole worlds of unexpressed emotion. At the time, I was terrified I'd never escape from my vows, wherever I lived, never experience a world outside of my father's rigid precepts. As for my father, faced with me, his careless accidental son, he probably felt deep regret, along with the fear that trumped all others for the ambitious man: what if my existence hasn't made the slightest bit of difference in the world?

I pulled into the carport and sighed. I had a lot to learn before my second rule became second nature. I was still doing daily battle with my ferocious attachment to rightness; just ask Bill.

Heather was standing by the big eucalyptus, taking in the tree-spired nightscape: the dark silhouettes of scrub oak and balsam, the amber glow of houses tucked throughout the canyon, and the distant, inked-in ocean.

She turned to me.

"You live here. *This* is where you actually live."

"I wake up grateful, every morning," I admitted.

A coyote chortled in the distance. Heather wrapped her arms around herself.

"Ten?"

"Yes?"

"Do you ever, I don't know, do ever feel like your angle on time and space isn't quite right?"

I realized she was asking a question that wasn't really a question. "Can you tell me what you mean?" I said.

She shook her head. "I don't know if I can. I've had this experience since I was a little girl. It's like I'm in a dream but I'm fully awake. Like now. I'm standing here next to you, and, we're talking, and there's this stream of thoughts, but there's also this other reality. Like two different dimensions, but wrapped in one. Does that sound crazy?"

I smiled. "No. Not crazy. The monks used to talk about that kind of thing all the time."

"Really?"

"Really." My mind drifted back to a dusty classroom and the slightly rank scent of yak butter candles. "My teachers liked to say, 'You *are* time and space. There's no "I" over here and time-space over there. It's all one thing, and you're it.'"

Her smile was uncertain. "So, which reality is real?"

"Neither. Or both. You get to choose."

"But . . . but we can't just make it all up as we go, can we?"

"Sometimes I think we can," I said. "It sounds complicated, but in a weird way it keeps life simple."

"Simple," she said. "There's a concept. How does that work?"

I laughed. "Well, sometimes—and understand, I'm talking here about me on a good day—but sometimes, if my angle on time and space feels all wrong, I just change the angle. We think we're stuck in fixed positions. But the Buddha says nothing inside or out is static. Everything's always in motion, and guess what? You and I are part of that everything."

"That's actually how you see the world?"

"Yes." Heat flooded my face. I'd been caught with some of my deepest beliefs exposed. With my father, such exposure usually led directly to an ice-cold shame-dunk.

"What's wrong?" Heather again read something from my face.

I told her. She reached for my hand. "Thank you for

explaining," she said. "It makes me feel closer to you. And by the way, I love how you see the world."

I decided then and there to make my life more complicated. I leaned forward and touched my lips to hers. Her mouth was soft and welcoming, as earthy and tart as the faint taste of wine that still clung to her lips.

We walked inside, our arms around each other. Tank padded into the kitchen to greet me and stopped short, his green eyes narrowing with suspicion.

Heather turned to me, but before she could comment on my cat, I gently shushed her. I pried open the pint of lavender ice cream, which had softened slightly, and used her forefinger to dip up a mouthful.

"Go on," I whispered. "Let him lick it off. You'll be his friend for life."

She walked close to Tank and knelt, her ice creamed finger outstretched. Tank studied Heather with some suspicion, but curiosity as to her offering won out. He took a few dainty steps forward, stretched out his neck, and lapped off the sweet treat. Then he did a little happy-shiver and strolled back to the bedroom, looking at us once over his shoulder as if to say "Coming?"

Heather and I smiled at each other.

"Heather," I said. "I'd really like you to stay." Blood accelerated through my arteries. I wondered if she could see the skin at my throat pulse. "But I kind of made a promise to myself to be more mindful in matters of the heart. To take things slowly."

Her smile was mischievous. "Fancy that," she said. "Me, too," and brushed my lips with hers. The kiss was gentle, but the current reached all the way to my toes.

I discovered something with Heather that night, a new, big truth: The only thing sexier than making love with a beautiful woman for the first time is making everything-but with a beautiful woman for the first time.

Chapter 16

I stood on the deck, breathing in the early morning smells of the canyon—the minty bite of eucalyptus, the faint hint of sea and salt. A lone bird warbled in the distance as a light, fresh breeze feathered my cheeks. Heather had left at dawn, after a hurried mug of my best Sumatra. She had an early autopsy to attend at the USC hospital, but I was guessing she was glad for the excuse to slip away. Our physical connection had been intense, more intense than I, at least, had expected. Both of us had woken up shy. But I didn't feel any regret, and if her warm kiss and promise to call me later meant anything, she didn't either. I considered that huge progress, at least on my part. I inhaled deeply, released a long, full out-breath, and went inside for a second cup of dark-roasted ambrosia. Maybe I'd finally have time to check out the contents of the Robinsgrove's trash bags before Bill got here. Surely they held a clue to Marv's demise.

But my fax machine began to buzz and chirp from my office area. Zigo's first regiment of information had arrived. A series of pages marched end to end out of the machine and into the tray. When the whirring stopped, I riffled through, counting five pages in all.

The first three pages were typewritten, that is to say, hammered out on an actual typewriter; faint, spidery script, old-fashioned and neatly looped, filled the final two pieces of paper, indicating a personal hand from long ago. As for the actual contents, I was stumped. Zigo had neglected to mention his information was coming in the motherland's mother tongue, and they don't teach German in Dharamshala.

"Hey, Tank," I called into the bedroom, and tried out the only two words I knew. "Spreck-en-zee Doitch?"

Tank's silent retort was interrupted by the familiar clunk of Bill's cop shoes, crossing the deck to my kitchen door. Just like that, my morning ease evaporated.

Bill stepped inside, a half smile on his face. "Was that the good doctor's car I passed driving up here?"

"Maybe."

"She makes house calls?"

"Maybe."

"Can I tell Martha?"

"Not on your life."

He chuckled, and I felt like I might survive this conversation after all.

I poured him a coffee, choosing the black-and-white mug he'd given me for my last birthday—he'd snagged it from the county coroner's odd little homicide-related gift shop. At the time, we had shared a good laugh over the skeletal Sherlock, pipe clamped between exposed jawbones.

Bill blew across the rim, sipped, and grunted with appreciation. We stood awkwardly in the kitchen.

"Let's sit outside," I said.

We sat facing the ocean, hidden under a blanket of early morning mist.

"It's so quiet here," Bill said. "I've forgotten what that's like." He sighed. "Ten . . ."

"No, let me go first," I interrupted. "I need to say some things before I lose my nerve." I breathed through the knot of fear, a hardened ball in my belly. "I realized something, after we hung up yesterday." I swallowed. "Bill, part of me hasn't wanted you to succeed, not without me. I wanted this change, but I've also been afraid. Afraid of failing. Afraid that leaving our partnership might mean losing our friendship, losing your respect. I think I've been overcompensating. Acting out. Completely disregarding your wishes.

I'm very sorry." I checked Bill for a reaction. Wait, was he
. . . ? "Why are you *laughing*?"

"I'm laughing, because you just stole all my lines,
asshole. Not wanting you to do well without me? Check.
Overcompensating? Check. Afraid of losing your friendship
and respect? Double-check, with a cherry on top. And as for
failing? How about doing it on prime time, in front of the
entire world?" Bill set his mug down and turned to face me.

"The truth is, this fucking case has been biting my ass
from the get-go. I pride myself on making quick sense of
things, but nothing about Marv Rudolph's death does. Sully
and Mack are next to useless, and now I've got four more
homicides crowding my desk at work, an irritated boss, and
a fed-up, overwhelmed mother of twins at home. But you
know what really grassed me when I woke up this morning?
Why I'm maybe the bigger jerk? When the captain suggested
I call you for help, did I thank him? No. Inside, I cursed him.
What's worse, I blamed you. And why? Because I didn't want
to need you. But I do need you, Ten, and that's the God's
honest truth. This is my first homicide as a D-Three, and I
am royally screwing it up, all by myself. Talk about ego." Bill
shook his head. "So please tell me you've been the cowboy
I know and love. Please tell me you've been working this
bastard behind my back and have come up with something
more than my fucking zippity-doo-dah-day."

I patted Bill's knee. "Friend," I said, "you know this
cowboy well."

We moved inside and sat across from each other at the
kitchen table, home to so many late night case reviews in
our past. It was still too early for beer, so I made a fresh pot
of coffee, and toasted two thick slices of farmer's market
corn bread. Using my notes as a memory aid, I told Bill about
sitting shivah, Harper's venomous glare, and my kitchen-
knife reconnoiter. The visit to the T-Bird tattoo parlor and
Thunder's interactions with Marv. I handed him copies of
my research on Marv's past and Clancy's telephoto shots of

Tovah Fields-with-an-*s*, driving away from the Robinsgrove. I passed over the exed-out surveillance photo of me, and described Pretty Boy and the wild stadium chase. I even owned up to my Halloween night fiasco with the teenagers.

Bill listened intently, stopping to jot in his little notebook from time to time. Finally, I talked about Raul Martinez. I showed Bill the fake identification card and retraced the thinking that led me to finding Charles Raul Montoya, aka the Low-riding Lawyer, our Getty meeting, and Raul's threats.

To my surprise, Bill shrugged off that part of the conversation. "Creeps say that sort of shit about me and the family on a daily basis. Forget about it. What's more interesting to me is, this Charles, or Raul, or whatever the hell he calls himself, rings a bell. You say he rides a Harley?"

"Yup."

"Hunh. There was this guy, back when I was still on patrol. He got his start doing slip-and-falls, kind of a joke around town with his shiny suit and his chopper. Then a few years back he gets this young gang-banger off scot-free—a Mexican, someone connected to someone else much bigger in the gang world. Big big, I mean. Anyway, he gets the creep off. Next thing you know, he slips and falls off the face of the earth himself."

Bill sat back, pulling on his lower lip. I smiled. I knew that gesture. Bill was hatching a plan.

"I'll put a trace on Tovah Fields right away. Even Sully ought to be able to handle that. As for this other thing, I need a little time to figure out the angle of attack. It's beginning to smell gang-connected. Or maybe bigger. You by any chance remember the name of the kid that lawyer got off?"

I checked my notes.

"Morales. Daniel Morales."

"Fuck me. I knew it."

"What? Cartel?"

"You might say that. You ever heard of Chaco Morales?

Started out a player in Mexico's casino trade, before he set his sights north. He's smart, ruthless, and everywhere—drugs, restaurants, casinos, you name it. He's up there with Joaquin 'El Chapo' Guzmán. Chaco's known for taking care of his own—hiring from within, setting relatives up, getting them out of jail, paying any legal and medical bills. It's all about family members, and Chaco's got a shitload of them. He's somewhat of a legend. His nickname's El Gato—on account of his nine lives. He's survived two assassination hits by organized crime. And rumor has it that once, when he was cornered by two Sinaloa bad boys, he just disappeared into thin air." Bill frowned. "What the hell was Marv Rudolph doing anywhere near Chaco Morales?"

"Hard to know," I said. "But in L.A., where's there's money, there's usually dirty money. And like Arlene Rudolph said, Marv was a movie producer."

"In any case," Bill said, "we've got to tread lightly here. When you're in cartel territory, you're not just dealing with DEA and the Feebs, you're dealing with Homeland Security, ATF, and God knows what else. I'll make some calls. See who has fingers in which pies. Jesus, what a clusterfuck."

"Glad it's not mine," I said.

"Ten, you're on a roll here," Bill said. "You want to piss me off all over again?"

"Maybe you should tell me to go fuck myself. I've got a nice streak going."

"Don't tempt me, kiddo."

We grinned at each other. He stood up and stretched. "Okay, Cowboy, I'll catch you later, after I clear some fences of my own. Speaking of, I want you to resist, I repeat, resist the temptation to ride solo into gang territory, okay? Now that I've got you back on my team, I don't want to lose you in a shoot-out."

"Hasn't crossed my mind," I said. And it hadn't. There was such a heavy undercover police presence involved in L.A.'s gangland, I was as likely to be shot by a cop as a banger.

"Here." Bill passed over a manila envelope. "Preliminary autopsy report, for what it's worth. Load of crap."

"That reminds me," I said, "as long as I'm confessing . . ."

Bill went very still.

"I might have done a little garbage cover the other evening, at Robinsgrove, just before the trash pick-up."

"Might?"

"Well, maybe more than might."

A smile played around Bill's lips. "How much garbage we talking about?"

"Let's just say there's enough stashed in my carport to fill a small Humvee."

Bill grinned. "In that case, my son, you can skip the Hail Marys and go straight to dumpster-diving." He made a sign of the cross over my forehead. "I absolve you of your sins. And happy hunting."

I walked Bill out to his car. "How's the other job going?" he asked. "The paying one?"

"Slowly," I said. "You wouldn't happen to know anyone who speaks German, would you?"

Bill stared. "Ten, for someone so smart, you can be remarkably thick sometimes."

I said nothing.

"You've met my wife, Martha? Raised-in-Germany Martha?"

I did the mental equivalent of slapping my forehead with my palm.

"Give her a call," he said. "Please. She'd kill for a little adult conversation right about now."

I walked inside and did just that.

"Bohannon house of horrors," Martha answered. "Morticia speaking." The high-pitched, background squeals told me that Maude and Lola were riding the crest of an energy wave.

"It's me. Ten."

"Lola, don't put that up your sister's nose!" Martha sighed. "Sorry, Ten, I'm dealing with the aftereffects of too much sugar. Thing One and Thing Two somehow found the hidden stash of Halloween candy. I thought Bill was coming to you?"

"Came and went," I said. "This call's for you." I explained what I needed. "How's your German these days?"

"Sharp," she said. "Especially after three solid days of my mother barraging the girls with *danke's* and *bitte's*—she's convinced she can make them fluent in a week."

"Cool," I said. "Can I bring the documents over now?"

"If you don't mind a little background noise," she said. "I'm all alone with the hooligans."

"I live for happy hooligan noise," I told her.

Tank was still napping. I dumped a scoopful of dry treats into his bowl to tide him over until dinnertime. I downed a handful of dried granola for the same reason.

I took the Shelby over the hill to the 101, and ran into a wall of unusual late-morning sludge through the San Fernando Valley. Another hour and a half of my life, sacrificed to the Freeway Gods. I practiced slow breathing, and then fast breathing, and then a prolonged bout of not-yelling. I finally parked in front of Bill and Martha's house at almost two in the afternoon. I stood still for a minute, working the commuter-crankiness out of my shoulders. The sun was at a slight slant; the warmth felt good across my shoulder blades.

Martha opened the door, wearing black leggings, a yellow tunic, and my scarf.

"You look fantastic!"

She gave me a hug. "Thanks. Dreading turning forty turns out to be a lot worse than actually doing it." She took a closer look. "You need a beer."

I nodded gratefully and she disappeared back into the house. She was a great wife—great wives know how to make observations like, "You need a beer." I added that to my growing just-in-case wife wish list, along with "smarter than me," and "laughs at my jokes."

"Unh Tey! Unh Tey!" Two balls of energy in bright blue wigs and red pajamas flaunting the labels "Thing One" and "Thing Two" careened around the corner. They held their arms high, and I bent low and lifted them into a two-girl hug. I carried the wriggling armload into the family room, while they chattered about their day, in perfect German gibberish, as far as I could tell. I deposited the girls on the floor. Maude did her one-armed thrust-and-march to the toy basket. She reached in and pulled out a striped rubber ball.

"Baw," she said to me, solemnly.

"Yes," I answered. "That is, indeed, a ball."

She squatted and rolled it through the doorway.

"Baw."

"Baw!" Lola echoed with great excitement, and they scampered after it.

"Nice outfits," I said, as Martha walked in with a bottle of dark ale and a clear glass stein.

"They refuse to believe Halloween is over," she said, and set both in front of me. "Bottle or glass? I can't remember."

"Glass," I said, pouring. "Light beers are fine out of the bottle, but sturdy ones need the glass to open up in."

"Ten and the art of beer-drinking," she teased. Her tone became serious. "You and Bill okay now?"

I nodded. "Back on track," I said.

"Thank God, because I honestly worried this little tiff might kill him. That's if I didn't kill him first. Between the two of us, this has not been a happy household, Ten."

I took my first sip. The crisp bite of hops coursed over my tongue, rinsing away the dusty taste of traffic.

"Girls? Nap-time," Martha called. She stepped into the hallway. I heard faint protests, followed by a low, warm voice, singing a lullaby. Followed by silence.

Martha rejoined me. "Fingers crossed," she said. "The

postcandy sugar crash seems to have kicked in. Okay. Let's take a look."

I laid out the papers, in the order in which they'd arrived. Martha looked them over, one by one.

"Right," she said. "The handwritten parts are notes, like the notes a doctor takes, only these seem to be by a Sister Ursula. I'm guessing the director of the orphanage, maybe? Do you want me to write these out for you in English?"

"That'd be great, but for right now, can you just give me a quick sense of what they say?"

"Sure," she said, and gave me a quick smile. "This is exciting!" She studied the page. "The first note is dated June fourth, nineteen forty-four. Right before the Allies came ashore at Normandy. 'Frau Engel brought young Sadie to us today,'" Martha read. "'She is five years old. Thought to be Jewish but not confirmed. In good health though of course malnourished. Will seek counsel from Mother Superior.'"

"June of forty-four," I said. "Must have been a crazy time."

"The next is June eleventh, one week later." She scanned the handwriting. "Actually, each of these notations is a week apart. That must have been Sister Ursula's procedure. Very organized. Very German. Anyway, June eleventh says, 'Sadie still withdrawn and uncommunicative. Taking nourishment every day. Sleeps soundly but is fitful and shy during day. Does not interact with other children.'"

"June eighteenth?" I asked.

She read on, "'Sadie began speaking this week. Asked for more soup at evening meal. Made a face when she tried to eat a, *ein Gurken* . . . a pickle! Smiled when we laughed. Frau Engel came yesterday and brought Sadie a scarf. We saw another smile. Mother Superior is making inquiries.'"

Martha looked up. "Angel."

"What?"

"Her name. *Engel* means angel. Sadie's angel." She lowered her head to the page. "Okay, June twenty-fifth. 'Learned

Sadie's last name: Rosen. Now we know. Frau Engel expressed fear about possible punishment. Sadie is adjusting, speaks and listens well. We cannot keep her. Mother Superior will make a decision this week.'"

Martha stopped reading. She knuckled a few tears away. "Whew," she said. "This poor girl was only a few years older than Maude and Lola. My God."

I pictured the twins in such a place. It made the horror so personal, so painful, that my heart wrenched for Sadie, and for her big brother, Julius.

Martha straightened up. "Should I keep going?"

I nodded, unable to speak.

"'July second,'" she said. "'Sadie packed and ready to leave. Frau Milz and husband to pick up at ten a.m. tomorrow. We feel sad to lose her. Little Sadie has become a spot of sunshine in our days.' That's it. The last entry."

Martha laid the paper down as if it were made of spun glass.

I pictured Sadie's face. That innocent smile.

"Anything else about Sadie?"

Martha scanned the typewritten pages. "These are forms," she said. "Records of when children came, how long they stayed, and where they went after they left the orphanage." She tapped her finger on a line toward the bottom of the third page. "There's Sadie," she said. "Let's see—arrival date, departure date, and oh, look, there's a signature." She squinted. "I can't read this, can you?"

I held the page close. The tight scrawl was faint.

"No."

"Hang on." Martha rummaged in the toy basket and came up with a neon pink plastic magnifying glass, shaped like a hippopotamus. "Never say mothers aren't resourceful," she said.

We peered through the lens at the faded handwriting.

"The last name is Milz," I said. "But I can't make out the first name."

"It looks like Rain . . . , um, Reinhold?" Martha said. "Yes, that's it. Reinhold Milz."

Once she said it, I could see it. "Wow. Good work. Many thanks, Martha."

"No problem," she said. "I can't say it was fun, but I'm glad I could help. Why don't I do a complete written translation of everything? I can consolidate it into a single document."

"That'd be great," I said. "How long will it take?"

"Two hours, max, allowing time for kidlet interruptions." As a former court reporter, Martha's typing skills were legendary.

I counted out four $100 bills. "You're hired," I said.

"Ten, you know I'm happy to do this for you, for free."

"Sorry. When I get paid, I pay others. It keeps everything freely flowing." I pressed the bills in her hand. "Call it Ten and the Art of Economics."

A short time later, I was back on the road. Happily, one thing that immediately flowed more freely was the traffic. I decided to drive straight to Julius, now that I had something concrete to report. I left him a message that I was on my way, and was at the gatehouse in half an hour.

There was a new guard. Early forties. Latino. His eyes were muddy with aggression, and he had a mean underbite. A scar slashed his hatchet features. I liked the old guy better, and he wasn't exactly a sweetheart.

"Tenzing Norbu, here to see Mr. Rosen," I said.

Underbite made a quick call and wordlessly thumb-jabbed me through the gate. As I drove away, I felt his hard gaze on my back.

I parked in my usual spot. The fountain was quiet, today, no flow happening here. No Julius bursting out the front door, either. I knocked and then buzzed. I knocked again. I even tried the handle, but of course it was locked.

I was turning to go, when the door opened, very slowly.

"Ten. Do come in." Julius was short-winded.

I stepped inside and was greeted by a startling sight—Julius, leaning on his two galactic canes, dressed in black-rimmed glasses, a semitaped man-diaper, and nothing else.

"Don't mind me," he said. "I was just getting into the shower." He indicated his minimal covering with a lopsided smile. "Believe me, it could have been worse."

We both started laughing as Otilia hustled into the foyer, her arms full of fresh towels. She pulled up, taking in the scene, and a smile teased one corner of her mouth. We met eyes, and she gave a little nod. Otilia had finally allowed me into her very small circle of trusted ones.

"Why don't you head on over to the ruminating room," Julius said. "I'll meet you there when I'm decent. It might be a few minutes—it's medicine time."

I crunched the graveled path to the little round cottage. Removing my shoes, I crossed the thick carpet to the closet and retrieved the white easy chair. I positioned its chrome stand across from Julius's matching black one. Each chair had a hinge, connecting the base to the frame. Hmmm. I grasped the front section of mine and lifted. It opened like a wing, concave seat becoming convex footrest, transforming the chair into a chaise lounge comprised of one uniform curve. Clever chair. I leaned against the back, put my feet up, and closed my eyes, happy to have a few minutes alone. My breath slowed and deepened. I'd like to say I experienced a deep dive into the great transcendent is-ness of life, but the startling *clonk* of chin on chest both woke me up, and pointed to that much more pedestrian occurrence known as catnap.

I paid a quick visit to the bathroom, to splash cold water on my face. The room was tiny and pristine, tiled in white, with some sort of complicated electronic toilet armed with a long row of buttons to push for various services. I didn't want to know. The pedestal sink was simple and elegant, with a mirrored cupboard overhead. Even the curvilinear trashcan was uniquely shaped, as if it had been oblong until a giant toddler squeezed its middle. My detective training, also known as a natural tendency to snoop, kicked in. Julius's swings in and out of clarity made me curious as to his medical regimen, and as any cop will tell you, bathrooms are the mother lode of pharmaceutical clues. I opened the cupboard. Nothing inside but a few expensive soaps, individually wrapped. Too bad.

I rinsed my face and dried my hands on a disposable guest towel. As I went to drop it into the can, I glimpsed something inside. I bent to look more closely. I couldn't tell what I was seeing, so I fished the waxy object out. It was also oblong, maybe two inches across—the kind of covering you'd peel off a Band-Aid, only bigger. There were a few more just like it in the bottom of the trashcan. No markings. I put the backing in my pocket, for future study. Maybe Heather would know what it was.

I returned my napping chair to its original form in one quick motion—very cool design—just as the door opened. Otilia wheeled Julius over and transferred him into his own chair. She left without a word, angry about something again.

Julius gave me another odd, uneven smile. "Tell me everything," he said.

I opened my notebook. Taking my time, I described as precisely as I could how and what I had learned about Sadie. I don't know what I was expecting in return, but it wasn't what I got. Although Julius responded several times with a "That's interesting," or "I see," he registered no feeling, that is to say, his expression was flat, almost as if his features were frozen. I had started off enthusiastically, but the lack of reaction was deflating. Also interesting. How people *don't* respond can be just as important as how they do.

He must have sensed something. "Sorry I'm not more animated," he said. He pointed to one corner of his mouth. "Botox shots. Helps with the drooling, doesn't help with the smiling. Plus, some of my medications make me spacey." He shrugged. "You know what they say—aging ain't for sissies."

Julius's glasses made it hard to see his pupils, but from what I could tell they did appear to be dilated. "Shall we talk another time?"

"No, this is fine. You're doing fine. Tell me more."

I returned to my notes, and relayed Martha's deciphering of the signature of Reinhold Milz. I retrieved copies of the three typewritten pages from my folder and started to hand them over. I blinked. Now it was his chin, on his chest. Julius was completely out.

Botox or not, something about this entire interaction was worrisome.

I sat back, caught in a momentary swirl of confusion. I let it pull me deeper, into its core. My mentor, Rinpoche, called this uncertain state "spacious confusion." *No, no, Lama Tenzing! Do not resist spacious confusion. Do not judge. Pure not-knowing is a good thing; it is one breath away from the void itself, the nonplace from which all reality is manifested.* Though the Buddha might take issue with the term, I sometimes called this state the Ultimate What-the-Fuck. If I can tolerate the discomfort and simply let the uncertainty play out, it can stun me to stillness and sometimes lead to a clearer comprehension of things as they are.

I expanded past my confusion, extending delicate filaments of awareness to encircle the unconscious man opposite. I was worried. I wanted to feel my way into his current state, as best I could. Rinpoche's words again floated to me across space and time. *Everything and everyone is connected. Let your body mirror another's and your consciousness will follow. Let the two overlap and become as one.* I studied the grooved flesh at the outer edges of Julius's downturned lips. I deepened the corners of my own mouth, mirroring the carved lines. I closed my eyes and dropped my chin to my chest. I again reached across with focused attention to the sleeping Julius.

A wave of profound and utter depression swept through me, followed by a sharp gust of grief-wind, accented by anger, and gone almost as quickly as it came. So painful, so human—all losses suffered over time, concentrated into a single sharp intake. It pierced like a whetted blade. I took a moment to honor his sadness and another to honor my own. *We are all as one, in joy and in grief, in love and in loss.*

I slipped out of the room, closing the door softly behind me. As I pulled on my shoes, I saw Manuel across the lawn, leaning against an olive tree. Watching. I gave him a little nod. He stepped back into the shadows.

For a man who claimed to relish privacy, Julius had an awful lot of people keeping their eyes on him.

My traffic-luck held. Even with a stop at Whole Foods, or as Martha calls it, Whole Paycheck, I was walking into my kitchen in under an hour.

Tank hovered by the door, dinner on his mind.

"Time to play Choose the Food," I announced. I placed three different tins around him in a neat semicircle; salmon, chicken, and beef. I stepped back—everybody likes a little space to think. Tank deliberated, his tail curling and uncurling behind him. Like me, he takes his food very seriously. Finally, with great gravitas, he approached the salmon can and touched it with his nose.

"Salmon it is," I said. I peeled open the can and forked the fish onto his plate. He was whiskers-deep in seconds.

I grabbed a cold ginger beer and stepped onto the deck. The spicy carbonation pricked my nostrils as I sipped. The canyon was winding down for the day. Lights blinked on here and there, as the lowering sun stained the sky in shades of peach and violet. Magic hour. *The hour of the seventh ray.*

Heather answered on the fourth ring. "Hey, Ten."

"I'm watching the sun set. It's too beautiful not to share. Can you come over?"

"Can I come over? Are you serious?" she said. "This room smells of chlorine and stale Lemon Pledge. I've been sneezing for the last hour. When do you want me?"

"Now. Don't eat. I'm fully stocked."

Tank settled on the kitchen counter as I unpacked my groceries. I put away the yogurt and fruit, and took inventory of what remained. Never shop hungry—I'd bought enough for a small army. Containers of tabouli, babaganoush, salad greens, hot and cold soup, Indian samosas, and an assortment of raw vegetables lined up single file across the counter, a parade of temptations. I set aside the pint of rice pudding, plump with cardamom and raisins. The mango, lemon, and coconut sorbets got tucked in the freezer.

I rearranged the food into a fancy display, and rewarded myself with one veggie samosa. Tank leapt off the counter and rubbed against my ankles.

"All right. All right." I put a tiny taste of the rice pudding on the end of a spoon. Tank's eyes widened with pleasure. One tongue-flick, and it was gone. He cocked his head.

"Sorry, Tank. That's all you get. I have a guest coming. We don't want to set off the smoke alarms." Too much dairy makes poor Tank fart like the night shift at a refried bean factory. Los Angeles has enough pollution problems as it is.

Heather's car wound up the road.

"Good times, Tank," I said. "Good times."

I hurried outside. We hugged. Her damp hair was pulled back into a ponytail. I inhaled the clean scent.

We walked into the kitchen. "My favorite way of eating," she said. "Little bites of lots of different things. Saves me from stealing off your plate."

"It's a lot easier being a hunter-gatherer if there's a Whole Foods nearby. Are you feeling hungry?"

Heather gave me a mischievous look.

"I'm feeling frisky," she said. "How about you? Are you feeling frisky?"

"Um," I said.

"My mother taught me to never arrive at a dinner party empty-handed," she said. "Now it may look like I'm empty-handed, Ten, but no one's searched my pockets yet." She put her hands in the air. "This girl needs to be searched. Is there a policeman in the house?"

I had no idea where she was going with this, but I played along.

"Ex-policeman," I said. "Okay. Turn around, ma'am. Place your hands against the wall." She spun and planted her palms, leaning.

"What about my legs," she asked.

"Uh, okay, um, spread your legs, please. Ma'am." I was feeling incredibly self-conscious. Heather's game was pushing me right up to my edge of ease, if not beyond it.

Heather, on the other hand, appeared to be thoroughly enjoying herself. She adopted a limber, wide-legged stance, complementing all the right body parts.

"Okay," she said. "Frisk away, detective!"

I glanced at Tank. He looked as befuddled as I felt. *Spacious confusion, Ten. Do not resist.* I patted Heather down, starting at her shoulders, and working my way south. The curves at her waist and hips were warm and firm to the touch.

"You're clean," I said.

"Don't forget my jacket pockets."

I obliged. "Suspicious round object in your left jacket pocket. Permission to search that pocket, ma'am?"

"Permission granted."

I came up with a small black plastic canister. I popped it open. A neatly-rolled joint nestled inside.

"Busted!" Heather said brightly.

Her delighted expression reminded me of Lola's triumphant *Baw!* and it made me laugh. "I don't know," I said. "I might arrest you. Or I might let you go with just a warning. It depends."

"Does this help?" She pulled a laminated card from her

purse. "I'm street-legal. Exhibit A: one medical marijuana prescription card."

"Did you write yourself a prescription?" I asked, amused. "How handy."

"Nope. I just happen to suffer from a mild anxiety disorder, not to mention, I'm connected. Don't you just love California?" Heather nuzzled against me. "Actually, I'm feeling a little anxious right now."

We walked onto the deck, and soon the joint was traveling back and forth between us. The pungent herb flavored up my bloodstream immediately. My head filled with a light fizz.

"Wow," I said. "Strong."

"Got to love my local dispensary. You should try their Cannabis Caramels—like hash and childhood rolled into one." Heather exhaled a stream of smoke and giggled. "Hmm. Floaty. Uh oh. I sense my first big confession coming on. My deepest, darkest secret."

I smiled into the darkness. She pouted.

"Aren't you going to ask me what it is?"

"Okay. What is it?"

Her smile was sly. "I guess you could say I was your opposite in high school. The oppo-monk. I was a cheerleader." She peeked at me. "No mocking."

"I can't mock you, because I have no idea what being a cheerleader entails. Except pom-poms, I'm guessing."

"Short shorts, push up bras, and a lot of wiggling. And yes, pom-poms, on occasion. Play your cards right and you might get a sample cheer later."

She was such an interesting woman.

An owl hooted in the distance. We finished off the joint. Heather glanced at me.

"I wasn't sure you'd want to partake."

"It's been a while," I admitted. I smiled, remembering the last time I'd smoked marijuana. That, too, was the direct result of a medical marijuana prescription, belonging to John D, an elderly cancer-stricken almond farmer with a heart as big as the Pacific. "I smoked dope in India, you know. Ganja, I should say."

"You're kidding."

"Nope. There wasn't a drop of alcohol within fifty miles of our monastery, but we lived smack in the middle of a region that's been producing ganja for centuries. There was this Hindu temple near us, totally rundown, but it was dedicated to some little-known ganja-smoking Hindu deity. A bunch of scraggly, bloodshot-eyed devotees lived there. They'd taken a vow to smoke weed every day until they reached enlightenment."

"Ha! The original wake 'n' bakers. No wonder the place was rundown."

"Exactly. Anyway, we were strictly forbidden to go anywhere near them. Naturally."

"Naturally."

"But somehow our elders forgot that the fastest way to get a teenager to do something is to forbid it."

Heather laughed softly.

"What?"

"Nothing. It's just that you're not at all what I expected."

"Is that good?"

She patted my arm.

"Yes, Ten. That's very good."

It was getting cold. I tucked my hands in my pockets. Something crinkled. I pulled out the circular covering from Julius's bathroom.

I showed it to Heather. "Do you know what this is?"

"Looks like the backing of a nicotine patch," she answered. "You know, for quitting smoking." She looked more closely. "Strange, though. Usually they're well marked. So you know what you're taking."

"Huh." I pocketed it. I was positive Julius didn't smoke. Maybe Otilia was a secret, three-pack-a-day gal in her other life. I snickered.

The night sky shifted. "Is it getting darker out here, or lighter?" I said.

"Okay, that's it. Time to get some food in us," Heather answered. "Doctor's orders."

We weren't a small army, but we were two people who had just shared one very potent joint. We mowed through the containers of food.

"Best for last," I said, moving to the freezer. I lifted out the coconut sorbet and tossed it to her. "Sorbet!"

Heather's palms flew up and she jumped back, as if I had lobbed a grenade. The container landed on the floor between us. I must have looked as startled as I felt. "Sorry," Heather said. She picked the container up and handed it back. "I don't do sorbet." She craned her neck. "Hey, can you aim me toward your bathroom?"

I pointed her in the right direction. Tank, who detects people's anxiety spikes better than a Geiger counter, lifted his head from his bed, the tip of his tail flicking.

"I know," I said. "And we were doing so well."

When Heather returned a few minutes later her eyes were slightly reddened, as if she'd had a quick cry.

"So, no sorbet then," I said, trying for humor.

"I'm sorry. It's a sore point for me."

"That's okay. You don't have to . . ."

"No. I kinda do." Heather sat at the table. "Confession number two. I was the chubby kid in the family."

"Really?" I said. "I find that hard to believe."

"Yeah, well, eventually I grew out of it. I mean, I look at pictures from my childhood and all I see is a happy, slightly chunky little girl. But my Mom was pretty plump herself as a child, and apparently her classmates teased her mercilessly. I guess it kind of scarred her, and she decided to spare me the same fate. So she put me on a low-fat regime pretty early on. Skim milk. Steamed vegetables. And no second helpings for Heather!" Her bright little laugh hurt my heart. "When I was eleven, Mom and Dad took the three of us kids to

England. We're Anglo-Saxons up and down the genealogy tree, and they decided it was time for us to connect with our roots." Heather shook her head. "Big Ben. Changing of the guards. Winchester Cathedral. Do you know the only thing I remember about the trip?"

I waited.

"Everywhere we ate, my older brother got to finish with a Knickerbocker Glory—this fabulous tower of ice creams and syrups. My younger brother would order an enormous banana split. And me?"

"Sorbet?"

"Fucking sorbet. One scoop." She laughed that brittle laugh again. I felt a surge of anger toward her parents.

Heather checked my expression, and her smile wavered. I let the tightness in my neck dissipate.

"In that case, how do you feel about rice pudding?" I asked. She relaxed.

"Bring it on," she smiled.

Dessert devoured, we moved into the bedroom, and climbed under the covers. We lay side by side, still fully clothed.

"The second bowl of pudding may have been a mistake," Heather murmured to the ceiling.

"Unh," I answered.

We drifted off to sleep.

I was awakened by the insistent buzz of my cell phone. I grabbed it off the table.

"Hello?" I croaked. I heard labored breathing. "Hello?" I said again.

"Lossssht." The voice was slurry, and familiar.

"Julius? Is that you?"

"Losssssht," he repeated. "No point."

"Who's lost?" I said. "Sadie?"

"No," Julius breathed into the phone. "Me." He hung up so gently it took me a moment to realize he was gone. I checked my watch: 3:20 A.M., the witching hour. Heather had slept right through the whole thing. I pushed "return call," but Julius didn't pick up.

I stripped down to my boxers and climbed back into bed, pulling the duvet over both of us. I nestled against Heather and was asleep in an instant.

I woke up at dawn to a delicious sensation: Heather's warm hand circling me in its clasp.

"Lean to the left," she chanted softly, illustrating. "Lean to the right. Stand up, sit down, fight, fight, fight!" I groaned with pleasure. "Give me a *T*," she continued, squeezing lightly. "Give me an *E*. Give me an *N*, give me a . . ."

I rolled on top of her miraculous, naked body, cutting her off mid-cheer with a deep kiss. Tank thunked to the floor and padded out the bedroom door. I pulled away.

"Are you . . . is it safe?" I asked.

She nodded. Then her eyes seemed to darken. "Define safe," she whispered, and drew me to her.

Afterward, there we lay, side by side on our backs, as if nothing, instead of everything, had changed. Heather reached for my hand.

"Oops," she said. "Now what?"

"Now, I don't know," I answered, honestly.

"Me, neither."

I gave her hand a squeeze.

"Coffee," I said.

Chapter 17

I served up two French-pressed Sumatras and two bowls of rough-cut oatmeal, drizzled with honey, and topped with sliced banana and Fuji apple. We avoided any heavy heart-to-hearts, by mutual agreement. Instead, as we ate, I told Heather of my concerns about Julius. I wanted her professional take on my employer's extreme mood and energy swings, not to mention last night's mysterious call.

"How advanced is the Parkinson's?"

"I can't really tell. Like I said, sometimes he's razor sharp, others, he's pretty loopy."

"Well, everything you're describing could be caused by the PD. I mean, it's a brain disease. The slurred speech. The freezing and lack of affect. And some people, especially in the later stages, do develop memory problems and a loss of mental clarity, though at his age, that can happen anyway. With PD, the main thing is to keep on top of the medicine."

"He has his caregiver, Otilia," I said. "Plus a boutique, live-in doctor."

"Then he should be fine."

I couldn't stop looking at her—the way her blonde hair cupped her face, the depth of blue in her eyes.

"What?" she smiled.

"Nothing. It's just—don't you have any flaws?"

For a split second, something darted from behind her eyes, some small fear perhaps. Then it was gone. She smiled across the table at me.

"We've all got flaws, Tenzing. Some are just harder to spot than others." She glanced at the clock. "Sorry, gotta go.

215

FYI, I have a crazy day ahead, between a pathological science seminar and this insane toxicology rotation."

My intuition tapped me on the shoulder. "You're doing toxicology?"

"Yeah. Why?"

I handed her the waxy backing. "Would you mind seeing if you can determine what this patch is for?"

"Sure. No problem." Heather stood up. "So, are we really doing this thing tomorrow?"

"What thing?" As I said it, I remembered. "Ah. The retreat . . ." I made a small face. Heather smiled.

"I know, right? It seemed like such a good idea a few days ago." She put on her coat. "Your call. I will if you will."

I so wanted to back out. I was feeling swamped with unfinished business. But the terrified faces of two teenagers—looking for treats and finding a stressed-out man with a gun—floated before me. I sighed.

"See you there. Nine A.M. sharp."

After Heather left, I jotted down her observations about Julius. Something still didn't feel right over there, but there were too many variables to lock in on one cause. I'd call him later, in any case, to check in.

My plan was to keep busy enough today to avoid thinking about how "taking things slow" with Heather had become anything but.

I put in a call to Mike.

"Hey," he said. "I thought you'd dumped me."

"Sorry. It's been pretty crazy around here."

"Me too. I got promoted to the one A.M. slot this weekend. That makes your old pal 'dj mk' super-cool, in case you're wondering. So what's up?"

"Can you come by this morning? I need some virtual-sleuthing. I'll throw in a Harpo's thin crust. With meat."

"On my way," he said.

I called in an order at Harpo's Oven for a large

pepperoni, sausage, and mushroom, thin crust, plus two Red Bulls. I knew Mike's dietary habits almost as well as my own.

I washed the breakfast dishes and set them to dry on my slotted wooden rack. Tank and I played five minutes of "chase the beam" with a red laser pointer, and I followed that with 35 minutes of weights and 10 more on the meditation cushion—if I was in for a full day of sitting tomorrow, I figured I could cheat a little today.

After a quick shower, I sat at my computer and organized all the Sadie information for Mike. I was getting much better on the Internet, but this next stage of the chase required the services of a genius-level computer jockey; one who made unerring leaps of logic and didn't mind engaging in a little unauthorized hacking. Mike was all this and more.

Next, I called Julius. He answered on the first ring.

"Tenzing," he said. "Just the person I wanted to talk to." His pronunciation was crisp this morning, his tone rigorous.

"Me, too. How are you doing?" I said.

"Fine, fine. Listen, I've been thinking things over, and I'm . . . I . . . well, quite frankly, I've decided I no longer need your services."

I said nothing. My right hand clenched into a fist. I uncurled it.

"Ten? Are you there?"

"Yes. Can you tell me why?"

"Yes. Quite. Well, it's just . . . " He started over. "I've spent most of my life chasing a ghost, Ten. That's not how I want to spend what little is left of it."

Again, I waited.

"Keep the money, of course." He was breathing a little faster now.

"Julius, you know I can't do that."

The next few words were delivered in a rushed whisper. "It has to be this way. Don't contact me again. I'm sorry. Good bye."

Tank must have picked up on my distress. He hopped onto my desk, and lay across the keyboard, facing me.

"Hgjjjjjjjjjjjjjjjjddddddddddkkkkkkkkkkk," he wrote.

"I know. Not good. Not good at all."

I peeled him off the keyboard and carried him onto the deck to ponder this unexpected news, just as Mike, long legs askew, motored up the driveway on his unique hybrid bike. The eRockit is skinny but streamlined, a little weird, and a lot street smart, exactly like its rider.

Mike pulled off his helmet. Not to be denied, his mop of dark hair immediately sprang to life, a wild crown of curls.

"Hey, boss. Hey, Tankster."

Mike grabbed his bulging commuter backpack of equipment and followed me inside. He started setting up his gear on the kitchen table.

"So, there's been a slight change of plans," I said. "Maybe."

Mike looked up.

"Julius Rosen just called me off the hunt. He told me to stop looking for Sadie."

"For real?"

I considered the question. For not-real was more accurate. Simply put, I knew Julius was lying to me about something. But I didn't know what, and I didn't know why.

"Technically, officially, I'm no longer hired to do this job. Are you okay with that?"

Mike's eyes glinted. "Off the proverbial grid. Now we're talking."

Mike hates when I hover, so I paid a visit to my carport. The heap of heavy garbage bags beckoned from the corner, and my Shelby sat waiting for a long overdue tune-up. Let's see: sift through overripe garbage or get my hands dirty cleaning an engine?

I glanced at my watch. I only had enough time for the latter. Oh, well.

I opened the hood of the Shelby and got to work. First, I wrapped the connectors and distributor in foil. Pulling on a pair of rubberized work-gloves, I doused a wet sponge with Simple Green and worked my way in, around, over and under all the tiny crevices, widgets, hoses, and pipes that made my Mustang run. Soon, the sponge was filthy. I ran it under the outdoor faucet and did a second round of scrubbing. After one more rotation, I was satisfied, and I hosed out the soapy insides until the water ran clear. I started the engine, and let it idle for about ten minutes, until most of the moisture had evaporated. Using a torn T-shirt, I wiped away every remaining droplet. I peeled off the foil, closed the hood, and gave the shiny yellow finish a pat. Next week, I'd change the oil.

"Thirty more seconds," Mike called to me, as I crossed the deck. "I'm about to snag something I've been chasing for an hour."

I stayed where I was, counting five slow, easy breaths while I waited.

"Oh, snap!" He pulled away from the computer and grinned at me. "Come and get it."

I sat beside him and studied the screen, which was now a map of Europe.

Mike had marked three places with red pushpin icons. He clicked on the first. Up came an image of what looked like a small European city, complete with cobblestones and a Gothic cathedral.

"Cobblestones. Nice touch, Watson." I said.

"Schwerin, Germany. This is how it looked at the end of World War Two."

"Never heard of it."

"Me, neither," he said, "but Sadie Rosen was sent to Schwerin, after the orphanage."

"So the Reinhold Milz family lived there?"

"Yes. Turns out they were quite prominent. Mostly in the cheese business."

"Do you have actual, reliable evidence Sadie was there?"

Another click, and another page—a computer scan of an ancient town hall record. On one of the lines, written in careful script, was the name Sadie Rose Milz, followed by: "adopted daughter of Reinhold Milz. Date of birth unknown."

She had found a family of sorts. I was glad. "Anything else?"

"Boss. Please." Mike's hands flew over the keyboard. My printer whirred on my desk. I crossed the living room, and grabbed a printout of the name and phone number of Ulrika Milz in Schwerin, Germany. I looked over at Mike.

"Ulrika?"

"Great-niece. Working number. Hey, it's the best I could do on an empty stomach. Hint hint."

"Right, I'll check on the pizza. And Mike, I mean it. You put Dr. Watson to shame." He had already moved on to the next challenge, but I could tell he was pleased.

The pizza was "On its-a way! Five-a minutes! Five-a minutes!" Let's-a hope.

I checked local time in Germany. It was 7 P.M. over there.

"Hey, Mike? Do I have conference calling?"

"Does a wooden horse have a hickory dick?"

I sighed. "Mike, a simple yes or . . ."

"Yes, Ten. You do. Just push the button on your phone—the one that says 'conference.'"

Call one: Martha Bohannon. Martha was home, and happy to translate. "Don't go away," I told her.

Call two: Ulrika Milz. Here goes nothing. I hit the conference button and initiated a second call, this one to Germany. A few moments later a female voice said, "Hallo?"

"Martha?" Martha trotted out some German. I heard "Ulrika Milz?"

"*Ja,*" the voice said. "*Ich bin Ulrika.*"

"*Sprechen sie Englisch?*" said Martha.

Now I knew two German phrases.

"Yah," Ulrika answered slowly, a thick accent coating her pronunciation, "but not so well. What this is about?"

I jumped in and introduced Martha and myself. "I would like to ask you some questions about Sadie, a little girl from long ago," I said.

Ulrika fired off an excited stream of German. I heard "Sadie" several times.

Martha translated. "She says certainly she remembers little Sadie. She says, 'Who could forget the way she looked at you with those clear, gray eyes?'"

Martha asked another question in German. The response was long and involved. Toward the end, Ulrika's voice sank, as if weighted by sadness.

"Oh," Martha said. "Okay. Shorthand? Sadie was with Ulrika's great-aunt for almost a year, until something *schrecklich,* umm, terrible happened."

"*Schrecklich! Ja. Schrecklich,*" Ulrika echoed, and rattled off another few sentences. I heard Martha's sharp intake of breath, and feared the worst.

"Mr. and Mrs. Milz were killed in a bad car accident," Martha said. "Sadie was with them."

"And Sadie?"

"Sadie survived."

That poor child. She'd endured more hardship and loss by the time she was six than most of us faced in a lifetime.

"Who took care of Sadie after that?" I asked.

Martha translated the question. Ulrika spoke quietly for nearly a minute.

Martha said, "Here's the gist. None of the other family members could take Sadie. According to Ulrika, different groups were combing Europe looking for survivors, especially children. She says a small group from one organization came to talk to Sadie. They concluded she was a Jewish refugee and took her away with them. Ulrika says nobody in the family ever heard from her again."

We digested this information in a silence, broken only by Ulrika's halting English: "I am hoping you . . . *finding?"*

"Find," Martha said.

"Yah. I am hoping you finding her."

We said our goodbyes and hung up. I called Martha right back. "Thank you. You have no idea how helpful this is."

"You have no idea what a treat this is," she replied. "To be useful, I mean, outside of changing diapers and reading *The Cat in the Hat* for the seventy-five thousandth time."

"Hugs to the hooligans."

I returned to Mike and stood there until he registered my presence and surfaced from his computer trance. I'm always afraid if I interrupt too abruptly he'll get the mental bends.

"Breaking news," I said. "I need Jewish charitable organizations with the mission of reclaiming Jewish children during or right after the war, in this case, from Northern Germany. According to Ulrika, Sadie got picked up by one of them."

He nodded, his fingers already airborne. Then Mike began to mutter. When Mike mutters, it's a very hopeful thing. I felt a little thrill in my belly as I sat beside him.

Like a concert pianist, he lifted his fingers from the keyboard with a flourish. He pointed to the screen. "Looks like there are quite a few. Any way to narrow it down?"

"Let me check."

I called Martha.

"I'm talking to you more than my husband," she said.

"This is a quick one. Did Ulrika say anything specific about the group that picked up Sadie?"

"Not really. Wait a minute, she did use the word *fremd."*

"What's that mean? Friendly?"

"No. Foreign. As in not German. She didn't seem to like them very much."

"Okay, thanks, that helps."

"You're welcome. Ten?" Martha's voice took on a tone I knew well, the not-to-be-denied tone. "Bill and I just had an interesting little chat on the phone. Are you planning on telling me about your new friend any time soon?"

"My new . . . ?"

"Don't be coy, it's not becoming. Heather. The good doctor Heather." I couldn't even blame Bill. Martha was a bloodhound when it came to sniffing out potential girl-friends, and Bill was a lousy liar.

"Oh. Heather. Well. Nothing much to tell, really."

Martha snorted. "You guys are all the same. You have no idea how much 'nothing much' actually means."

Ooph. I hung up fast. Mike's look was pointed. I pur-posely misunderstood.

"You should concentrate on any non-German Jewish organizations that paid visits to northern Germany, spe-cifically Schwerin, in 1946," I said, as the crunch of tires announced a timely delivery. The boxy little Harpo's Oven Cube rolled to a stop. Soon Mike was loaded up with pizza, Red Bull, and a new data trail to track.

My phone buzzed. Bill.

"Hey, traitor," I said. "Remind me never to give you any state secrets."

"You know Martha. There isn't a double-agent out there she couldn't crack."

We laughed.

"Want to join me for lunch? I'm thinking Mexican, spe-cifically, La Cantinela, on First Street in Boyle Heights. The boys say we might find some interesting customers there. Can you get there in an hour?"

"What's the plan?" I asked.

"Fuck if I know."

"Oh, goodie," I said. "My favorite kind." I left Mike hunched over his screen, Tank watching him from the windowsill.

This was a job for me, my Wilson Combat, and my clean-engined Shelby Mustang. I wasn't getting caught with my pants down again. Within the hour, I was at the restaurant. I circled around to the back and cruised by its private parking lot, set in a narrow alley. A young attendant stood guard over luxury Beamers, Mercedes Benz SUVs, and a couple of high-end, fully loaded choppers. I checked, but I didn't see Pretty Boy's there.

I looped around again, and found Bill one block south, on the opposite side of the street. He had a clear sightline to the front of the restaurant. La Cantinela was a pristine stucco and stone structure the warm color of saffron. Like a beauty queen flanked by bums, it was tucked between a grimy pawnshop and a dilapidated check-cashing facility, both heavily tagged with the angry calling cards of rival gangs.

I pulled in behind Bill, glanced up and down the block, and slipped from my car into his. My Wilson lay snug under my windbreaker, tucked in the Jackass rig shoulder holster. Bill scanned La Cantinela with binoculars.

"Can't see a fucking thing," he grunted.

"I have an idea," I said. "There's a private lot in the back. How about you position yourself near there, in case anybody decides to do a quick split, while I go inside for a look."

He thought that one over. "You know what I call that kind of plan?"

"What?"

"I call it 'Ten having all the fun.'"

"Maybe, but what I don't have is Thing One and Thing Two back at home."

We'd had this debate before. I had a high desire to make sure Bill was around for the next 20 years. He had an equally high desire to prove that having kids hadn't blunted his edge.

"How about this? Give me ten minutes. If you don't see anyone taking off, including me, you can join me inside."

"Deal." Bill put away the binoculars and stuck on a Dodger cap. "Do I still look like a cop?"

"Yeah, a cop in a Dodger cap."

He headed for the back alley. I strolled across First and up the block, and pushed inside the carved wooden doors marking the entrance. It may have been midday, but the room was dim. My eyes adjusted. The owner obviously had a lot of disposable income to spend on décor—the walls and floor were a stunning interplay of decorative tile and distressed wood. The hand-carved booths and tables were peopled with mostly well-dressed clientele of every nationality. Not your usual gangland eatery.

I noticed an opening in the far wall, the size and shape of a large picture frame. It overlooked the busy kitchen, where cooks in hairnets chopped, fried, and folded various ingredients. A waitress passed me with a tray of sizzling, skewered shrimp surrounded by an assortment of salsas. The scent made me rethink everything I thought I knew about shellfish and Mexican food. I wondered if being a vegetarian was such a good idea after all.

A dark-eyed beauty hurried up. "Do you have a reservation?"

"Didn't know I needed one," I answered.

"I'm sorry," she said. "We're fully booked."

I leaned closer. "Chaco didn't say anything about making a reservation."

She stared. "Wait here," she said.

She scurried across the restaurant, ducked into a side door, and reappeared inside the kitchen. I drifted left, shifting my viewpoint, until I found her again, standing over a table at the back of the kitchen itself. Six men were seated at the table. She was bent close, talking to one who sat with his back to me. He was of stocky build, and his hair was slicked into a kind of ducktail. Something about him seemed familiar. Intensity radiated from him in waves. I sensed it from across the room.

Turn around. Turn around so I can get a good look at you.

He made a small gesture, and the girl shot a glance in my direction.

"*Vayase,*" a voice hissed in my ear.

Way to stay alert, Tenzing. He was about my age, but a lot worse for wear, with flat, high cheekbones, teeth rotted by a steady diet of meth, and a Gila monster tat curled around his neck. He was so in my face, I could have tallied up his acne scars for extra credit.

"That means get lost," he said.

"What about my lunch?"

"Sorry. Kitchen closed."

"Fine. I'll just get a beer," I said.

"Bar closed, too." He moved even closer. He reeked. I thought about pulling my gun on him then and there. With body odor this deadly, I'd get off on self-defense.

Instead, I backed off. I didn't want him to feel the Wilson rigged against my chest. No need to pour accelerant on the situation, especially with Bill two minutes from joining me.

"No problem. I'm going," I said.

"Good," he said, and started to walk away, his limp pronounced.

"Hey, Daniel?"

He turned, startled.

"Thunder sends his best."

Before he could respond, I slipped outside and trotted around back to grab Bill.

"Time for us to vayase," I said.

CHAPTER 18

We drove to Langer's for a late lunch. Jean herded us to a corner booth and loaded us up with coffee. I ordered an egg salad sandwich, and Bill went with his usual, pastrami with pastrami, and a side of pastrami. I provided Bill with a soundtrack to the silent drama I'd watched in the kitchen.

"So you think it was Chaco?"

"I never saw his face, but I'd say yes. Whoever he was, he was 'the Man' in there. And the presence of Daniel Morales is definitely suspicious." I frowned. "I keep feeling like I've seen that guy Chaco before."

"Mug shot? He's been around a while."

"Maybe."

Jean plopped down our plates. She put her hands on her hips. "Ten-zing, don't be mad, but look what I got."

She pulled a little keychain out of her pocket. I squinted at the logo.

"L.A. County Sheriff's Department? Jean, how could you go to the other side?" LAPD and County have kept a nice little feud going for years.

"Sheriff Baca gave it to me," she said. "You're not the only regular in here." She lowered her voice. "He also gave me a little pillbox. Empty, unfortunately. Should I be worried?'

I laughed.

"Only if he asks you out for dinner."

A man shouted from a nearby table. "Hey! Sweet Cheeks! Little service here, please?"

I met Jean's eye. "You want Bill and me to help that fellow with his attitude?"

"Now, now, Ten-zing. You know what I always say. 'Bless them, change me.'" Jean headed for the diner, armed with a smile.

"Have you ever considered a career change," I called after her. "His Holiness the Dalai Lama is looking to retire soon."

Bill's phone buzzed.

"Yeah? Yeah. Be right there." He stood up. "Captain needs me. Another gang-banger just turned up dead. Fifth this month."

"Any idea what gang?"

"Does it matter?" He strode out.

I was itching to take action on some front, any front. I called Mike from the parking lot.

"Do you know," he said, "that there are about eight hundred Sadie Rosens in the world, and nine of them live in Beverly Hills?"

"No, I did not know that," I said. "Any luck on the refugee groups?"

"Maybe," he said. "You can't rush genius, boss." He yawned. "I'm beat. I'll get back on this tomorrow, okay?"

"Sleep tight." I was getting another call. "Hello?'

"Hey, Ten. It's Clancy. Clancy Williams."

I waited.

"So listen, sorry about bailing on you the other day. I mean, fuck. Look at what I spend my days doing. I don't have a leg to stand on when it comes to moral superiority."

"Who does?" I said.

"So anyway, I've been keeping an eye on the Rudolph home, but Harper's pretty much been in lock-down since her one little escapade."

I counted the days.

"Right. They're still sitting shivah."

"So I was just wondering if you, uh, if you can point me to some other work? I'll do anything. Stake out anyone, anywhere." He swallowed. "I'm desperate, man. The wife and I had a little sit-down today. We're four months behind on the mortgage, and the bank won't budge. Three years ago they couldn't throw enough money at us, and now . . ."

"I can send you a couple hundred," I said. "For work done."

"Nah," Clancy said. "Thanks, man, but a couple hundred isn't going to cut it. I should pay you, for making me feel useful for once. Just keep me in mind for the future, a'right? And let me know how it all turns out." He hung up gently, another potential drowning victim of the current financial tsunami.

It was too late for the freeway, so I tacked and jibbed down Sunset. I was almost at Pacific Coast Highway when my phone made a booping text-received sound. I needed gas anyway, so I pulled into the 76 Station at the base of Sunset. I checked the phone screen.

ARE YOU OUT OF YOUR FUCKING MIND? It read.

Well, maybe, but I didn't much care for the tone. Then my phone buzzed, announcing an incoming call.

"Hello?"

"You get my text?" The voice belonged to Raul Martinez, aka Charles Raul Montoya, biker-lawyer extraordinaire.

"Yes."

"Well, then, let me ask you again, hombre. Are you out of your fucking mind?"

Nobody'd ever called me "hombre" before. I tried it on for size. Hombre. Hombre Norbu. I liked it.

"Why didn't you stay the hell away from those guys?" he pleaded and let out a sound somewhere between a grunt and a hiccup. It occurred to me he might be drunk.

"Raul, what's going on?"

"Aw, fuck," he said. A gull cried in the background.

"Where are you?" I asked.

"I'm up on the bluffs. Point Dume. You know it? S'beautiful here," he slurred.

"What are you doing there?"

"None of your business." He breathed heavily into the phone. "Not that it matters. I'm fucked from here to Sunday, either way." He faded into silence.

Yeshe believes four simple words, when asked sincerely, are the fastest path to right action in certain situations, especially tricky ones.

It was worth a try.

"How can I help?"

"How can *you* help?" His laugh was bitter. "*You* want to help *me*."

"You called me. Why?"

He said nothing.

I waited.

He sighed. "I want to get out."

The moment had an electric quality. My skin tingled. A threshold had been crossed. I looked across the highway to the slow-rolling waves—the same waves Raul was watching. A flock of pelicans swooped and spun over the water.

"I'm looking out at the ocean," I said. "I wonder where those waves started out."

"Somewhere north. Alaska, maybe." There was a long pause. "I hear it's pretty there."

"So, you want out," I said.

"Yeah, but with this *hijo de puta*, you don't just turn in a letter of resignation, tell him you're moving on."

"Right," I said. "It's complicated."

He made a little half laugh. "Complicated. No shit." I heard him take a swig of something.

"How about if I come to you?" I asked. "I can be there in fifteen minutes. We'll talk this through."

"Don't bother," he said. "They'll never let me out. Not how it works, you know? I got nobody to blame but me—I dealt my own goddamned hand. This is it."

This is it. I put things together: the call, the drinking, the cliff. He was about to play the last card over which he had any control, the suicide card. I jumped in the car and peeled onto the coast highway. I plugged in my Bluetooth earpiece so I wouldn't lose him. I figured I was about fifteen miles from Point Dume.

"Talk to me," I said. "Tell me what's going on."

"Tenshin. What kind of name is that?" he asked.

"Tibetan." I pronounced it for him. "Now you try." But his tongue was two swigs past the point of navigation.

"Just call me Ten," I said.

"Might as well call me Charlie, then. My mother gave me that name."

"You're going back to your roots?"

"I guess you have to someday, don't you?"

I said nothing.

"You and me, we're not so different," he added.

That was news to me, but I was too busy steering through Malibu at a high speed to disagree.

"The way I see it, we're both refugees. Both trying to get to someplace, and away from someplace else at the same time. I saw that in you, up there at the Getty."

I never turn down an insight, no matter what the source. It did feel odd, though, to be seen so clearly by a drunk thug preparing to jump off a cliff.

"I know what I'm running from," he said, "but what's a guy like you running from?"

A guy like me?

"What kind of a guy is that?" I asked.

His words drifted over the phone. "You know—a guy trying to do the right thing. A good guy. I never could figure out how that game worked. How did I get here?"

"Same way we get anywhere. You can figure it out now, Charlie. You got where you are one small, bad choice at a time. You can make a different choice, right here. Right now."

His breath wheezed into my ear.

"Charlie?" The quick double-beep signaled a lost connection. I urged my car forward. *Come on! Come on!* The coastal road left the ocean and curved inland. I hooked the

Shelby up Westward Beach Road and wound around to the public parking lot. Above me, high-end homes with beach views sprinkled the hillside. Below lay the curved sandy bay known as Smuggler's Cove. Set between the two, the scrubby cliffs and jutting headland of Point Dume State Preserve. I jumped out of my car and ran to the end of the lot, where the trail began. The sun was lower in the sky, and the empty asphalt was streaked with light and shadow. I was relieved to see a custom Harley, with its S&S twin-cylinder engine, parked at the base of the trail, across from a dumpster. The rest of the lot was empty—it was November and close to closing time.

I jogged along a sandy footpath, past scrubby chaparral and succulent ground cover, and darted up the trail as it narrowed and grew steeper alongside the rock-faced point. Soon the sharp incline was bracketed by thick wire hand-holds, and stapled with railway ties. I slipped and skidded and cursed my leather-soled shoes. Close to the tip of the point, a lone figure took shape. Charles Raul Montoya, Esq. was perched on the edge of the promontory. He had climbed past the lookout deck with its cozy bench and safety railing. He was clutching a bottle of tequila, staring out to sea.

I stepped onto the deck, catching my breath. I didn't want to startle him, so I called out softly.

"Charlie?"

He swung his head around. He nodded once, swiped the mouth of the bottle with his sleeve, and held it out to me.

I shook my head. "No thanks."

He looked confused. "You won't drink with me?" He sounded more hurt than angry.

"Sorry. I've never tried hard liquor," I said, "and now's not the time to start." He shrugged and took another pull. I sat down on the wooden bench, next to a pair of binoculars—Barska Gladiator zooms. Someone—Charlie—had abandoned them there.

"Join me?"

After a moment, he stepped away from the rocky lip of cliff, and made his stumbling way back onto the wooden lookout deck. He sat next to me. A sea bird screeched overhead, and we followed its flight, low over the water. Just two guys watching a gull on an early November afternoon.

"We got ourselves into some deep shit here, hombre," Charlie said. "But maybe there's still time for you to climb out."

"Tell me what's going on," I said, "and I'll decide if I want to."

He shook his head slowly. "You act like you have a choice. It's too big."

"Too big for what?"

"Too big for anybody who isn't a billionaire or a stone-cold killer."

I chose my words carefully. "I think you're telling me Chaco Morales has got a deal underway that teams up big money and murder. Is that what you're saying?"

He nodded. "That table in the kitchen at La Cantinela? Every one of those guys has innocent blood on his hands. Men, women, children, you name it. Chaco, his brother, Pepé, and their boys took down a whole village in the Sierra Madre, back when he was building his business. Shot them and loaded the bodies up, well, just the heads, actually, and delivered them to the biggest town in the region. Seventy heads, stuck on pikes. Think he had any trouble getting the area organized after that?"

"How did you know I was at La Cantinela?" I asked. "How did you know I saw that table?"

"Chaco's nephew Daniel called. 'I just met a guy,' he said, and described you to a T. 'That the guy we've been hearing about?' he asks me."

"What did you say?"

"After I got through crapping my pants I said, 'Yeah, that's him.' And Daniel says 'Chaco told you to scare him off, but he don't look too scared to me.'"

"Then what did you do?"

"I bought myself two pints of tequila and came here to pay my respects. This is sacred land, you know. Chumash tribe. My great-grandmother was part Chumash. I can think of worse places to die."

"Me, too," I said. "But maybe not today, okay? How about I give you a lift to a motel? You can take a hot shower. Call your daughters. Get some rest. You can come back for the chopper later."

He studied the horizon. "Yeah," he said, "maybe." I followed his gaze, and located a tiny flat smudge—like a distant hyphen on the water. Charlie started to reach for the binoculars. Then he changed his mind. He met my eyes, his hollow. "I got something for you. A present."

"What kind of present?" The way he said it made me nervous. I was glad for the gun, snug under my arm.

"Information. Something that's going to piss you off—a con they're all running on you."

"Who's 'they'? Chaco? Marv?"

"You're the fancy detective," he said. "You figure it out." He fished around in his jeans pocket and came out with a small key. He handed it to me.

"Lockbox on my bike. Get what's in there for me? I think I'm too drunk to make the hike just yet."

"Sure."

I skidded downhill to Charlie's chopper. The sun was slanting sharply now. I located the lockbox, bolted onto the back of the frame. A small fragment of my brain registered that one of the Harley's fiberglass saddlebags was hanging open. Empty . . .

Crack! The sharp report of a .44 Mag split the dusk in two. My ears rattled like tin as I heard Charlie shouting. A second blast rang out as I dove and rolled. A huge puff of sand kicked up to my left, and I tasted grit. Someone out there was big game hunting, and I was the rogue elephant.

I grabbed for my .38 as I swept my eyes over the hillside.

Where are you? I heard Charlie cry out and another *crack!* I scrabbled onto all fours. *Whang!* A bullet tore through the metal skin of the Harley's fuel tank, maybe two feet from my head. I swung my Wilson upward, about to take a shot. *No. Don't. People live up there.* I did a tuck and roll over the bike, onto the sandy asphalt behind it. *Take cover!* My eyes whipped across the lot. *There is no cover.* A steady stream of gasoline spilled out of the tank and onto the metal motor casing. I focused on the dumpster, about ten yards away. I pushed into a crouch and did a quick zig and zag across the open space. *Crack!* The next bullet must have grazed the fuel tank. The bike exploded into flames. A blast of heat bit the back of my neck as I wrenched open the lid and dove inside the dumpster. I thought about how 44 mag bullets could pass through metal like a knife through warm butter. I burrowed deeper.

Dead silence, except for the hard pant of my breath. My nose registered the stench of rotting fruit, stale beer, plus some other things I didn't want to identify. I stifled a gag, as my trip-hammer heartbeat finally began to slow. I dialed 911, and then Bill.

"Stay put," Bill said.

Right.

After a few minutes, I had to look. I pushed up the lid of the dumpster, only an inch or two. No movement that I could see. I gulped the sea air, as my eyes found the Harley. The flame had died off. The burnt carcass of the chopper looked like an incinerated scorpion. But somehow, the lockbox still seemed intact, and the key was still in my pocket. I lifted the lid higher. I sighted my gun and swept it across the lot, and up into the hills. Nothing. The shooter, too, had gone underground.

Shouts broke out. Happy man-shouts. Welcome shouts, under the circumstances. A swarm of bicyclists, all wearing helmets and dressed in colorful Lycra tights, sped along the hillside road above me, spread out like colorful prayer flags.

They paused to take in the view, and then pedaled away. Maybe they'd scared my hunter off.

I stayed where I was, as silence settled in their wake. I counted ten long breaths, then ten more. A faint siren wailed in the distance. I listened. *Yes. Getting closer.*

Okay. Enough.

I clambered out of my smelly safehold. I ran to the lock-box, worked the key into the lock, and turned. It released, and I forced the slightly jammed lid open. I pulled out a quart-sized Ziploc bag as a fire engine, followed by two L.A. county sheriff's patrol cars, tore into the parking lot. I shoved the bag in my pocket. It was Charlie's present to me, and I'd earned it. Then I ran back up to the deck, before the sheriffs spotted me. "Charlie? Charlie!"

Nothing.

My eyes fell on the binoculars. I used them to scan the area. My heart caught at a figure holding his arms up, but it was a cactus.

"Charlie Montoya!"

The quiet was ominous. I lowered the binoculars, and looked out at the ocean. My eyes narrowed. The dark smudge seemed a little larger. I raised the binoculars and focused. A long narrow fishing boat filled my vision—maybe thirty feet long. No cabin that I could see, only two little outboard motors, side by side.

My phone buzzed.

"Hey, Bill."

"I'm here. Where the hell are you? I thought I told you to stay put."

"In a dumpster? No thanks. Take the footpath up." In a few minutes Bill was by my side, huffing from the climb. We went looking for Charlie, as I did my best to explain the sequence of events. Bill grunted a few times, but mostly just listened. We picked our way across the scrubby ground and inched to the lip of the promontory. We looked down.

Charlie lay in a still, spread-eagled heap, far below. A

gory carnation bloomed in the middle of his back. The force of the bullet must have blown him over the edge as he was trying to run away. Or maybe he decided to jump after all, and the shooter just gave him an extra push. I would never know. The sand around Charlie was soaked dark. His legs and neck were bent at odd angles—the sight of his broken bones bothered me more than the blood.

Bill got on his phone. I gazed at the sprawl of body, motionless on the beach.

How can I help?

You can't.

I thought about Charlie giving me the key to his lockbox. One small, good choice, before he died. Maybe I had helped after all. I closed my eyes and offered this: *Through the merit you have accumulated, however small, may all your hopes be fulfilled in an instant. Om mani padme hum.*

"Okay," Bill said. "I called off the ambulance. He clearly doesn't need one." Bill scratched at his head. "This crime scene is going to be a mother. Get ready for a couple of hours of explaining, Ten. No way to avoid it."

"I know," I said.

Bill's mouth twitched.

"Just so you know, the county coroner's on his way. With Heather. You might want to think about rinsing off. You smell like a sewer."

The next couple hours crawled by at a miserable pace, as I told my story over and over to the Malibu/Lost Hills Sheriff's Department. Deputies sifted through chaparral, looking for footprints and bullet casings. Others combed the cordoned-off, lush gardens and side-yards of Cliffside Drive, as worried residents peered from behind their curtains. The gated community was home to Hollywood royalty, secreted in some of the priciest real estate in Malibu, so the powers that be weren't taking any chances. Nobody looked in my pockets. And nobody found my shooter, either. Chaco's guys had a disconcerting way of melting into thin air.

Heather arrived just as I was leaving. She moved as if to give me a hug.

I held her off with one arm.

"Sorry," I said. "But after half an hour in a dumpster, I not only feel like crap, I smell like it. Better stand downwind."

She nodded. "Thanks for the warning. You okay?"

"I'm okay. Just beat."

"Will I see you tomorrow?"

"I'll see you tomorrow."

Bill caught the end of our exchange.

"Hot date?" he asked, as he walked me to my car.

I thought about what lay ahead. Eight hours of enforced sitting and noble silence.

"Something like that."

Charlie's "present" was calling to me from my pocket. A few miles past Point Dume, I pulled into a deserted parking lot. I opened the baggie and scanned the contents as well as I could—the Shelby's dome light is pretty dim. What I was hoping for was a neon sign's worth of unmistakable answers to all my questions. What I got was a smudged, hand-scrawled list, at first glance in some sort of Spanish code, and what appeared to be a scrap of material wrapped in plastic. Both required a lot more light and a far fresher brain to decipher further. I tucked the baggie back in my pocket and pulled onto Pacific Coast Highway, no wiser.

CHAPTER 19

Tank was not happy. His personal butler was not only late, he smelled like a toxic waste dump. If a cat's nose can be said to wrinkle, Tank's did. But what he didn't know was that I was packing liver.

On the way home I'd stopped off at Harpo's Oven for a pizza to go—this one all for me. All I'd had to do was walk in and Harpo knew to shout "Double mushroom, pesto sauce, pan-style, large" to the kid in the back. Then I'd nipped next door to the butcher shop. After such a long, unexplained absence, it was going to take more than love to repair my relationship with my feline friend. The butcher and I have an understanding. He had reached into the cold case and brought out a little half pint of calves liver trimmings to go. He'd refused to charge me, as usual, and as usual I'd assured him that the merit of his action promised wealth beyond measure. I'd picked up my pizza and headed home.

Now I revealed the glistening treasure to Tank. His eyes glazed over, and he rolled onto his back. A four-legged salute was more than I could have hoped for. I dished out the liver trimmings. Tank fell upon them like a savage, and I did the same with my pizza, washing it down with a Sam Adams, straight out of the bottle.

It was late, and I craved a hot shower more than *samadhi*. But the Marv trail was getting colder by the minute, and I'd already done some time today in trash. It only made sense to finish my sentence before getting clean.

I had parked in the driveway, leaving the carport empty—you need a well-ventilated space for this job. Now I spread out a tarp, and clamped two spotlights overhead, positioning them for maximum visibility. I dragged the black bags to the middle of the tarp, pulled on a painter's mask and thin blue latex gloves, and started scavenging.

I soon knew a lot of useless information about the upstanding residents of Robinsgrove: there were snorers (nose strips), mothers (diapers), diabetics (syringes), and debtors (late-payment notices); gossipers (*In Touch* subscriptions), dieters (Getslim meal containers), drinkers (tallboys), and dog-owners (don't ask). Lots of flossers of teeth and grinders of coffee beans. A few smart souls knew enough to shred their paperwork, but most disposed of everything casually, exposing their innermost identities to scrutiny without a second thought. I sifted and separated the soggy waste, an archeologist on a dig from hell, but turned up no clues as to Tovah's life, or Marv's for that matter—either Marv was an expert at covering their tracks, or Tovah had forgotten to take out the trash. There was no joy at all, in fact, until my fingers recognized something inside one little plastic bag, and my heart hammered in response to the find.

I held up the two rectangular waxy covers, familiar backings to as-yet-unidentified patches. I went very still inside as I tried to digest this information. *Impossible. Must be a coincidence.* But any good detective will tell you that coincidences, like vampires, don't survive long if exposed to sunlight. I bagged the backings and tackled the rest of the trash with renewed energy.

I was rewarded again, this time with a Hollywood gem. I had pulled out a pile of discarded fashion magazines, their pages glued together by moisture, and was flipping through them, when a three-holed script, pages dangling from a single brass brad, turned up mid-stack. The damp pages were well thumbed, and most of the corners were turned down. I looked at the cover and whooped at the title. I was now the proud owner of my own personal copy of *Loving Hagar.*

That was it, but it was enough. I refilled the bags and

stuffed as many as I could into my own garbage cans, carefully separating the recycling from the rest. I loaded the remaining trash in the trunk of the Toyota and delivered them to a dumpster I knew of down the hill—in my mind, I was merely fulfilling their original fate.

Back at home, I barraged my skin with hot water, soaping away every last remnant of a long, stinky day. I set my alarm for 6 A.M.—that would give me a whopping five hours of shut-eye—and collapsed next to my softly snoring cat.

A high-pitched *meow*, accompanied by the prick of claws kneading my thigh, told me I had slept past the alarm, and then some. I squinted at the clock; it was 7:15.

I bolted out of bed, pulling on clothes, cursing my late night activities. I dumped two cans of mixed grill into Tank's bowl. His look was so piteous I ran into the living room and hastily rearranged his fort, adding another chair and towel to expand his choices of places to hide.

I drove my Mustang as if possessed, and squeezed into a space two blocks past the Sweet Spirit Meditation Center, 30 minutes late, and anything but sweet of spirit.

I added my shoes to the pile outside and tiptoed into the hall. A woman in her 50s, with close-cropped hair, a gray cotton jumpsuit, and an easy manner, was sitting on a cushion set on a slightly raised platform at the front of the room. She was addressing the group of about 50 people, some on the floor on cushions, others in chairs lined along the walls. The resident red-robed Western monk was right by the door. He smiled, handed me a schedule and a hard, round cushion, and motioned toward a spot in the back row between two sheepish-looking middle-aged men, trying to get comfortable on their own hard cushions. I looked the crowd over, and soon spotted a perky blonde ponytail. Heather was in the front row. Well rah-rah for her.

I took a deep breath and used the long exhale to send my hostility outside, where it belonged. I was here. I was doing this. I had almost put a bullet in a teenager the other day and almost taken one myself yesterday. Maybe this woman could help me.

"Listen, I understand," the teacher was saying. "I was in law enforcement for twenty-five years. We all shut down emotionally around stress. How many of you have found yourselves turning to alcohol, drugs, even infidelity just to cope?" She put up her hands. "Don't answer that question. God knows I didn't, at my first retreat."

Everyone laughed, and the room opened up a little. I glanced at the schedule. The leader's name was Marcie Whitney. I had missed most of her opening remarks. I was sorry I had.

"This day isn't about changing human nature," Marcie said. "And it certainly isn't about me telling you guys how to do your jobs. It's about acquiring tools—tools for examining our intentions, our hidden biases. It's an invitation to approach your work not with anger and cynicism, but with love and fierce compassion."

There it was again. That word, *fierce.*

A red-faced man squirming in his chair raised his hand. "This is bullshit, pardon my French. You should see the scum I deal with every day. I'm here because I have to be—the brass wants me to manage my anger better. Manage it, not get rid of it." He snorted. "Only tool I really need is my Beretta."

Marcie nodded. "I respect that. No one is asking you to put away your gun. But I would ask you this. Who do you think is better at serving and protecting, someone blinded by anger and fear, or someone centered and taking action from a mindful place?"

She had a point.

She invited us to close our eyes and led us into a process of counting breaths while allowing thoughts, a process deeply familiar to me. The initial restlessness around me settled—I never ceased to be amazed at how quickly the simple act of closing one's eyes and counting breaths resulted in ease—and I soon sank into a place of deep relaxation, all the more powerful because it was multiplied by the power of 50. *I take refuge in the sangha.*

I've missed this.

The morning was a seamless flow of sitting and walking meditations, and I slipped into the silence as easily as if it were a warm bath. At lunchtime, we were given a few simple instructions in mindful eating. I had run out of my door without breakfast, so the flavor released with every slow, thoughtful bite was enhanced by my appetite. Even so, I couldn't remember when I'd last enjoyed a meal so much. Heather and I sat next to each other, our eyes lowered to our plates. She was focused and serious about eating mindfully, like a little girl learning to trace. I smiled inside.

She gets it.

My heart gave a little twist and cracked open. Sweet appreciation, like warm syrup, spilled out of my center and widened its path to include Heather.

Heather put down her fork. She pressed her hand to her heart. She closed her eyes, inhaling deeply, and smiled. Then she turned to look at me, as if to say, "Whatever it is you're doing, don't stop."

She gets me.

We followed lunch with another walking meditation in the garden area. Placing light attention on the lift and press of each foot, I paced a ten-foot path between a stone bench and a clump of rose bushes. I guess my banished hostility decided to camp out behind the bushes, because within minutes, resistance started nipping at my heels, followed closely by doubt, worry, and the howling hounds of horniness. *This is a waste of time. Who are these people? Why am I here? I need to get back to work. Look at those curves—maybe I can get Heather to spend the night tonight. What if she won't? What if she never does again?*

I paused, to regroup. I looked around. Everybody but Heather had taken on the shape and personality of deluded fools. She, on the other hand, looked like a tantric goddess. I recognized my wild mind from long sits in Dharamshala: the Buddha talked of the five hindrances to meditation, and except for sluggishness, I was, as Bill might put it, batting a thousand.

The sluggishness hit the instant we returned to the hall, and I spent most of the next sit with my chin on my chest. But right toward the end, the fatigue dissolved, and my mind opened into a wonderful, spacious clarity. I decided to take advantage of it and do a little work.

I mentally addressed a few of the many uncertainties regarding my case. Once in a while, if I phrase the questions just right, the answers come spontaneously, as if they already lay waiting, right beneath the surface of my mind.

Who is running a con on me?

What is the con?

Are Marv and Julius connected?

How?

I came up blank, four times.

Instead, an observation pushed its way forward, a painful one that had lurked in the background like a lingering sore. *We're both refugees. Both trying to get to someplace and away from someplace else at the same time.* Charlie's words had struck a minor chord in me. I rephrased them: What am I running from? I let the question resonate and then let it go.

Longing for Yeshe and Lobsang pierced my heart area. They would surely know the answer—they understood me better than anyone. The three of us had shared a bond so close growing up that we'd practically heard each other's thoughts, read each other's intentions. Like any other close-knit crew of kids, we'd had each other's backs.

I smiled, remembering our favorite game, *sgom rgyab*, a game that would probably mystify most children. The name meant "meditation," but we played it with a twist. First, we'd put a bunch of random objects in a box—anything from chunks of turquoise, to feathers, to pictures of cars torn from magazines. We'd meditate for 15 minutes or so to get tuned up. Then, taking turns, whoever was "it" would reach into the box, select one object, mentally "picture" it, and attempt to send the image telepathically to the others. Whoever correctly identified the most items won.

It wasn't Angry Birds, or Wii tennis, but we worked with what we had.

Once we hit puberty, we started linking up telepathically for more practical purposes. If one of us had a problem with a teacher, "one of us" meaning me, the other two would link up telepathically to neutralize the situation. And when Lobsang and I started getting pimples, we linked up with ever-clear Yeshe, letting our skin learn from his how to be blemish-free. Call it crazy, but the pimples didn't stand a chance; our skin was usually clear within a week.

You're wandering. Come home again. I gently returned to my breath. The outer edges of my mind melted. I entered a deep domain of spirit and light, both above and below the surface ramblings.

Yeshe. Lobsang. Are you there?

I opened up to our shared field.

Unh!

Instead of expanding into that familiar home-space, it was as if I'd crashed into a wall. I took a few conscious breaths and tried again. *Yeshe?* Nothing. *Lobsang?* A bolt of fear jolted my core. What had happened to them? "Slowly, mindfully, become aware of the body," I heard. "Take your time."

I tried to breathe through the tightness in my chest and shoulders. Rinpoche used to warn us never to end a sitting with residual fear or anger—we might end up wearing it for the rest of the day, like a thick *chuba*. I rolled my shoulders, inhaling, exhaling. The coat of worry was still pretty heavy.

I realized Marcie was giving a few more simple

instructions. We were finishing up the afternoon with a loving-kindness meditation practice, known as *metta*.

Maybe that would help.

She asked us to close our eyes, and settle into an awareness of our breath. To feel into our heart area. Then she asked us to picture the person in our lives who most easily opened our hearts. The furry face of a Persian Blue wiggled his whiskers at me. *Tank.* I sent him a series of wishes for safety, joy, strength, and ease.

Next, she asked us to expand our loving-kindness to a mentor . . .

Bill. Safety, joy, strength, ease.

To a friend . . .

I considered Heather, but knew any loving-kindness was sure to be high-jacked by the gravitational pull of our powerful physical connection.

Yeshe. Lobsang. Safety. Ease.

To a parent . . .

No! My heart slammed shut as my eyes snapped open. I wanted to run from the room, and only the thought of disturbing the peaceful row of fellow meditators stopped me. I forced myself to close my eyes again. I imagined Tank, his soft paw patting my cheek in the morning. My breath calmed a little.

Tank. Health. Strength. Ease.

"Now include yourself."

I couldn't. I just couldn't.

I sat as still as I could, stretched tight as the skin on a drum. I hoped no one here knew how to play *sgom rgyab*. If anyone read my mind, all they'd find was resistance.

Allow, allow.

Like a rogue wave, my father's stern, unyielding presence invaded my space, as vivid as if he were standing in front of me, glowering.

Now I knew with absolute certainty what, or who, was blocking my connection with Yeshe and Lobsang. More important, with myself. *What are you running away from?* The same thing I'd always been running away from. The same thing I had to turn and face, if I was ever to be free.

I slipped past still meditators as they sent out silent waves of safety, waves of ease. I hoped some of their blessings adhered to me—I was going to need all the protection I could get.

As I paused at the door, Heather slowly turned her head in my direction, as if pulled by an invisible string. She met my eyes, hers questioning.

I have to go. I'm sorry.

Again, she touched her hand to her heart. Then she closed her eyes. This time I was the one who tasted a sweet stream of loving-kindness, sent like a benediction from the front row.

CHAPTER 20

I was home by 5:00 P.M., and by 6:30 I had somehow, impossibly, landed a cheap seat on Thai Airways, the red-eye to Delhi, via Bangkok. When all the lights turned green like this, I knew I was taking the right actions. In Delhi I'd make the short hop to Dharamshala on Kingfisher. That put me in the belly of the beast around 1:00 P.M. on Sunday. Twenty-four hours, door-to-door, all made possible by the wonders of the Internet. I booked my return for Tuesday, which after another 20-plus hours of flying would get me back here on . . . Tuesday. I suffered a brief spasm of panic before remembering my U.S. passport was valid—when I'd turned 25 and could claim my mother Valerie's estate, I'd had to make a quick trip to Paris to clear up a Trust issue. Trust issues and my mother. Nothing new there.

All told, this impulsive venture would cost 25 percent of my Julius wages, and four days of my life in travel alone, plus and minus the day I crisscrossed time zones. Was I crazy to do this? Yes. Was I doing it anyway? Yes again. Sitting in meditation at the retreat, I had somehow slipped past the invisible net of denial inside, and now the sonar alarm was sounding from deep within. In the past, I have ignored such messages, whether they were tickles or slams, at my own peril. If I ignored this one, I might drown.

I packed next to nothing—a change of clothes, two extra T-shirts, a traveler's First Aid kit, my laptop and Kindle, the autopsy report, the bagged contents of Charlie's lockbox, and the tattered screenplay, *Loving Hagar*.

Tank was hiding under the bed, his fresh tuna water untouched. I pulled him into my arms and walked outside to the deck. We stood there for a few minutes, his weight warm against my chest. *I'm sorry, but I have to do this. I'll be home soon, I promise.*

Tank wriggled free, polished my ankles with a quick fur-swipe, and ran inside to his food dish. That meant he still wasn't thrilled, but he accepted my explanation.

I called Mike, waking him up. He agreed to be on cat-duty while I was gone. I cleaned Tank's box, loaded a second bowl with crunchy treats, and I was out the door by 8:00 P.M. With only one small carry-on, I made it through security in plenty of time to board my flight. At 11:20 P.M., I was wedged in a middle seat between two strangers, happy to be on board at all. Despite flying steerage, I had quite a bit of legroom. An exquisite flight attendant with honeyed skin and a jet-black bun, an orchid tucked behind one ear, delivered a blanket and pillow to me. She was trim, dressed in an elegant pink Thai silk suit, bisected by a vibrant purple sash. *Not purple. Violet. The Seventh Ray. The color of new beginnings.*

We shared a smile.

"I am Dok," she said.

"Ten," I answered.

"Traveling to Bangkok, Mr. Ten?"

"Delhi."

"Business or pleasure?"

Good question. "Neither one, or maybe both."

"Ahh," she said. "A mystery."

Indeed.

Moments after take-off, I fell into a deep and much-needed sleep. I didn't move a muscle as we headed west, a small speck in the sky, pursuing the sun. I awoke several hours past Fiji. I was ravenous. Dok had kindly set aside an Asian-vegetarian dinner. I devoured skewered fresh fruit and Pad Thai, washed down with a cold Singha and numerous glasses of water.

The plane was dark, most of the passengers asleep.

Time to get to work. I set up my laptop, and opened the

email function. Thai Air had no onboard Wi-Fi yet, but I began to compose a fuzzy explanation of my current status. "It's important that I do this," I concluded. "I will call as soon as I can to let you know where I am, and why."

I wasn't deliberately vague; I was vague because I only had a partially formed, mostly spiritual sense of what I hoped to accomplish. Hard to explain. I copied and pasted the message to Bill, Martha, and, of course, Heather. I would send off the e-mails during the brief layover in Bangkok.

Next, I pulled out Charlie's final, zip-locked bequest to me. I unzipped it and removed the smudged sheets of paper, along with the discolored piece of material, Saran-wrapped in plastic, the length of a business card and leathery, like a scrap of rawhide. I examined it first, and discovered pale blue numbers: 481632. My stomach heaved. I was holding a shred of Marv's skin, tattoo and all. It smelled slightly of embalming fluid, as if dipped in preservative. Some present. I swallowed bile as I hot-dropped it back in the baggie. I checked the woman to my left and man to my right. Asleep, thank goodness.

I clambered past the man and went to the lavatory to scrub my hands.

On to the papers. I was looking at some sort of inventory, scrawled in Spanish. With the help of the Spanish-English dictionary on my desktop, I started to hack my way through the handwriting. I sat back. I was reading code for a laundry list of activities, some checked off, some not, followed by sets of initials. A tidy little criminal's to-do list. I didn't know what "spice the salsa," or "teach Juan the tango" meant, but I could make educated guesses, and none of them were legal, or about eating and dancing. Nor did they necessarily concern me. But one checked-off item did:

Abrazo para el monje: R. M.

An "abrazo" is a type of embrace; a man-hug, clap-on-the-back greeting between friends. Apparently in this case it was also someone's—probably Chaco's—ironic term for

Raul Martinez's first meeting with yours truly. They'd sent him to "embrace" the monk, in other words, me, in their own special way, by trying to scare me off.

Okay, so the initials belonged to designated flunkies, assigned to do the dirty work.

Down at the bottom of the list was another chilling entry:

Abrazo largo para R. M.: B. P. solo

Poor Charlie. No wonder he was so despairing. He'd stolen the hit list only to discover he was the next hit. I sat back again to think. Now I also knew the initials of the hit man who'd been given the assignment of administering a "long embrace" to Raul/Charlie. B.P., whoever he was, must have followed Charlie to the bluffs to give him his long embrace, only to be pleasantly surprised when I showed up as well. He probably envisioned a nice bonus for the double hit—two for the price of two, were it not for a dumpster. He'd accomplished his main priority, though, and must have decided to split after missing with a couple of potshots.

I refrained from putting a tic next to that item.

Now that I had a loose understanding of the code, I tried to piece together a few other tasks. Charlie, or R.M., had one more assignment—*Pista la mula:* R. M.

Watch the mule.

I found another reference to this "mule," *Descarga la mula: los primos.* Not too hard to translate. Raul had been ordered to watch for some carrier of goods, at which point "the cousins" would unload them.

I circled both items, as well as another interesting tidbit on page one: *Distribuir los golosinas:* A. A. Hand out the candy? Subtle, boys.

I scanned the list for any other errands for "B.P. solo" and sucked in my breath.

Dar la vuelta - ¡Vindicacion!: B.P. solo.

The first part of the translation was weird—something to do with turning ones back, maybe? But I didn't need a dictionary to translate ¡*Vindicacion!*. And whatever B.P. was supposed to vindicate, he'd done so successfully. Two big tics next to that one. I was half expecting a smiley face, as well. I jotted down my thoughts, and tucked the contents away for future reference.

We had a short layover in Bangkok—just enough time for me to enter the terminal, send off my e-mails, and stretch my stiff muscles before returning to the plane for the second leg of the trip.

There was a new flight crew. I was sorry to see Dok go, but another stunning flight attendant soon came down the aisle with a drinks cart. I asked for two minibottles of Merlot, hoping they'd knock me out for a few more hours of sleep. The wine, plus residual fatigue, worked like a charm. Next thing I knew, my new Thai guardian was lightly shaking my shoulder. I just had time to brush my teeth and drink two cups of fresh-brewed, hot Thai tea before we began our descent into the dusty madness of Delhi.

New Delhi's multibillion-dollar airport may look like a modernistic sprawl of glass and steel, but its true identity is *naraka*, the hell realm. The customs area was a milling swarm of sweaty humanity. My first inhale captured a breath-holding mixture of curry, diesel fuel, urine, and hair pomade, accompanied by a mind-searing din of screaming children, angry tourists, bellowing baggage handlers, and, oddly, a small brass band blaring out welcome music, no doubt for some incoming, corrupt Indian politician.

I had added International/Asian service to my iPhone before I left LAX. I called Heather's number, got her voicemail, and held up the phone to give her the latest soundtrack of my life. I told her I'd give her another call when I could.

My plane had landed in Delhi a half hour late, making for a very tight connection to the Kingfisher puddle-jumper to Dharamshala. This was going to take some maneuvering. I studied the seething crowd as they awaited permission to enter. As a boy, I had waited in these endless lines numerous times, shuttled as I was between parents and countries. But rather than using the interminable waits to practice equanimity, I had instead honed my resentment, as I observed over and over again that a privileged few always seemed to jump the lines. Soon, a pattern emerged.

As anyone who lives in India will tell you, where there is a want, there is always a "fixer," whether he be in charge of train schedules, chapatis, or even ganja at a hippie temple. All I had to do now was ascertain where the fixer was. I already knew how to speak his language—it was universal.

The restless masses funneled into the narrow customs booths, where officials inspected passports and other paperwork with glacial precision. I waited and watched from the back of the room until I noticed a dark-complexioned man dressed in a three-piece suit and wielding expensive luggage, visually scouring the long row of officials. Watched as he caught the eye of one thin, balding man with a long face and precise moustache, also wearing a dark business suit, standing behind the row. Three-piece suit gave a small nod, and moustache-man hurried past the crowd, to his side. *Gotcha.*

Their business concluded, I moved into the fixer's line of sight. I bowed. In a moment, he was in front of me, his long face giving nothing away.

"We haven't met," I said. "Inspector Tenzing Norbu. From Los Angeles."

His eyes widened slightly. "Jay Gupta, at your service."

"Mr. Gupta, I am traveling on a mission of great importance to Dharamshala, the seat of His Holiness the Dalai Lama." First rule of working with the fixer? Drop a name. Strictly speaking, I was telling the truth, as well, because I *was* going to Dharamshala on an important mission and it *is* the seat of His Holiness. Mr. Gupta didn't need to know the undertaking was important only to me, and that Dorje Yidam was three monasteries up the road from His Holiness' headquarters.

He bowed back. "It would be my pleasure to assist you

in any way possible." Only a trace of Indian singsong spiced his precise Oxford English.

"I wonder if I could engage you to help me move through customs quickly," I said. "My flight leaves in half an hour."

"Of course," he said. "It would be my great, great pleasure."

Two greats. That meant it would cost more than I'd estimated.

This was confirmed when Gupta waved at the line of officers. "These men see their brothers and sisters making fortunes in high-tech jobs. But do not they, too, have a value in this world?"

"Absolutely," I said. "And who would not choose to honor those who serve, so that when they go home at night, it is with a deep sense that their worth has been appreciated?"

He leaned close. "Three hundred U.S. gets you out the door and to your connection in ten minutes or less. I will, of course, make the appropriate distributions." I was guessing that meant two-thirds for him and the remaining third spread among the other worthies.

"Deal," I said. He spun on his heel and walked briskly toward a senior inspector, overseeing the 20 or so others dealing with the throng. They had a short whispered conversation, and he beckoned me over.

I was at the Kingfisher gate with enough spare time to down a cup of vendor chai. Soon we were bucking severe up-and-down drafts of the Himalayan foothills for a white-knuckling hour before landing with a bump.

I stepped outside and took several deep breaths. I may have landed safely, but my stomach continued to lurch and my chest to tighten. The real danger still lay ahead.

I climbed into a taxi for what I hoped was the final leg of my journey. The airport is about ten miles from the town. I stared out the window at the lush forests and jagged peaks. The route is simple, basically two turns and you're there, and soon we had reached the suburbs. We buzzed through lower Dharamshala, past local government buildings and schools, and headed uphill for the other government seat, the exiled one. We slowed to a crawl, weaving between scooters, buses, monks, and tourists, all jostling for space in the sprawling but narrow hill village of McLeod Ganj, home to His Holiness for more than 60 years. Tibetan snow lion flags snapped from every hotel roof and shop window, announcing beds and spiritual trinkets. I felt for the wide-eyed backpackers who had trekked here from all over the world, no doubt looking for tranquility. Their stunned expressions reminded me of the early-rising tourists standing in the heart of Hollywood, looking for stars and finding hookers. My own eyes widened as we passed café after café boasting Internet connections. *Everything changes.*

We rounded a bend. There it was, nestled in the hills, backed by mountains. Butter yellow walls, curved turrets, flapping flags. Half a mile, and light years, away.

"Let me off here, please."

I set my shoulder bag down and leaned against a pine tree, breathing in pure mountain air still scrubbed clean by September's late monsoons.

I remember this smell.

I shivered. I pulled out my fleece and zipped it on. A small blue-gray cat hair clung to one sleeve. I left it there.

I walked up the hill to find my friends and face my demons.

CHAPTER 21

I pushed open heavy wooden double doors, the same brick red as the steps leading up to them. I entered a dim, deserted foyer—afternoon classes were in session. I almost buckled under the sensory assault—the musty scent of yak-butter candles, the thick mantle of dread—and I reached for one wall to steady myself. I'd spent half my life here, and I still felt lost and alone, and anything but at home. A shimmering veil of darkness dropped over my eyes. I ducked my head below my knees and breathed deeply, waiting for it to dissipate.

I heard him before I saw him—the familiar, ponderous footsteps, perhaps a little slower, but no less relentless. *Father.*

I raised my head to look. I was wrong. This man was shrunken and stooped and, like Julius, propelled himself with the help of a cane. He was thin to the point of emaciation, and a grayish pallor clung to his skin like mold.

No.

A sharp, dark jab, somewhere between pain and anger, bit into my heart. *Father.* The last time I saw him walk this hallway, he was a giant, trailing a wake of threat and judgment. Now I towered over him. But his eyes glowed with the same ferocious fire, and as he rested both hands on his cane to observe me, his face seemed to shift into the same expression of suspicious irritation, as if once again I had interrupted him from something more important. The pain inside intensified. The wound may have had years to heal over, but it felt fresh—I was a 13-year-old boy, who had just lost his mother and knew his father didn't want him.

"Father." My touch to the forehead was so slight as to be imperceptible. Even so, I regretted it.

"Tenzing." He returned my gesture with an even slighter dip of his chin.

So. It begins again.

He smiled. "I woke up today feeling I might be receiving a visitor. I had assumed it would be Rinpoche. Now I see it is you who has showed up."

A grenade of rage exploded in my belly. *You never bothered to show up for me. You didn't show up when she died. You never even acknowledged her passing, or my pain. I was just a child!* Intense heat rippled throughout my body. My armpits flooded with sweat and the back of my eyeballs burned.

"Will you take tea?" he asked.

I nodded, unable to speak. He pulled a cord by the wall. Somewhere down below, a bell rang. He gestured for me to follow him. I did.

Entering his office was like stepping into a time warp: nothing had changed since the day I'd left. Even the dust motes' dance was the same. My father, wincing, lowered himself onto a wooden chair next to the window. I sat opposite, on a square meditation cushion on the floor. I looked up at him. Years of mindfulness practice evaporated. I was caught in a churn of feelings.

A young monk walked inside, bowed, and delivered a tea tray. *Same chipped tea pot.* A lump of yak butter and a salt shaker flanked two cups. *Same cups.*

"Tibetan or English?" my father asked, his eyes boring into mine. It felt like a test.

"I'll have what you're having," I said. He filled the cups with tea, and stirred a spoonful of yak butter and a pinch of salt in each. He pushed one cup in my direction. Picked his up, and slurped noisily, following up with a drawn-out "Ahhh" of satisfaction. I sipped and was happy not to gag.

My father's voice was amused. "You've lost your taste for the old ways."

"Maybe I never had one to begin with."

My father set down his cup. "Why did you come back?"

"You mean why, when you put so much effort into throwing me out?"

His voice was mild. "The front door is never locked. You walked out of it voluntarily thirteen years ago. Nobody forced you to leave, and as far as I know, nobody forced you to return."

I was suddenly overtaken by an urgent need to lie down and sleep. I was so tired of fighting. My father's stubbornness was monumental, my resistance exhausting.

Breathe, Ten. Breathe.

I inhaled deeply and exhaled fully. My father observed me, his face impassive. I tried to release my own stubbornness with the long exhale. I had wasted so much time waiting for my father to change. I would try not to waste a moment more.

"I didn't come here because of you," I said. "I came here because of Yeshe and Lobsang. I still link up with them, or at least I did until a couple days ago. When I reached out to them during meditation I found the connection broken. An image of you stood in its place."

A slight smile played at the corners of my father's mouth. To my mind, it was condescending. "So, still meditating?" he asked. "Still playing at sgom rgyab?"

How dare he? What gives him the right? I wasn't here to discuss my meditation practice. As far as I was concerned, he had lost the right to know. "I'd like to see my friends. Now, please," I managed to say.

My father turned to look out the window. "They're gone," he said, fixing his eyes on the snow-capped crags. "Sent away. I'm sorry."

"Why?"

"Ah. Why. That is an interesting question," he said.

"What have you done with them?" I spat out the words.

He shifted his gaze back to me. "As the years passed, with

no word from you, not one, I finally accepted you had left all of us absolutely. Then I discovered you hadn't, not really. I found them, you see; all those letters you'd sent to Yeshe and Lobsang over time. Pages and pages filled with descriptions of your new life. So I sent your friends to a simpler place, where they would not be distracted. I told myself it was better."

"Where?"

"Over the border," he said. "The old country."

"*Tibet?*"

"Yes, to Dip-Dorje. It's still home to twenty of our monks. Twenty-two, now."

Dip-Dorje. Our original monastery. When we were kids, Yeshe loved to locate it on the old map of Tibet hanging in one of our classrooms. He would find Lhasa, place his finger on Potala Palace and move it up a few inches to the hilly region that lay north. The map showed where our centuries-old monastery lay, but not what happened to it in 1959, when all of Tibet was "liberated" by the Chinese Red Army. Along with thousands of others, our temple was ravaged, and any surviving monks joined the massive spiritual exodus to India. Dip-Dorje lay in ruins until right around the time I'd left for America, when word trickled in that local volunteers had begun reconstruction. My father and the other abbots had dispatched a few brave lamas to reopen the monastery as best they could, given the watchful eyes of the local government. But that was a decade ago, before the recent crackdown.

"The Chinese allow such things?" I said. "Monks can go back and forth? It is safe?"

"No," he said. "Not back and forth. Not safe. Our relations with the Chinese are no better. Now that His Holiness has half retired, perhaps worse."

I stared at this shrunken version of my father. Smaller, but no less vindictive. "And still you sent Yeshe and Lobsang? How could you do this to them? I always knew you to be a cold man, Father. Cold and angry. But never unfair."

"Unfair?" He shook his head. "Such a Western concept. The spiritual life, like any life, is neither fair, nor unfair. Life just is. And our feelings about its fairness are completely irrelevant."

I wanted to throttle him. Then, like a pendulum, a deep ebb tide of fatigue again replaced the flow of anger. My father, too, seemed to slump under the wear of this ridiculous dance between us. He leaned back and closed his eyes. I blinked. His skin was giving off a faint pulse of grayish-green energy, like a discharge of poison.

He isn't well.

"Father . . ." I started, just as he opened his eyes, and said "I'm dying, Tenzing."

My body was kneeling next to his before my mind had fully registered the words. He took off his glasses, exposing brackish eyes.

"But . . ." My own stung. "You can't . . ."

He put his glasses on again. "I've got a cancer, deep inside. I cannot fight it—it's stronger than I am."

"Where?"

"I think they call it 'prostate' in the West."

"But that's good, then. There are treatments."

His smile was weary. "There's no treatment for karma," he said. "No pill, although I'm sure your drug companies would disagree."

Now they were "my" drug companies. *I am his metaphor for all things Western and therefore wrong.* I pulled back from heading down that sour alleyway. Not now.

Next came panic, irony fast on its heels: No one prided himself more than me when it came to the subject of death—accepting it, allowing it, helping others to deal with it. But this? *Not my father.* "I don't know what to do." I said. My voice broke.

My father touched the back of my hand. I almost flinched, though whether from fear or disgust, I couldn't say.

"Tenzing, do you remember what I told you when you left?"

"Every word. You said I had shown once again that my commitment to the Dharma was insufficient."

"That's right, son." He sighed. "I'm sure I meant it at the time."

Son.

A tiny heart-space opened, and a droplet of hope formed inside. I hardened around it.

"You meant it," I said. "I'm sure you still do."

"Tenzing, please. Look at me. Not who you think I still am. Me."

I forced myself to look. And saw a fearsome monster that would live forever, claws eternally dug into my heart.

"Let it go," he said.

And saw a frail man, old before his time, with little of it left.

I had fought against this person for my whole life. He had a permanent outpost inside me. *Because he is your father.* To eliminate him completely was to kill myself. *Because you are his son.* My body was the living host of his presence, and there was no way to root it out without jeopardizing the rest of me. *Because we live in each other.*

"Tenzing, I'm trying to see things differently now," my father said. "Can you allow that to be true?"

He was asking me to reexamine a core fact of my existence—that my father's rejection was the source of all my problems. The challenge was terrifying. As I took a deep breath, my vow, the one I had outlined to Yeshe and Lobsang in that fateful returned letter, plucked at my heart. If ever there was a time to let go of an outmoded, limited model of thinking, it was now.

"I'm listening," I said.

"Thank you, Tenzing." My father's voice was heavy. "I think . . . I think our struggles have their roots in resentment."

"Whose resentment?" I said, and braced myself.

He touched his chest. "Mine." His face twisted. A tear formed. Rolled down his cheek. More tears followed. *Impossible. My father does not cry.* But there they were—and something loosened inside.

I opened my mouth to speak.

"Please. There's more," he said. "Rather than addressing this resentment, I told myself I did you a favor. That I gave you something to rebel against, something that might propel you into a new life and make you strong enough to succeed." His smile was wan. "Is there any truth to that? Or am I simply a failed father trying to make himself feel better?"

"Yes," I said. "And yes."

He nodded. "I understand. Just as I now understand why I sent Yeshe and Lobsang away. How much easier, to condemn intimacy and trust among others, rather than acknowledge one's own utter lack of either."

We remained silent for a few long moments.

"I am haunted by the thought that my life is almost over, and I failed in everything I did," my father said.

"That sounds like the cancer talking," I said. *Welcome to the human race,* I thought.

"Maybe. But there's truth in the cancer nonetheless," he said. "And the pain is teaching me things I couldn't learn any other way."

Fear put a choke hold around my throat. "Father, are you sure there's nothing . . . ?"

He stopped my words with a raised palm. "I missed my chance, Tenzing. Now all I can do is regard the process of dying with equanimity. Try to stay open to learning from it."

"Long may you learn, then," I said.

"No," he said. "Short may I learn."

Our eyes met straight on. His crinkled in what looked like genuine good humor.

"I never gave you my blessing, did I?" he said. He opened a drawer in his desk and pulled out a soft, silken object, a white *kata*. "His Holiness gave me this when I was installed as head abbot. He will be pleased to hear that I have passed it on to you." He draped it around my neck.

A seed of feeling blossomed in my chest area, a sense of warm expansion I had never associated with my father. Was it love?

He pushed upright and took hold of his cane.

"There is a Sikh in the village," he said. "A merchant. Mr. Mohan. He will help you. Now go. I'm very tired."

"Father . . ."

"Go."

I went. On my way out, I glanced into the courtyard, now filled with young monks, heading for their afternoon assembly. I thought I might recognize some of them, but I didn't.

There are fixers everywhere. Inside India, most of the really good ones are Sikhs. Their network is nationwide, they won't cheat you, and if things get dicey, their ceremonial daggers are known to have sharpened edges.

I soon tracked down the white-turbaned Mr. Mohan in his rug shop. He was wide across the shoulders and a long, full beard, held neatly in place with a hair net, rested on his well-fed belly, a sign of distinction among the merchant classes in India. I explained who I was.

"Your father's a great man," he said. "How wonderful you come from America to visit him."

I just smiled.

"What you need?"

I told him I needed to somehow get to Yeshe and Lobsang's monastery. As I said the words, a feeling close to panic swelled in my lungs, making it harder to breathe.

Tenzing. Brother. Where are you?

Yeshe and Lobsang. Something was wrong.

"As quickly as possible," I said.

Mr. Mohan nodded. "I arrange passage for them," he

said. "But no 'quick as possible.' One full day by truck, followed by ten-mile hike where truck cannot go."

"No!"

He raised his eyebrows.

"I'm sorry, but no. I don't have a day," I said. "Please. It's urgent."

He eyed me, and somehow deduced I had enough money to grease the right palms.

"Good. You fly Lhasa, then drive 3-wheel ATV to Dip-Dorje Yidam. I arrange both. Maybe you get there today, things go your way."

"Is that the fastest way?"

He chuckled. "No. Fastest way helicopter. Fastest way get there. Fastest way die. Chinese don't shoot you out of sky, they burn down monastery." He waved me off. "Come back in one half hour."

I was starving. I crossed the street and purchased three *momos*, plucked from the heated metal vat of a colorful street vendor. She beamed at me as I devoured hot dumplings of shredded cabbage, carrots and potatoes, savoring the sharp bite of ginger.

I hurried back to find the amazing Mr. Mohan had fixed all my problems. Within the hour I was back at the Dharamshala airport, catching a ten-seater to Lhasa. This plane, too, bucked and lurched until I wondered if I would outlive the journey. I distracted myself from worrying about my safety, and that of my friends, by mentally rearranging fragments of insight from the time with my father. Maybe I could piece them into a new quilt of understanding.

Half the cells in my body come from my father.

There is no escaping him. He lives in me.

I give him power every time I argue with him in my mind.

I give him power every time I spot some thought of his in my mind and curse him for putting it there.

He will trouble me as long as I continue to give him permission to do so.

Accept. Allow. All will be well. My father's voice, the newer, kinder version, seemed to float to me from somewhere outside. *No, not from outside. Inside. Inside me.* I had to smile. One part of my mind busily clung to regrets and resentments and heartaches from years ago. Meanwhile, another part piped up, trying to shift the direction, a wise voice like that of a good parent. Marvelous instrument, this brain, even if often an instrument of torture.

The "good father" voice spoke up again, encouraged by my brief willingness to listen. *Accept him as he is, and maybe he'll quit bothering you. While you're at it, accept the parts of you that are just like him, and maybe you'll quit bothering yourself.*

As I wrapped this new understanding around my shoulders, trying it on for size, the aerial bumps stopped bothering me, too.

A dour Chinese official at the Lhasa airport took in my dark eyes and high cheekbones with suspicion. I met his gaze steadily, though my heart was pounding.

"Reason for your visit?"

"Tourist," I said.

He grunted and returned to my passport. But no matter how long he studied it, it still said "American."

He stamped me through.

I stepped outside, breathing in the crisp air. I spun round and round; at home in a place I'd never been to before. A chill wind whipped my face, and I was shocked to notice my cheeks were wet.

I was some kind of Tibetan mess, wasn't I?

During my years in the monastery, Tibet shimmered in the background of every conversation, salted every bite of bread, sweetened every sip of tea. But it was never completely real. Now, as I stood in the wind, facing the jagged ridgeline of the Himalayas, I absorbed the deep pulsation of the Dharma and the land, and finally understood the depth of their connection to each other, and my connection to them. I felt the power and innate happiness of my tradition, felt how the wild heart of the land beats in the earth, and in the air. I understood how it was that my ancestors knew how to reconcile the animal and spiritual nature of our species.

Two hundred and fifty years ago, the sixth Dalai Lama, too, was called Tenzing. He, too, had a wild heart. He, too, was a spiritual man blessed, or cursed, with an erotic nature. As a young lama, I fell upon his poems for reassurance. Now my favorite verse of his paid a visit:

> I dwell apart in the Potala.
> A god on earth am I.
> But when the sun goes down,
> I roam the town,
> A master of boisterous revelry.

He was my kind of monk, and Tibet was my kind of country. Fierce.

Tenzing. We need you.

I had to find the local Lhasa fixer, Chubchen, and quickly. The second person I asked pointed me toward the two-acre square of rubbled ground on the edge of the airport that served as a parking lot for a motley bunch of rental vehicles. Mr. Mohan was correct. Chub was there, squat, merry, raggedy, and gap-toothed. He stood guard over an equally well worn 3-wheeler. Even with his broken English and my almost nonexistent Tibetan, it was an easy deal. I handed him six hundreds, he handed me the key. If I returned the ATV in one piece, he'd give me three hundreds back. If I, or the vehicle, didn't survive, all bets were off.

"*Gzab gzab,*" Chub warned. I vaguely recognized the word: *helmet.* Chub pointed to my Dodger cap and frowned—his fixing hadn't extended to a *gzab gzab.*

I might scrounge up safer covering for my cranium in

the center of town, but there was no time. I had to get to my friends as fast as possible.

I fired up the 3-wheeler and took a few laps around the parking lot to get a feel for the vehicle before I started the long trek. I concluded the experience was somewhere between steering a burro and straddling a trike. Over an hour later I trundled around a curve and saw the Potala for the first time, a magnificent multileveled palace perched on a hill overlooking the Lhasa valley. I smiled. The location actually reminded me a little of the Getty. I pulled over to the side of the road to take a quick look, since I wouldn't set foot on its holy ground, not this trip, anyway.

For a brief moment, I soaked in the silent grandeur of the immense, sprawling structure, a monument to the Buddha that took thousands of workers many years to complete. Some said the hillside itself still harbored a sacred cave, used as a meditation retreat in the seventh century. Centuries of contemplation, centuries of compassion. It was humbling. *I take refuge in the Buddha, the Dharma, the supreme Sangha.* I bowed to the home of my spiritual ancestors. *I take refuge in my teachers.*

I restraddled my ungainly mount and hit the throttle.

I steered around the outskirts of Lhasa and up into the hills. The gravel road petered out, replaced by narrow yak trails skirting high above a river gorge. A gust of wind sent my Dodger cap soaring to the bottom of the thousand-foot ravine. My trusty ATV and I dodged boulders, branches, and piles of yak dung. On the positive side, since I'd left the main road, the only bipeds I'd seen were Tibetan hill people—no Chinese officials in evidence.

I was hungry, thirsty, and battered from the bumps in the road. I was beyond jet-lagged as well—Monday or Friday, morning or evening, I hadn't a clue. But I pressed on. I had to find Dip-Dorje before I lost the light. The final few miles of twisted, rocky trail required my final few ounces of focus. Close to the top, the wind changed direction, blowing hard down the slope and straight into my face. I paused to put on my wraparound sunglasses, tightening them in the back with their little leash. I'm sure I looked ridiculous, but at least I could see where I was going.

Finally the trail widened, and I saw the whipping prayer flags and colorful turrets of a little monastery up the slope to my right, just past a few stone huts. A gaggle of children, streaked with grime, giggled and shrieked as they played some sort of jumping game in the courtyard. I chugged up the path and braked to a halt. They fell silent, staring at me in astonishment.

In an instant I was surrounded. I tried out a greeting in my rusty Tibetan, and they hooted and crowed at my pronunciation. Then they asked me where I was going—at least I'm pretty sure they did. In any case, I pointed to Dip-Dorje. They led the way, filling the trail with happy chatter as my machine and I crept behind them. I was still wearing my sunglasses, and I was sure no movie star ever had a better entourage.

I dismounted and bowed my thanks. They scampered down the hill to their homes.

I stretched my creaky bones and tight muscles.

"Tenzing! Is it possible?" a familiar voice cried behind me. I straightened up and spun around, grinning at the sight of my soul brother Lobsang. I threw open my arms. "*Tah-shi de-leh*, Lobsang. I am happy to see you, my friend." My smile faded. Lobsang's round face was pinched with worry.

"No time," he said. "No time! It's Yeshe!"

He grabbed my arm and hurried me to a small door in the back of the monastery. He lit a candle and pulled me inside. The flickering light illuminated our way up the narrow wooden stairs to the second floor. He opened a door in the hallway and whispered "Yeshe. Our brother, Tenzing, is here." He pushed me inside.

Yeshe lay still, on a rough mattress on the floor. His face was slick with sweat.

"Yeshe!" I ran to his side and knelt. I took his hands in mine. The palms were hot, and papery dry. Yeshe moaned.

"How long has he been like this, Lobsang?"

"Three days," Lobsang said. "He scratched his ankle, gathering wood. It seemed like nothing."

I pulled the covers down. The scratch was badly infected. His right ankle was swollen to twice its normal size, and the hot, red skin was speckled with white spots.

I thought of Heather's autopsy—how quickly untreated sepsis can kill.

I jumped to my feet and ran downstairs and back outside to the ATV. I grabbed the first aid kit. *Please. Please have what I need.*

My fingers trembling, I unzipped the kit and rummaged through its contents.

"Hah!" I pounced on the small tube of Neosporin and Z-pack of six miraculous pills.

I ran back upstairs. "Antibiotics. These will stop the infection," I said. Lobsang hurried over with a cup of water, and together we lifted Yeshe upright. I placed a pill far back on his tongue and Lobsang tipped the cup to Yeshe's lips. He swallowed the pill, his throat working.

"Can you bring me a clean, wet cloth and some hot water?"

I washed the infected area, trying not to press on the painful swelling. Then I applied the cream to his wound. The simple act touched my heart deeply, and I had to blink back tears. As I wrapped his ankle with a second clean cloth, Yeshe's breathing slowed. In moments, he was asleep.

"He has to take all six of the pills, Lobsang." My words came out in a rush. "Do you understand? All six. He could have died. One more day and . . ."

"Tenzing."

I looked up. Lobsang met my eyes, his full of compassion. He opened his arms. I stood up and walked straight into his rough embrace.

I took a step back. We studied each other. His squat powerful body had thickened over the years.

"At least one of you looks healthy," I said. A grin plastered his face.

"Come eat with me," he said. "Then we will talk."

I followed Lobsang downstairs, through the kitchen and into a dining room, where monks were slurping and ahhing over yak-butter tea. They were all in their 50s and 60s, their skin leathered from the harsh Tibetan climate.

Lobsang ladled out lentil soup and a generous mound of rice. We sat cross-legged on the floor, guzzling straight from our bowls, using fingers to convey little wads of rice into our mouths. After my afternoon trek, a boiled shoe would have tasted pretty good, but this simple soup of yellow lentils, flavored with cumin and some other spices I didn't recognize, was delicious—deep and rich, and tasting of comfort.

Lobsang poured two mugs of homemade beer, or *chang*. Chang tastes more like fermented orange juice than ale, and I'd gotten a gloomy headache from it more than once in my past, but under the circumstances, it would do just fine. Anyway, I owed it to Lobsang to keep him company—he had always loved the tart brew.

I stopped after half a mug—the fermentation was speeding directly to my brain. Lobsang drained his mug and eyed mine. I handed it over, and it was gone in one gulp. I waited, smiling.

"*Brrraapppp!*" There it was, the traditional post*chang* belch of appreciation. Between the three of us, Lobsang had always been the champion burper. It was our signal to talk.

He leaned back and folded his hands over his stomach. He cocked his head, as if measuring my features.

"What?"

"You won't like hearing this, but you look very much as your father did, when I first met him."

"You're right. I don't want to hear it."

"Still the same Tenzing. Still denying your inheritance." Lobsang smiled. "So you saw him?"

I'd forgotten how few words we actually needed to communicate.

"Yes," I said. "But I'd rather wait for Yeshe to talk about it."

Lobsang nodded.

"So how are you?" I said. "How is . . ." I waved my arm around the room. " . . . all this?"

Lobsang's domed forehead furrowed slightly. "I must confess something. There are times I think of you with envy in my heart, my friend. Your life is . . . Well, the things you used to write to us about, the people you've met, your work. Since we've moved," he gestured. "Nothing ever happens here. Nothing."

I understood completely. That's why I'd left Dharamshala in the first place. I hadn't wanted to spend my existence with my eyes closed, life happening elsewhere. But leaving was not without its own consequences.

"Sometimes I think of your world with envy in *my* heart," I said.

He nodded slowly. "Just so. The things you see must sicken you. I can imagine you might long at times for a place where nothing happens."

"I'm sorry you were sent here," I said. "I know my father gave the order, but I am responsible."

"You must not worry yourself. Nobody is in control of anybody else's existence. Our karma brought us here; yours brought you to where you are. Your father's karma . . . well, let's just say it will take him wherever it takes him."

"Still, there's something I don't understand," I said, when a cheer swelled from the dining room, where monks were still congregated. In a moment Yeshe limped his slow, unsteady way to us.

"Yeshe! What are you doing? You need to stay in bed!" Lobsang scolded.

Yeshe smiled. "Yes, mother. It's just—I had to make sure Tenzing was really here, and not some spirit, conjured up by fever."

He swayed a little, and we both sprang to our feet.

"Bed," Lobsang repeated.

We helped him upstairs and back under fresh covers. His fever had already broken. Lobsang marveled at the healing power of western medicine, and I puffed up a little, as if the credit was mine to claim. Lobsang made a bed for me on the floor, using two yak-hair blankets for a mattress, and another to cover up with. He blew out the candle and we were enveloped in dense darkness. Soon, though, we were speaking to each other across the shadows, just as we'd always done.

"Yeshe, are you still awake?"

"Yes."

"Lobsang?'

"Yes."

"I have to ask you both. I know my father sent you here to Lhasa, so my letters could no longer find you. But why couldn't I find you with my mind?"

There was a long silence.

"You have lived for some time now in a world where the practice of obedience is perhaps not common," Lobsang said. "We took a vow, Tenzing."

"Your father forbade us from contacting you," Yeshe added. "He is still our abbot."

I tasted anger, and beneath it, hurt. "We also vowed to always stay in touch," I said. "To take refuge in our sangha of friendship."

I could hear the smile in Lobsang's answer. "As you may have realized, I recently came to the same conclusion. Especially when our mutual friend here managed to force the issue by hurting himself."

"I'm sorry. It won't happen again," Yeshe said.

"Hurting yourself?"

"No. Hurting you."

We breathed together quietly.

"Anything else?" Lobsang said. "Just so you know, Yeshe, I've already admitted my envy to Tenzing."

"I envy you as well," Yeshe said. "But not for your adventures. I envy your access to books, your exposure to different philosophies and spiritual systems." He sighed. "I only know the one."

"Hey," I said. "It's a great one to know."

"I know, I know, the Dharma is a perfect transmission, but what about the rest? Don't others find theirs perfect, too?"

It was a big question, especially for this time of night. Too big for me, but maybe not too big for technology. Anyway, I was dying to see my friends' expressions at my new toy. I felt my way to my backpack and pulled out the Kindle. I turned it on—the battery was still strong. I shone my little clip-on light onto the screen. Lobsang and I joined Yeshe on his bed, and we huddled around the Kindle, like cavemen clustered around the first fire. I clicked a few times until I could pull up my latest favorite spiritual tome. I found the page I wanted, and pressed the Kindle into Yeshe's hands. I pointed to the first line.

"Go on. Read it. It won't bite you."

Yeshe read slowly, his eyes shining. "The secret of happiness is knowing this: some things are within your power to change and some things are not. Place your attention on those things that are within your power to change."

He looked up. "This man—he was Buddhist."

"Nope. Greek. Epictetus. He lived in another time, on the other side of the world. I doubt he'd even heard of the Buddha," I said.

"But he is teaching the Dharma, don't you think? This is so . . . so . . . ." He returned to the page.

Lobsang patted my knee. "I think you have given Yeshe a medicine more powerful than the pills."

Yeshe happily clicked through a few more pages before

erupting into a huge yawn. "My eyes will not let me continue," he said. He set the device aside.

The three of us lay side-by-side-by-side on the floor, friend next to friend, candle next to Kindle.

I thought about change.

I asked into the darkness: "My father wants to know if you'd like to come back to Dharamshala. He has shifted out of blame and into a place of greater awareness. Or so he says."

I listened to their breathing—when I remember to listen, breath can tell me everything I need to know. Theirs caught for a split-second, then quickened slightly.

Finally Yeshe answered. "This you've seen with your own eyes?"

"He is dying. He wishes to be free."

They met this news with a silence that was full of feeling.

"So what do you think?" I asked.

"This brings up a conflict of desires," said Lobsang. "I am just now beginning to accept that here is where I live."

"In one way it is better," Yeshe added. "Not so many distractions, as your father suggested. But there is," Yeshe lowered his voice, "growing fear here. Fear, and . . ." Yeshe said a Tibetan word, foreign to me.

"Paranoia," Lobsang translated.

"Paranoia," Yeshe repeated. "The Chinese have started coming into our community disguised as lamas, pretending to be friends. They pave their way with gifts, offering money, food, even television sets, in return for information and cooperation."

"And the monks go along with this?"

"Those who refuse are banished," Lobsang said.

"Banished," Yeshe said. "And worse."

"We are hearing of protests breaking out in other provinces." Lobsang quieted his voice to barely a whisper. "It is bad, Tenzing, as bad as long ago. From the outside, it seems peaceful, but inside, everything is boiling."

"Some are setting themselves on fire," Yeshe said. "Students. Monks. Twenty at least, in the last year alone."

I raised myself up on one elbow. "Here? Here in Lhasa?" I could scarcely bear to think of it.

"Not here yet, but elsewhere in China. Our brothers in Labrang are expected to attend 'patriotic education' sessions. The authorities call it monastic management."

Lobsang's voice tightened. "Management! They kick in doors and tear up photographs of His Holiness, replacing them with portraits of Mao Zedong. Hang surveillance cameras from the temple's eaves!"

"And I thought Los Angeles was scary," I said. "You should seriously consider coming back with me."

We laughed, and the air lightened a little.

"Maybe we will, some day," Yeshe said.

Lobsang pushed onto one elbow. "Tenzing, we have had no stories from you for months. Tell us what you are working on."

I gave them the short and not-so-sweet version of all my latest detective work, paid and unpaid, beginning with my first introduction to Marv Rudolph and ending with the brutal demise of Charlie Montoya.

"Good story," Lobsang said.

"Not really," I said. "It has no ending, and it doesn't make sense."

"Then change it," Yeshe said, after a moment

"What?"

"Change the story. Isn't that what they are always doing in Hollywood? Changing the . . . what do they call them? Plays?"

"Screenplays."

"Yes. It's just like the mind. Don't like the story it is telling you? Change it!"

"I wish it were that simple." I felt a little bubble of irritation rise and pop. Yeshe's naiveté was legendary—and one of my favorite things about him.

I drifted toward sleep, when I heard Yeshe again. "Shouldn't we . . . you know."

"Yes," Lobsang said, finishing the thought. "We should bless these problems you are working to solve. Especially as you are here with us."

They began to chant quietly, Lobsang's voice a lower scale than Yeshe's. I absorbed the pure duet of ancient sound. Soon my own voice joined in, lower still. After chanting in harmony for a moment, we softened our voices until the notes melted into a linked silence.

"Go on," Yeshe whispered.

I offered my questions to the dark: "What happened to Sadie Rosen?" I let the words settle. Then "Who killed Marv Rudolph?" Finally, as I was trained to do, I added, "It is my belief that knowing these things will help ease suffering and promote truth."

Lobsang answered back with the ancient, familiar refrain. "If a monk's desires are pure, the desires of the monk will become manifest."

I thought about this.

"I hope I'm still enough of a monk to qualify," I said.

"I think you probably are," Yeshe said. "What do you think, Lobsang?"

Lobsang's answer was succinct.

"*Brrraapppp!*"

Chapter 22

I am here again, lying face down on a concrete floor. I look around. A man watches me from the shadows in the corner. Is it me? No. It is my father. He lifts a finger, as if in warning, then points outside.

I step into a garden. The garden is beautiful, lush with blooms. A cat runs by, not Tank, a black cat. I hold out my arms and spin around and around, and my arms lift me into the sky, until I spin far above the garden. The sky darkens around me. Is it day? Night? What time is it?

I look at my watch, but the numbers are distorted, like little scratches.

I am not surprised. I have been in this lucid dream before.

"Show me," I say. And I am standing at the base of a tall stone watchtower. It is dark inside. Dangerous. I climb the steep stairs to the first level. It is as far as I am willing to go. I look out a narrow window, and see two dark-skinned men wrestling on the ground below. They look alike. Are they twins? No. But related.

A low voice speaks into my ear. It is neutral, neither male nor female.

"What do we inherit?" it says.

"Nothing," I answer.

"Everything," the voice replies.

The struggling men turn and stare up at me, and I am paralyzed, unable to look away, unable to move.

"Help me," I say. "I don't know what to do."

"Yes, you do," the voice says. *"Change the story."*

I jolted awake, my eyes opening to strange smells, strange sounds. My heart thudded against my ribcage. *Where am I?* I touched the rough weave of my blanket. Became aware of Lobsang's soft snores.

What time is it?

The glow of my watch told me, 3:20 A.M. Of course. I'd slept only four hours, and now adrenaline sang in my veins. I sat up and again closed my eyes, allowing my breath to smooth. *That dream, again.* I'd had versions of it before. Recurring, disturbing, yet also, at times, illuminating. I allowed the dream to clarify from wispy image into description and stored the words as memory.

Fathers and sons. It always came back to that for me, didn't it? Fathers and sons.

What do we inherit?

A deep shift started inside, and I wavered between fear and excitement. I was locking in on a homing beacon, I could feel it, though whether the shift was personal or professional, I didn't yet know. But a new shape was forming, something bigger than anything I'd dealt with before. Maybe more sinister, too. I shivered.

It was action time.

Lobsang and Yeshe must have sensed my urgency, because they stirred awake.

I have to go," I said. "I can try to arrange safe passage for you as well." They met each other's eyes. Lobsang's shake of the head was slight.

"Not now," Yeshe said to me. "Not yet."

He pushed himself upright. I walked over, and we exchanged a warm hug.

"Take your pills," I said.

Lobsang insisted I join him in the kitchen for a bowl of rice and a mug of hot tea before I left.

He walked me outside. I pressed some bills into his hand.

"In case," I said. "Ask for Chubchen."

"Tenzing . . ."

"Just think about it. Otherwise, buy Yeshe a Kindle, and yourself a computer. It's the new way of keeping in touch." I climbed onto the ATV. "E-mail, my friend. Skype. Everybody's doing it, even His Holiness. Why not us?"

Lobsang laughed. "You seem to forget where we live, Tenzing."

"Lobsang . . ."

"Go! Go!"

I left before I changed my mind and stayed.

It took me no time at all to get back to the airport—it was downhill most of the way, and the road through the village was deserted. That said, I still arrived at the lot feeling like I'd gone through ten rounds of kickboxing. I left my wheels with Chub, collected my refund, and jogged into the airport, three hundred dollars the richer, ticket in hand, ready to bargain my way home. I talked myself onto a flight to Katmandu, and by noon I was in the transit area, scanning the big board for Thai Air departure options. I got lucky again, and found a flight to Bangkok that left in 45 minutes, and connected with a nonstop to L.A. (Katmandu has fixers, too.) I boarded immediately and somehow snagged an aisle seat.

The next leg of my journey would take a little over three hours. Before I did anything else, I jotted down my early morning dream-thoughts. Then I sat back and let my mind twist and turn the pieces into different formations, a kaleidoscopic review. Julius would call it rumination.

Two men, grappling in a garden. Gardening. Gardener. *Julius has a beautiful garden.* My father. Me. Wrestling. A black cat, running away. Men. *I look like my father.* Fathers and sons. *What do we inherit?*

My eyes snapped open.

Manuel, the gardener. Manuel, and the man who I thought was Manuel, both on Julius Rosen's estate. Not one man. Two. Both broad-shouldered. Both squat. And those same wide shoulders on "the Man" in the back table at La Cantinela. Two men: the older one a gardener called Manuel, the younger a killer called Chaco. *El Gato.* The Cat. Not brothers, but related. Father and son. And working with Julius.

Why had I not seen this earlier?

Because you expected to see only gardeners in the garden. And friends inside the house.

What else was I missing? What other limiting thoughts were still blinding me? In how many other ways had I ignored my second rule?

I opened my laptop, my brain on fire. My fingers flew, and we were landing before I knew it.

I had to change planes in Bangkok, and without much time between. I was unable to retrieve my e-mails —the airport Wi-Fi was down. I did manage to take a quick paper-towel bath in the restroom, scrubbing off the top few layers of travel grime. I changed into my one remaining clean T-shirt. The rest of me would have to wait until I got home.

Window seat this time. As the plane climbed out over the ocean and banked toward the east, I had a panoramic look at the steaming mess called Bangkok. Streets choked with traffic, a thick haze of pollution—I could practically smell the rank air. It made me very glad I didn't live there, until I realized a version of the same thing awaited me on the other end.

I was tempted to close my eyes and sleep, but I still had work to do. I started with the autopsy report. I scanned it quickly. Most of the information I already knew. *Careful, Ten. Don't assume you know what it says.* I reread the report, slowly. Sure enough, a small item toward the bottom caught my eye: "Trace adhesion, upper left bicep." It must have turned up when they used the ultraviolet light to scan Marv's body, after Bill and I left.

So innocent: trace adhesion.

My skin tingled. Adhesion meant at one point Marv, or

someone else, had stuck something on his arm. Something like a patch, maybe.

Another connection between Marv and Julius.

The flight attendant delivered a tray of food to the man on my right.

"Here is your special meal, sir."

I eyed it curiously. Looked like ordinary food to me, though mighty tasty, even with the meat. My hollow stomach calculated the enormous gap between the here and now, and my meager, predawn breakfast bowl of Tibetan rice.

My neighbor answered my avid stare.

"Kosher," he said. "I'm Jewish. We don't mix meat and dairy, not even on planes. They are always to be eaten and cooked separately."

"You mean in separate pans?"

"No. Separate ovens. Sometimes even separate kitchens."

"Hunh."

At that point I received my own, nonspecial meal, some kind of cheese-filled pasta this time. Not pretty, but my stomach didn't care. I ate everything on my tray, including the ice cold dinner roll and a square of yellow cake glazed with a pink, translucent slick of unknown flavor and origin.

One final task awaited me, before I allowed myself a movie and a nap. I pulled out the screenplay to *Loving Hagar*, its pages slightly curled. I had read Shakespeare's *Romeo and Juliet* soon after I arrived in America, as part of my crash course in Western ways. I'd liked it okay, though more as a cautionary tale regarding the perils of attachment than anything else. Talk about bad karma.

Anyway.

I leafed through the whole thing first, and saw that someone had not only highlighted all of Hagar's lines, but also turned down the corners of every page that mentioned her. I was guessing that someone was Tovah. Very industrious of her.

I started again, from the beginning. FADE IN, it said. Okay . . .

This was my first screenplay, and it took me a little while to get used to the format. But I soon caught on— and soon was totally confused. I'd thought this was a love story between a holocaust survivor and a Palestinian refugee. Surely that was what Julius had told me? But when the young man of this love story was introduced, his name was Fernando, and he was described as "20s, hunky, think early Banderas meets Robert Pattinson, plus tats."

I knew that description. Word for word, I knew it. I grabbed my notebook, and leafed back through the pages to my first meeting with Marv, months and months earlier. *Where is that name?* I found it: Bronco, Bronco Portreros. Harper's first man-crush. Drug dealer. Wannabe actor. And according to Marv at the time, a big star in the making.

What had Mike said about *Loving Hagar*? Rewrites—after Julius dropped out, there had been rewrites to the script.

Change the story.

Why was this flight taking so long?

I forced myself to read the rest of the screenplay, which was 100 pages of lameness, to my mind. Whoever had done the rewrite, he or she was no bard. Then, I watched a disturbing film about an international plague that made me want to spend the rest of my life washing my hands.

Then, I thought about Heather, which was much more pleasant. I couldn't wait to see her, to touch her and kiss her. I couldn't wait to tell her everything, and hear everything back. I pictured her, the way she threw her head back when she laughed. The way she opened her heart to silence and could both receive and send affection—or maybe something stronger—across a room . . .

A solid seven hours of dreamless sleep later, I was gazing at another smudgy skyline. Home sweet home. Soon I was shuffling through the huge customs and immigration area, one among an exhausted horde. The officials gave me a hard look, and my backpack a major search. Nobody in their right minds made the kind of trip I'd just made, unless they were on something, smuggling something, or both. Fortunately, the only suspicious item I was carrying was a package of Indian crispy snacks for Heather.

I stepped outside the terminal, squinted at the blue-gray Los Angeles sky, and felt an odd jolt of displacement. I'd been gone for four days, but it felt like a lifetime. Ideally, I'd have allowed myself at least two more days just to process everything, but not today. My work was waiting.

I checked my voicemail before I left the lot in my Mustang. The stack of e-mails would have to wait. Six messages. Bill's said, "Hey. You back? Give me a buzz." Martha's said, "Thanks again, for everything." Mike's said, "Dude, your cat's crazy," which was a little worrisome, and Heather's said, "Hi! It's me. How was your trip? Are you talking yet? I have some information for you." A quick one from Clancy: "Are you going to Marv's memorial service Thursday? Just wondering." And finally, from an hour ago, Bill again: "Call the minute you land." I caught the urgent undertone. *Something's up.*

I called back in order of importance. I got Heather's voicemail. "Call me," I said. "Better yet, come see me. I'm home."

Bill next.

"Thank God," he said.

"What's going on?"

"Not on the phone. Listen, we tracked down Tovah Fields. She was staying with friends in Newport Beach. I'm meeting her at the Robinsgrove in an hour. Can you . . ."

"See you there."

I called Mike next. He answered on the tenth ring, voice foggy.

"It's yesterday morning my time," I said. "What's your excuse?"

"My excuse is, your cat has boundary issues, as in he

doesn't have any. Doesn't believe in anyone sleeping during the day, either, unless it's him doing it."

"It's good for you," I said. "What if you get a real job someday, with real hours?"

Silence.

"Anything on Sadie?"

He seemed to cheer up at that. "I struck gold. Sadie Rosen never came into contact with the big three organizations, but I did find her mentioned in the records of a private group calling themselves The Refugee Center. Bad people, it turns out."

"How bad?"

"They were snatching up Jewish orphans and charging exorbitant fees to return them to their relatives, ransom demands, essentially. And guess whose family was right in the middle of it all?"

What do we inherit?

"Helmut Zigo's?"

"Boom. Two brothers, Albert and Dieter Zigo. Helmut's daddy and uncle. Both did some prison time, both now deceased."

"Anything else?"

"Plenty. Sadie was logged in somewhere in Northern Germany and logged out in Brooklyn, New York. An unnamed family member took her."

"And the trail ends there?"

"No. I took a nap, okay? Out here on the deck, where Tank the Obliterator couldn't jump on my chest and knead me into submission."

"It's good for you," I said again.

"Oh, yeah, one more thing. May explain why your friend Julius called you off. I mean, there's something extremely fishy about this. I turned up a bunch of donations to different Jewish organizations given anonymously, only the small print says "in celebration of Sadie Rosen." Could be a coincidence, with all those Sadie Rosens floating around out there, but still . . ."

"Any way to find out who made the donations?"

"Working on it, boss. Working on it."

"Well while you're working on that, do me one more favor," I said. "See if you can track down a photograph of a guy called Bronco Portreras."

"Who's he?"

"Besides being a scumbag, I think he may be an actor."

"Is there a difference?" That was his exit line. I've heard worse.

I parked on Arden, two cars away from Bill's. He walked over and started to give me a quick half hug. He stepped back quickly.

"What'd you do over there, roll in camel dung?"

"More like sleep in yak hair," I said.

"I don't even want to ask."

"Before we go in, I've got a big chunk of news," I said.

"Me, too. You first."

I described my dream-insight, and the connection I suspected between Chaco and Manuel, the gardener at Julius Rosen's estate.

"So now we've got Marv looping back to Rosen at least two different ways?" He shook his head. "I don't get it. You get it?"

"I think I'm starting to, maybe."

"Well chew on this. Word's out something big is going down with Chaco's crew. Tonight. Some big shipment coming in. DEA's going ape shit. They know the who and the when, but they don't know the where."

We were at the front entrance. Something nibbled at the edge of my brain.

"Give me a second." I paced the sidewalk, breathing in and out, feeling each foot lift, and press against the asphalt. *Lift. Press. Lift. Press.*

Mula.

Pista la mula. Watch the mule.

Descarga la mula. Unload the mule.

I hurried back to Bill. I told him the "where."

"If you didn't smell like last week's diaper I'd kiss you," Bill said. "I guess I know where I'll be tonight." His finger hovered over the button next to apartment 710. "Shit. I know you're exhausted, but any chance you can drop by Rosen's place later? Check out the Chaco connection for me?"

I hesitated, thinking about Heather.

"I wouldn't ask if we weren't dealing with this other shit storm."

"No problem. Glad to help."

"Thanks." He pushed the doorbell. "Let's see what Miss Tovah has to say, shall we?"

We were buzzed in. We took the ancient elevator to the seventh floor. Apartment 710 was located between the elevator and a small stairway leading to a metal door, blocked off by yellow tape.

"That the way to the roof?"

"Yup. Scene of the crime."

We moved to Tovah's door. "What about this apartment?"

"Sully and Mack already checked it out," Bill answered. "We got whatever was gettable: his and her prints, the second deck chair, a package of unused condoms. That's about it. One of Marv's personal holding companies has had it on the books for years."

I swayed a little. Bill grabbed my arm to steady me.

"You okay?"

"I hope Tovah drinks coffee," I said.

She didn't, not exactly, but she did provide us with bottled Frappuccinos, over ice. Except for the huge wide-screen television dominating one wall, the spacious one-bedroom apartment was deco-deluxe meets Ikea, with a healthy sprinkling of fingerprint powder on the side. The bone structure was impressive, with large built-in cupboards and shelves, decorative trim everywhere, scrolled archways, and a picture window overlooking a courtyard, with a wide, cushioned window seat Tank would have immediately claimed. The furniture was functional-hip all the way. Someone had spent as little as possible to make this place likable and livable, short-term. As a sugar daddy, Marv was noncommittal.

Tovah was pale, her oval face dominated by huge dark eyes. Mid-20s, though she seemed younger. I shot a look at Bill, and his eyebrows elevated slightly. He'd seen it as well. Tovah looked like Arlene Rudolph, only thirty years younger. Everybody has his type, I guess.

Tovah took the window seat. Bill and I pulled up matching, neutral armchairs and sat facing her. A set of church bells outside gonged the time: 5 P.M. If you'd dangled me out the window by my heels, though, I couldn't have told you the day.

"Thank you for seeing us, Ms. Fields," Bill said. "I know you already spoke with Detectives Sully and Mack, but Detective Norbu and I have a few follow-up questions, if you don't mind."

She nodded, attempting a smile. Her teeth were very white.

"Please tell us what happened the night Marv Rudolph died."

"I already told them. He came over around nine, after some big reception deal—he was always going to those things. He was already pretty tight. We went onto the roof with a bottle of red wine. We wanted to look at the city lights and . . . " she darted a look at us, "and smoke a doobie, okay? Marv loved it up there. He said it was the only place he could ever get any peace. Anyway, we both got pretty shit-faced. He passed out—he did that a lot. I was freezing, so I came back down here around midnight and went to sleep. Next thing I know, it's morning, and there's a shitload of cops all over the place. I got scared. So I split."

She spoke in a monotone, and her eyes kept shifting away. She was lying through every polished tooth in her mouth.

Bill caught my eye. *You take it.*

What would tie a beautiful young woman to a fat angry man old enough to be her father? I thought about a well-thumbed screenplay, with highlighted lines and corners turned down. About naïve dreams and ruthless ambition, and how disappointment can harden the one into the other if we're not careful, mindful.

"Ms. Fields," I said. "*Hagar* was your big break, wasn't it? "

Her eyes grew huge.

"You were on the brink of having all your dreams come true. Because of Marv. Then everything crashed. Because of Marv. How did you get from hope, to here?" I waved around the room. "From an up-and-coming-star to Marv's secret plaything, tucked away in an apartment he paid for so he could have you whenever he felt like it?"

Now her eyes flashed with hatred. Still, she said nothing.

"He stole your innocence, didn't he? Your hope. I wouldn't blame you for wanting him to die. But I'm also pretty sure you didn't kill him. So why don't you help us figure out who did? Maybe it's time to tell the truth, and then you can move on with your life. Make some new dreams."

I stopped talking.

We waited. Tovah said nothing.

"Or, we can take you downtown," Bill said.

Nothing.

"Aiding and abetting. Always a plus on a girl's résumé," I added.

That turned out to be the persuader.

"He said he just wanted to talk to Marv," she whispered. "He told me to get Marv loaded, loaded enough to pass out. That it would be easier that way."

"What would be easier?" Bill asked, gently.

"He said he just wanted to talk! To change his mind about making the movie!"

"Who, Ms. Fields?" Bill said. "Who came to see Marv?"

She clammed up. *She's scared. She should be.*

"I'm going to say a name," I said. "And you just nod if I'm right, okay?"

She wrapped her arms tight around her knees.

"Bronco Portreras."

As I said the name, another piece of colored glass clicked into place.

Tovah nodded. Her face crumpled and she collapsed into sobs. Bill shifted into good-cop comfort-mode. My phone pinged. I stepped into the hallway. Right on time, an e-mail from Mike. Subject: Bronco Portreras. A JPG was attached. I opened it, though I already knew: Bronco Portreras, initials B.P., was also my attacker. Pretty Boy. *¡Vindicacion!*

It all led back to Chaco.

Bill took Tovah downtown to make a statement. As for me, if I didn't take a shower soon, my skin was going to curdle. I also had a burning desire to bond with my furry, four-legged brother. Then I was going to take a run on the beach, then I was going to invite Heather over, then I was going to . . . *Brrrrt.*

I checked my phone. Mike again. He was unstoppable today.

"What's up?"

"Got something. Are you coming home soon?"

"On my way."

I pulled into my carport 20 minutes later and trotted up to the house. As I opened the kitchen door, a mass of warm cat launched itself into my arms.

"Hey, Tank. Hey, little buddy!" I lowered my head into his fur. *Yes, I'm happy to see you, too.* I carried him inside, holding him close to my heart. The minute we crossed the threshold, he launched himself from my arms and ambled over to his bowl, lest I think he'd lost his edge in my absence.

Mike was exactly where I had left him four days earlier, sitting at the kitchen table, eyes glued to the screen. Except it looked like he'd lost a few pounds.

"Give me fifteen minutes," I said. He waved one hand at me while the other tap-danced across the keys.

I squeezed Tank a full can's worth of tuna water. He funneled it up as I headed for hot water.

The scalding shower revived both my skin and brain cells. One clean T-shirt and a pair of jeans later, and I was ready to face Mike's computer screen.

He pulled up a spreadsheet with donation amounts, followed by names.

"Meet Mr. and Mrs. Anonymous," he said.

"How did you get hold of this?" I asked.

He said nothing. That meant he'd hacked in illegally and didn't want to contaminate me with the details.

"So check this out," he said. He pointed to the first name, responsible for multiple donations.

I read: The Rosen Foundation.

"Now this."

A second donor: The Sadie Rosen Foundation.

"I think you've been had," Mike said.

"Okay," I said, "but how do we know it's not just something Julius started in her memory?"

"It is. And we don't, but look," he said: *click, click*. The screen showed contact information for The Rosen Foundation: Julius Rosen's address, along with phone, fax, and email information.

"Okay . . .?"

He clicked again. Now the screen showed a Beverly Hills address for The Sadie Rosen Foundation. I didn't recognize the street. No phone listed, or any other contact information.

"I still don't . . ."

"So check it." Mike pulled up Google Earth and tapped.

I squinted. There, in slightly fuzzy but recognizable detail, was Julius Rosen's estate and the surrounding neighborhood. One small house, less than a mile away, had a flashing red star on it.

"There it is. The Sadie Rosen Foundation. Also, the address of one Sadie Rosen." Mike cocked his head. "Coincidence? We think not!"

A second detour before quality time with my cat and my girl. But I had to go, while I was still standing. Once the jet lag really hit, I might not function properly for days. I threw some protein powder and almond milk into the blender, added a handful of frozen organic cherries, and buzzed it into a shake, which I downed while Mike looked on in horror.

I grabbed my windbreaker from the closet.

I'm sure this is all nothing. False alarms.

I started out the door. A second thought stopped me in my tracks.

What was Julius Rosen afraid of?

I got my Wilson and shoulder holster out of the closet, grabbed my car keys, and left.

A sense of urgency was building in me, for no immediately discernable reason. I jumped in the Shelby and tried to unlock the glove box so I could stash my Wilson. The key jammed. Wrong set of keys. *Great.*

I switched to the Toyota. I locked my gun and holster in the glove compartment, and took off for what I hoped would be two quick, uneventful visits to Beverly Hills.

As I drove down Topanga, I hooked on my earpiece and called Heather.

"Hi, Ten," her voice sang, and I was grinning like a schoolboy. "I was just about to head your way."

"Hold that thought until later," I said. "Believe it or not, I have to go out again. Something's come up."

"As long as it stays up." Heather's voice was husky. I shifted in my seat. This woman certainly knew how to get a rise out of me.

"I'll call you when I know what's what. Lots to talk about. I . . . I've missed you," is what I said. *I may be falling in love with you*, is what I didn't say.

"Me, too. Bye," she said.

Two seconds later, I got a text from her. FORGOT TO TELL YOU. FOUND OUT ABOUT THE PATCH. FENTANYL. MAJOR PAINKILLER. MAJOR. XXXOOO

Fentanyl? As Mike would say, *boom*.

The Sadie Rosen Foundation was an unobtrusive bungalow on a side street just off Summitridge, a half mile before Julius Rosen's high stucco wall began.

I knocked on the door. An elderly woman with pure white hair and a pleasant smile opened it.

"Yes?"

I stared. Despite the passage of six decades, there was no mistaking the curious, open expression, the clear gray eyes. I was looking at Sadie Rosen. My brain tried to grapple with the information.

"Can I help you?" Her eyes clouded over. "I'm sorry, am I supposed to know you?"

"Miss Sadie," I heard from inside. "Everything all right?"

I swallowed. "Your brother is going to be very happy," I finally managed.

"Julius? Why?"

"Because he claims he's been looking for you for sixty years."

She smiled. "Silly. I had tea with Julius yesterday."

"Miss Sadie?" A slender middle-aged woman appeared behind Sadie in the doorway. She frowned at me.

Choosing my words carefully, I said I was a private investigator, and that I'd been working for Mr. Rosen. That he'd hired me to track down his sister.

"I am Señora Rodriguez. Miss Sadie's caregiver. Please, come in."

I followed her into the living room, my mind skittering.

Sadie didn't move from her spot in the foyer, as if she hadn't noticed we were no longer there. Señora Rodriguez returned to Sadie, and led her to a chair, where she sat, upright, prim, and a little anxious, like a child waiting to be picked for a game.

"I take Miss Sadie for tea with her brother three times a week," Señora Rodriguez said. "I know Mr. Rosen is not himself these days, but did he think Sadie was somehow missing?"

"Well, yes," I said, "that's why he hired me. But he had me start the search in Germany. Sixty years ago."

"Oh, dear," she said.

"Oh, dear?" That was one way of putting it. A small tongue of anger flicked at the edges of my brain. *I thought you were my friend.*

A phone rang in the hallway. Señora Rodriguez excused herself and soon was engaged in an emotional rapid-fire exchange in Spanish. Sadie blank-smiled at me. I forced a smile back.

Señora Rodriguez hustled in with the phone. "It is Otilia," she said. "I told her you were here. Can you talk to her?"

"Otilia?"

Her voice cracked. "Please, she's very upset."

Sadie buckled over, stuck her fingers in her ears, and started to rock back and forth.

"*Please.*"

I took the phone and moved into the hallway. Señora Rodriguez crouched next to Sadie and stroked her back.

"Otilia?"

"They trying to kill him." she said. "*Venga, venga*—they doing bad, bad things to him."

"I'm on my way."

"*Pero cuidado! Tienen armas.*"

No translation necessary.

Well guess what? I was armed, too.

CHAPTER 23

The guard stepped out of the gatehouse. His dark scar glowed in the moonlight.

"I'd like to see Mr. Rosen," I said.

"He's busy right now."

"Can you at least call him? Tell him I'm here?"

"Don't need to. He's busy." He took a menacing step toward me. I backed my car out of the driveway to think things through. A hundred yards down Summitridge, I pulled my car onto the shoulder and called Bill. He was on his way to Point Dume. I filled him in; my sentences, like my thoughts, choppy and confused.

"It definitely sounds like something strange is going on," he said. "You want me to try to get someone out there with a warrant?"

"No time."

He sighed. "I know, and anyway, what would I say? Hey there, judge, my private detective friend got a distress call from a cook. Can we please raid the home of one of the city's richest philanthropists? I don't think so."

"I'm going in there, Bill, one way or the other."

I could practically hear Bill's teeth grinding. "Shit. Okay. How about this? I'll try to send backup, but they can't go onto the property, not unless there's cause. You check out the situation, and I'll tell them to stay just out of range unless and until you need them. But don't move until they get there, Ten. Deal?"

I said nothing. Bill sighed again.

"Right. Have fun," he said, code for "Don't get your ass shot off."

I checked the action on my Wilson, and slipped it into the shoulder holster. I locked my car, tucked the keys in my back pocket, and trotted to the stucco boundary bordering the Rosen estate. I ran hard along the western face, hugging the wall, as I tried to picture the grounds within. The moon was a filled bowl, the milky light enough to guide my way. Just before I reached the farthest northwest point, my feet crunched on something. I reached down. My fingers found the brown, dried husks of fallen carob beans. I looked up, and saw the overhanging branch of a giant carob tree. Now I knew exactly where I was, and what to do next.

I steadied my breath. Bending my knees, I launched upward and grasped the branch with one hand. My shoulder socket screamed at me and I dropped back to the ground, hard. I tried again. This time both hands grabbed, and I was somehow able to chin-lift close enough to hook my ankles around the branch. I clung upside-down like a giant sloth, catching my breath. Then I swung right side up, and pulled, scraped, and crawled across the bobbing branch, trying to avoid looking down.

I reached the trunk, skin raw from traversing the rough bark. I shimmied and clambered my way through a thick tangle of branches, down to firm ground.

I was in.

I hunkered low and trotted through the grove of leafy sentinels; past the guesthouse, bathed in darkness; past the koi, feigning sleep; past Julius's round, white Roomful of Wonders, probably wondering, like me, what the hell was going on. I pulled up short. Loud voices, more "drunk loud" than "arguing loud," sounded from inside Julius's rumination cottage. The tone was boisterous, the language Spanish. I dropped to the ground and crept around to the back window to take a look.

The gauzy curtain softened a hard scene. Chaco Morales sprawled in Julius's black and chrome easy chair, thick-bodied, broad-shouldered, a Corona in one hand, a lit Cohiba cigar in the other. Manuel the gardener squatted against the wall across from him, an older, grayer mirror image. Up close, the family resemblance was unmistakable between father and son, though the son, alone, emanated menace, as palpable as poison.

I heard a low moan. I located the source of the sound. What I saw chilled me.

Julius slumped on the white easy chair, now elongated into a chaise longue. His head lolled, and behind his glasses, his eyes were empty plates. Dr. Alvarado knelt next to him. She was checking his pulse, her medical sports bag of tricks opened next to her. Bronco Portreras stood guard. Pretty Boy wasn't so pretty tonight—he had a fat lip and a pretty good shiner going. He also had a Sig Sauer P2xx tucked in his belt. No sign of Otilia or Señor Beefy.

Doctor Alvarado lifted Julius's arm and let go. It flopped like a wet towel. She said something, and everyone laughed, everyone except for Julius. The joke was on him, but he was too far gone to get it.

I melted back into the shadows. Julius was out of it, sure, but as far as I could tell he was in no imminent danger. I trotted over to the main house, avoiding the gravel path, and headed for the kitchen. I checked the outside door. The knob turned. It was unlocked, a huge piece of luck. I moved to the kitchen window. Light poured out, giving me temporary cover. I peered inside. Otilia stood next to the stove, arms wrapped tightly around her chest. Her lips moved. *Not alone, then.* I couldn't quite hear her, but I could read the twist of her mouth. She was disgusted by something. I ducked back into darkness to think. By all counts, there was one of me, and four to five of them, not counting Otilia and Julius, and counting Señor Beefy, wherever he was. Not a good ratio, and that's disregarding the firearms.

How close is help?

I pulled out my cell phone to call Bill. No service. Not even half a bar. They must be using a cell-signal blocker.

Get out of there, Ten. Be smart.

I turned the knob and slipped in the door with barely a whisper of sound. Otilia's voice was rattling nonstop in high-velocity Spanish. The undertone of desperate pleading tugged at my gut—and made up my mind. I fingered the safety off the Wilson and banged straight through the nook into the kitchen.

"*Cuidado*, Señor Ten!" Otilia pointed. I spun right, sighting my Wilson. Sure enough, Señor Beefy was reaching for a shotgun, resting against one wall.

I flicked my barrel at his chest. "Easy," I said. "Move away from there." I motioned with my chin, and he moved about ten feet away. I grabbed the rifle and laid it on the floor in the pantry area, out of reach.

Keeping my gun sighted on Beefy's broad chest, I returned to him, reached down, and removed a .22 popper out of his ankle holster. It must have looked like a toy in his massive hand. He crossed his arms and glowered, his equally massive biceps bulging.

I set the .22 on the kitchen table. Otilia met my eyes. "These men, they bad," she said. "They making Señor Julius sick. They making him do things that he no want to do."

"Shut the fuck up!" Beefy hissed.

Otilia shot him a look of blind rage. "*¡El puerco moron!*" She snatched up a pair of kitchen shears and lunged across the room.

"Otilia, no!" I said.

Otilia stopped, her body trembling. But she didn't let go of the shears. The words tumbled out of her: "Ever since they come, Señor Julius, he get worse. And that doctor?" She bit off the words. "*Bruja!* Witch! She here for his money, like everyone else."

She raised the shears and edged closer to Beefy. "And always they coming in my kitchen telling me to make things. Telling. Señor Julius always *asking*!"

Height-wise, the little woman barely reached Beefy's chest. The brandished shears waved back and forth in the general vicinity of his crotch. One snip, and he was a soprano. But before that happened, he would snap her neck in two like a twig. I had to get her away from him.

"Otilia, *por favor*," I said. "I am asking nicely, see? Please put them down." She glanced at me, taking her eyes off Beefy for a moment. That's when he made his move.

His arms shot out. He yanked Otilia into a bear hug that whooshed the wind right out of her. He transferred her to one arm, lifting her until her feet dangled. I sighted my gun at Beefy, but big as he was, he kept moving Otilia back and forth, using her writhing body as a shield. He grappled for her shears. Otilia let out a piercing shriek, twisted an arm loose, and rammed the shears point-first into his forearm. He bellowed like a wounded bull, swinging her to one side like a doll, but he didn't drop her. So I dropped him.

I shot him in the meat of his left thigh. He crumpled, howling. Between his roars and Otilia's screeches, I didn't hear anything else. Until I did.

"Don't move, asshole," a familiar voice said.

Bronco Portreras jabbed the cold shaft of his Sig Sauer into the small of my back.

"Lose the gun," he said.

I set my Wilson down on the kitchen table, next to Beefy's .22.

Bronco pushed a kitchen chair against the wall.

"Now sit."

I sat.

"You move, you die," he said.

Bronco looked over the two guns. He passed over my .38, opting instead to snag the popgun. He crossed the kitchen and stood over Señor Beefy.

"What we tell you?" he snapped. "Didn't we tell you to watch the cook? Chaco give you the job because you too fucking stupid to do anything else around here. And this is how you do it? You watch so good you end up getting stabbed by the fucking cook and shot by the fucking Chink?"

301

Tibetan, I thought, but for once didn't say.

Señor Beefy whined through gritted teeth, "Can't you just get the fucking doctor in here?"

"Don't need no fucking doctor," Bronco said. "You already dead."

He raised the .22. *Pop!* A small hole appeared in the middle of Señor Beefy's forehead—a bloody bindi marking a cruel end to a sorry life. His body twitched twice and came to rest. Bronco smiled, setting the small gun back on the table. Otilia crossed herself.

Now.

I lunged across the room, but Bronco was waiting, as if he'd planned it that way. He dealt a blow to the side of my head with the butt of his gun. I fell to my knees, trying to shake the pain off.

Bronco raised his Sig Sauer at Otilia. Her body contracted into a tiny ball.

"Don't shoot her," I said. "Shoot me."

"Fuck you, *pendejo*. I don't need nobody telling me who to shoot." Then Bronco shrugged. "Relax. I ain't gonna kill her, man. She make the best *mole* I ever put in my mouth!" He aimed the gun my way, aiming for my chest. He was enjoying playing cat-and-mouse. "You, though. Yeah. Maybe I shoot you."

I met his gaze, my own steady. *May I be safe and protected. May I be . . .*

He jabbed his gun toward the door. "Move," he said. "Chaco wants to meet you."

He pocketed the popgun and grabbed my Wilson, holding it in his left hand as he used the Sig Sauer to prod me toward the door leading outside. Turning back, he aimed it carefully. The explosion blew a splintered hole in the kitchen floor. Otilia backed further into the corner, tight with terror.

"Don't move," Bronco said. From the icy clutch of her body, I assumed she'd obey. But just in case, I shot her a look, jigging my eyes between her frozen face and the shotgun Bronco had inexplicably overlooked.

Bronco marched me out the back door and up the graveled path toward Julius's cottage. Halfway there we met up with Manuel and Chaco, on their way to find us. Chaco stepped close, his dark eyes appraising. He was maybe two inches shorter than me, but a considerable amount wider, a solid block of muscle, smoldering with energy.

"So, *monje*," Chaco said. "We meet. *Soy feliz.* I am glad."

He gestured toward the cottage. "Come." I paused at the doorway to take off my shoes. Bronco gave a quick jerk of his head. "No need."

Inside, Dr. Alvarado was leaning against one wall, leafing through a magazine. She barely glanced at me.

Julius saw me. He struggled to sit upright.

Chaco nudged me closer. "You two *putas* ready to kiss and make up?"

"Hello, Julius," I said.

"What are you doing here?" Julius whispered. "Tenzing, I . . ."A cloud of pain floated across his features. He gestured around the room. "I'm so sorry. I didn't mean to bring you into all this," he whispered.

"I found Sadie," I said.

His face crumpled.

"Hey, don't blame the old man. The missing sister was my idea," Chaco interrupted. "When you started nosing around here, I told him, you want to keep a snapping *perro* off your heels? Throw it fresh meat." He shrugged. "You did pretty good, too. Better than most of us thought you would. Except the old man. He knew." Chaco's sudden smile was scarier than his scowl. "Who knows, *monje*? Maybe I can find something for you to do. I'm always looking for smart workers." I listened hard for irony, but he was all business. I was being offered a job.

"Think about it," Chaco said.

"I will," I said. "I'm always looking for smart bosses, too." I listened to Chaco's breath as I watched his chest. The one quickened, and the other puffed slightly. *He's flattered.*

Good. I sensed a small opening, and pushed through. "So what are you up to, Chaco? What kind of game is this?"

"Big game," Chaco said. Again, everybody but Julius laughed. Chaco pointed to him. "That old man's a fucking genius. You wouldn't believe what he came up with."

My head started to throb. *What does the hum of betrayal sound like, Julius?* Julius winced, as if he could hear my thoughts.

"Tell him, *Viejo.* Tell him what we been planning."

Julius said, "It was the only thing that helped with Dorothy's pain, Ten. The only thing that sustained her."

"What was? What are you talking about?"

"Manuel's marijuana."

Chaco's chest swelled again. "My papa grew the best *mota* in the village, before he moved up here."

Manuel rattled off a long sentence in Spanish. He clapped Chaco on the back.

"Sorry. Didn't catch that," I said.

"He says he is proud of me," Chaco boasted. "He started with one small plant and now I control Sinaloa."

"Manuel grew it for her specially," Julius said, his voice weak. "Only thing that helped." Sweat beaded on his upper lip. "I don't feel very well. I think I need my medicine. Dr. Alvarado? Can you give me my medicine?"

She looked over at Chaco. He shook his head slightly.

"Soon," she said.

Time to step things up.

"That's it? That's your big idea? Selling Manuel's marijuana to treat cancer?" I shrugged. "Sorry, already taken. In case you hadn't noticed, Chaco, there's a whole industry out here built around that notion."

Bam! Chaco's fist split my lip, and I tasted metallic blood. "You think I'm stupid?" He said. "You think he is? No! That old man, he decide to buy up *all* the places that sell dope as medicine. Get a monopoly. Squeeze everybody else out of business."

That *was* a big idea. There were hundreds of medical marijuana dispensaries throughout the state. Somebody with a monopoly could make a bundle, assuming the crusading politicians didn't declare a new prohibition first. And where better but California, where the current laws were as lax and confused as any state in the country?

"I see," I said. "And let me guess, to do that, he'd need a single supplier . . ."

Chaco patted his chest. "One-stop shopping. Best shit around, too. I give him a great price, he buys only from me. Everybody wins."

Truth be told, it was kind of ingenious, setting aside the crawling into bed with cartel killers part. But clearly something must have gone wrong. What had happened? Again, Julius seemed to catch my thoughts midair. He roused himself. The effort to speak made him gasp a little.

"Greedy," Julius said. "These men are too greedy. They want to start sucking money out before we've set up a proper infrastructure. I keep telling them, the trick is patience. But no, they can't wait. They can't keep their word."

"Shut up, old man," Chaco snapped. "Now you said enough." He took a step toward Julius.

Julius groaned.

"So where is it, Chaco?" I said, hurriedly.

"Where's what?"

"The patch," I said. "I'm guessing the small of his back? Or did you stick it on his arm, like the one that killed Marv?"

Dr. Alvarado's intake of breath was more like a hiss. Bronco whistled. "Shit, man, the Chink's smarter than he looks."

Chaco backhanded Bronco across the face, whip-fast. "Smarter than you, fuckhead. If you hadn't been so *stupido* none of this would be happening!"

Bronco rubbed his cheek, but he didn't say another word.

"I still don't understand," I said to Chaco. "Who came first? Julius or Marv?"

"Chaco," he boasted. "Chaco always comes first."

"You know what I mean. Why did Marv have to die? Did he find out about your scam?"

"Nah. Nothing like that. Look," Chaco said. "I got a big family to support. I'm always looking for opportunities, you know? And this city's lousy with them." He pointed to Julius. "Take him. Rosen. The man's got nothing but money to piss away. When my father starts working for him, I keep an eye open and an ear close to the ground. Rosen's wife getting sick, some might call that a tragedy, *verdad*? Me? I call it *una opportunidad*. So Papa and me, we make sure Señora Rosen gets the best pain medicine there is, legal or not. Right, Papa?"

Manuel bobbed his head from the corner of the room

"And Marv?" I said. "That was ingenious, by the way, how you put Bronco and him together."

Chaco's eyes widened. "You're good. What a waste." He returned to his favorite subject: Chaco Morales. "Like I said, family is everything. So when my brother tells me his *muy guapo* son Bronco doesn't want to deal no more, wants to be in the movies, I think, who do I know that knows somebody in the movies? Rosen, that's who. And the man already feels like he owes us. So my papa talks to Señor Julius. Didn't you, Papa?"

Manuel smiled and nodded.

"And Julius helped you?"

"Si. Rosen puts in a word with this big producer, Marv Rudolph. Bronco gets an audition. And Bronco almost gets the part. But after all that, my brother Pepé's boy can't be in the movie, on account of Pepé's boy's got a record."

Pepé Morales. Chaco's Sinaloan killing partner.

And now I knew absolutely. Chaco was bragging to me, because Chaco was planning on killing me. And if Julius didn't change his mind, Chaco would kill him, too.

I might still have a chance. *Keep him talking.*

"But you still owe Pepé," I said.

"But I still owe Pepé. So I wait. And I watch. And I find

out Julius Rosen and Marv Rudolph are getting into business together. On another movie."

"*Loving Hagar.*"

"Si. And then? Just like that!" Chaco snaps his fingers. "Julius stiffs Marv. So Marv's hungry. I like hungry, hungry means desperate. Hungry means he'll do whatever it takes. And if all it takes is money? Even better. Land of opportunities, *monje*. One thing leading to another."

One death leading to another, you mean.

He sighed. "Until it all went to shit. Fucking Marv."

I heard the tiniest crunch of stone outside.

"Why kill him?" I said. "Why risk drawing attention to yourself like that?"

"What attention? No one was supposed to know. But he had to die. That asshole made me invest a couple million dollars in his movie before he'd go near Bronco."

"So what, then?" I said. "Marv ripped you off?"

"He blew a lot of money, sure. But if he'd just come to me, I wouldn't have been so pissed." Chaco leaned forward. "The fat fuck put my movie in turnaround. Nobody puts Chaco Morales in turnaround."

"*¡Puta!*" Bronco screamed, raising his Sig Sauer.

Blam! The window shattered, spraying the room with fragmented glass. Bronco let out a hoarse cry. I dove behind the black chair as Bronco grabbed at the ragged hole in his chest. Otilia had hit him with the shotgun blast, dead center. The blood between his fingers spread until his shirtfront was drenched. His knees buckled. He fell face forward, staining the white carpet crimson.

She stood outside, ramrod straight, shaking with rage. Señor Beefy's shotgun was pressed to one shoulder. She took a small step forward and rested the heavy barrel on the windowsill. She swung it slowly from side to side, like the muzzle of a tank. She had everyone in her sights. Nobody moved.

"You," Otilia said to Dr. Alvarado. "*Venga.*" Dr. Alvarado edged toward her. "*¡Mas rapido!*" She reached the window.

Otilia leaned inside, the shotgun inches from the doctor's belly. "This is for putting drugs in Señor Julius."

Dr. Alvarado squeezed her eyes shut.

"*¡Abierta sus ojos!*" Otilia shrieked. Alvarado's eyes popped open. Otilia drew back and spat into the other woman's face. Dr. Alvarado crumpled to her knees. As Otilia went to spit again, her gun muzzle canted to one side, Chaco lunged for the barrel and I lunged for Chaco. He twisted the gun away as I tackled him from the side. It was like hitting a brick wall, but at least I knocked him off his feet. He rolled sideways, barrel in his hands, butt pointing toward the ceiling. I grabbed the butt, and we started a deadly tugging match. I had the advantage. Unlike Chaco, I wasn't looking into the wrong end of the shotgun.

White-hot pain ripped through my shoulder. *What the . . . ?* Chaco reached back again and drove his palm hard on the muzzle, stiff-arming the butt into my shoulder, loosening my grip. Chaco wrested the shotgun from my hands. *Gutsy move. If I get out of here alive, I'll remember that one.* Now I was looking down twin tunnels of death. I kicked the barrel sideways as he pulled the trigger. *Blam!*

"*¡Hijo de puta!*" Manuel fell, howling. He was hit. His screams merged with the wail of sirens, growing close.

Chaco and I gauged the distance between our bodies, the rifle, and the door. We came to different conclusions. I lunged for the shotgun. Chaco leapt for the door, flinging it open and disappearing into darkness. By the time I made it outside, he was already nearing the edge of the property. I'm pretty fast, but somehow that fireplug was faster. I was losing ground—the shotgun didn't help—as Chaco streaked through the shadows. *El Gato.* He veered toward the grove of trees. I could only hope he was better at up than down, like another cat I knew.

The sirens were deafening now. Then I heard loud shouts, doors slamming. I glanced back. A half dozen cops spilled down the path toward the cottage, illuminated by pulsing squad-lights. They'd be picking through that mess all night, what with the two corpses, and the bullet casings from . . .

Idiot! I was carrying a double-barreled shotgun that had fired twice. I dropped it, and pumped into top speed. Up ahead, Chaco scrambled up the wall, using the hydrangea vines for purchase. Watery moonlight briefly illuminated his squat body, balanced on top of the wall. He jumped. I heard a sharp grunt. I shimmied up the carob tree, the bark sandpapering my skin raw, and pulled into a straddle atop the wall. Unlike Chaco, I used the overhanging branch to swing lower before letting go. I landed in a soft roll, and was up in time to see Chaco limping along the far end of the wall toward Summitridge Drive.

I'm fast when I need to be. I caught up with Chaco scuttling across the road, favoring his left ankle. I tackled him from behind, and we tumbled onto the soft shoulder, my arms wrapped around his middle, our ribcages heaving in tandem.

"Listen," Chaco gasped. "You could make a lot of money working for me. Have some fun, retire in a couple years."

"I'm having too much fun doing this," I panted. "Plus, the money isn't all that bad."

"You got no fuckin' idea what real money is," he grunted.

Probably true.

I hauled Chaco further off the shoulder and propped him against the trunk of a Sycamore tree.

I pulled out my phone. I checked to see if I finally had a signal. I did. I called Bill. The call went straight to voice mail.

"Bill. I bagged El Gato," I said.

I turned back to Chaco. I couldn't resist.

"So I guess your big mistake was using Bronco," I said. "Instead of doing it yourself."

"Fucking Bronco," Chaco muttered. "Good-looking boy, but nothing between his ears, you know? Me and the doc— she's my second cousin's oldest and smart," Chaco made a whipping motion. *"Como un latigo, verdad?* We worked out the perfect crime!"

"Fentanyl overdose. Hard to detect. Looks like a heart attack."

"Si."

"So you sent Bronco to stick the patch on Marv's arm . . ."

"Big enough dose to kill even that *puerco*. All the kid had to do was wait a couple hours and peel it off. Guy that size, no one would think twice about it. Natural causes, no questions asked. But no, Bronco decides he should also peel off the fucking tattoo. Save it, like some kind of trophy."

"You can't get good help these days."

"Fucking telling me."

I knew the answer, but I asked anyway. "I take it the knife next to Marv wasn't yours?"

"Knife?" Chaco shook his head. "No knives. Not for business, anyway. Knife is for personal."

"Right."

"Monje?"

"Yes."

"You smart. But you not as smart as you think. Get you in trouble some day."

My phone buzzed.

"Hola," I said. The jet lag was starting to really hit.

"Where the hell are you? I'm still ten minutes away. I'm dealing with a bunch of headless chickens up there."

I looked across the drive. Flashlights bobbed in the fields. Squad lights were flashing in front of the house. *They drove right in. How did they . . .*

I shifted my eyes. The wrought iron gate stood open. The gatehouse?

Empty. Where was the guard?

You're not as smart as you think.

"Bill, I'm . . ."

My head exploded into splintered shards of light. Then everything went black.

Chapter 24

"Okay, sir, you're good to go. Just take it easy for a few days, okay?"

The attendant walked back into Julius Rosen's house, where two other EMTs were strapping Manuel onto a gurney. Julius was already headed for Cedars in the first ambulance. I stood up and winced.

"Easy, cowboy," Bill said, walking up.

I had to ask. "Any luck?"

"Not yet."

I groaned. Chaco was gone. So was the guard. They had just melted away, invisible as black cats in the dead of night.

"I had him, Bill. And I lost him." My head hurt, but my pride hurt worse. I'd refused painkillers. Some part of me wanted to hold on to the ache a little while longer.

"The helicopter's on its way," Bill said. "I called in more uniforms. We'll find him, Ten. They won't get far on foot."

"I'm so sorry."

"Please. You're okay, which makes the rest of this okay." Bill met my eyes. "When they told me there was a man down in the white room, I was scared it was you." He laughed softly. "Jesus, this turned into a royal goat-fuck, didn't it?" He took out his notebook. "I know you feel like shit, but . . ."

"No. I understand." We moved to the edge of the fountain and sat. "They find the other dead body, the one in the main house, yet?"

"Yup. Any guesses?"

"Another one of Chaco's plants, disguised as help. I call him Señor Beefy."

"Wait. So who shot Beefy?"

311

"Take your pick. I shot him in the thigh, to get him off Otilia—that's the cook—and then Bronco, that's the nephew, finished him off for being a fuckup." I was starting to babble now. "In between, Otilia skewered Beefy in the forearm. So basically, you've got three shooters: Bronco, the cook, and me. Plus two bodies, Señor Beefy and Bronco. Oh, and the gardener, wounded by accident."

Bill shook his head. "Only you, my friend."

"Which brings us to Otilia and Bronco," I said, ignoring him.

"I got that one already. Don't worry. The way I see it, the cook's a hero. Bronco was armed and aiming at her. She stood her ground. Self-defense, all the way."

I could live with that.

We both looked up as the *whumpa-whumpa* announced an approaching copter, sweeping the hillside with its powerful lights.

"Here comes the cavalry," Bill said. "*Wa-hoo!*"

"Why are you in such a good mood?" I asked. "I screwed up, Bill. I just let a big fish slip the hook."

"Yeah, well, you hooked me a bigger one. I haven't even had a chance to tell you yet. Your hunch paid off. Two hours ago the feds seized two tons of prime Sinaloan marijuana from a *panga* beached at Smuggler's Cove, along with Chaco's brother Pepé Morales and three more henchmen. That'll set a cartel back. Caught them red-handed, just like we'll catch Chaco." Bill clapped my back. "Add to that Marv's probable COD? You made me look good tonight, pal."

I yawned.

"Ten?"

"Yeah?"

"Go home."

"Yeah."

"Where's your car?"

"My Toyota?" I patted my back pocket for the car keys. "Summitridge, right below the gatehouse entrance." Patted the other back pocket. Moved to the front pockets. Patted the back pockets again.

"Bill?"

He took one look at my face and he knew.

"Fuck," he said. "Don't tell me."

"Yeah. Looks like they weren't on foot."

Chapter 25

I'd arrived early on purpose. After a quick reconnoiter, I entered the main auditorium of the Director's Guild and claimed three seats in the back row of the empty theater. Now it was filling up nicely. If the number of paparazzi out front was any indication, this was an A-list event.

I did a quick physical inventory. My lip was still swollen, the bump on the back of my head still knobby, but at least the spring in my step had returned. I straightened my tie and ran a hand over my black thatch. I was doing okay.

By the time the squad car had dropped me off Tuesday night, it was 4 A.M. Wednesday morning, and every cell in my body was screaming. I'd found poor Tank lying in the dark, a tight curl of woe in the middle of my bed. I'd plopped next to him, and somehow found the courage to listen to Heather's message, to see how big the trouble was. I'd had to listen three times, because even in my exhausted, prone-to-exaggerate state, I'd been unable to detect a speck of anger or resentment. "Hey, you," she'd said. "Listen, I have an early morning, so I'll just assume you got delayed. Sleep tight, and call me when you can. Can't wait to see you. Bye."

This woman was setting the relationship bar pretty high.

I'd sent her a brief text and taken her advice, "sleeping tight" on and off for the next day and a half, minus brief food and pee breaks. Tank's idea of heaven.

Bill's call early this morning had woken me up. "We found your heap. Dumped downtown. Keys inside. I'll have S & M drop it off later."

"Chaco?"

"Still in the wind. Guys like Chaco, they're really good at not getting caught."

"Sorry," I'd muttered.

"Don't be. Right now, I'm flavor of the month. Marv's killer's dead, which saves the city a fortune, and we look like geniuses for figuring out the cause."

"Did you get the print off the cup?"

"Yup. Right again, Norbu. It was a match."

I'd told him my theory, and what I wanted to do next.

"Go get 'em," he'd said.

"Thanks. And Bill?" I took a moment to breathe. "We good?"

"Better than good, pal," he'd said. "Family . . ."

A hand tapped my shoulder.

"Hey! If it isn't The Monk. How you doing, dude?" Keith Connor's famous mug beamed down at me, and my insides did a little jig. My hunch had been right.

"Ten, right? Nice to see you here," he said. "So, what? You stayed tight with Marv?"

"Not exactly," I said. "Congratulations on the film, by the way."

"Yeah, well, you saved my ass on that one. You ever need anything, bro, just let me know. Seriously."

"Funny you should say that." I explained what I wanted, and he barked with laughter. "You got a twisted mind, my man," he said. "Cool. Let's do it."

He continued down the aisle, greeted as if he were the mayor of the world. I studied the stream of Hollywood's best and brightest filing past. The ages and genders varied. Marv's contemporaries wore expensive watches and clothes designed to flatter. Their skin was starched, any telltale sign of aging ironed out. The younger set seemed to be aiming more for an "I run a meth lab in Bakersfield" look. But they were all coated with the same veneer. *Look at me!* their strut seemed to bray. *Look at how great I am!* They were taking refuge in the *sangha* of self-promotion, obsessed with their own bright reflections.

I knew better. I could see it in their eyes. Beneath the glittering confidence ran a hidden vein of fear. Fear of aging. Fear of failing. Fear of being found out. What had Julius said this morning? *Never start anything fueled by fear . . .*

I'd stopped by the hospital on my way here. Apparently, there are benefits to being a major donor. His room was more luxury hotel than medical infirmary. Even the monitoring equipment was super-shiny and expensive-looking. I'd found Julius propped up in bed, watching a golf match on a huge flat-screen. The colors were so vivid I'd half expected the greens to give off a grassy smell.

"Can you believe this?" Julius had said. "I get over four hundred channels."

He was doing pretty well, for an octogenarian on an opiate detox program.

"They tell me I'll walk out of here clean in a week, 'walk' being a relative term," he'd said. "Sadly, there's no detox for Parkinson's."

He'd met my eyes, and then looked away.

"I wasn't sure you'd come."

"I almost didn't."

In truth, I'd gotten past the Sadie issue fairly quickly. Who was I to blame Julius, really? I knew early on something was off. Some things weren't adding up. Julius was paying me a fortune to do something his own people could have easily done. Finding Sadie was a little too easy. And I'd made Julius's betrayal even easier. My need to make money had stopped up my ears and blinded my eyes. So we were both complicit. In the end, all that mattered was that Sadie was alive and in good hands. I'd come here to make sure my path was clean.

"So, do you want your money back?"

"Hell, no! You confirmed that Zigo's family was behind

the orphanage scams in the first place. He's agreed to turn over to the authorities whatever other records he has. For free. No, Ten, you more than earned your fee."

"In that case . . ."

I'd handed him my get-well gift, lox and bagels from Nate 'n' Al's, and his eyes had grown moist.

"I've been doing some thinking," he said, "now that I have my brain back. Ruminating on this whole *meshugganah* fiasco."

"Ruminating is good."

"I feel I owe you an explanation. A confession, if you will. Remember that money my Aunt Esther gave me?"

"The pickle jar money?"

"Yes. The thing is, it didn't come from selling candy."

"It did seem like a lot of caramels."

"My uncle was, well, let's just say he was into some slightly shady activities. Gambling. Horses. Like that. Once my Aunt died, I took up where he left off. I was headed down the wrong path. Until I met my Dorothy."

I said nothing.

"We started stepping out together, and I fell hard. When I saw what she was like, how good, I made a deal with God. I told Him I'd change my ways. Become the man she'd be proud to marry . . ."

"And in return?"

Julius's eyes were pleading.

"I'd already lost so much, Ten. All I asked in return was that I be the one to go first. I didn't want to be a survivor again. And I was terrified of life without her."

"Ahhh." There was something so honorable about his pain, even though it had made him dishonorable.

"Dorothy's death sucked the air right out of me. I was paralyzed at first. And furious. I didn't know what to do. And then I did. All bets with God were off. I'd show Him. I'd show everyone. I'm a businessman, so I came up with a big business idea to distract me from realizing how afraid of life I felt without her. Never start anything fueled by fear, Ten. It never ends well."

"Noted."

"I lied to you," he added. "I let you down. Can you forgive me?"

"Maybe," I smiled. "But it'll cost you something. Three somethings, in fact. I'm not leaving here until you give up those three life lessons you keep hinting at."

Julius had burst out laughing.

"What?"

"It's just . . . Given the recent . . . It's ironic, that's all." He'd collected himself. "Okay, ready? Here they are. Number one: Feel your feelings. Number two: Tell the truth. Number Three: Keep your commitments." He'd grinned. "Me? I keep learning them the hard way. By not feeling my feelings, not telling the truth, and not keeping my commitments. Might want to do as I say, not as I do."

"Excellent insights," I said. "And timely. Thank you."

"Thank Dorothy. They're hers. High time I put them into practice again, with whatever time I have left . . . "

The auditorium buzzed with conversation as more and more people arrived. Clancy slipped into the chair to my right. He leaned close.

"How many narcissists does it take to save a reputation?" he murmured.

We laughed.

"Hey. There's the missus." Arlene, loyal wife to the last, was making her way to a seat in the front row. The rigid set to her back told me she wouldn't be loyal for long.

I wished her well. She was in for her own dose of life lessons, and very soon. Our meeting at her house this morning was only the beginning . . .

I'd parked outside. The paparazzi were long gone, leaving behind patches of flattened grass where they'd camped out.

Arlene had answered the door in a terry cloth bathrobe, belted over dark stockings and low black heels, as if she had been too tired to finish dressing. Her eyes were red, the flesh underneath small pillows of pain.

She'd led me into the living room, where Harper waited on the sofa, her expression unreadable. Arlene stood next to her, arms tightly crossed.

"I'm here about the knife found next to Marv's body," I said. "Your knife." Both bodies stiffened. "You see, at first I was confused, because the last time I was here, I checked your kitchen. And nothing was missing from the knife block."

Arlene had lowered herself next to Harper, her eyes never leaving my face.

"But then I realized. I was working on a limited assumption. A habit I'm trying to break, by the way. Because you have two kitchens, don't you?"

"For keeping kosher," Arlene had whispered.

"Right. Two separate kitchens with two sets of knives. Which makes two possibilities, sharing one alibi. So the only question is, which one of you was there when Marv died?"

Arlene thrust out her wrists. "Arrest me! It was me!"

I kept my voice gentle. "Nobody's getting arrested, Arlene. And I don't believe that's true." I'd turned to Harper. "That's why you went back, wasn't it? To get the knife?"

Harper looked at her mother with something like pity.

"Can I talk to you alone?" she said to me.

"No!" Arlene crossed her arms. "No. I need to hear this."

Harper's eyes flashed. "Fine. It was happening again, okay? The late nights. The way he was always whistling. My father's so obvious. We both knew, didn't we Mom? He was fucking somebody again. And you did what you always do. Bail."

Arlene bit her lip. Gave a tight nod.

"That lecture you took me to? At the temple? 'Women and redemption'? Those women kicked ass! We came home, and you started making excuses for why he wasn't here, and I just couldn't take it anymore, you know?"

"How did you know where to find him?" I asked.

"Dad, like, he took me there, lots of times. I even knew the code. Did you know that, Mom? He called it his little getaway. Told me not to tell you. He'd bring me to the apartment, and there she'd be. His latest chick, whatever, he called them his 'discoveries.' We'd eat take-out, and then we'd go on the roof and look at the city lights. When I got older, he'd let me smoke a joint with them." Harper's voice was oddly matter-of-fact. "I think it made him feel less guilty, you know? Like we were both just having our little fun. So yeah, I knew where he was. And the later it got, the more pissed off I got. I waited until Mom's Ambien kicked in. Then I grabbed the knife and drove over. Nobody answered the apartment, so I checked the roof, just in case. And that's where I found Dad."

Arlene reached toward Harper. "Honey."

"No, Mom, just listen for once. He was passed out. Oblivious to everything. Me. You. Everything. I was so angry, I wanted to stab him. But he looked so weird. His lips . . . I . . . I dropped the knife, and I shook him! And shook him! And . . ." Harper's voice cracked. "And I . . . He . . . He didn't wake up! He didn't . . . he was dead!"

Arlene touched her daughter's back. Harper wheeled on her mother. "Go away! I hate you! I hate you both!" Then she'd fallen into Arlene's arms, sobbing . . .

Now I craned my neck around the amphitheater. No Harper to be seen; she'd taken a pass on her father's memorial, and I couldn't fault her. Someday she, too, would discover the parts of her that were just like her parents. Someday, hopefully, she'd trade in the painful pleasure of blaming others for the subtler but more rewarding joy of accepting herself. Someday she'd let go of the knife blade she held to her own heart. But not today.

A hand touched my arm, sparking a tingle that radiated throughout my body. "Sorry," Heather whispered, slipping into her seat. "Got trapped with an acutely inflamed liver." She had pinned her hair up, and her skin smelled like fresh strawberries. One fingertip lightly traced my swollen lip. "You get that in the monastery?"

I grabbed up her hand and kissed it. "Practicing fierce compassion," I said. We smiled at each other, a matched pair of goofy grinners, and kept smiling until Clancy cleared his throat.

"Heather, this is my friend Clancy," I said. "Clancy, this is my . . ." I swallowed. Heather gave my knee a little squeeze. "My girl, Heather."

A microphone crackled. The first speaker walked up. With his schlubby brown suit and bald fringe, he stuck out like a . . . I smiled. *Like a monk at a police academy.*

"Marv . . ." The mike gave off a loud *Pop!* He started again. "Marv and I, we go way back." His accent was thick, his voice shaking with nerves. "We grew up on the same block in the Bronx. We went to the same schools. He could be a jerk sometimes, but I never met a guy who dreamed bigger or loved movies more." He swallowed. "Anyway, I like to think I'm the reason we're all here. I took him to Atlantic City on his 21st birthday. And he won big that day. Roulette. I still remember the numbers."

My pulse sped up. I knew what was coming. I was betting Arlene did, too. 481632, I thought.

"Forty-eight. Sixteen. Thirty-two," he said. "He made a bundle. 'It's my seed money,' he told me. 'You just watch. I'm going to make it big one day.' Well I watched. And he did."

Marv's lucky numbers. Until he used them, viciously, and for the wrong reason. Karma.

The childhood friend was the highlight. A painful parade of self-congratulation, artfully disguised as reminiscence, followed. I was glad for the little band of spiritual warriors I'd briefly joined last week, sitting *shivah* to ease the passage of Marv's broken soul.

I glanced at the program. We were just about done.

"Let's go," I said. We slipped out, and I led Clancy and Heather across the lobby to a private screening room.

"What's going on?" Heather asked.

I explained. Clancy yelped and started struggling to set up his camera.

"You okay with this?" I asked Heather.

Her eyes gleamed. "Only if I get to tell my mother."

The door opened. Keith Connor slipped in, swaddled in a scarf and dark sunglasses.

"It's cool," he said. "Nobody saw me."

I had Heather unclip her hair. Clancy helped me pose the scene, making sure that only Heather's slender back and blonde tresses were visible. Beautiful, but unidentifiable.

There was no missing who Keith Connor was.

Click.

Tomorrow morning, some lucky gossip site would be emblazoned with the image of Keith Connor, caught in a close-up embrace with a mysterious blonde. Keith's movie would get a nice big bump of free publicity. And Clancy? He finally got his money shot.

I walked Heather to her car. She'd be joining me at home later. But what I had to say couldn't wait.

"Heather?"

"Hmmm."

"I . . ." I paused. I wanted to get the words right. *Feel your feelings. Tell the truth.* "I'm really nervous right now. I'm not very practiced with romantic stuff."

She inhaled, as if breathing in my words.

"But here's the thing." My heart was pounding so hard I felt sure she could hear it. "I've held people at arm's length my entire life. Especially women. I don't want to do that anymore. I don't want to keep running away. Playing it safe. I need . . ." I swallowed. "I need a *sangha*. A spiritual home.

A safe haven, where I can love, and be loved back. And I think I'd like to start with you. And me. With a, you know, a *sangha* of two. Us."

Heather's smile started in her eyes, and proceeded to spread, like sunshine, until it included us both in its warmth.

"Do you know," she said, "I think that's the most romantic thing any man has ever said to me." Then she kissed me.

Chapter 26

I sat on my deck, Tank purring like a chainsaw on my lap. Inside, a decanted cabernet did deep breathing exercises on the kitchen counter. I'd set out a selection of Seventh Ray salads: cashew-crusted tofu, roasted beets with candied walnuts. The wild mushroom flatbread was keeping warm in the oven.

I was smitten. That was obvious. I knew the time would come when I'd start discovering her flaws, and that was okay with me, too.

My fingers found the fluffy undercoat beneath Tank's chin, and his whiskers quivered.

"We have company coming tonight," I said.

Tank's steady *prrrttt* paused for an instant, then started right up again. *If she makes you happy.*

"She does. You're a good guy, you know that?"

I savored the snap in the air, the eerie sheen of canyon rock, steeped in the blue light of the full moon.

I thought about family. Marv and his daughter. Julius and his sister. Bill and Martha and their two little girls. Something twisted, deep in my heart.

The moon nudged at me, urging me to stay with the pain. To hear, maybe even to embrace, the message it carried from the other side of the world.

Somewhere out there, in a small bed, in a cold room, a man was dying.

Seven thousand miles away, another man—a man, not a boy—was grieving the father he never had.

What do we inherit? Sometimes, it's up to us to decide.

I stroked Tank's ears, translucent in the moonlight. They fluttered beneath my touch, like fierce, delicate wings.

"I'm going away again, Tank," I said. "Just for a bit. My father needs me."

ACKNOWLEDGMENTS

GRATITUDE FROM
GAY HENDRICKS

First, a deep bow of gratitude to Tinker Lindsay, who began as a gifted co-author and became a treasured friend. You are a bundle of wonders, Tinker. Long may we write together!

I'd like to send a big thank-you to our growing community of Tenzing Norbu fans. I've been deeply moved by the reception Ten has received from readers and reviewers around the world. The reviews have been not only heartwarming but also remarkably insightful.

I'm grateful to Louise Hay, Reid Tracy, and the Hay House team for giving a good publishing home to Ten, Tinker, and me. It is deeply satisfying to work with people who are not only trusted professionals but also good friends. I'm especially grateful to Patty Gift for her early enthusiasm for Ten; it meant a great deal to me that a person of her experience and stature would see the potential of the series.

Our agent, Sandy Dijkstra, is an author's dream. Sandy has a passion for books, authors, and the whole literary enterprise; the power of her passion has made a profound difference in my life. Thanks also to Sandy's team, Andrea Cavallaro and Elise Capon, for their efficient help whenever we need it.

Many thanks to the detectives of the Santa Barbara Police Department for their graciousness in taking calls from harried mystery novelists about obscure criminal topics. Just up the road from SBPD, the good gentlemen of the Far West gun shop were always there when I needed to tap into their expertise.

I also want to thank two undercover ATF agents, who must of necessity remain nameless, for helping me understand many unsavory aspects of life such as tactical nuclear weapons and drug cartel management styles. I admire your courage and appreciate your generosity. Next time you're going to let me pick up the tab.

Lucy, our beloved 17-year-old Persian cat, can almost always be found sitting near me when I'm writing, as she is at this moment. Her good vibes and purrs are an essential nutrient for the creative process around the Hendricks household.

I've been richly blessed for 32 years to have a magnificent mate, Kathlyn Hendricks, who is also my muse, best friend, and creative partner. She is always the first audience for the adventures of Ten; her generous listening and keen feedback are crucial elements in everything I write. Katie, my gratitude to you is infinite.

GRATITUDE FROM
TINKER LINDSAY

First and foremost, gratitude and thanks to my co-author, Gay Hendricks. Gay's talents are huge, in exact proportion to his heart, and I wake up every morning in a state of happy shock that I get to play with him and the products of his abundant imagination. (And special thanks to his wife, Katie, for welcoming me into a world of warmth, creativity, and unbelievable cooking.)

My heartfelt appreciation to the entire Hay House team for their enthusiastic support, including our lovely editor, Patty Gift, Reid Tracy, Quressa Robinson, Charles McStravick, and the amazing Louise Hay.

Deep appreciation, as well, to Sandy Dijkstra and Elisabeth James of the Sandra Dijkstra Literary Agency for helping shepherd our detective, Tenzing Norbu, into future incarnations. He is in capable hands.

The following generous people made researching this book more fun than I can say. I owe them an enormous debt of gratitude. Whatever I got right is thanks to their knowledge and experience. Whatever I got wrong is due to my own inadvertent missteps:

Ed Winter, assistant chief of the operations bureau, L.A. county coroner's office, shared his time, expertise, and thoughtful observations, especially regarding how high-profile homicides in L. A. play out publicly and privately.

John L. Grogan, private eye extraordinaire, patiently walked me through the specific steps necessary to the journey from cop to private investigator and regaled me with his behind-the-scenes professional adventures.

My nephew and favorite techno-DJ, Roddy "the Ride" Lindsay, served as translator and guide into the mysterious warehouse-world of traveling underground techno-shows.

I panned much gold from the work and words of Cheri Maples, Dharma teacher, former police officer, and co-founder of the Center for Mindfulness and Justice. Thanks, too, to co-founder and Operations Director Maureen Brady, for providing me with a sample daily retreat schedule, as well as her warm support.

Rabbi Jason Van Leeuwen offered a moving perspective on the bereavement process and spiritual purpose of sitting *shivah*, and he gave me invaluable insights into how and where orthodoxy and grief intersect.

Rod Fracascio invited me to ride along with him up and down the Hollywood Hills so I could experience a day in the life of a working paparazzo. It was a fascinating time, and he applies a lot of Tenzing-like intuition to his work.

Tattoo artist Howard Teman, owner of the eclectic T-man Tattoo parlor, gave freely of his time, sense of humor, and expertise in all things pertaining to skin and ink.

Former police officer Dave Brown, Jr., both suggested

the action and ensured the accuracy of "how and when to shoot through a door," and "Sully" O'Sullivan loaned out his wonderful name.

Thanks to Tessa Chasteen, artist and avid mystery buff, for her multiple manuscript readings and helpful plot tweakings, not to mention for negotiating access to the roof-top wonders of Ravenswood Apartments.

What would I do without my brilliant writers group? Buckets of appreciation to Bev Baz, Monique de Varennes, Kathryn Hagen, Emilie Small, Pat Stiles, and Barbara Sweeney for taking precious time away from their own creative endeavors to assist Gay and me with ours. To say they helped edit our baby is an understatement—they had a big hand in shaping it.

My love to Daisy and Addie Pidduck, deep sources of delight and hilarious providers of ongoing material for the intrepid Maude and Lola; and to Jon, Blossom, Thomas, and Dorothy—children of my heart, my prides and my joys.

Finally, my love and gratitude to Cameron Keys: partner, ally, and friend. You encourage me with your courage and enliven me with your life. You make me laugh. You make me think. You make me better.

ABOUT THE AUTHORS

Gay Hendricks PhD has served for more than 35 years as one of the major contributors to the fields of relationship transformation and body-mind therapies. He is the author of 33 books, including *The Corporate Mystic, Conscious Living* and *The Big Leap*, and with his wife, Dr Kathlyn Hendricks, has written many bestsellers, including *Conscious Loving* and *Five Wishes*. Dr Hendricks received his PhD in counseling psychology from Stanford in 1974. After a 21-year career as a professor of Counseling Psychology at University of Colorado, he and Kathlyn founded The Hendricks Institute, based in Ojai, California, which offers seminars worldwide.

In recent years Dr Hendricks has also been active in creating new forms of conscious entertainment. In 2003, along with movie producer Stephen Simon, Dr Hendricks founded the Spiritual Cinema Circle, which distributes inspirational movies to subscribers in 70+ countries around the world (www.spiritualcinemacircle.com).

www.hendricks.com

ABOUT THE AUTHORS

Tinker Lindsay is an accomplished screenwriter, author and conceptual editor. A member of the Writers Guild of America (WGA), Independent Writers of Southern California (IWOSC), and Women in Film (WIF), she has worked in the Hollywood entertainment industry for over three decades. Lindsay has written screenplays for major studios such as Disney and Warner Bros, collaborating with award-winning film director Peter Chelsom. Their current screenplay, *Hector and the Search for Happiness*, with Egoli Tossell Film, stars Simon Pegg, Rosamund Pike and Christopher Plummer, among others, and will be released in 2014. She also co-wrote the spiritual epic *Buddha: The Inner Warrior* with acclaimed Indian director Pan Nalin, as well as the sci-fi remake of *The Crawling Eye*, and *Hoar Frost*, with Cameron Keys, the latter currently in pre-production.

Lindsay has written two books – *The Last Great Place* and a memoir, *My Hollywood Ending* – and worked with several noted transformational authors, including Peter Russell, Arjuna Ardagh and Dara Marks.

Lindsay studied and taught meditation for several years before moving to Los Angeles to live and work. She can usually be found writing in her home office, situated directly under the Hollywood sign.

www.tinkerlindsay.com

READING GROUP GUIDE

A NOTE FROM THE AUTHORS: We're thrilled you have chosen *The Second Rule of Ten* for your book group. First and foremost, we hope you enjoyed the ride! But we'd also love to think that Tenzing's adventures can provide a little food for inner thought, as well as a cracking good story. The following questions are ones we have asked ourselves in the process of discovering "Ten," and following his unique path through life. (Makes for an interesting journey, at times.) Have fun with them!

Questions for Discussion

1.   Tenzing Norbu is a complex character, a 21st century detective trying to balance his inner and outer worlds. In what ways are you like, and not like, Ten?

2.   Tenzing's second rule deals with his unconscious beliefs. What are they, and how do they help or hinder his investigation into Marv's death, his search for Sadie Rosen, and his pursuit of Chaco Morales?

3.   What "life rules" have you developed? How are they the same as—or different from—the rules you learned as a child?

4.   Along with his police training and trusty .38, Tenzing has a number of intuitive skills in

his detective's arsenal, honed through years of spiritual practice. How do they come into play as he seeks answers to Marv's murder? Have you ever relied on intuitive flashes to solve personal dilemmas?

5. Ten is a bit of a hybrid, shaped by an upbringing in two very different cultures and environments. Have you or anyone you know had a similar experience of living in two different worlds? How did that impact your/their life choices?

6. This detective series represents the collaboration of a male and female author. How do you think this affects the way in which the male and female characters come to life and interact?

7. Tenzing has a deep longing for a good father figure. In what ways does this shape his interactions with the male characters he encounters in this story?

8. Ten also has a complicated relationship with his mother (more on this in future books!). Do you think Ten's feelings for Heather (and Julia in *The First Rule of Ten*) are impacted by his mother issues? Does this ring any bells?

9. Ten's greatest test is to be present in a world that is largely "anything but." How do you handle the challenges of staying mindful in a fragmented world?

THE THIRD RULE OF TEN

Beep Beep Beep!

My eyes snapped open, the high-pitched warning tone piercing my sleep. It was 2:58 A.M., and somebody had just breached my perimeter.

I slid my hand under the pillow next to me, gripped my Wilson Supergrade, and thanked the various gods that Heather hadn't spent the night. I swung out of bed. Sure enough, a shadowy figure was moving across the screen of my high-tech Guard-On system, captured in the eerie green glow of the infrared camera. I couldn't tell if it was the same kid who had paid a night visit here before, but whoever he was, he was heading straight for my garage.

My cell phone buzzed. Mike. He must have received the automatic alert over at his place.

"I'm on it, Mike. Can you call Bill for me?" He grunted and hung up.

I pocketed the phone, pulled on some shoes, and slipped outside the bedroom. Moving quietly, I crept across the slick, hardwood floor, making my silent way through the living room and into the kitchen. I needed to get a better sense of what I was up against. I crouched low and looked out the kitchen window. About 100 yards away, past the trees that line my property, a sliver of moonlight glinted off the big, square windshield of a Hummer. Did that mean I had more than one visitor?

Homeowner outrage hummed in my bloodstream. *This is private property. This is my safe space. You don't belong here.* I racked a round into the chamber of the .38.

I knew I should yell out to the intruder—most intruders flee at the first sign of an inhabitant, armed or not. But I could feel the sizzle of adrenaline in my bloodstream urging me to deal with this guy the old-fashioned way.

I cracked open the kitchen door and swept the barrel of the pistol across the grounds. Nothing. I dropped low and snuck around to the back of the garage, where my two cars were stabled. I peered into the small back window. It was Miguel, squatting behind the locked trunk of my Shelby, a crowbar in one hand and a flashlight in the other.

He was about to jimmy a trunk I'd spent at least 20 hours restoring. *Not my Mustang, Miguel, not in this lifetime.*

I crept silently to the door between the kitchen and the garage. I took a deep breath and banged open the door, reaching through to hit the switch illuminating the over-head light. I yelled at the top of my lungs and aimed the Wilson at him.

Miguel jerked his head up. The flashlight clattered to the floor and rolled across the concrete, coming to a stop at my feet as he groped in his pocket and pulled out a small pistol.

I pointed my gun at his chest. "Drop it!"

His arm jerked upward. Bad move. I lowered the sight and shot him in the meaty part of his left leg. He howled and fell like a stone, his head clunking against the Mustang's back bumper as he went down. He was out cold.

I was starting toward him when I heard the sound of two car doors slamming.

I crouched down behind the Shelby and aimed into the inky darkness. Now I regretted switching on the light. It put me at a disadvantage. I could just make out a man—no— *two* men sprinting through the trees and running straight for me. When they were about 20 yards out, I grabbed the flashlight and slung it to my right, aiming for the Toyota. It hit the sheet metal with a clang. They started firing in that direction but spotted me immediately when I stood up to return fire. Two muzzles swung my way.

There was no time for niceties. I aimed for center mass, just like the Academy taught me. Two shots, two hits, square in two chests. The guy on the right toppled backward with a loud cry. The other one must have been wearing Kevlar because he just staggered for a moment, stopped in his tracks, but still very much alive. He got his footing back and fired, hitting the wall behind me.

My police training sent up another instructional flare: *Take cover and hold fire until you can get a clean shot to the leg.* But I wasn't a cop anymore, was I?

By my count, this guy had already fired eight or nine times, leaving plenty of zip in what was probably a 17-shot magazine. I didn't like the odds. I sighted the Wilson in for a headshot but missed low, hitting him directly in the Adam's apple. With no oxygen or equipment to make a sound, he sank to his knees and fell forward onto his face with a wet flop.

I let out a deep breath I didn't realize I was holding. With the smell of gunpowder lingering in the air, I realized I was witnessing karma happening right before my eyes. The second shooter had gotten a reprieve when my first shot bounced off his bulletproof chest. But then he'd spurned that subtle gift from the universe and called in his destiny.

I heard a loud *thwock* and my left foot jerked. Miguel! I took cover and checked the thick bottom of my running shoe—the ridiculously expensive running shoes I'd just treated myself to a couple of weeks ago. A .25 caliber bullet was now imbedded in its ruined sole.

Miguel was running out of strikes. Strike One: trying to jimmy the trunk of my Shelby. Strike Two: he blows away my new sneaker. The kid was clearly escalating.

I scooted backward so the Mustang's axle and wheels were between him and me. I heard the scuff of jeans against the concrete floor.

"Hey, Miguel!" The scuffing sound stopped. *"Habla Ingles?"*

"Un poco." A little. That's about how much Spanish I spoke.

"I don't want to kill you," I said. "And you don't want to die. Give me the gun."

I waited. The silence grew. I curled my finger around the Wilson's trigger. Then I heard the scraping slide of gunmetal across concrete. I peered around the back of the Mustang and saw the flimsy little Browning on the concrete. I stretched down and got it.

"You carrying anything else?"

"No. Don' kill me, okay?"

I stuck the revolver in my pocket. Miguel was lying on his back, arms overhead, palms facing upward. Blood had pooled under his left thigh, but I was pleased to see I had just grazed him as I intended. I did a quick over-and-under frisk and came up empty, as he'd promised.

"Okay," I said. "You can put your arms down."

He lowered his arms.

"Now roll over. Put your hands behind your back."

I used a bungee cord to secure his wrists.

"Stay put," I said. I stepped outside to survey the damage to my other two assailants. It was extensive and permanent. The end for both of them had come quick. The first body had a hole in the chest, just right of center. The man lay flat on his back, so I couldn't tell if it was a through-and-through. The other sprawled facedown, his head at an odd angle. I rolled him over and saw that his throat was a ragged mess.

I stood up, feeling slightly light-headed, and focused on my breathing to center myself. A river of feeling was flooding my body.

Relief.

Sorrow.

Remnants of rage.

Swimming up through it all was a deep and sure knowledge that this was a turning-point moment in my life. I had never killed anyone—not in the line of duty as a police officer, not as a private investigator. Now everything was different. I had killed. Not once, but twice.

I had taken two lives.

Nothing in my training as a monk or a cop had prepared me for the feeling that welled up from down in the middle of me, a hot wave of revulsion that felt like my stomach was turning inside out. I tasted the bile on the back of my tongue and bent over to throw up.

The sudden roar of a big engine broke through my nausea. I stood up just in time to see the rear lights of the Hummer receding, wheels spitting gravel like grapeshot.

I went back inside the garage and saw the bungee cord on the floor, sliced in two. During my quick frisk of Miguel I must have somehow missed a hidden blade. I wanted to swear, but in my current brain-overloaded state I had reverted to thinking in Tibetan, which has no real curse-words. My mind just kept repeating the Tibetan phrase that would translate as "I'm upset! I'm upset!"

The Hummer disappeared down the twisting curves toward Topanga Canyon Boulevard. I decided not to give chase—he'd be long gone by the time I got my car cranked up and hit those steep turns myself. I could feel the adrenalin, nausea, and other feelings fading in my body, replaced by grudging respect for the kid. Miguel had managed to get away on a badly wounded leg. He'd done it quickly and so quietly I hadn't even noticed. Even though he hadn't come to my house for honorable reasons, he'd certainly made a skillful escape. He was one tough kid. I found myself wishing him well in spite of his abuse of my hospitality.

Then that feeling subsided and I was left with the consequences of my actions rattling around inside me.

What have I done?

The cell phone in my pocket vibrated. I glanced at the screen and saw it was Bill Bohannon, my ex-partner. In that moment, it felt like light years since we'd been Detective II's in LAPD's elite Robbery/Homicide division. Now Bill was a Detective III, and I was about to be one of his cases.

"Hey," I said.

Bill's voice was thick with sleep. "Your buddy Mike said something triggered the security system. Everything okay?"

I looked at the two still bodies.

"Not exactly," I said. "I got two men down, one more wounded and at large."

Bill woke up fast. "Two men down. How down?"

"As down as they can get," I said.

Bill groaned.

"The kills were righteous," I said, but I wondered if that was true.

A siren wailed in the distance, drawing closer. My night was about to get even more complicated.

"Bill, I hate to ask, but . . ."

"I'm on my way," he barked. "Don't say a word to anyone until I get there."

The two lifeless bodies lay sprawled on the ground like a pair of unanswerable reproaches. I studied them as a wave of shivers passed through my body.

Tank.

Suddenly I remembered I wasn't the only member of my household that might be having some feelings. I hurried across the driveway and into the kitchen.

"Tank? Where are you, buddy?"

I heard a muffled squawk from the living room. I ran to the sofa and dropped to my knees, peering underneath it. Tank was huddled flat in his place of ultimate refuge, usually reserved for the rare thunderstorms we have in this part of the world.

"It's okay," I said. "I'm okay." I stretched out my hand to stroke his head.

He shrank against the far wall and made a small hissing sound. Maybe he was rattled by the smell of blood on me.

As I sat back on my haunches, unsure what to do next, my computer made that odd Skype sound, like a bubble popping.

I looked at the screen.

It was a Skype video call, from "lamalobsang." My heart rose, choking my throat with bittersweet relief. Yeshe and Lobsang—my lifeline between past and present, Dharamshala and Los Angeles, monk and detective. Always there for me, whenever I needed them.

For years after I'd moved to California, we had communicated through snail mail, and the occasional whispered telephone call between Dharamshala and Los Angeles. Then my father had discovered our ongoing, forbidden contact, and banished them to Lhasa, Tibet, where even snail mail was impossible. But a few months ago, they had been called back from Tibet to become head abbots of my old monastery in Dharamshala—my father's final act of healing before his death. This change in leadership at Dorje Yidam had brought with it many other changes, a lot of them technological. But I knew my friends' decision to get in touch with me this morning had nothing to do with modern technology, and everything to do with ancient intuition.

I sat down at my desk and clicked on the icon. Within moments, the gleaming, shaved heads and warm features of my two friends swam into view.

"Tenzing, dear Brother! Greetings to you." Lobsang touched his forehead. Just to his right, Yeshe did the same.

"Lobsang. Yeshe. I am happy to hear from you," I said. As I said the words I felt my chest compress, as if two giant hands were squeezing it.

"Are you all right?" Yeshe's voice was breathless. "We had to reach you. I felt something . . . Something dark."

I pictured the fresh corpses outside. I opened my mouth to answer, but the words stuck in my throat. These were my dearest friends in the world. But they were also Buddhist monks. They had dedicated their lives to the practice of *ahimsa*—to doing no harm to any and all sentient beings. How could I tell them that I had just killed two men?

Just weeks ago I had made a new vow: to be more mindful of the difference between privacy and secrecy—to make sure my natural shyness wasn't causing me to hide things from others I ought to be revealing. Now here I was at a crossroads again, deciding whether to risk a relationship by being totally honest. If I told the blunt truth to my brothers, would I lose the rock-solid respect we'd built up over a lifetime of shared secrets?

And if I lied, would I lose even more?

"I'm fine," I said. "Everything's great. How are you?"

We hope you enjoyed this Hay House book. If you'd like
to receive our online catalogue featuring additional
information on Hay House books and products, or
if you'd like to find out more about the
Hay Foundation, please contact:

Hay House UK, Ltd., Astley House,
33 Notting Hill Gate London W11 3JQ •
Phone: 0-20-3675-2450 • *Fax:* 0-20-3675-2451
www.hayhouse.co.uk • **www.hayfoundation.org**

Hay House, Inc., P.O. Box 5100, Carlsbad, CA 92018-5100
Phone: (760) 431-7695 or (800) 654-5126
Fax: (760) 431-6948 or (800) 650-5115
www.hayhouse.com®

Hay House Australia Pty. Ltd., 18/36 Ralph St., Alexandria NSW
2015 • *Phone:* 612-9669-4299 • *Fax:* 612-9669-4144
www.hayhouse.com.au

Hay House SA (Pty), Ltd., P.O. Box 990, Witkoppen 2068
Phone/Fax: 27-11-467-8904 • www.hayhouse.co.za

Hay House Publishers India, Muskaan Complex, Plot No. 3, B-2,
Vasant Kunj, New Delhi 110 070 • *Phone:* 91-11-4176-1620
Fax: 91-11-4176-1630 • www.hayhouse.co.in

Raincoast, 9050 Shaughnessy St., Vancouver, B.C. V6P 6E5 •
Phone: (604) 323-7100 • *Fax:* (604) 323-2600 • www.raincoast.com

Take Your Soul on a Vacation

Visit **www.HealYourLife.com**® to regroup,
recharge, and reconnect with your own magnificence.
Featuring blogs, mind-body-spirit news, and life-
changing wisdom from Louise Hay and friends.
Visit **www.HealYourLife.com** today!